A SHAMELESS ANGEL

ALSO BY ELIZABETH COLE

Honor & Roses

Choose the Sky

Raven's Rise

Peregrine's Call

A Heartless Design

A Reckless Soul

A Shameless Angel

The Lady Dauntless

Beneath Sleepless Stars

Daisy and the Duke

Heather and the Highlander

Rose and the Rogue

Poppy and the Pirate

A SHAMELESS ANGEL

ELIZABETH COLE

SKYSPARK BOOKS

PHILADELPHIA, PENNSYLVANIA

SkySpark Books
Philadelphia, Pennsylvania
skysparkbooks.com
inquiry@skysparkbooks.com

Publisher's Note: This is a work of fiction. Names, characters, places, and incidents are a product of the author's imagination. Locales and public names are sometimes used for atmospheric purposes. Any resemblance to actual people, living or dead, or to businesses, companies, events, institutions, or locales is completely coincidental.

Ordering Information:
Quantity sales. Special discounts are available on quantity purchases by corporations, associations, and others. For details, contact the "Special Sales Department" at the address above.

A SHAMELESS ANGEL / Cole, Elizabeth. – 2nd ed.
ISBN-10: 1-942316-26-7
ISBN-13: 978-1-942316-26-8

Chapter 1

♉

THEY NEVER LET HER SEE the body.

Sarah had been engaged to her Charles for over two years. Now he was dead, and she hadn't even got the proper chance to say goodbye. She wouldn't be able to see the face she loved so dearly, or touch him one last time.

The churchyard was a sea of black, full of mourners come to pay their respects. She wore a gown of dark grey bombazine, too hot and heavy for summer. Sarah had no proper mourning dress, and no time to have one made before the funeral. The late August heat did not allow for longer than a few days before the body had to be committed to the earth.

Her head was mostly concealed by a black bonnet, loaned by her mother. Was she wearing jewelry? She scarcely remembered putting it on. Oh, yes. The jet beads around her neck, also from her mother. All the dark colors would wash out her blonde hair and fair skin. She looked like a corpse herself: pale, thin, hideous. Not that it mattered. No one would be looking at her.

To judge by the crowd, Charlie touched many lives. Sarah was permitted to stand close to the grave, for although she wasn't family, she almost had been. *A few months until the wedding*, she thought. How quickly things could change. She felt as though she was in a dream. Perhaps she might wake up.

But she did not wake up. The parson completed his homily. The casket was lowered into the ground while she watched, her heart aching. At the sound of twinned, stifled sobs, she raised her eyes briefly to see Charlie's sisters, their hands tightly entwined as they watched the coffin sink into the earth.

This wasn't supposed to happen, she thought for the dozenth time that morning. Charlie and she were in love. Sarah was a practical girl, and never loved tragic romances. She planned to marry Charlie and live happily ever after.

But now Charlie was buried, and she was alone. Sarah took a long, shaky breath. Alone didn't begin to describe how she felt.

Not fair, Sarah told herself. Not fair. Nothing about it was fair.

After the family had done so, she also tossed a little handful of dirt into the grave. Looking down at the wooden surface of the coffin, now partially covered with soil, she had a sense of vertigo. Then she noticed a worm industriously working its way through the soil exposed by the grave diggers, and felt pure horror. She didn't want to think of Charlie like that, at the mercy of those worms.

She turned away so abruptly she lost her balance. She started to stumble, but then someone caught her by the elbow, stopping her from falling further.

Sarah found her footing, then glanced at the hand, following it up to the arm and the attached face. The man wasn't anyone she knew, but she thought he was one of the pallbearers, though she couldn't say for certain.

"Are you all right?" the man asked. His voice was pitched low, keeping the question discreet.

"I misstepped," she said, realizing she hadn't spoken a word all morning until just then. Looking down again, she tugged at the black gloves on her shaking hands. She had been a wreck since hearing the first news of Charlie's accident. She couldn't sleep, she couldn't think. "But I have my balance now."

He released her, but didn't move away. "Do you intend to go to the wake?"

She nodded. The procession would head to the Wolvertons' home nearby, where the wake was to be held. "There's no need to shepherd me, though."

"All the same, since we're heading to the same place..." he said, falling into step beside her. Without making a show of it, he offered an arm.

Sarah accepted his decision, slipping her hand onto his arm. She was too overwhelmed to do anything else but follow as the group passed out of the cemetery. The man was another mourner, and that was that. It didn't matter that she didn't even know his name. She had no interest in the living.

But if this man had been a pallbearer, he must have been a friend. Yet she never even met him? Odd.

"How did you know Charlie?" she asked the gentleman. She kept her gaze lowered, not willing to fully engage in a conversation with a stranger.

"We were at school together," he said. "And we both did some work for the government. I knew him well. And since you used the name Charlie, I assume you did, too."

"We were to be married."

His step hesitated very slightly, then caught the rhythm of hers again. She had surprised him.

"I'm sorry," he said. "I'm engaged, too. I can't imagine what it must be like for you."

"I hope you never have to," Sarah whispered.

At her words, he unconsciously put one hand on hers for a moment. "That means you must be Miss Brecknell," he said. "Charlie mentioned your name."

"Sarah Brecknell," she confirmed.

"Well, since we have no one else to properly introduce us, I'm Theodore Drayton, Lord Markham. I expect we never met because your fiancé didn't want you to know what reprobates he associated with." Markham's tone was just a little teasing, perhaps in an effort to snap her out of the worst shock.

The name was vaguely familiar, and something in his voice reminded her of another conversation she once had with Charlie. She looked at him fully for the first time. He bore her examination without any sign of discomfort. Indeed, he seemed almost to welcome it. He was not particularly tall, perhaps two or three inches above her own height. His reddish brown hair was cut a little shorter than was popular at the moment. She barely noticed his features, or really anything beyond the black clothes, because she was caught by his eyes. They were a warm green, and familiar. She had seen those eyes somewhere. "Are you sure we haven't been introduced?" she asked, trying to place him.

"I promise you I would have remembered," he said. "Why?"

Sarah looked down again, finally conscious of her manners. "Forgive me. I must be mistaken."

They reached the Wolvertons' home, where the guests would eat and drink and remember the dead…and gossip.

Sarah had been in the house the previous night, for the sitting up. At the invitation of the family, she'd sat up with the body for a few hours, and could only stare at the closed wooden box. How could Charlie be in there? she wondered. How could Charlie be so *still*? That wasn't Charlie. He was always quick, talkative, engaging…*alive.*

It was traditional for a casket to be open, for that way family and friends could look upon the deceased one last time before they were buried. But Charlie's death had been violent: a horrible accident. Thus, Charlie's sweet and charming face would be hidden, because it was no longer sweet or charming. His mother declared no one would look upon her son that way. He would be remembered as he had been in life. Hence, the closed coffin, shutting Sarah out in another small way.

His family—especially his mother and sisters—was so kind to her after the news, but Sarah felt an outsider that day. She was only Charlie's fiancée, not his wife. She was not family. And now she never would be. The ache in her heart was unbearable.

The night before, the house had been nearly silent. At the wake, it was already lively. True, all the guests wore sober colors and expressed heartfelt condolences to the family. The late Charles Wolverton had been in the prime of life, and his death came as a shock to everyone in society. Such a tragic accident!

Lord Markham hadn't left her in the few moments since they arrived at the house. He seemed to take the role of escort seriously, and Sarah was rather glad. He directed her to the receiving line the family had set up.

They both spoke briefly to Charlie's parents. His mother was crying, his father looked devastated. His younger sisters Georgia and Bryony had taken over as hostesses, putting their own grief aside for the necessary job of greeting guests and accepting condolences on the part of the family.

"Oh, Sarah," Georgia said when she saw her. "I feel you should be standing right here with us." Georgia's blonde hair was pulled back severely, and her normally bright blue eyes were red-rimmed.

Sarah said, "I only wish we didn't have to be here at all. Please let me know if there's anything I can do. I don't know what that could be, but..." she trailed off, feeling useless.

"We were going to make the same offer," said Bryony.

She was just young enough to wear her blonde hair down in braids, which had the effect of making her look especially vulnerable in a black gown which didn't quite fit her. "A few months' difference, and you'd be a sister. So you must remember that."

"I'll never forget that," Sarah promised.

"And it's fitting that you're joined by our not-quite brother." Georgia looked at Markham and smiled tremulously.

"Miss Wolverton, Miss Bryony," Markham said then. "I'm so sorry."

"Thank you for coming, my lord," Georgia replied. "I was just thinking about how you and Charlie would play chess for hours on end. We still have the set out in the drawing room, you know, halfway through a game."

"Perhaps I can call on you both and play a game or two," he said.

"That would be wonderful," Bryony said. "You are welcome any time. We won't be out much..." She suddenly broke off and turned her head away. "Excuse me. I'm just not *prepared* for this..."

"No one could be, Miss Bryony." Theo offered her a handkerchief, seemingly without even noticing he did it.

Sarah watched the younger girl with concern. Bryony was supposed to have her debut in a few months. A period of mourning for her brother would no doubt affect her socially as well as personally. "Everyone will understand," Sarah added, hoping to reassure the girl.

"You both understand," Bryony whispered. "I just don't know about the rest of the world."

"Where is Lady Alyse?" Georgia asked Markham then, looking beyond him for another guest.

"Not in town, I'm afraid. She is at home in Cheltenham until the fall," he said. Sarah realized they must be talking about Markham's fiancée.

"So you escorted Miss Brecknell instead. How kind."

Sarah shook her head. "I came alone. I only met Lord Markham this morning."

"Truly?" Georgia asked curiously. "But you both knew Charlie so well! How is that possible?"

"Charlie lived in several different circles," Sarah said, with a little shrug.

Markham cleared his throat. "Let's move on. We've no wish to keep others from offering their sympathies."

"Please come see us soon, both of you," Bryony urged. "You will, won't you? The house is so quiet now. I don't like it."

They both promised, and then left so the sisters could speak to the many other guests.

Sarah allowed Markham to lead her to a quieter corner of the room. As she surveyed the chattering guests, she heard several rumors regarding Charlie's life and death.

He had a mistress, and they fought....

He was fleeing from a gang of thieves he fell in with...

He was mistaken for someone else, and it was all a tragic misunderstanding...

Sarah tuned out the words. She knew the correct story from the Wolvertons. Charlie had been driving his brougham to Woodforde, which was his private retreat outside of the city. But he'd gone rather late at night, and on the road a group of highwaymen waylaid him. Highwaymen did not usually kill their victims, but something had gone wrong during the robbery and Charlie had been shot. The highwaymen, of course, fled the scene, leaving Charlie to die alone in the night. The truth was horrible enough. Why did people always want to add embellishments to it?

She noticed Markham watching her with those oddly familiar eyes. "You said Charlie lived in several circles," he said quietly.

She nodded. "His family, his own friends. Me, when he was in town. He was busy, you know. Always off on some important function abroad. That's all I meant."

"He told you about what he did?" Markham's voice sharpened a bit.

Sarah looked out the window, feeling a jolt of alarm. "Not the particulars," she said quickly. "He did not speak of any business or other such affairs with me, my lord." She couldn't look at Markham while she spoke, because she was not a good liar. The fact was that Sarah knew more than she should about Charlie's real work. He'd been a spy, part of a highly secret group called the Zodiac.

"So he didn't talk about his work," Markham said, in a more normal tone.

The weight of it all seemed to bear down on her again, making it hard to even speak. She said, "No. When we were together, we spoke of other things. Just silly things."

"You don't strike me as a particularly silly person, Miss Brecknell."

"I'm sure you can't judge at this point." She spoke too sharply, but his questions had put her on edge.

He immediately looked contrite. "I'm sorry. I didn't mean to disturb you."

"You're not what disturbs me today," she said.

He must have understood that a long conversation with her wouldn't look well at a funeral. He offered her a final condolence and began to turn away.

"Lord Markham," she said, putting out one hand. She arrested the movement before she was anywhere close to touching him, but she'd caught his attention.

She took a breath to steady herself. "I was wondering. Do you think...do you think anything could have been done? When he died, I mean. Do you think there was any other outcome?"

Markham looked once at the crowd, then deliberately turned his back on the room to face her alone. "There have been a lot of rumors about his death," he said candidly. "I've heard some, and I expect you have too."

She nodded slowly.

"I don't know the whole truth," he said. "I wasn't there, so how could I? But I knew Charlie. He was my friend. Whatever happened, he was not at fault."

Sarah breathed out, more relieved to hear those words than she'd expected. That was her secret fear. If Charlie had done something rash to provoke the highwaymen, if he'd been too bold.... But of course he was too careful to do such a thing. It was bad luck. It had to be. "It helps to hear that."

"If I can be of any assistance to you, Miss Brecknell,

please let me know." He took out one of his cards, and scrawled his street direction in town on the back side with a pencil stub from his pocket. "Anything. No matter how odd or minor the request may be."

"Out of mutual friendship?" she asked, taking the card and reading both sides.

He nodded. "Of course."

Sarah looked at him steadily, trying to remember where she knew him from. "Thank you."

She turned away then, shutting him and everyone else out of her private grief. She didn't know when Markham left, and she didn't care. But she kept his card held tightly in her hand, the edge of the paper digging into her skin through the black gloves.

Chapter 2

♉

THEODORE FLED THE WAKE EARLY, leaving the quiet, stunned Miss Brecknell alone in the crowd of mourners. He would have liked to stay a bit longer and talk to the others, but he had somewhere to be.

It was an almost offensively sunny day, especially for a man in Theo's frame of mind—rain would have suited him better. August heat had settled over the city of London, bringing with it the peculiar, brackish scent of the Thames, at least to some neighborhoods. The air would make the residents pray for the first breezes of autumn.

He'd been to plenty of funerals before; he'd go to many more after today. Why did this one feel so different? Because Charlie and he were almost the same age? Perhaps. Nearly the same station, too. Theo would inherit a title, and Charlie came from generations of landed gentry. They were also linked by one more fact, though this was a closely held secret. Both men were members of a group called the Zodiac.

The Zodiac was an organization of spies, dedicated to protecting England against all manner of threats. He worked for years as a member of the group. He never worked with Charlie—or anyone else for that matter. The signs of the Zodiac were solitary. But as Pisces, Charlie sometimes briefed him on a matter of diplomacy, or informed him of news that would affect his next assignment. Theo was sure Charlie saved his life more than once.

But now Charlie was dead. Theo believed it had to be connected to the Zodiac. An enemy working against them overpowered Charlie. Or perhaps someone was taking vengeance against the Zodiac and Charlie was just a first assault. There were too many possibilities and no way to get answers until he met with his superior.

And then there was Sarah Brecknell, who Charlie never bothered to even introduce to his friends. When Theo first saw her, he briefly wondered if the fact that she was dressed in grey—rather than black—meant she wasn't particularly upset by Charlie's death. Once he saw her face up close, he knew that wasn't the case. She looked frozen, her wide grey eyes unfocused and her skin unnaturally pale.

But the whole conversation with her left Theo rather nonplussed. At times, she seemed to almost know Charlie's secret. *He lived in several circles*, she said. But Theo told himself that she couldn't have meant *the* circle, which was what the Zodiac agents often called their group. It had to be a coincidence—if Theo wasn't so on edge, he wouldn't have thought twice about it.

As he walked, his mind drifted back to Charlie. Theo had gone to school with him, and he always admired Charlie's intelligence and humor. Theo was higher-born, but it never got in the way, because both boys had similar interests: riding, games, girls, and pulling pranks. The pranks got more and more elaborate as they grew older, often involving weeks of planning and sneaking into the headmaster's office at night to get whatever they needed. The payoff was always worth the punishment.

Over the years, Theo learned how to pick locks, hide in plain sight, lie to his elders, and keep a secret. Who knew such childish tricks would be so useful later in life?

After school, Charlie had begun work in the government, and Theo had been aimless, living the life of a lord's son awaiting his full title. Charlie showed up one day, as giddy as he used to be when he thought up a new trick.

"Enjoying yourself?" he had asked, knowing full well that Theo was bored to death. "How would you feel about pulling some more pranks…but with higher stakes?"

Of course Theo was hooked. If not for Charlie, Theo would likely still be drifting through London, living a dull and ordinary life. Instead, he risked his life for his nation, and he liked it far better.

Theo's father, the Baron Markham, was a member of the House of Lords, though he wasn't terribly active when not defending his own neck of the woods. Theo would eventually succeed his father, and he hoped he'd do well. But he dared not wait for his father to pass away before he started living. Besides, Theo liked his father better alive.

Theo's father never would have permitted him to join the military—he was the oldest son, and thus the heir. But Theo wanted to do something. He couldn't imagine a worse fate than watching as events across the continent and across the world seemed to explode. His work with the Zodiac filled that need.

Lost in these thoughts, Theo walked back to where Charlie was buried. He didn't hurry. In his severely black clothing, he was already overheating. All too soon, he stood at the entrance to the churchyard again. He glanced over at the eastern side, where Charlie lay underground.

Theo didn't linger, but turned in through a side door. The church appeared deserted at the moment. He found the stairs to the choir loft and climbed them, suddenly dreading the meeting he was about to have. Some terrible feeling came over him, perhaps inspired by the fresh grave and the silent church. It was as if he were about to discover something hideous.

But the only thing awaiting him in the choir loft was a man with sandy colored hair and mild blue eyes. His short stature made him seem unassuming. But Julian Neville was more than he seemed.

Julian was Theo's superior. He was Aries, the First Sign of the Zodiac. Theo reported to him and received all his assignments from him. And now, Theo hoped Julian would be able to explain Charlie's death.

"Morning, Taurus," Julian said quietly, using Theo's code name. "I won't say good morning, because it won't be. I'm afraid I have bad news."

"Worse than Charlie being dead?"

"Far worse."

Julian said nothing more, and Theo got worried. "Why are you waiting?"

"Because there's no easy way to say this." Julian took

a breath. "Charlie was a traitor."

"No, he wasn't," Theo said instantly. He rarely contradicted Julian, but that was over the line. "How could that possibly be? He was a *sign*. He was my friend."

"He was a traitor." Julian's face was calm, but underneath, he was seething.

Theo knew better than to argue, but he did anyway. "There's a mistake. He must have been set up. Framed."

Julian shook his head. The light from the stained glass window hit him oddly, making his face and hair suddenly red, then blue, then gold. "Believe me, I wish to God that were true. But Charlie confessed it before he died. He'd been acting against England for over two years."

"Confessed to who? How do we know this? He died in an accident." Theo was getting angrier by the minute. How could such a thing happen and he didn't even have a hint about it? "Tell me how you found out. Tell me how he *died*."

"It's complicated. Not too long ago, I sent two agents on an assignment. In the course of their work, they discovered there was a traitor linked to the Zodiac, and then discovered the traitor was actually a sign. Pisces."

"Charlie," Theo said, to make absolutely sure he wasn't going insane.

"Yes. One of the agents, Libra, tracked him down in order to get him to confess the details. The chase led to that road outside London. Charlie wasn't driving alone, waylaid by highwaymen. He was with Libra, who had followed him with the hope of gaining more evidence. Unfortunately, Charlie resisted and was accidentally killed."

"Accidentally?" Theo echoed, skeptical.

"Libra wanted him alive, trust me. But Charlie preferred death to explaining himself. We didn't have much time to concoct a story that made sense—highwaymen were something believable, and we discouraged any investigation into the matter."

Theo sat down in one of the long pews. "A traitor," he said. It was too much to take in.

"Yes." Julian looked at him steadily. "I'm sorry to bring you this news, Theo."

Something in the way Julian said it made Theo look up. "Do you think I'm complicit?"

Julian raised one eyebrow. "Should I?"

"I was one of Charlie's best friends," Theo said. "He's the reason I'm part of the Zodiac. You know that. Why wouldn't you think I was involved?"

"I don't."

Theo sighed. He hadn't realized until that moment how tense he'd got. "For a moment, I thought…"

"You thought I'd set up a meeting in the church in order to kill you and have a convenient place to bury the body? If I were going to do that, I wouldn't have given you any warning."

The terrifying part of that was the utterly indifferent way Julian said it. He would have killed Theo without a second thought if he considered him a traitor like Charlie.

A traitor like Charlie.

"I'm not going to say you're wrong," he told Julian. "But I'm going to need a while to come around to this."

"Of course."

"Can you…" Theo paused. "Can you tell me anything about what he was doing?"

"He was selling documents he was able to procure in the course of his work, both during his Zodiac assignments and as part of his cover work in the department. Though he seemed to sell to various players, we know he was in contact with Arceneau, at least indirectly."

Theo knew that name well. Over the past decade, the man called Arceneau had emerged as an extremely powerful criminal mind. Though French by birth, he had no sense of loyalty or patriotism. He was particularly interested in supplying governments with weapons and war supplies. To be sure he'd always have customers, Arceneau frequently meddled in politics and did everything he could to worsen hostilities between nations.

"Well, I suppose Charlie decided if he was going to turn traitor, he might as well aim high."

"Indeed. He told Libra he intended to stop. He would use the excuse of his marriage to leave both the Zodiac and his position in the government. I have my doubts."

"What else?" Theo asked.

"We don't know much more. Charlie wasn't particularly forthcoming, as Libra's multiple knife wounds prove."

"He's alive?"

"Libra is surprisingly difficult to kill," Julian said, with an odd smile.

"But no one is searching for any papers left behind?"

Julian shook his head. "Don't go looking for an assignment. I have another agent cleaning up after Charlie, and besides, you're too close to it. I wouldn't assign you anyway."

"But I could talk to his family. His fiancée. What if he told them something, even a slip of the tongue?"

"No. Charlie was nothing if not smart. Too smart to share a secret like this with his sisters or his bride-to-be."

"But there's a chance…"

"Taurus. Stop it."

"Yes, sir." Theo nodded, accepting the reality of the situation.

"I'm telling you the truth because you deserve to know how and why Charlie died…and why you shouldn't lose too much sleep over it."

"I was at the funeral. Everyone was devastated."

"Let them remember the man Charlie used to be." Julian stood up. "He was a good man once."

"When did he stop?"

"I wish I knew." Julian looked hard at him. "Have I got your word? You won't go poking around? If this whole thing disappears, we'll all be better off."

Theo stood up as well. "It's not my assignment. I understand that, sir."

"That's all, then," Julian said quietly.

Theo watched the other man walk out. He didn't move, still shocked by the unwelcome revelation. If Charlie had gone so wrong, there must be a reason for it. And Theo intended to find it.

Thank God Julian hadn't noticed Theo's promise wasn't a promise at all.

Chapter 3

♉

January 1807, five months later

SEASONS PASSED, AS SEASONS WILL. At first, Sarah knew nothing would be the same after Charlie's death. In those first numbing and dark days, she thought about Charlie every minute. She cried nearly as often.

"You look like a widow, my dear," her mother had said. "You are far too young for that."

Sarah shrugged, unwilling to talk about it. Her mother was as unlike Sarah as it was possible for a woman to be. She was graceful, witty, and adored the intrigues of polite society. She had not gone to the funeral because she felt that black was unflattering to her complexion—the same complexion Sarah inherited.

Her mother went on, "The worst will fade. I know you don't believe me now, but you will recover."

"I don't want to recover," Sarah said.

"But you will," her mother said firmly. "Just you see. Next year at this time, you'll have a new beau, and a new life..."

"A new beau? Mama, how can you talk about such

things at a time like this?"

"Because I'm older than you, dear. You will mourn, but not forever. Trust me."

Sarah pressed her lips into a thin line. She would not argue with her mother. She would not speak of her life after Charlie. If her mother thought she was just a fickle girl who didn't know what love was, she was much mistaken. Sarah promised her whole soul to her love. She even gave him her body, eager to prove her love to him. She gave Charlie everything, because he was the only person in the world for her.

And then her grief mixed with fear. Only a few weeks before Charlie's death, on a warm summer night, they had been alone. They were often given time alone, thanks to the impending marriage. The legitimacy of the engagement gave them leave to be together without offending propriety. But on that particular evening, seduced by summer and love and her fiancé's charm, Sarah allowed him to do something she knew she shouldn't. But he loved her, and she loved him. And they would be married soon. What difference would a few months make? She let him take her virginity, because he said he adored her and couldn't wait. She wanted to make him happy. And she was curious.

It had been, if not magical, mostly pleasant. She thought she understood why men and women did such things. And she did love him.

But then the tragedy of his death put all her silly, dreamy notions to shame. Once the first shock and grief passed, Sarah was seized by a new fear. What if she was with child—a real possibility, considering the timing. She turned nervous and jumpy. Her prayers alternated between begging for evidence that she wasn't carrying, and begging for forgiveness for committing such a great sin. For two weeks after the funeral, Sarah didn't leave her house.

Then, she awoke one day to find blood on her sheets. Oddly, she broke down in tears when she discovered she wasn't pregnant with Charlie's child, because that meant he wouldn't live on. Her maid Naomi had to coax her out of bed just so she could change the linens.

But somehow, life was indifferent, and went on regardless. Weeks later, she realized with a start she had gone a few hours with no thought of Charlie at all. Then she felt a horrible sense of guilt for forgetting him for even an hour, and she cried again, but this time alone in her room.

Summer came to a gentle close, and Sarah ate food, slept, and held conversations like a perfectly normal person. She dressed in mourning and refused nearly all invitations. But the worst grief—and the worst fear—seemed to pass.

As the weather grew cooler, so did her heart. She sometimes went a day or two without thinking of Charlie, and when she did, the tears didn't always come. Some of the memories were happy, and some were simply there. Was it possible she might endure?

Sarah's parents began to prevail on her to go outside of their home. Her mother, always alert to social niceties, counseled Sarah to accept more invitations and to put off her full mourning clothes. She said Sarah's fair coloring suffered in black—and that was impossible to refute.

Her father's requests were easier to accept, since he only urged her to go with him to her favorite place in the world: the Athenaeum. The building housed a society for the advancement of science and knowledge. While only men—such as her father—were permitted full membership, Sarah had been there so often over the years she was practically considered a sort of communal niece. She was as common a sight around the place as Cassius, the Athenaeum's Chief Mouser.

Cassius was a sleek, beautiful black cat with an affectionate manner and the soul of a murderer. He more than earned his keep with his dedication to keeping the building free of mice and rats. The books were protected from rodents' teeth, and Cassius was well fed at no cost.

The Athenaeum liked such practical arrangements.

Sarah's arrangement was also practical. As a child, the old men (they all seemed like very old men to her then) were amused and delighted by her interest in their subjects.

As the years went by, Sarah was educated in a manner befitting her station…and indeed far beyond it, for Sarah proved to have an insatiable appetite for learning. So it must have seemed quite natural to give the very young lady a space of her own, where she could study or read or perform some administrative tasks for the society while her father pursued his own work in the larger reading room where all the men gathered.

It was a happy compromise. Sarah got her privacy and a space to read, and all the proprieties were observed, since Sarah was surely adequately chaperoned by dint of having so many elders surrounding her.

Sarah loved her little office. It was tiny, scarcely more than a closet. But she had a desk to work at, a chair to sit in, and another, more comfortable chair to read in if she chose. Because the room was all the way at the end of the hallway, she did not disturb the gentlemen going to and fro. Not that the usually silent Sarah disturbed anyone. She was a model of a young lady, all the members said.

As she gradually came out of mourning, Sarah felt comfortable attending lectures, because it appeared she was being social, when she in fact barely remembered half the topics. But it kept her mother from hounding her about other commitments for the length of autumn. By the time winter settled on the city, she had established a routine, one centered on avoiding society in favor of hiding with the academics who populated the Athenaeum.

One day in January, she was ensconced in her office. She had accompanied her father there in the early afternoon, just when her mother settled into the drawing room to accept any callers who might come by. Sarah hated the idea of sitting and waiting for callers, so she was doubly glad to escape the house. This afternoon, she was curled in the chair, reading. Cassius prowled around the office, listening for mice. She was thoroughly lost in her book. For the moment, she was a Roman general, exploring the dark, barbaric forests of Gaul at the height of the Republic. That the book was in Latin made no difference at all. She could read Latin as easily as English ever since she was young.

A noise at the door brought her back to reality for half a moment. The sound was like that of claws scratching the wood.

"Cassius!" she said sharply, without dragging her eyes from the page. "Stop that or you won't get the fish I saved for you!"

"What a shame. I do love fish." The voice was almost a purr, but it was no cat.

Sarah jumped when she heard it. Her eyes snapped up to see a huge man standing at the door, overcoat still spotted with snow. His dark hair was long, and damp from the weather outside, so it gleamed in the light of the single lamp on her desk.

He stepped inside the room, pulling the door shut behind him.

She was trapped with him.

Cassius took one look at the newcomer and hissed, his back arching up. The man ignored the cat.

"Who are you?" she gasped, regaining her voice. "Get out!"

The man shrugged aside his overcoat to reveal the pistol he held. "You're not in charge. I have an item of business to discuss with you, Miss Sarah Brecknell, and *then* I will be on my way." His voice was accented, but he spoke his English perfectly, adding special emphasis to her name. The man's bulk was almost entirely muscle, and the width of his shoulders implied a vicious level of strength. She would never get past him.

"How did you get so far into the building? Please leave. I am sure that I have no business with you," Sarah returned sharply, despite her racing heart. The pistol held her gaze.

"You do," he said. Sharp eyes surveyed her from head to foot and back. His expression shifted from indifference to appreciation.

Sarah noted his appraisal and shivered. She looked instinctively at the letter opener lying on the desktop. It was the only thing she had which even remotely resembled a weapon.

He saw it too, and smiled, showing surprisingly white teeth. Before she could do anything, he leaned forward and seized the letter opener with his free hand. He twirled it with three fingers, and she saw his hand was completely missing the last two. The detail made him even more alarming.

He said, "The business I refer to involves a gentleman you might remember. Charles Wolverton."

He may as well have pulled the trigger of the gun. Sarah moved backward, her breathing erratic. "Charlie?" She sank back onto the chair.

"Charlie," he confirmed. "So you do remember him. Of course, since you were his lover."

"His fiancée, you mean," Sarah corrected weakly, too weakly. "But Charlie died."

"And good riddance to him." The man sneered. "He was weak at the end. Made mistakes."

"What can you want with me?" Sarah asked plaintively. How dare he say that? Charlie had been unlucky. An accident could happen to anyone.

"He left something behind," the man said. "Something

important. You are in a position to get it for me. If you do, I will disappear from your life and you will have nothing to fear."

"And if I don't?"

"Then you'll have plenty to fear." He looked at her again, showing those white teeth once more. Sarah knew exactly what he meant by that gaze. She shuddered.

"What am I supposed to find?" she asked, striving to keep the terror she felt from surfacing in her voice.

"There were some letters and other documents he was, ah, keeping safe. You must find the hiding place he used, and bring the items to me."

"But I don't know…"

"You can find them, Miss Sarah," the man said. "Surely a gentleman so close to his fiancée told her a few little secrets, passed her a few little love notes. You must remember his quirks. Where he might have hidden a letter…or concealed a message. Wolverton was good at that sort of thing. But you know that already." His smile was cruel then, hinting at many more secrets.

Sarah nodded before she could stop herself.

"I can try," she whispered. What else could she say?

"Excellent. I give you to the end of the month, the night of the 31st. If I do not see what I want by then, you will regret it for the rest of your very short life. I will send you a note to tell you where to go. Do you understand me?"

"Yes," Sarah whispered, her mind whirling.

With a negligent gesture, he flipped the letter opener past her, onto the desk. He waved his malformed hand in a mocking gesture of farewell, then turned his back and slipped out of the door, utterly unconcerned that she might attack him or cry for assistance. He didn't bother closing it after he left.

She stood up shakily, but made no move to call for help. What would be the point?

Cassius chose that moment to rub against her legs, and she snapped at him out of sheer shock. The cat hissed in response. Sarah bent to pick him up. "Oh, Cassius. What am I going to do?"

The cat, now nestled in her arms, began to purr. However, true to his species, he offered no solutions.

She shivered. "What can I possibly do?"

Sarah remained in the little office until her father rapped on the open door an hour later. She jumped in alarm, and Cassius, who had been curled on her lap, sprang up in irritation, streaking out of the room.

"That cat!" her father exclaimed, his voice going up a register. "He'll give us all heart attacks one day!"

"Is it time to go?" she asked.

"Far past. I lingered over some work and the building is nearly deserted."

He was a thin man, shorter than Sarah by an inch. He had greying hair, worn in a queue, just as he had worn it for decades previously. His grey eyes were weak, requiring him to wear spectacles all the time. But he nearly always wore a smile on his face, and had a habit of humming to himself while he worked.

"I thought you would come find me, dear," he went on. "It's well after dinner. We'll be lucky if Bette gives us some cold meat." He chuckled, knowing his words to be spurious. Their cook Bette pampered the family, and they never lacked at meal time. He expected Sarah to laugh too, but when she didn't, he squinted at her. "I say, are you feeling well?"

"Yes, yes," she said hastily. "I was distracted. Let's return home. I'm famished. And we ought not neglect Mama, or she'll be cross."

Sarah put on her heavy pelisse. On the street, her father hailed a driver to take them back home. Behind her, the Athenaeum stood dark and silent. Until now, she thought of the place as some inviolable sanctuary. But the man had no trouble getting inside. Who would stop him?

She did her best to hide her anxiety from her father. It was not difficult. Stephen Brecknell was a man devoted to study, often to the point of ignoring the outer world entirely. He could go for a day without eating, and he was not to be trusted to pick out his own clothing. Sarah thanked her stars for his absentmindedness that night. She wouldn't dare get her family involved in whatever madness just happened.

But she couldn't solve the problem on her own.

Chapter 4

♉

WHEN THEY ARRIVED AT THEIR house, Sarah hurried her father inside. She saw nothing out of the ordinary, but she still felt watched, and she glanced around her as if she would see the hulking form of the stranger there, too. The man knew where her office was. Surely he knew where her home was as well. So why did he need Sarah to find something Charlie left? Or was this all a trick of some kind?

Inside the modest home of the Brecknells, everything appeared normal. The fires in each room were kept going against the cold and damp. Both Sarah and her father were given a very hearty late dinner by Bette, who had kept the food warm and even managed a perfectly timed sweet cheese soufflé for dessert.

After dinner, they went into the parlor where Mrs Brecknell usually spent her time. Sarah found her mother asleep in a chair.

"Mama?" Sarah asked, nudging her shoulder. "Mama, you ought to go to your bed now."

Her mother blinked and yawned. She was a proper lady, and even her yawns were delicate. "Sarah, are you back at last? Your father keeps you out too late at that place. You ought to be at home instead."

"I want to be there, Mama," Sarah reminded her. Then she thought of the incident again. If that man could simply walk into the building and accost her, perhaps she *didn't* want to be there. "You were asleep already. Should you go off to bed?"

"Not yet," her mother said. "I have a few things to discuss with you."

Sarah sighed. She knew exactly what was coming.

The social season had begun earlier in the month. Invitations were trickling in again for parties and teas. The Wolvertons even sent a dinner invitation, despite the fact that they still mourned their son's death. However, with Bryony's coming out to consider, life had to go on.

A few cards from gentlemen she had known also came to the house—names of those who courted her before she accepted Charlie. Sarah often said she was not at home, but some of those gentlemen would not be put off forever. Perhaps they had found no replacement since then. They would all be quite disappointed in her now. She was not the same girl she had been three winters ago.

Her mother picked up a short stack of papers. "I saw several invitations on the table. Have you responded to these yet, my dear?" she asked.

Sarah said, "I will send my regrets tomorrow. I was too busy to write today."

Her mother frowned. She was a pretty woman, still mostly blonde like her daughter, though she had rich brown eyes, where Sarah inherited her father's eyes. "I would council you to accept at least one of these. If you keep refusing, eventually you will no longer receive any invitations."

"Thus saving me the bother of sending regrets."

"If you don't want to venture out alone, join me to make some calls." Seeing Sarah's wrinkled nose, she added, "Or ask your friend Chloe. She's always happy to go visiting! You need not be alone, dear. People wish to see your face."

Sarah stifled a huff. "Mama, no one cares in the least. *You* are the person they all want at the parties. You're the witty one. Why don't you accept an invitation?"

"So councils the hermit!" Her mother sniffed.

But Sarah did see the point, so she said, "You know, the Wolvertons are hosting a dinner in two days. I said I will go. Georgia had been after me about it."

"A dinner is better than nothing." Her mother smiled a bit. "Then I shall go to Lady Mathering's little event next week. You see how your obedience heals your mother's heart."

Sarah rolled her eyes. "Yes, Mama."

Her father sat on a chair near his wife. She turned to him, but didn't let Sarah off the hook.

"Though a dinner with the Wolvertons will hardly better your chances at another proposal. It would be good for you to consider future prospects and put the past aside."

"Put myself on the market again, you mean." Sarah's own coming out had taken place three years ago. She would not be seen as a catch next to the young debutantes this winter, even with her respectable dowry. "Besides, I won't catch any eyes in my grey gowns."

Her mother sighed. "Then wear a color. You were not his wife. Five months, six months…you have shown very proper grief. But you still have a life to live."

"Ah, let her be," her father interjected in a mild tone—his tone was always mild, truth be told. "Sarah goes out nearly every day when she comes to the Athenaeum with me. She is such a help. And what is the point of having a brain if not to use it? Let her be."

"Of course, dear," her mother responded, though she waved another invitation at Sarah meaningfully.

"I will consider them," Sarah said, hoping to appease her mother.

"Truly?"

"Of course." Of course she would consider attending meaningless parties and dances. And then she would choose not to go.

Her mother sensed her recalcitrance. "I will insist."

"Can you insist tomorrow? I have a book I'm keen to finish."

"You and your endless books. Your father is far too indulgent of your habits," she groused.

"And too indulgent of yours, Madeline," her father said. "You should go to bed. Let me take you there."

Once her mother was on her feet, she kissed Sarah on the forehead. "Don't stay up too late. You will get shadows under your pretty eyes."

"Yes, Mama."

After her parents went up to bed, Sarah walked over to

a bookshelf and hunted for a particular title. She found the book, bound in red leather, and took it up to her room. She had read this one before. It was not the book that interested her.

She opened the front flap and a card fell out. *Theodore Drayton, Lord Markham.*

Sarah picked up the card and traced the edges. She needed assistance—badly. But was that the sort of favor Markham had in mind when he handed her the card? Probably not. In all likelihood, it had been a meaningless gesture of comfort. What else does one say at a funeral?

And yet. She thought back to that painful day, trying to recall the man and the conversation. She couldn't remember what he looked like, but she could call up the words. *If I can be of any assistance to you, Miss Brecknell, please let me know.*

He just appeared at the funeral. There was no reason to seek her out at all. But he did. Perhaps there was another reason he spoke to her. Charlie had a secret life as a spy. He was more than he seemed. What if this man was too?

She didn't sleep, but lay staring into the darkness for a long while. She had to get help from somewhere. Georgia spoke of him as an almost-brother.

"I'll ask her about him at the dinner," she said out loud to the darkness. "She can tell me if he can be trusted."

Chapter 5

♉

THE NEXT MORNING, THEO WOKE up long before the dawn. He hadn't been sleeping particularly well for the past few months, whether he was at the family estate or in his own townhouse, tucked in a quiet corner of Berkley Square.

It was better since his sister and her husband came to stay with him for the duration of the Season. Katherine and Harry lived near the Markham home in rural Gloucestershire, not far from Cheltenham. But they always managed to come to London for the Season. Katherine was older than Theo by three years, but she had never lost her love for the gaiety of society, even after she bore two girls and settled down to a considerably quieter life.

Theo found the presence of his family comforting. He always wanted a family himself, but his work with the Zodiac meant he kept putting it off. Luckily, his Alyse was understanding. As the first daughter of a wealthy earl, she had a comfortable life already, and little need to rush into a marriage.

Theo dressed, then sat down to look over a few notes he'd made for himself. He liked working at this time of day—all was quiet, so he could think. For the past few months, Theo had been pursuing a few lines of investigation into Charlie's past, despite being told not to. Theo simply couldn't leave it alone. In the guise of his legitimate role as an attaché for diplomatic work on the Continent, Theo exploited his contacts and chased down any potential lead regarding the possibility of stolen documents offered for sale.

As Theo carefully talked with people he could trust—or bribe—he learned of Charlie's past sales, which revealed his sometime friend as a shrewd businessman. Charlie sold a few stolen documents nearly every time he went on an assignment for the Zodiac. How he smuggled the documents to the buyers was another question. He was never caught by either British or Continental authorities, so he must have devised a wickedly clever way to hide the contraband. Smuggling one letter one time was difficult enough. Charlie crossed the Channel so often that he couldn't possibly have escaped the occasional run in with authorities. Whether it was custom officers, police, or military intelligence…someone must have searched him and his belongings occasionally. All spies knew it would happen. The best ones had good hiding places, good stories, or a good amount of money to pay off their interrogators. Charlie must have had all three to succeed as long as he did.

He did find out that Charlie was interested in things such as troop movements and plans for war machines. All of Theo's investigations kept pointing to Arceneau as a main customer. Charlie often sold the documents to assistants because the man himself was mostly above such transactions, but the money came from Arceneau.

And yet, with Charlie's death, everything seemed to have stopped. Perhaps Julian was right; chasing down more clues would only risk exposing there'd been a mole. With every passing day, the risk diminished. If Theo listened to logic, he'd give up his hunt. But Theo also listened to his gut, which told him if Charlie was involved, nothing would be simple.

Throughout his investigation, he kept returning to Sarah Brecknell. Though he only met her once, she became a symbol in his mind. She stood for all the people Charlie betrayed. The young woman had done nothing, yet she—like so many others—suffered because of Charlie's selfishness.

She should not have had such an effect on him. It was silly. He built her up into a beautiful, tragic heroine. But he didn't know much about her. She was respectable. She was extremely well educated. And she was engaged to Charlie. Nothing about her situation gave Theo a reason to see her again.

But for some reason, he wanted to.

He made a sound of frustration, and packed away his notes. In any case, he could do nothing more without a new lead. He glanced outside and saw the sky was much brighter as dawn came.

The door opened and Theo's valet walked in. "Oh," he said, on seeing Theo up and dressed. "Why did you not ring?"

"I am capable of dressing myself, you know, Baxter.

I'm twenty-nine, after all."

"Indeed you are, my lord," Baxter replied, artfully avoiding whether he was referring to Theo's age or his abilities. "Started your work early?"

"Yes, but I will be leaving the house after I have some breakfast. I have a few things to attend to." Theo put his notes in a drawer and locked it.

"Do you want the carriage brought around?" Baxter asked.

"No, I'll walk. I want to think." Theo always thought best when he was moving.

Baxter nodded and tidied up a few things around the room, while Theo went downstairs to find something to eat. He frequently ate long before the rest of the household, so the cook never bothered with a sideboard for him, instead bringing hot food directly from the kitchen. He drank his tea and ate some ham on bread without tasting much of anything.

While Theo sat at the table, two servants entered. He looked up, seeing the two newest employees at his house, Jem and Ivy. "Good morning," he said. "What brings you both here?"

After checking that no one would overhear the conversation, Jem said, "We'd like to know if you've any assignments for us particularly."

The young man was taller than Theo by a few inches, and his lanky frame increased the effect. He possessed mouse brown hair and plain brown eyes and a forgettable face. Those features had no doubt been an asset in the boy's former life, when he worked as a pickpocket on the

London streets. His proper name was James, but the casual Jem fit him better.

"Aye, my lord," the maid named Ivy added. "Your windows are clean and the silver polished, but that's not truly why *we're* here." Ivy was an unassuming girl with a head of dark glossy hair that was pinned back and almost entirely hidden under her maid's cap. Indeed, she was so properly turned out and starched in her uniform that she disappeared behind it, which was a great advantage both in servitude and spying.

Both servants had been in the house about a month. Theo hired them at the express order of the Zodiac. Julian first learned of this odd group of disreputable servants during another agent's investigation into missing plans for a warship, which led to a woman named Miss Bering. Her servants, it turned out, were all former criminals she hired out of mercy. A criminal history would destroy the reputation of a servant, condemning him to low paying jobs or yet more criminal activity just to make ends meet. Miss Bering offered some of those people a new life, and her faith was repaid. Her servants were both uncommonly loyal and competent.

Julian realized the implications right away. History had many examples of servants who spied on their masters. But to train servants as spies…that was a step further. Servants were so often invisible. With the right letters of introduction, or the proper references—both easily fabricated—a uniformed servant could practically turn into a ghost, floating through the most secret rooms and overhearing the most sensitive conversations without drawing attention.

But first they had to be prepared, which was why Jem and Ivy were working at the Markham townhome. Theo leaned back in his seat, surveying them. "Ivy, how many guests have come to this house in the past week?"

"Seven, if one counts your aunt Lady Amelia as a guest," she said.

"And we must," he said, with a hint of sympathy. His aunt was the definition of a cantankerous old woman. Her arrivals were viewed with dread and her departures with elation. "Of those guests, whose rooms did you see to personally?"

"Lady Amelia's, your sister's, and her daughter Melissa's."

"Did you look in my sister's jewelry case?"

"Yes, sir," Ivy said, without a trace of shame. Most servants would deny such an act until they drew their last breath. But he wasn't accusing Ivy of theft, and she knew it. "She has an interesting collection, and she favors blue stones. Melissa, of course, is only permitted to wear the coral ring and beads."

"Does she read? My sister, that is?"

"She has a few books on her own table—the Bible, Mrs Radcliffe's latest novel, and *Christian Thoughts for Ladies*. Melissa has been given *The Road of Life: Improving Stories for Young Boys and Girls*, but she only reads it when her mother orders her to. She has dogeared a few passages in the Radcliffe novel, though—her mother underestimates her abilities." Ivy was sharp-eyed.

"If she were hiding something in the room, where

would you look?" he asked then.

"Under the bed," she said. "Or perhaps on top of the wardrobe. Your sister, begging your pardon, is not an original thinker. If I could do so without seeming suspicious, I'd just ask Miss Melissa. She has her nose in everything and likely found whatever it was by accident already."

He nodded. "That's all too true. Well, Ivy. You've more than proven yourself as an observer."

"Does that mean you'll give me a real assignment soon, sir?" she asked eagerly.

"As soon as I have one to give," he promised.

"Not that we're complaining," Jem added. "Had worse jobs than this, by far."

"How are you getting on?" Theo asked Jem. He knew the boy's skills already. Jem was able to get along with fellow servants, gentry, and common folk alike. His ready smile disarmed most people, and his various skills—legal and not—made him a good man for odd jobs. He also had a way with horses. He mainly worked as a hostler and driver, though he'd been a footman in the past.

"Nothing to speak of, sir," Jem said. "I exercised your horse Lightning this morning. That's a fine beast. The stables are cleaned and all the equipment mended."

"You're dying to do some real work, aren't you?" Theo said. "But you'll have to be patient. Remember that this experiment is still quite young."

"We know, sir, and we are grateful," Ivy spoke up. "It's just that we want to help, sir."

"I'm sure you'll get the chance, Ivy." Theo sent the

servants onto more mundane tasks, and then realized he needed a dose of normalcy. So he did the most normal thing he could think of: he called on his fiancée.

Theo usually went round to visit Alyse once a week or so. She smiled when he walked into the lavishly decorated drawing room of the Templeton family's home. *She is beautiful,* he thought. He'd thought so since she was about twelve years old and he was not that much older. She was petite and had long, dark curling hair she wore pinned up for the morning. Her sweet brown eyes crinkled at the corners when she laughed, which was often. She also possessed a dimple in each cheek, which he *knew* had got her out of trouble on many occasions during child-hood.

"Theo," she said warmly. "I didn't think you'd be over today."

"I should have sent word," he said.

"Don't be silly," she said, laughing. "You're always welcome here."

"Would you mind getting out for a bit?" he asked. "It's cold, but sunnier than it's been for the past week."

"That sounds splendid. As a matter of fact, it's good you came. I have something I need to discuss with you today."

Despite the chill, they walked through the park. As they were engaged, Theo was granted far more indulgence than a man normally would be toward the unmarried Al-yse.

She was well bundled against the cold, and her cheeks were a healthy pink after a few moments. She talked amiably enough for a while, but Theo could tell her mind had wandered.

He asked, "What's troubling you? You're drifting along and barely aware of where we are."

"Well, it's just that Mama has been after me to set a date."

Something lurched a bit inside Theo's brain. "She knows I'm content to wait, correct? It's not any great concern."

"Believe me, she is profoundly unconcerned with our unconcern," Alyse said, with a wry look. "*Her* concern is paramount."

He said nothing, taken somewhat aback. He knew they had to set a date for their wedding at some point, but he'd got used to the idea of the marriage being in a misty future, at a time when he was not so involved with the Zodiac and when he'd have more attention for Alyse and his own duties as a husband and—presumably—father.

"I told her we would discuss it today," Alyse went on.

"And we are discussing it."

"Yet I'm not sure that will satisfy Mama, who has been pointing out any tiny baby in her line of sight."

He couldn't stop a laugh. "So, that's the issue."

"Yes, issue is the issue," Alyse quipped, though she quickly sobered. "Not that I don't want children. Of course I do."

"But…"

She looked around the quiet park. "I am quite spoiled, you know. Since I have you, I have neither to impress a brigade of hopefuls nor worry about making a wrong step.

I can simply *live*."

"I hope you don't think you'll be shackled to a wall once we're married. Much will be exactly the same as before." Why did that seem damning, rather than reassuring, as he'd meant it to be?

Alyse didn't seem to notice. "Oh, Theo, I know that. But you have your interests and I have mine, and we're not rushing to please everyone else, so why must we bend to the will of the mothers?"

"You'll not look at it that way when you're the mother."

She laughed, suddenly looking carefree again. "That's true. I *am* spoiled. Listen to me!"

"I am listening to you, Alyse. And I happen to agree… with you and with your mother."

"Meaning?"

"We ought to set a date, if for no other reason than to reassure the world we are dedicated to the marriage."

"Yes, you're right. You're always right, aren't you."

"Perhaps in spring?" he suggested, thinking it sounded far off.

"Spring," she mused. "Maybe. At the end of the Season…that way the wedding will be an event Mama can plan to death. All the other events will be done, so she'll know which ones to top."

"Late May," he said. "Lots of flowers around then. Much better than a dreary winter day."

"Indeed." Alyse nodded, looking decisive at last. "Thank you, Theo. It always helps to talk to you."

"I hope so. It's what I'm here for, after all."

"Mama will be quite happy to hear it."

"Are you?" he asked.

Alyse looked at him, her head tipped to the side. "What does that mean?"

"I don't know," he said, suddenly doubting himself. "Nothing. Don't mind me. I just wasn't expecting to set the date today."

"I sympathize. But we have to do it sooner or later, don't we?"

"Yes." Theo smiled, hoping to reassure both her and himself it was a happy occasion. He loved Alyse. He always had. So why wasn't he eager to marry her?

Chapter 6

♉

FOR THE NEXT TWO DAYS, Sarah couldn't sleep. Every time she closed her eyes, she saw the man again, with his cruel smile and his hand with the missing fingers. She had literally no idea what to do about his threat. What could he have meant by his implication that she could somehow get hold of Charlie's secret papers? And indeed, how did the man even know Charlie was a spy? She turned over possibilities in her mind, and came to no conclusions because there was no one but herself to talk to.

She didn't go to the Athenaeum, too afraid to encounter the man again. Instead, she stayed at home, sitting near her mother and fretting silently. She looked composed from the outside. She was actually quite good at hiding her own thoughts, which was a skill she learned when defending her intelligence against various men and women who thought her interests frivolous. But all the same, she worried.

Thus, by the time Naomi dressed her for the dinner at the Wolvertons on Sunday evening, Sarah was a wreck. She wore a gown of dark grey wool, and she insisted on restrained jewelry and hairstyle. Naomi groused that her skills as a lady's maid were being squandered. When given free rein, she was capable of turning any woman into a stunning work of art. She'd learned her craft from her mother, who brought her from the West Indies to London when their old employer died.

"Your mother at home so often, and you darting back and forth from here to that place where there isn't a gentleman under the age of fifty," Naomi said, her smooth brown hands working efficiently to brush Sarah's hair to gleaming. "What do you need me for? I may as well give my notice."

"We'd never survive without you," Sarah said. She watched the maid's face in the mirror, and caught the teasing light in her wide set, brown eyes. "Would you like to curl my hair?"

"I would, but you'll be late for the dinner then," Naomi said, with regret. "I'll put it in a twist tonight. And may I use the coral pin? You must be sick to death of jet."

Sarah raised her eyebrow at Naomi's choice of words, but merely said, "The coral won't match my outfit."

"Nothing matches charcoal grey. I remember dressing you in colors. Like a garden. And now you insist on winter all the time."

Sarah sighed. She missed the colors, but the grey clothes made her nearly invisible, and she did not like the idea of attracting attention, particularly after the incident the other night. "Someday, Naomi. I need time."

The maid paused in her efforts and gave Sarah's shoulders a friendly squeeze. "Yes, miss."

After a moment, Naomi asked, "Who will be there tonight?"

"Oh, just the family, and a few friends," Sarah answered. "It's quite a small dinner." She wouldn't have gone otherwise. Since the Wolvertons were practically family, she didn't need to have a parent or chaperone along. The truth was that Sarah found herself in an odd space with regards to how people saw her. She was no longer a young miss under anyone's watchful eye. And since she'd been engaged to Charlie for so long, she was seen almost as a widow, despite not ever being married. She was so quiet that most people didn't even notice her, and no one was ever concerned about her behavior. Thus, Sarah slipped through the usual social requirements without anyone making a fuss.

When she arrived at the Wolvertons, Georgia was there to greet her. "Come along, and I shall make sure you are acquainted with everyone. There may be a few you don't know."

Inside the parlor, Sarah surveyed the faces. She had seen the family several times since the funeral, but this was the first proper dinner she had attended. Mr and Mrs Wolverton greeted her kindly. Bryony, healthier and happier now, chattered about her upcoming Season. Sarah also knew Mr Faber, who was courting Georgia.

Then she saw someone else, a gentleman who had remained in the background while she was speaking to the others. Sarah felt a slight shock when she noticed him. At first she thought it was simply because she didn't see him right away. He really was that unobtrusive.

Yet how could he be unobtrusive? True, he was not so tall, only a few inches above her height. But he had narrow, almost foxlike features, and interesting green eyes that appeared to miss nothing. Reddish brown hair only added to the notion of him as a fox. The dark green jacket contrasted with his natural coloring, and the cut of his clothes was superb, showing off a lean, athletic figure. She would wager her dowry he was a rider.

He was also unnervingly familiar. She felt as if she knew him.

"You met Lord Markham before, of course," Georgia said.

Lord Markham! The same man she had wanted to quiz Georgia about. "At the funeral," Sarah said. How could she have forgotten what he looked like?

Markham looked at her, his expression unreadable. "Yes, though I would not be surprised if Miss Brecknell didn't remember me, under the circumstances. I hope you are well, or at least on the way to well," he said in a quiet voice. "I wish I had something more diverting to say, but I've never been known for my charm."

"Thank you, my lord," was all she managed in response. She hoped she did not seem horribly rude.

Georgia noticed her difficulty and quickly moved on to the final guest. "And may I present you to Lord Carlin. He has been a delightful friend to us all in the past months. My lord, this is Miss Sarah Brecknell. You may know her mother's family, because they have land in Kent."

Carlin bowed. He was an older gentleman, with silver

hair and a quick smile. "Kent, you say. Whereabouts?"

"She grew up on an estate called Wheystoke."

"Wheystoke? I know of it. Not very far from my own seat. Do you go there at all?"

"Nearly every summer," Sarah said.

"I should like to hear your impressions of it at some point."

"You'll find she is a font of information," Georgia put in eagerly. "Miss Brecknell is a scholar all on her own, and can tell you the history of nearly anything!"

"That is an exaggeration," Sarah said. "But I do like to read."

"You like to read in five languages!" Georgia laughed. "Don't let her be modest, gentlemen. She is all brain!"

"Not all brain, for there is beauty too," Lord Carlin said. "May I take you in to dinner, Miss Brecknell?"

"Thank you, my lord." Sarah looked down, feeling very shy. She knew Carlin was just being kind.

Markham then offered to escort Miss Bryony in, and they trailed Sarah and Lord Carlin into the dining room.

Sarah had sharp ears, so she heard when Bryony whispered to him, "Georgia is a matchmaker. And not a subtle one."

Markham responded in an even lower tone. "Not that it's my business, but isn't he too old for her?"

"That's what I said," Bryony agreed. "But Georgia was certain they'd get on. But honestly, can you picture a man *less* like Charlie?"

She lost the conversation in the bustle of being seated. So that's what Georgia was about when she urged Sarah to come to dinner. Sarah wasn't quite sure how she felt about the effort.

True, Lord Carlin was amusing as a companion. He told stories Sarah couldn't help but smile at. She did her best to respond to Carlin, and to be as polite as possible. But even something as simple as a chat took so much effort. She couldn't wait to get away.

Was Bryony right? Sarah wondered. Granted, Carlin was charming and certainly not decrepit, but he might have twenty-five years on her. Or thirty.

Sarah's gaze flickered to Lord Markham across the table. He must be the same age as Charlie, if they were old school friends. He kept Bryony giggling, his manner just like an older brother, half teasing and half protective.

Further down the table, Georgia was discussing some of the recent events of the *ton*. Mindful of her age, Bryony kept relatively quiet, allowing her older sister to control the conversation. But the naturally bubbly young lady could be easily encouraged to talk, especially when Markham asked about the upcoming ball, which would be her official coming out.

"Just a few weeks left, Miss Bryony," he noted. "Are you prepared?"

She nodded. "My gown for Almack's is ready. The gown I'll wear for my ball is nearly done too. I hope it will look all right. My friend Susanna said she got three proposals the night of her coming out. What if no one proposes to me at all?"

Georgia rolled her eyes. "She's been insufferable on this point, my lord. Will you please tell her she has nothing to fear?"

"You have nothing to fear, Miss Bryony," Markham repeated dutifully. "And, if I may add, any gentleman who proposes to you on a single evening's acquaintance is unlikely to be a good match."

"*Thank* you," Georgia stage whispered.

"But it would be so romantic!" Bryony sighed. "Just like Cinderella."

"Who had to run away, and lost her shoe in the process," Carlin pointed out with a laugh. "And any marriage would certainly have to be approved of by your father first."

"Too right," Mr Wolverton said, jabbing a finger on the table to emphasize his point. "No daughter of mine will make a poor match."

Theo nodded. "By spring, you'll be swimming in proposals."

"But how do I know which is the right one?" Bryony asked. She turned to Sarah. "When Charlie asked you, you knew right away he was the only one for you, didn't you?"

"Bryony!" Georgia hissed.

Sarah's eyes rounded at the question, and for a second, she wanted to bolt out of the room. The table was momentarily silent.

"Oh!" Bryony said, realizing her gaffe. "I didn't mean to…I didn't think…"

After a moment, Sarah recovered. "It's all right. When Charlie proposed, I thought myself the luckiest person in the world. That is the simple truth."

Mrs Wolverton said, in a slightly too loud voice, "Of course. We all knew our son had good taste. A girl with a good head on her shoulders! Smart enough to keep up with him, the dear boy."

"And Charlie must have loved that," Markham said.

Georgia nodded. "True enough. When they talked together, it was like another language! And no one could join in. It was just them."

Just them. Sarah looked down, hoping she wouldn't do something embarrassing, like cry.

Hoping to rescue the evening, Georgia cast about for another topic of conversation. "My lord," she asked Markham, "are you traveling again?"

"Not until March," he said. "A delegation to Vienna, though I'll admit I don't think anything will come of it. Still, it's a break from my usual round of work."

"What sort of work is that?" Carlin asked.

"Not trade, of course. Lord Markham lends his services to the government," Georgia explained. "Much like Charlie did, you know. Diplomatic missions to various places."

Sarah looked up again. "Is that so?" she asked.

"Yes," he said, his eyes flickering towards her, "though I should stress it's not glamorous work. I assist the undersecretary in preparing materials and making sure His Majesty's government doesn't stumble into some horrible political morass at the meetings."

"So you are familiar with the issues causing so much strife on the Continent at the moment?" Carlin guessed.

"As much as any other man," he hedged. "Well, a little

more, perhaps."

The way he said it caught Sarah's attention. She remembered what he had said at the funeral, his questions about whether she knew of Charlie's work. Sarah didn't look at him again, but she made a decision in that moment. She *would* ask him for help.

But how? On such slight acquaintance, Sarah could hardly arrange to meet him anywhere. And she couldn't ask him to call on her, where they would be under the watchful eye of a parent the whole time.

So how was she to speak to him alone?

Chapter 7

♉

THEO WAS GLAD HE CAME to dinner. He always liked the Wolvertons, but he was especially glad he got to meet Sarah again. The lady had been hovering in the corners of his mind for months. Maybe seeing her as an ordinary person—not some tragic figure—would get her out of his head.

True, she wasn't exactly ordinary, Theo thought. She was a little taller than most women, and her head was crowned with thick blond hair likely to reach her waist if it were not bound up so tightly. Theo also noted how her simply cut gown displayed a figure that hinted at ripeness. He wouldn't want her any slimmer. Her body would probably be luscious to touch. At that thought, he deliberately made himself think of something else. He should not be considering Sarah Brecknell in such a light.

After dinner, the guests idled some more time in the parlor. But as the hour grew later, they left. Lord Carlin was first, content to leave after securing Miss Brecknell's permission to call upon her at home. Theo watched the exchange without seeming to. Her response was polite rather than effusive, but Carlin seemed quite pleased.

Georgia was smug, while Bryony shot Theo a look of disgust.

Miss Brecknell left not terribly long after Carlin. She thanked the Wolvertons for inviting her, and gave a modest little curtsey—not much more than a nod, in fact—to Theo.

"My lord," she murmured. She did not look at him directly, and he had the odd impression she was trying to fade away.

"Miss Brecknell, I hope to see you again sometime," he responded.

"It's possible," she said, with a ghost of a smile. Then she told the group good evening, and drifted out of the room.

"Well," said Georgia, still taken with the initial success of her matchmaking. "I think that went perfectly!"

Bryony shook her head. "You can't seriously contend she'll fall in love with Carlin. He's the same age as her father!"

"Oh, you exaggerate. Lord Carlin is a dear, and he ought to marry again."

"Yes, but not to Miss Brecknell! My lord," she appealed to Theo, "what is your opinion?"

Theo wanted no part of the debate. "It's not my place to say."

"Oh, I wished for better from you." Bryony pursed her lips in profound disappointment.

"Theo is well aware the world requires practicality," said Georgia. "Both Miss Brecknell and Lord Carlin ought to marry. She will gain a title, and he'll get her dowry. And they'll both have security and friendship. What's wrong with that?"

"Security and friendship!" Bryony wailed. "How can we be sisters?" She stood up. "Good night, my lord!" She flounced out.

Theo bit back a smile. It must be pleasant to be as sheltered and idealistic as young Bryony. "That is my cue, I fear," he said. "I should not wear out my welcome."

"You could not do that, Theo," Georgia said. "You are the next best thing to a brother, you know."

"Well, I have a lot of practice," he allowed. And indeed, with four sisters and a younger brother, that was true.

"Oh, that reminds me," said Georgia. "Remember a few months ago, you asked whether Charlie left any journals. Well, when I was puttering around this week, I found a few notebooks tucked away with a box of oil paints and brushes in a corner of his room, which I thought was a strange place to keep them. But I put them aside for you. Please take them if you like."

Theo's heart quickened. "Thank you. I'll be sure to return them."

She waved it away. "No need. I glanced at a few, and it seemed to be mostly nonsense. Charlie was always trying new little hobbies, and I suppose that's what these were. But I thought them gibberish."

"Yes," he said, trying to sound calm. What Georgia considered gibberish might very well be a code. "Charlie always had a new hobby, didn't he?"

"I'll say. Last spring and summer it was art collection.

I never dreamed Charlie would care about art."

Theo frowned. In all the years he knew him, Charlie never showed the slightest appreciation for art. "He was collecting art? For pleasure?"

"Or investment," Georgia said. "I hope so, because none of the pieces were remotely interesting. And the way he hung it all up…just a mishmash. No order at all."

"Hung up where?"

"Oh, at Woodforde, his lodge. I went there once in September to check on it after Charlie passed away. I've never seen such poor taste as on those walls. One doesn't speak ill of the dead, but he was lucky he couldn't hear me laugh."

Georgia walked Theo to the door, where she offered him a small box. "All the journals are in there. I don't expect you'll get much out of them. What were you hoping to find?"

"Nothing in particular," Theo fibbed. "I just wanted to know what he was doing in his last days."

"You're more sentimental than you pretend, my lord," Georgia said, squeezing his arm. "But don't worry. I'll never tell."

"I'm at your mercy, Miss Wolverton." Theo bid her goodnight. He then saw Jem at the front door, probably just come from the kitchen where he would have stayed with the other servants, keeping warm during the long wait.

"Ready to go, sir?" he asked. "I brought the carriage up a few minutes ago."

Theo followed Jem out into the cold night, walking

through the light dusting of snow which had fallen during dinner.

Jem held the door, then leaped up into the driver's seat and already had the reins shaken out by the time Theo settled himself. So it happened Jem was already urging the horses forward when Theo first looked across to the other seat. He barely suppressed a curse.

Sarah Brecknell was sitting opposite him, her pale face seeming to float in the air, surrounded by her dark hood and the greater darkness of the carriage.

"Good evening," she said. "Again."

Chapter 8

♉

SARAH SAW THE SURPRISE ON his face.

"What the hell are you doing?" he hissed. "You shouldn't be here."

"I'm aware of that, my lord. But I need to talk to you, and I wished for some degree of anonymity." She knew as well as he did the scandal she was inviting by riding with him, particularly at this hour.

His eyes narrowed as he surveyed her. "How did you even get in here?"

"Your family crest is painted on the side," she explained. "So I knew it was the correct vehicle. The footman ordered a carriage for me, but I dismissed the driver when the footman's back was turned. I told him I had to go back inside. Then I snuck into yours when I passed by the whole clutch of carriages. I was a little worried your driver would check inside, though in the dark he might have missed me even so."

"What would you have done if I lingered over another drink?" Markham asked.

"My cloak is really rather warm," she said. "I would have waited."

Markham sat back. He was either still surprised, or he

just didn't know how to react to her presence. Finally, he said, "Either you misread something I said this evening, or I have mistakenly given you the wrong impression about…"

"My lord," she cut in. "Despite my unconscionable behavior, I am not here to throw myself at you. At least, not for the reason you seem to think."

"No?" He raised an eyebrow, looking rather devilish.

"No," she said, her voice rising. "And besides, I'm not the sort…. Never mind. Let me just begin with this. I think it will explain…" She looked nervously at him, then took a deep breath, and spoke a single word: "Pisces."

Instantly, Sarah wondered if she had made the mistake of a lifetime. As soon as she said that fatal word, Lord Markham's whole attitude shifted into something very cold. He did not look benevolent at all.

He knocked twice on the ceiling of the coach.

"Sir?" a muffled voice called.

"Jem, if we get too close to home before I knock again, keep driving in circles," he said.

"Yes, sir!"

Sarah asked, "Won't he wonder at that?"

"My driver's curiosity is the least of your worries, Miss Brecknell."

The way he looked at her made Sarah question the wisdom of her move. It was beyond the pale, by any standard. She was alone with a stranger, she had no legitimate reason to be with him, and she had no idea how he might treat her.

"Tell me what made you say that word," he ordered.

"It...belonged to Charlie. You know what it means, don't you?"

"I do."

His confirmation was not reassuring. But Sarah had to know she was on the right track. "You know because you're part of it too. I didn't realize it when we first talked, but Charlie once hinted you were like him. Aren't you?"

"If I was, do you think I'd admit to it?"

"It's not as if it's shameful," Sarah said heatedly. "You should be proud to be part of something so important. Charlie was! He said he was protecting the whole natio—"

Seeing his expression, Sarah choked off the last of the word.

Markham stared at her, assessing. Sarah waited in agony as the silence stretched out. He had to say *something*.

Finally, he did. "It's not shameful. But it *is* secret."

He offered nothing more. She remembered him as being kind, when he spoke to her at the wake. And his eyes were so familiar. But perhaps she had been too shocked to properly assess the man at the time. His features were sharpened by the odd light in the carriage, and his eyes, which had been green, now looked black. But she couldn't look away.

Why had she revealed Charlie's secret to him?

Because she needed his help.

Before she lost her nerve completely, Sarah hurried on, "Please. Charlie once told me when he was in trouble, he turned to you. That you were the man for a crisis." Her voice broke then. She swallowed hard and forced herself to finish her prepared speech. "I realize you have no reason to trust me. Or listen to me. I must appear half-mad. But I am in a crisis now, my lord. And I have no one else to turn to."

"You'd best explain your crisis," he said. The tone was calm, not encouraging, but at least not disdainful.

Sarah told him the story of two nights ago, right down to the mysterious man's implied punishment should she fail to deliver. She watched Markham's eyes narrow as she went on, until he looked less like a man and more like a predator. Sarah instinctively leaned against the back of the seat, as if she could flee that way. She finished her story with another plea for assistance.

"You are right to characterize your problem as a crisis," he said quietly. He did not offer to help her, though, and Sarah quailed. She *had* made a mistake.

Perhaps he was considering whether to dump her on the side of the road and be done with her. She would not have been at all surprised if he had. She did not know what went on behind his scrutinizing eyes, but she felt the chance slipping away, and tried to plead one last time.

"I know I have no claim on you, but I have no idea what to—"

"I'll help you," he said.

Sarah sighed in relief.

He went on, "If someone approached you so recently, there is clearly some current danger concerning those papers Charlie possessed, or else no one would care. A danger to the country as a whole. That's my main concern."

Sarah nodded. "What will we do?"

"I need some information from you. Tell me everything Charlie told you about his work."

"You mean, as…as Pisces?" Sarah looked at Lord Markham, and realized how deadly serious he was.

"Precisely." There was anger in his voice. It wasn't directed at her, but she felt it all the same.

"Charlie should not have told me anything," she said, understanding his fury.

"But he did," Markham noted coldly.

"Yes. I think he may have wanted to impress me. To convince me he led an exciting life. Does that make sense?"

Theo raised an eyebrow. "I can see why he might do that. Go on. What did he tell you? And don't leave anything out."

"Well," she began. "He didn't tell me anything about what he did until well after we were engaged. He was always off on some matter, and I made a comment that he must not find me very interesting. And then he told me his business was vital to the Crown. He told me all about his latest assignment to Paris—he was meeting with some contact to learn about the Emperor's troop movements at the time. That would have been over a year ago. It *was* very exciting to hear, but even then I felt it was wrong for him to tell me. Rather indiscreet."

"To say the least. You realize he told you his code name."

"Yes," said Sarah. "But I suppose I pressed him."

"If an eighteen year old girl could press him, he had no business in…" Markham suddenly stopped.

"No business being in the Zodiac?" Sarah finished.

Markham looked supremely annoyed. "So he mentioned that name, too."

"No!" she said quickly. "That is, not exactly."

"How did he not *exactly* mention it?"

"Well, I guessed. From the name of Pisces, you see. I asked if there were only twelve, or if they had to exploit other myths. And Charlie said no, it was the Zodiac for a reason…" She broke off, watching his expression.

"You *guessed*." His tone was skeptical. No, incredulous.

"It's not as if it were a particularly challenging puzzle," she said, suddenly defensive. "A random collection of names would have been better."

"Charlie keeping his mouth shut would have been better," he growled.

"I'm sorry," Sarah said, worried she'd goaded him.

He suddenly put his head back, closing his eyes. "No. I don't mean to snap at you. You aren't to blame for his—" A sudden thought occurred to him, and he looked at her sharply again. "You didn't tell anyone else about the code names, did you?"

Sarah frowned at him, managing to convey censure despite her turmoil. "No! Do you imagine for a second I would have done *anything* with that information?"

"I don't know you, Miss Brecknell," he countered coolly.

"No, you don't," she snapped back. "You don't know a thing about me."

"I know you're unusually brave," he said quietly.

She blushed, thinking he was referring to her scandal-courting ride in his carriage. "I don't feel brave, my lord. I have no choice but to beg you to help me."

"And I will." His voice, at last, offered some support. "I'm not going to leave you to twist in the wind."

She winced at the reference to hanging, but assumed he'd spoken like that to shock her into paying attention. She began again. "I don't know why the man thought *I* knew anything, but he was convinced I was the key. He was sure I'd be able to find this hiding place. It must be a mistake. But I don't think I can explain that to *him*."

"Unlikely," Markham said. "But it's also unlikely he would risk accosting you unless he was certain of his information."

"Speaking of that, I don't know why he would have waited so long to contact me. Doesn't it seem odd?"

His eyes brightened. "You're right. And the specific deadline of the 31st is interesting. Why do you need weeks? If you had the documents, why wouldn't he simply force you to get them immediately?"

"But I *don't* have the documents," she insisted. "You must believe me."

He looked at her, his expression skeptical, and then a little sympathetic. "Is it possible Charlie gave them to you without your knowing it?"

"How would I not notice that?" she asked tartly. "'Hello, dear, here's a few letters I'm keeping safe for the

Crown. Tuck them away for me, but don't peek, Pandora!'"

Markham actually smiled at her words. "I didn't mean it quite like that. He could have hidden something at your home while he called on you. Perhaps slipped something onto a book shelf? Or left something behind?"

"That's possible," Sarah said. "Though it's more likely he hid something in my office at the Athenaeum."

"What's that?"

She quickly explained what the Athenaeum was and why she was associated with it. "I could look through my shelves there."

"May I call on you tomorrow?" he asked. "At the Athenaeum, I mean? I'd like to see your office myself. The whole place, actually."

Sarah nodded slowly. "Say you're there to see my father, if anyone should ask. We'll have to tell him we met before, and somehow convince him he's forgotten you—which shouldn't be too difficult. He doesn't pay attention to most events after 1500."

He nodded. "Don't worry. I'm fairly good at making stories up. I will call on you there around two. And now you'd better return home yourself."

She couldn't agree more. Though he hadn't done anything untoward, the fact that she was alone with him at midnight was frankly terrifying. She told him where she lived, and he called the street direction up to his driver.

As the carriage wound its way through London's twisting streets toward her home, she looked at the man across from her. "I have a question for you. Will you give me an honest answer, seeing as we're as alone as we're ever likely to be?"

"That sounds ominous."

"Do you know how Charlie died?"

"He died in an accident," said Markham, his expression suddenly closed. "You heard the story."

"Do me the courtesy of not taking me for an utter child." Sarah refused to look away from him, even though she dearly wanted to. His gaze was disconcerting. "While I only know a little about Charlie's secret life, his death could not possibly have been an accident. Highwaymen! On that road? I assume your little club didn't have much time, or you wouldn't have created such a flimsy story."

Markham wouldn't give an inch. "I can't tell you the details of his death."

"Can't or won't?"

"Won't."

She sat back. "Well, at least you're honest."

"You're generous with your terms," he said. "I refuse to tell you a thing, and I'm honest for it?"

"You didn't lie," Sarah said. "I don't think I could take another lie. Since that man appeared, I feel like I've been dropped into some sort of mirror world. Everything looks the same, and yet feels completely different. I look at books and wonder if the words are the same inside them. I look at people and wonder who they really are. I look at myself and wonder how I could not have known that something was happening so close to me. It's one thing to learn the one you love is a spy. It's quite another to be drawn into his life…especially after he's dead."

The carriage came to a halt. So did Sarah's confession.

She looked outside where the carriage had stopped on the street, a few doors away from her own. The incurious driver did understand discretion.

"Thank you for taking me home."

His lip quirked. "No inconvenience at all. Should I see you to the front door?"

"No," she said. "I appreciate the chivalry, but I had best go in by myself." She didn't want anyone to see her alighting from a carriage with only a strange man in it. But on the street at night, she supposed, it would be anonymous enough. She stepped out.

"The carriage will wait until I see you go into your home. Good night, Miss Brecknell," he said, before he shut the door again. Suddenly, he smiled at her. "And for what it's worth, I do think you're brave."

Sarah smiled back, feeling much better than she ought to, considering the situation.

She turned to walk back to her house. The light snowfall of the evening left everything dusted white, and the world was quiet as she moved. Her nerves were practically singing after the encounter with Lord Markham. Hiding in his carriage was one of the most daring things she'd ever done. Asking for his help took even more strength.

But he did say yes. Sarah sighed, her breath clouding the night air. She thought she might actually sleep that night, unlike the previous two evenings, when she'd lain awake until dawn, praying things were different.

Now things *were* different. She had an ally. Not a friend, but an ally. Tomorrow she would see him again.

And they'd find the secret Charlie left behind.

Chapter 9

♉

THEO WOKE UP MONDAY MORNING feeling as if he hadn't slept a minute. After he dropped Miss Brecknell off the previous night, he returned home as soon as possible. The journals Georgia gave him were suddenly even more exciting. If he could match something found in those notebooks with what Sarah told him, he might be able to put the whole business to rest.

He couldn't believe it. Months of waiting for a lead, and it turned out Sarah might be exactly the person he'd been hoping to meet. Such a strange moment, finding her there in his carriage. She was not at all like the image of her he'd created in his head based on their brief meeting at the funeral. The real Sarah Brecknell was more composed, more practical. And obviously intelligent.

He wouldn't have been surprised if the woman had been in hysterics after the encounter she described to him. Yet Sarah showed very little fear. She laid out the problem plainly, merely wondering about the oddity of the request surfacing after so many months of silence.

Which was an excellent question to ask. Why *did* the

stranger confront her after so long? Had something happened to bring Sarah to the man's attention? And who the hell was he? Did he work for Arceneau? Was he another opportunist like Charlie, but for another side?

Theo groaned at all the possibilities. He had so much work to do. He had to reexamine all the puzzle pieces he'd already gathered. Unfortunately, once he got home and had the privacy to examine Charlie's notebooks, he discovered they were virtually unreadable. He spent three hours poring over them, burning several candles more than usual. He could read a few lines written in plain English. But the majority of the notebooks appeared to be in some sort of code. Several codes, perhaps, to judge by the many different pages of letters, columns of numbers, and even sketches. He wasn't skilled enough to break a single one. Nothing made sense. But Theo refused to believe it was useless. Charlie never dabbled. If he did something, he always had a reason for it.

After he gave up on the notebooks for the night, Theo lay in bed, eyes wide open as he turned over all the new information in his mind. Sarah kept reappearing, her grey eyes asking questions he had no answers to.

One other thing he realized from speaking to Sarah was that although she knew about Charlie's work and about the existence of the Zodiac—a fact that would give Julian a seizure when he learned of it—she did *not* know Charlie had turned traitor. And thank God. She was obviously so proud of him, and in love with his memory. Learning such a thing would only hurt her, which Theo didn't want to do.

And of course, if she did know about Charlie's perfidy, she would be far less inclined to help him recover the papers. She wouldn't want to summon any sort of proof of her beloved's fall from grace. No, Theo had to keep the truth from her if he expected her to cooperate.

Eventually, he slept a little, and when he woke, it was full daylight.

Downstairs, he encountered his sister Katherine in the sunny parlor. She was sewing, and her youngest child Estelle was crawling around at her feet.

Theo came in, happy to be distracted for a moment. "Good morning," he said. "How's my favorite niece?"

Estelle turned at the sound of his voice and held her arms out imperiously. "Up!"

"Yes, my lady," he said, bending to scoop her up in his arms. Estelle squealed in delight as he swung her around.

Theo gave her a kiss, then sat down opposite Katherine. Estelle laughed as she bounced happily on his knee.

"See what I told you the other day?" Theo told Katherine. "She's going to be a rider. I can tell."

His sister smiled indulgently at both of them. "You promise to teach her?"

"Naturally. Who else would you trust to do it? Estelle," he said. "Listen carefully. It will be my duty to teach you to ride and jump fences and chase carriages and race and perform all manner of stunts that will have your mother cursing my name."

Katherine shook her head. "Not if I have anything to say about it!"

He bent his head and mock-whispered, "As soon as

she turns her back, little star, we'll be off."

"You look ten years younger when you smile, Teddy," Katherine said.

He cringed at the old family pet name. "Don't call me that. What do you mean?"

"You've looked so dragged down these past few months."

"I have not."

"Of course you have." She looked at her baby and then back to him. "When you have to seek out a toddler for solace, I know something's wrong."

"Nonsense."

"Mama was by to visit yesterday. She said you finally set a date with Alyse."

"The end of May," he confirmed. "There's no reason to put it off longer."

"No, indeed." Katherine shot him a sharp look, but then held up her work. She appeared to be embroidering the hem of a baby's outfit. "What do you think?"

"You're asking me?" he said, amused. "I suppose it's pretty."

"A word of advice, dear brother. When Alyse asks you a similar question, you need to be much more effusive."

"Is that so? Let me try again. How *darling*," Theo said, putting false enthusiasm into his voice. "How do you manage to stitch all that and still be a perfect wife and mother?"

Katherine muttered, looking skyward, "I wonder if Alyse knows what she's getting."

"Alyse and I understand each other very well. And in

any case, we have over a year before I have any chance to be interrogated over the stitching on a baby's outfit."

"Theo," Katherine said, more gently. "You're never so short tempered. I know something's wrong. Can't you tell me?"

No, no he could not. Katherine was his sister and he loved her dearly. But the truth wasn't something he was entitled to share. "If I've been distant, I apologize."

"I don't want your apology. I want you to be happy."

"Happy!" Estelle echoed.

He smiled at her, then said to Katherine, "Don't worry about me. I've had a few concerns over the past months. But they are nearly concluded. And when I marry Alyse, I'm sure all will be well."

Katherine didn't look as if she believed him, but let the matter drop.

Later, when Theo walked to the front hall dressed to go out, Jem was waiting patiently.

"Where to, sir?" he asked as they stepped outside.

Theo said, "We're going to the corner at Adam and Manchester Streets."

"Oh, the Athenaeum." Jem nodded confidently.

"How did you know that?" Theo, asked, exasperated. Did everyone know everything now?

"Could find that place in the middle of a fog, sir. Didn't I drive milady there nearly every month?" he said, referring to his former employer.

"So you know what the place is like?"

Jem shrugged diffidently. "Only the outside and the mews nearby. I'm not exactly the typical lecture-goer, sir."

Theo laughed as he climbed into the cab. Jem had a gift for understatement.

He arrived a few minutes before two, just as he said he would. Not surprisingly, the building was a model of classical architecture, though in wood and brick rather than marble. It sported columns all along the front façade, and the windows glowed from within, for even the afternoon did not bring much light in winter.

Theo found little difficulty in gaining entrance. The name of Mr Stephen Brecknell was well known to the people there. He did not seek out the gentleman, however. Following Sarah's instructions, he instead found his way to the end of a long hall. He knocked at the last door on the left.

Sarah was waiting. She stood up when he entered, looking as if she were nervous.

"Thank you for stopping by, Lord Markham," she said formally. "We are lucky," she added in a quieter voice. "Papa is quite busy preparing for an upcoming lecture. So you shouldn't have to explain yourself at all."

Theo nodded, looking around the small room. "This belongs to you?"

"I have the exclusive use of it. They think it more seemly than if I were out among the men."

He glanced at her. "Are they worried you'll show them up? What do you study?"

"Oh, I just dabble. Classics. History. Languages. Whatever catches my fancy."

"Have you looked through your books yet?"

Sarah nodded and pointed to a stack of books on the desk. "These were all gifts from Charlie. I had to start somewhere."

"He gave you books?"

"They last longer than flowers," Sarah said defensively. "And I enjoy them considerably more."

Theo looked through the stack. Titles in German, Latin, and Greek. Many were well-thumbed. Sarah was probably not a dabbler, but a very serious scholar. Theo wondered if she downplayed her dedication because some men were affronted—or intimidated—by it.

"I'm twenty-one," Sarah said suddenly, as he was still examining the titles.

He looked up at her, puzzled at the announcement. "What?"

"Last night, you said if an eighteen year old girl could press Charlie…" She paused. "In fact, I am twenty-one. Nearly twenty-two. We were engaged for years, ever since he proposed to me at the end of my first Season."

Theo was amused at her precision. "I stand corrected."

"It's important to tell the truth," she said.

Theo's sense of amusement fled. "Indeed." The truth was the one thing he couldn't tell her.

They both looked through the books more carefully, but there was nothing hidden inside.

Theo did notice a rather odd inscription on the flyleaf of one book: a series of three numbers, in columns all down the page. "What are these?" he asked, pointing. It looked similar to a few pages in Charlie's notebooks.

Sarah looked at the inscription. "They refer to Bible

verses. That's all."

"Chapter and verse only explains the first two numbers."

"The third is the word of interest in the verse," she said shortly. She pulled the book from his hands. "It doesn't have anything to do with anything he left behind. He gave this to me shortly after we became engaged."

Theo saw how nervous she was, and took the book back. "Are you sure?"

"Of course. Please forget about it." She moved as if to take it again, but she stopped when Theo made it clear she'd actually have to touch his hands to do it. A lady like Sarah would never be so bold.

"Why not tell me the significance, or do I need to look up all the words myself?"

Sarah looked down, then muttered, "She is my one love, until the end of time."

"What?"

"That's what it says," she said, her eyes glued to the floor.

He could see a blush spreading over her face. "This is a coded message?"

"Yes. It was just a game we played."

"Charlie taught you codes," Theo said.

"No," she corrected. She looked up at him, gauging his reaction. "*I* taught *him* codes."

Chapter 10

♉

Sarah watched Theo carefully, and saw his eyes widen when he heard her words.

"So you know about codes?" he asked.

She nodded. "It's always been an interest of mine, since I found references to them in my Greek and Latin histories. There's a number of people interested in cryptography around town. It's not so unusual."

"I know a few myself," he said. "I just didn't think Charlie was one of them. Beyond a certain practical interest, that is."

"Oh, he was obsessed with it for a few years. That's actually how we first met. We kept trying to borrow the same books on the subject."

Theo nodded slowly. Sarah had encountered men who refused to believe she could be genuinely interested in such things. But Theo accepted it without argument. In fact, he suddenly looked hopeful.

"If you communicated with Charlie that way," he said, "perhaps we can discover where this supposed cache is. I just received some of Charlie's notebooks, but I haven't been able to read them at all. If you can read his code, maybe you can learn where it is. Perhaps that's why your mysterious friend thought you could do this."

"Don't say friend. He was horrible." Nevertheless, Sarah felt a little jump in her heart. "But I can certainly look at Charlie's notebooks. Even if he invented a new code, I'd wager I could decipher it."

He smiled at her. "A bet I wouldn't take, Miss Brecknell. Something tells me you're quite good at codes."

"Oh, I like puzzles. Where are the notebooks? When could you get them to me?"

He straightened up. "While I think you are above reproach, I can't let those notebooks out of my sight until I know if they're valuable or not. We are going to have to solve them together."

"But how? It will take time, and we can't be seen together."

"But we can both enter this building," he said. "Is there any place here we could meet? Someplace we won't be interrupted."

"Oh! Well, perhaps I can find a spot that will be out of the way. But even so, I'm not sure it would be appropriate."

He frowned at her. "Believe me, Miss Brecknell, I would much prefer to do everything myself. But it appears I may need you, and you did ask for my assistance. Now, do you still want it?"

"Yes."

"Then you must accept it on my terms. We work together, and the notebooks don't leave my possession. As that man proved, even these walls aren't a safeguard."

Just then, a sound caught Sarah's attention. Familiar footsteps in the corridor. "Oh, bother," she said. "I think my father is coming to collect me. Are you any good at lying?"

"Would you believe me if I told you?"

Sarah smiled at his unexpected levity. "Say you were offering me condolences, and I'll say you were just leave —"

"Darling? Are you still working?" Sarah's father said as he shuffled in through the door.

Sarah said, flustered, "My lord, may I introduce my father, Stephen Brecknell. Papa, this is Theodore Drayton, Lord Markham."

"Good afternoon, my lord," the older man said, clearly puzzled at Markham's presence, though he didn't look concerned in the slightest. "Have we met?"

Markham stood up as soon as he entered. "Good afternoon, Mr Brecknell. We have not had the pleasure. I am sorry to say that this is a rather sad visit. I have been out of town, and hadn't yet had the opportunity to offer my condolences to those people Mr Wolverton left behind."

"Oh!" Sarah's father shot her a sudden, worried look.

"Lord Markham was a good friend to Charlie, Papa," she explained. "We talked a bit about him, and I must say it wasn't as painful as it used to be." Strangely, Sarah found that was true.

"Yes," Theo added. "I wanted to hear some things about Charlie's life last summer. You see, I was in the country, to be closer to my fiancée. Our families' estates join."

"Indeed? How fortunate." Mr Brecknell's expression was back to its normal calm.

"Miss Brecknell has been most accommodating, but I have taken up far too much of her time."

Before he could leave, her father held up a half-sheet of paper. "Before I forget. Are you quite sure all the invitations have gone out for the lecture tomorrow evening?"

"I did that last week, Papa," Sarah said gently. But the sight of the invitation gave her an idea. She plucked it from her father's hand and gave it to Lord Markham.

"Now that you're back in town, perhaps you could come to the lecture. Bring your fiancée. You can explore the building a bit," she added meaningfully.

He gave her a quick nod of approval as he took the invitation. "What a good idea, Miss Brecknell."

"Yes, do come," her father added. "A Mrs Heath will speak on her recent finds among the Egyptian ruins at Karnak and the Valley of the Kings. Should be fascinating."

"Really? I've always been interested in Egypt," Markham said. Sarah couldn't tell if he was lying, but she supposed it was an important skill for spies.

Mr Brecknell beamed at him. "Then you must come! Need not be a member of the Athenaeum! And do bring your fiancée. We need more bright young ladies like my girl around here."

"Papa!" Sarah said, blushing.

"We'll be here," Markham said. "But at the moment, I

should not intrude further. Excuse me. I will see myself out."

After he left, Sarah sat back down, suddenly drained.

Her father sat beside her in the other chair. "Sarah, dear. Are you sure that thinking of such sad things hasn't made you melancholy?"

"No, I'm quite all right. Lord Markham was only making a courtesy call."

"Very courteous, yes," her father murmured, already thinking of something else entirely. "I hope he was not affronted you were alone today. I know we don't hold you to the strictest standards at your age, but a family such as his must observe all the niceties…"

He saw the stacks of books on the table. "Cleaning out the shelves? Good, good. Well, we should be off home now. Your mother doesn't like to be alone all day. Tidy up and I'll see you at the front hall." He patted Sarah on the hand, smiled, and wandered out.

Chapter 11

♉

THEO LEFT THE ATHENAEUM FEELING as if something was finally going right. If Sarah was any good at codes—and something told him she was—the notebooks could be deciphered and the cache found. She would be able to confront her tormentor, and Theo would learn what Charlie had stolen. Everyone would win…except the tormentor, who Theo planned to capture or kill, depending on how he felt that day.

He was deeply annoyed at the idea of the man involving Sarah in his schemes. Why should he think the lady could succeed where trained agents—criminal or otherwise—had failed? How did he know Sarah would not simply have melted down in pure panic?

Theo had to find out who the man was as soon as possible. He'd begin with Sarah's description. Tall and muscular, she said. Dark hair. She had been frightened, but she didn't seem the type to misremember. Still, that wasn't much to work with. The last two fingers on his right hand were missing, she said. Such a detail was far more useful.

Wasting no time, he began to work his various contacts throughout the city. He knew people in high and low places. Some were genuine friends, who he'd got to trust over the years. Some were allies, willing to share a secret if the cause was good. And others were simply eyes on the street. They would give Theo the information he needed for a price, but they'd do the same for Theo's enemies. It was not always a simple matter to ask a question among London's underworld.

But after several hours of careful work, he was able to get a name from an unlikely place: a beggar who used to work in a freak show. His limbs had been malformed at birth: his legs mere stumps with no feet to speak of, his right arm whole but spindly, and his left only grown to the elbow, where a half-formed hand grew. Short Henry, as he was known, only had three fingers on that hand. He kept informed about other people in the city with similar deformities—he worried about rivals.

"Penny for the poor, good sir?" Short Henry called out piteously as Theo walked toward him, the darkness of a winter night already obscuring most of the scene.

Theo pulled a few coins from his pocket. "Got more than that, Henry, if you can answer a question for me."

"Down the alley," Henry muttered, recognizing him. "Two minutes."

Theo tossed a coin in Henry's cup and strolled on, turning down the next alley as if on a whim. He waited in a doorway well away from the street. Soon enough, Henry came down, by means of a little rolling cart he'd had made especially for him. He could reach surprising speeds with it.

"Well, now," Henry said when he drew up to Theo. "What brings you to my exquisitely-scented neighborhood?"

"I need information, Henry. And I think you might be the man who can help."

"Fire away," the beggar ordered, an eager light in his eyes.

"There's a man in town I'm looking for. He might be a newcomer, but perhaps not. He's a big man. Dark hair. Healthy. Tough, in the sense that he'll look muscular and mean. But he's missing the last two fingers on his right hand."

"Two fingers gone? But healthy otherwise?" Henry mused. "Maybe. Anything else about him?"

"He speaks with an accent. I've never heard it, so I can't say what. But my source is reliable."

"Accented, but he speaks the King's English?"

"Perfectly well."

"And a big man." Henry nodded to himself. "I have a name that comes to mind. But what's this worth to you?" he asked.

Theo held up two silver coins. "One to pay for the name, and the other to pay for your silence should anyone else ask about him—or me."

"That will do," Henry said, as Theo handed over the coins.

The beggar took them in his good hand and hid them away in a flash. "The name I have is Matteo Rossi. He may not be who you want, but I'd bet one of these coins he is."

"He's missing two fingers?"

"Aye, and he's a big fellow. From somewhere far south. Italy or Spain, if I recall. He used to work in a circus among the elephants and lions. He would wrestle a bear for the show, all mostly an act, but still one that requires real strength. He was mean among people, but kind to the animals, and strong enough to deal with them."

"Why did he leave the circus?"

"Run in with the law. He was said to have killed a man over money. I can't say what the truth of the matter is."

"But he's in London now?"

"Yes, but I don't know who he might be working for. He's not the type to work on his own—not that bright. There's a woman with him sometimes. But what their link is, I don't know."

"You're earning another coin with all this," Theo said. "Answer me one more question. Where was Rossi last known to live?"

"St Giles, so you'd best keep a gun with you if you look for him there," Henry replied. He accepted the next coin just as quickly. "I thank you, my lord. And now I'd best get back to begging."

"I'll leave the alley the other way," Theo said, before Henry could suggest it.

"One thing I'm curious about," Henry said as he prepared to leave. "What's this man done to bring you down here and pay me so much for a name? I doubt I'm the only coin you spent on this."

"I would have spent more if I had to. As for his crime,

he was rude to a lady," Theo said.

"Must have been quite the insult," Henry muttered. "Good hunting, my lord. Kindly don't seek me out again till your business with him is done."

"God keep you, Henry," Theo said, meaning it.

Armed with the name, Theo felt much better. He was tired from a night of no sleep and hours spent traversing the city, but he had one more place to stop before he could go home.

The offices of the Zodiac were tucked away in a building that housed several private firms and offices. Theo privately thought the architect must have been unfamiliar with the concept of a straight line. There were so many twists and turns one had to make before reaching one's destination that the place felt more like a maze. In that respect, it was an excellent location for a group of spies.

He arrived at the door on an upper floor and knocked once. It was opened by a woman in practical clothes and ash blonde hair. She moved aside as soon as she saw who it was.

"I'll tell him you're here," she said, shutting the door.

Theo nodded. "Thank you, Miss Chattan."

She ushered him into Julian's inner sanctum. Despite the hour, neither person showed any hint that they intended to leave at any time. "Do you live in these offices?" Theo asked suddenly.

"It sometimes seems so," Chattan said with a faint smile. She closed the door on her way out.

"I don't have you on an assignment at the moment," Julian said. "What's happening?"

"I found a link to Pisces."

Julian went cold. "I told you to stay well out of that."

"A lead landed right in my path," he said.

"By coincidence, I'm sure," Julian said.

"It surprised the hell out of me, I promise you." Theo explained about Sarah's appearance in his carriage, and her story about meeting Matteo Rossi.

At the end, Julian asked, "But why did she tell you about it? You said you only met her once before."

Theo took a deeper breath. "She knows about the Zodiac."

The other man's eyes narrowed to slits. "How did she find out about it?"

"Not from *me*," Theo said quickly. "Charlie told her. That is, he told her a little about his work and his code name. She guessed there must be twelve of us, and identified the name of the Zodiac on her own, which he confirmed."

"Why would he do that?"

Theo shrugged. "Miss Brecknell is quite pretty." It was a pat explanation, but essentially true. Theo could well understand why a man, even one as intelligent as Charlie, could have lost his better sense around Sarah. She was exactly the sort of pretty that made some men talk too much.

"My God." Neville leaned over in his chair. He called, "Chattan?"

The woman appeared in the doorway. "Yes, sir?"

"Can you make up a list, Miss Chattan? Just the names of the people in England who *don't* know about our clandestine organization?"

Chattan didn't even blink. "Certainly, sir. I'll be back in five minutes."

"See her? Not a flinch. She keeps me sane." Julian turned back to Theo. "I expect you to watch this girl carefully. Find out who she talks to and if she's spilled any other secrets. And don't start spilling any yourself."

"When have I ever done that?" Theo asked. "I've been engaged to Alyse for years and never breathed a word to her."

"These things have a way of getting out of hand. If Miss Brecknell knows a little, you might not think it a problem to tell her a little more. In for a penny, in for a pound."

"She's not in for anything at all, sir," Theo corrected. "I'm going to use her to decode Charlie's notebooks. Once she does that, I'll be done with her...other than to deal with Rossi, of course."

"Good," Julian said. "Maybe we can arrange for her to marry someone who lives very far away then. Do we know anyone who lives on the Orkneys? Or Ireland. Some man must need a wife in Ireland."

Theo rolled his eyes. "She knew Charlie's code name for well over a year, and said nothing. I'm not concerned."

"Her life wasn't in danger before. That tends to change people's outlooks."

"Her life isn't in danger now. We'll find the cache, I'll intercept Rossi, and it'll be done."

"God grant it. The sooner everything about Charlie

Wolverton is dead and buried, the happier I'll be."

Theo left the inner office and found Chattan sitting at her own desk outside. "Still working on your list, Miss Chattan?"

She gave him a wry smile. "It's not as bad as all that."

"I knew he'd hate learning a random citizen heard the name of the Zodiac, but the risk is minimal."

Chattan kept her voice low. "You have to understand. Wolverton's betrayal shook his confidence. He had such faith in his agents, and to be failed by one…that's never happened before. I mean, perhaps it did during the Zodiac's earlier history. But not under Julian's watch. He's furious. He's been simmering for months."

"We'll just have to make sure it can't happen again," Theo said. "Though I don't know how to go about it."

Chattan said, "A few of the agents—the ones involved in exposing Charlie—want to make the Zodiac a bit more open. They think the agents should know each other, and sometimes work together."

"Isn't that the Astronomer's decision to make? Or Julian's. He's the first sign."

"He's been considering it. Slowly. You might mention your opinion to him."

"And what's your opinion, Miss Chattan?"

"I think it's a good idea. Secrecy and isolation can be weaknesses as well as strengths."

"You talk like a spymaster yourself. Sometimes I wonder how you grew up."

She smiled. Chattan had never revealed a thing about her past in all the years he'd known her. "I leave you to wonder."

"And I'll leave you to work," he said. "I have to sleep at some point. Tomorrow I'm off to break codes with Miss Brecknell."

"Do you like her?" Chattan asked suddenly.

He stopped short. "What does that mean?"

"Exactly what it sounds like."

"Yes, I like her," Theo said slowly. "She's intelligent, discreet, and keeps her head when no one would fault her for losing it." He saw Chattan's disturbed expression and made an intuitive leap about her concerns. "Charlie didn't deserve her."

"That's what I feared," Chattan said. "Just one more person he hurt. Look after her, will you?"

He nodded. "Yes, ma'am."

* * * *

The very next morning, Theo sent a note to Alyse about the lecture. Her reply came shortly after, telling him she would be delighted to join him. So that evening, Theo drove to the Templetons' home. Alyse was waiting for him, having dressed with considerable care.

"Do I look scholarly enough?" she asked him, showing off an outfit of a rich burgundy velvet coat over a wool gown. "All my other frocks are so lacy and light. I wish I had spectacles."

Theo laughed. "It's a lecture, not a costume ball. Are you ready to go?"

"I suppose. I just don't want anyone to laugh at me."

"Who would laugh?"

"I don't know. There's probably a host of old dusty men who will blink at me with their owl eyes. What if I'm the only younger lady there?"

"I'm quite certain there will be others. Though I wasn't sure you would want to attend."

"Oh, it sounds interesting," she said. "And different. I was just telling Mama that if I had to attend another tea, I'd scream. How did you hear about it? It's hardly your typical event."

He shrugged. "A friend mentioned it. And I too can get bored of the usual entertainment." Personally, he was far more interested in exploring the building. If Sarah could find a safe place to meet, they could start working the next day. If they were incredibly lucky, they might even find Charlie's stash of papers in the building. Then the evening would be worth it.

At the Athenaeum, Theo noticed Sarah immediately. She was again dressed in a dark grey gown, and wore black gloves and a black ribbon in her blonde hair, which made her pale complexion look even paler. It was as if she wanted to fade away into the dark paneled walls.

She nodded in greeting, but didn't have time to come over before the lecture began, so Theo simply escorted Alyse into the main hall.

The talk was on advances in archeological study. Theo didn't have much interest in the matter—ancient history was a subject he merely endured in school. But the presenter was unusual and her talk far more compelling than he would have guessed. The explorer and scholar Mrs Elena Heath had spent years in Egypt, digging out the ruins of the pharaohs.

Mrs Heath was dynamic and entertaining as a speaker. She combined the dry facts of her work with amusing stories of the local culture, and often peppered her tales with humor stemming from her unique position; she was quite often the only woman at the digs, aside from a personal maid.

Alyse appeared completely enraptured. "Can you imagine!" she said more than once, under her breath.

At the end of the lecture, everyone applauded, and Alyse leaned over to him. "Theo! Wasn't that fascinating?"

Theo smiled at her. "Perhaps you can tell Mrs Heath directly."

"Oh, what could I say to her?"

"Just ask a question. You must have some." He saw Sarah then. "Let me introduce you to someone else first. She's the reason we're here."

Chapter 12

♉

AFTER THE LECTURE, SARAH SAW Lord Markham approach with a gorgeous dark-haired woman on his arm. She put on her most welcoming expression. "Good evening, my lord."

He smiled at her. "Miss Brecknell, may I introduce you to my fiancée, Lady Alyse Templeton."

Alyse gripped Sarah's hands warmly in her own. "So you invited us! I'm so pleased to meet you."

Surprised by the genuineness of the gesture, Sarah asked, "Did you enjoy the lecture, Lady Alyse?"

"It was marvelous. I want to go to Egypt posthaste!"

"Perhaps it would make a good honeymoon," Sarah suggested.

Alyse's face lit up. "I never thought of that. What an idea. Have you ever been to Egypt, Miss Brecknell?"

"No," Sarah said. "I have never been abroad at all. In fact, I've never been further away from London than Kent."

"So you live in town? How splendid. How have our paths not crossed yet?"

"I have not been particularly social of late," Sarah

said, subconsciously glancing down at the somber color of her gown.

Alyse's face fell as she took in the significance of the color.

"Miss Brecknell was engaged to my old friend Mr Wolverton. You remember him," Theo explained in quiet voice.

"Oh." Alyse's eyes widened. But then she smiled and said, "You know, my family is hosting a little party in a few days. I think it's dreadful to be all alone on a winter's night. Won't you come? I'll have an invitation sent round to your home."

Sarah knew the other girl was only being polite, but it would be extremely bad form to refuse. "That is most kind of you," she said. "I should be glad to."

"Oh, good. Wear your prettiest dress! I shall introduce you to everyone!"

After a few moments, Alyse glanced toward the stage. "If you'll excuse me, I was going to go up to Mrs Heath and ask her a few questions, if she'll spare me the time."

Theo laughed a little. "When has anyone not found time for you?"

"Well," Alyse pondered, "I'm sure I could think of one instance. Do excuse me." She went off to find Mrs Heath.

"So that's your intended?" Sarah asked, strangely jealous. Alyse was as bright and pretty as a flower, perfect in her petite figure and curling dark hair.

"We've known each other practically our whole lives," Theo said, looking fondly after Alyse. "We grew up together, and I knew from a very early age that she would be my wife."

"You're lucky," Sarah said, thinking it one of the most romantic things she'd ever heard.

Theo turned back to her. From his expression, she could tell he was about to apologize for what might have seemed a callous statement, considering Sarah's own dashed hopes.

"Please don't say anything," she warned him. "After all, we have more important things to worry about. Let's see if there's a space here that might suit our purposes."

"It's your domain, Miss Brecknell. Lead the way," he said.

They waited until no one was watching, then slipped past the heavy oak door to the main part of the library.

Sarah knew the layout of the Athenaeum well, and she had a place in mind almost as soon as Theo suggested the idea. On the top floor, there were several partially finished rooms. They had been built in anticipation of more scholars needing space, but the fact was none of them were needed yet, and so the whole floor was largely disused.

Sarah led the way up the back stairs, Theo trailing behind her. Once on the top floor, they investigated the rooms until she found one that boasted a small stove for heating, and a window to the street. A single table and chair occupied the center of the room.

Theo looked in and nodded in satisfaction. "This will do. We won't have to whisper."

"I'll bring up some coal, so the room will be at least tolerably warm," Sarah said. "And I'll bring another chair in for you."

A dark shape at the doorway caught her eye, and she stepped back further into the room.

"What?" Theo saw her movement and immediately whirled around.

"Oh," Sarah said with relief. "It's just Cassius."

"Cassius?"

"Yes. When we first found him in the alley, he had a lean and hungry look."

The black cat slinked closer, sniffing at Theo's feet. Then he deliberately bumped his head against Theo's shin.

"He wants attention," Sarah said.

But Theo was already bending down to scratch the cat's ears. Cassius immediately started purring loudly. "Speaking of attention," he said, pulling a notebook out of his chest pocket, "I want you to look at this."

She reached over to take the notebook from Theo, who was still close to the floor. Cassius made a sound of irritation when Theo stopped paying attention to him for a bare second.

"Oh, hush," Sarah said absently to the cat. She'd already opened the book and was scanning the pages. "This is Charlie's handwriting," she said.

"Do you understand any of it?" Theo gathered the cat in his arms and stood up, watching her.

"Give me a moment." Sarah pulled out her silver-rimmed spectacles and put them on.

Theo laughed.

"What?" she asked.

"Nothing," he said. "When I picked Alyse up before

we arrived, she wished for a pair of spectacles in order to blend in. I see she was right."

"A common ailment of the scholarly. We all ruin our eyes eventually."

"They suit you."

"Hmm." Sarah sat down on the one chair in the room.

With nowhere else to sit, Theo leaned against a wall, still holding the cat. He seemed content to wait while Sarah looked through the pages.

She guessed he was testing her. "You know that reading a code is not like reading another language," she said. "It's more like deciding which mathematical formulas to use, then putting the coded words through and seeing if you're correct."

He grimaced. "Mathematics."

"Not necessarily advanced, though. Some codes are simple, such as Caesar's cipher. It's quite basic, in fact, but effective in a world where so few people could read at all. It's just a shift of three letters. In English, you would replace a B with an E, for example. If one doesn't know what to expect, the words would appear to be gibberish."

"That's what Georgia called the notebooks when she gave them to me."

"Exactly. In her case, the code worked perfectly."

"How do you know all this?"

"I've read about it. In books, you know."

"Don't get salty. But you must admit it is unusual. You're obviously more educated than the typical girl of your class."

"Yes. My father was impressed by the argument advanced by Mary Wollstonecraft that girls should be educated and could be rational creatures if taught the same lessons as boys. I read her *Original Stories from Real Life* many times as a child. I had tutors in mathematics and classics. When I got older, Mama did feel I was overly bookish, but it was too late. I was always meant to be a bluestocking."

Theo shook his head. "No, no. You don't escape that easily. It's one thing to be a bluestocking. It's quite another to study codes."

"I've always found cryptography fascinating. And steganography, too, naturally."

"Um…that's what?"

"Cryptography is when one encrypts a message so another can't read it. Steganography is even more tricky: it's hiding the message so someone else doesn't even *know* there is a message to be deciphered. Combined, the two disciplines can protect even the most sensitive information."

"That makes a lot of sense."

"Your group," she said hesitantly, knowing Theo didn't like to talk about it, "You never use such things? Aren't you encouraged to study it?"

"The Zodiac uses codes and cryptography occasionally. But I've never had to devise a code on my own. It appears Charlie did exactly that."

"Yes," Sarah said. "And I'm afraid he was good at it. Ideally, what we need is his key book."

"Which is?"

"A place where he recorded all the code words and

phrases he might need while either drafting or decrypting a message. It might be among the notebooks you have."

"We'll find out when I bring them to you. But you said you knew of some of Charlie's codes already."

"In a way. You see, a code doesn't always mean you change the letters of words. Sometimes, it could be a picture, or even a whole phrase. It was a game we played when we first met. I would send him a letter with a phrase only he would understand. Some were silly. *There is a dragon in Jerusalem* meant my grandmother was in town. She never liked Charlie. But some phrases were more dire."

"Such as?"

"Oh, let me remember. That's right. If I wrote *she wore a long ribbon last night*, it meant 'Come quickly, I'm in danger.'"

"That does not sound like a call for help," said Theo. "It sounds mundane."

"Well, that's the point. The best codes don't even look like codes. In any case, I never had occasion to use that one. I don't know if Charlie would have even remembered what it meant."

"You had to keep them in your head?"

"It's what makes it a strong code," she said, speaking faster as she grew more enthusiastic. "Because only the sender and the receiver know the significance of the phrases, no one else can possibly break it—there's nothing to break. But obviously, it's limited in scope. One can only memorize so much, and it must be agreed upon beforehand, and you must always communicate with the same person. Of course, you could have a number of people share the phrases—a Zodiac's worth of people, for example. But the more people who know a phrase, the less strong the secret is. In cryptography, everything must be balanced. Ease of use nearly always means a weaker code…I'm babbling, aren't I?"

He smiled at her. "It's not babbling. It's expert knowledge."

"I hope so. But all the same, it will take a while to make sense of these. And I don't have long till I have to meet that man and give him something to convince him to leave me alone."

"I have faith in you, Miss Brecknell."

Sarah merely nodded and kept skimming the notebook for anything familiar. She looked up after a few moments to see Cassius putting a paw on Theo's face.

"He likes you," she said.

Theo said, "I imagine he likes anyone willing to indulge him."

"That's not true, actually. Cassius is rather particular. He nearly clawed that man's face off when he showed up in my office."

"The man's name is Matteo Rossi, by the way," Theo said.

Sarah was surprised. "You found that out quickly!"

"Finding things out is essentially my job."

"How did you manage it?"

"I asked around. Your description helped considerably."

"Oh, you asked around," she repeated. "I'm sure I

wouldn't have been able to get the same results."

"That's why we're working together," Theo said. "You decode, I do everything else."

"What if I can't do it?" she asked anxiously. "Whatever he wrote in here, he didn't want anyone to read. And I was hardly his confidante."

"Bryony told me you two were almost inseparable."

"Bryony is a very romantic young girl," Sarah said. "I assure you, Charlie separated himself from me whenever he wished. Partly, it was his work. I know he traveled. But there would be weeks when I didn't see him or get any letters. And he rarely talked about other parts of his life."

Sarah's tone had grown bitter by the end. She knew it, and she saw when Theo's eyes softened in pity. Abruptly, she held the notebook out. "Here. I know you want to keep it safe. Tomorrow, I'll have more time and can make a proper go of decoding something. I really do understand the process, my lord."

"I don't doubt you, Miss Brecknell."

"Why not? I've proven nothing thus far."

"I think you have," he said. "And you'll have a better opportunity tomorrow."

He let Cassius jump down, then collected the notebook from Sarah. For a moment, they were standing very close to each other. She then remembered that being alone with him was utterly forbidden by every set of rules she knew…and she wasn't nearly as scared of that as she ought to be.

"How long will Lady Alyse be distracted?" Sarah asked.

"Alyse?" he echoed, as if he had completely forgotten her. "I don't know. She was very keen to talk to Mrs Heath. And she can charm nearly anybody into talking for hours."

"Still, we shouldn't stay here too long," she said. "My parents indulge me, but I must not attract any attention."

"That would not do at all, or I'll have to break into your house to exploit your cryptography skills."

"Please don't even joke about that."

Theo leaned a little closer. "I'm not joking. If you're the key I need to solve my problem, nothing is going to stop me from getting to you."

"I suppose," Sarah said, feeling rather breathless, "that's what got you into the Zodiac."

"Well, it certainly wasn't my charm." But then he smiled at her, disproving his statement. "Come. Let's get back downstairs," he said, putting a hand on her back to walk her out of the room. "After all, you're too valuable to let wander out alone."

Chapter 13

♉

DOWNSTAIRS, ALYSE WAITED AT THE edge of the group surrounding Mrs Heath, feeling strangely shy. The guest of honor held court at the edge of the low stage, using it as if it were a pedestal. Several guests peppered her with questions and begged for more details of her work.

Mrs Heath answered them all with good humor, her blue eyes sparkling with wit. When one audience member said she must be parched, Alyse volunteered to fetch some water.

"Make it wine, my dear, and I shall be eternally grateful," Mrs Heath chimed out.

Alyse hurried off to find the requested item. It wasn't difficult, as there were plenty of wines available at the reception table outside the lecture hall. Alyse looked around briefly for Theo, but didn't see him or Miss Brecknell.

Securing a glass, Alyse returned to the hall. The circle around Mrs Heath had thinned a bit, and she saw Alyse approaching.

"Ah, Ganymede returns!" she said.

Alyse blushed, handing over the wine. "I very much

enjoyed your talk," she said. "I can't believe you tramped all over the Nile's bank all by yourself."

"Tramped is the word. The shoes I wear while on excursions would not be welcome in a London home. What is your name?"

"Lady Alyse Templeton, ma'am."

"Oh, don't you dare ma'am me. I'm Elena Heath, and you shall call me Elena."

"All right…Elena."

Elena smiled, and drank half the wine down. "Passable. Made more sweet by the hands that brought it, of course."

"Who is Ganymede?" asked Alyse. "I remember hearing the name in school, but nothing beyond that."

"Ganymede was the cupbearer to the gods. I think you will do very well for a Ganymede."

"I hope so," Alyse said. "I wish you could talk longer. I have so many questions. How do you manage dealing with so many men when your husband isn't about? And do men ignore you because you're a woman? Even if you're smarter?"

Elena laughed. "All good questions, my lady."

"Just Alyse, if you please."

"Well, just Alyse, I will do my best to answer." Elena began to explain some of the details. Alyse listened, delighted at the story. She only realized they were alone in the room when Elena fell silent at last, and no one said anything.

Alyse blinked, looking around. "Oh, I have kept you from everyone."

"I don't mind at all. Give me one interested listener over a hall full of indifferent ones any day." She slid off the stage to stand by Alyse, who was surprised to find that the other woman was actually not much taller than she was. Her impressive demeanor and brassy reddish hair made her seem larger. "I should find the hosts, though," Elena continued. "The evening is getting on."

"Oh," Alyse said, disappointed.

Elena laughed again, an enchanting sound. "Why don't you come round to visit me tomorrow, if you'd like to hear more? I have a suite at the Hotel Foster."

"I will, if it would not be an inconvenience."

"I would like nothing better. London is dull for me, especially in winter. I need good people around me."

The two women walked out of the lecture hall, finding a much thinner crowd than before.

"My goodness, nearly everyone has gone. I must find Theo," Alyse said then, realizing how much time had elapsed. "Lord Markham, that is."

"Your escort for the evening?"

"My fiancé," Alyse said, suddenly shy about it, though she had no reason to be. "I should not like to have kept him waiting. Mr Heath must be an uncommonly patient man!"

Elena gave her a conspiratorial smile. "I'll tell you a secret, Alyse. There is no Mr Heath."

"What does that mean?" She looked down at the other woman's wedding band.

"I made him up," Elena said. "He is a fiction."

"How did you do that? And *why*?" Alyse asked.

"Because it makes my life much easier if people think a man has a leash on me. I come to England, and tell folks he has stayed behind in Egypt to oversee things there. In Egypt, I say I have just seen my husband in England, where he has secured the needed funding. I hire a secretary in both places to manage correspondence, and voila! I am free to do what I wish," Elena said with satisfaction.

"That's marvelous," Alyse said admiringly. "I never would have thought of it!"

"Trust me, dear. Necessity is the mother of invention. I knew no one would take a single young woman seriously, whether in archeology or in any other sphere. So I created Mr Heath, and I must say, he is my favorite man in the whole world…next to Amenhotep III!"

Alyse laughed. "Oh, I love it!"

"You'll keep my secret, won't you?" Elena smiled at her.

"Of course! To the grave."

"Let's hope it doesn't come to that."

Then Alyse saw Theo enter the room. "Oh," Alyse said quickly. "I hope you weren't looking for me."

He smiled rather absently. "Not at all."

He was not the slightest put out by the time, which relieved Alyse. He greeted Mrs Heath and asked her a few questions about her talk, though Alyse could tell his mind wasn't on the conversation. She offered an invitation to Mrs Heath to come to the same party she previously invited Miss Brecknell to, and felt triumphant when the woman said she'd attend. "Oh, marvelous. But I still threaten to see you tomorrow!"

"I look forward to it, Lady Alyse."

Theo walked Alyse outside, and then drove her home. He was largely silent in the carriage.

"Theo?" she asked. "Are you well?"

"What? Oh, yes." He offered her an apologetic look. "My mind was wandering."

"I *know*." Alyse smiled at him. But she didn't press him on it. Her mind was wandering too, all the way to Egypt.

Theo escorted her to her door, and Alyse said good night. Up in her room, her maid helped her change out of her dress and get ready for bed. "Did you enjoy the evening, my lady?" she asked as she put away Alyse's clothes.

"I did indeed," Alyse said with a dreamy smile.

"Thought you must have, my lady. Lord Markham looked especially handsome tonight."

"Mmmm," Alyse said, not really hearing.

As she drifted off to sleep, she realized she had enjoyed the evening, not because of Theo being especially handsome, but because of meeting Elena Heath.

Chapter 14

♉

SARAH ROSE EARLY ON WEDNESDAY. Naomi dressed her, then braided her hair and put it in a crown around her head. She went with her father to the Athenaeum in the late morning, leaving her more than enough time to worry and doubt herself regarding the arrangement to work together with Theo. What if he thought better of it? What if he decided she knew nothing after all?

She gathered several books she thought would be useful and went up to the room on the top floor. She'd brought up coal already, and started a little fire in the grate. Soon the room was warm enough that she had to take off her shawl.

Just after two, Theo arrived.

"I wasn't sure you'd actually come back," Sarah said.

"When I say I'll do a thing, I will," he responded, with a warning glance.

He was carrying a box beneath one arm, which he put in the middle of the table. "I see you procured a chair for me. Thank you."

"Well, it would be rude to make you stand the whole time." Sarah reached for the box. "May I?"

"Go ahead." Theo watched as she opened the lid and looked in at the notebooks.

"These were all Charlie's?"

Theo nodded. "Shortly after the funeral, I asked Miss Wolverton if I might look at any papers Charlie left behind. She was most accommodating, but aside from a few items I got immediately, there was nothing else to be found. Until the day of the dinner party. She found these tucked away in an odd corner of the house, and boxed them all up and gave them to me."

Sarah glanced at Theo. "What made you ask for Charlie's papers? Is that something your group typically does?"

He looked uncomfortable. "Charlie was…in the middle of something when he died. I hoped to find some answers. That's all."

He helped pull the notebooks out of the box and started to stack them carefully side by side. "I was able to arrange them by date. The earliest ones are these," he said, tapping one stack. "Does it make sense to begin at the beginning?"

"Yes, indeed," Sarah said, reaching out to pull the stack toward her. She had no idea what sort of information Charlie recorded, but surely she would get another glimpse into his mind. Although she didn't miss him quite as keenly as she had in the first months, she was hungry to know anything he might have recorded about her.

She began to skim the pages of the first book. "This is interesting," she said.

"Found something already?"

"Not specifically. I just mean that it's interesting how Charlie chose to write. As you obviously know, there are coded passages. But he used different methods. This one here is mirror-writing, and a few pages later, he has a column of numbers I don't think is code at all. I think they're exactly what they look like: numbers, probably the amounts of payments made and received. He might have been testing methods."

"That actually sounds promising," he agreed. "This may be quicker than I thought."

"Don't get your hopes up. Decoding is art as much as science."

"Take your time, Miss Brecknell."

"We don't have that much time. And there are so many notebooks."

He leaned forward. "Just focus on the code. I won't let you wander into that meeting with Rossi unprepared. That's a promise."

Sarah tried to heed Theo's advice. She sank into the notebooks, and soon found herself absorbed in Charlie's secret writings. A few parts were easy enough to decipher, since they weren't proper codes at all. She read those aloud to Theo, who acted as secretary and wrote her words down on fresh paper.

"You're used to doing that," she noted, seeing him write so fluidly, without pausing or asking her to repeat anything.

"Often my task in a meeting between luminaries," he explained. "They don't want to bother to take notes, so I get to do it."

"And in the meantime, you're actually working for the Zodiac?"

Theo's expression closed immediately. "We're not going to talk about that."

She said, "Can you not say a little more about this group? It may help me as I work. Not anything too secret," she went on. "Though I suppose it's all secret. But I only heard a little bit about what Charlie did. What you do. Please. It sounds like every day could bring about a death. And for Charlie, it did."

He said nothing for a moment, but then gave a nod. "I can tell you a little. Only a little."

"As long as it's true."

He looked away for a second, considering where to start. "We were both part of this group. And as you guessed from the names, it's very small."

"Twelve members," Sarah said. "What do you call yourself? An operative?"

"Agent."

"So there are twelve agents. And you do what?"

"Whatever needs to be done, when it can't be done in the open. Perhaps it bends the rules of diplomacy…or breaks laws. Perhaps if an official representative were to be caught doing such a thing, it would spark a war. We have no official status as agents, and therefore His Majesty's government need not respond if we were to be discovered. It keeps the government safe."

"But it doesn't keep you safe. If anything were to go wrong…you're lost?"

"Yes."

Sarah didn't like that at all. "How can you bear it? You have to do such dangerous things, and you're alone."

"I knew the risks when I accepted."

"But still, it's hardly fair to ask one man to do something when you know full well you'll give him no support," Sarah argued.

"Fair is not a word one uses in espionage," he said. "Nothing is fair. You win by breaking the rules. Winner takes all. And the stakes are your country."

"That's appalling."

"It's life," he said, as if it barely concerned him. "Now, back to work, Miss Sarah. If you want to know what espionage is all about, this is your best introduction."

After a while, Sarah commented, "Espionage is considerably duller than I would have expected."

"It has its moments," Theo responded.

"You can't talk about those, though," she said with a laugh.

"I would prefer not to."

They kept working. Sarah was nose deep in all the books. She would read, her lips moving as she translated the coded words on page after page. But time after time, she shook her head. "There's nothing especially noteworthy here. These texts are all ordinary. This one is a speech from Hamlet. This other is a text on some French artist. It appears Charlie was simply practicing new codes, using ordinary texts to translate."

"You're holding the oldest notebook," Theo pointed out. "Perhaps he settled on one code and used it for the later ones."

"Oh, good idea." Sarah pulled out several notebooks and leafed through them. The image of the celestial Zodiac appeared on one of the pages, with all twelve signs in a circle, and some random lines drawn between each of them.

"Look. Charlie was making some sort of chart," she said, showing to him.

Theo looked at it, his eyes searching out the pattern of the lines. "He was trying to find out which signs were connected with the others," he said. "He wanted to know who was in contact with whom."

"Aren't you *all* in contact?"

"No," he admitted.

She was surprised, to say the least. "There are only twelve agents and you don't even know them all?"

"It's safer that way," Theo explained. "If an agent is captured, he can't give up the whole organization."

"Then why was Charlie making this chart?" she asked.

Once again, Theo's expression closed off. "I couldn't say. Charlie was always curious. Perhaps he just wanted to do it for his own amusement."

"That sounds like Charlie," she said with a smile. "He always had to know everything. The worst taunt I could offer him was 'I know something you don't know.' Drove him mad."

He laughed once. "I believe it."

Sarah was still looking at the chart. "Aries, Capricorn, Leo…" she said, listing the signs. Leo. Theo. "Your code name isn't actually *Leo*, is it?"

"It'd be a pretty poor code if it were," he said.

"You didn't answer the question."

"No, I didn't."

Sarah glanced at him. Even in the very short time she had known him, she understood that there were many questions he would never answer. She found that she liked him better for it.

"Can I ask something else?"

"You can ask," he said. "I may not answer."

"He'd done something dangerous, hadn't he? He exposed himself. Said too much. Or talked to the wrong person."

Theo clearly didn't want to tell her. Maybe he wasn't allowed to.

"He did." She sighed. "You don't have to say it. I *knew* it. I knew something wasn't right."

"What do you mean? How do you know?" Theo's eyes brightened as he asked the questions.

"He was so different the last few months before his death."

"Worried? Nervous?"

"Oh, no. Just the opposite. He was nearly euphoric. He kept saying that he was planning something spectacular. He wouldn't say more. But it was odd."

"Euphoric," he repeated, his tone thoughtful.

"Yes. He was so happy. And talkative. He'd go on about what he was planning for the future. For us. He wanted to tour Europe. India, even China. He said we've live like royalty. And he gave me gifts, far too often, really."

"How can a woman receive gifts too often?"

"These gifts were ridiculous. He got me a necklace with a single pearl, from Bahrain, no less. Shawls and silk gloves in a rainbow of colors. I didn't even like them. It was as if he was…fevered." She paused, recollecting the last few weeks of the summer, right before the tragedy. "He'd just…laugh sometimes, like he couldn't stop himself. Now that I think back on it, it was a little frightening."

Theo reached across the table to put a hand on her arm. "It's easy to think things have significance after an event like death. It may not have been that strange."

"Maybe," Sarah said, doubting herself. "He said he felt better than ever, the one time I dared to ask him what was going on."

"Did he say anything else?"

"I can't recall…yes." Sarah straightened up. "He said everything was falling into place. I thought he was referring to something he was doing for the Zodiac…" She trailed off, having remembered she shouldn't speak the name.

Theo sighed and sat back, thinking over her words. Sarah watched the man, wondering what was going on behind those green eyes. Theo was practically the opposite of Charlie. It was hard to believe they'd been boyhood friends. Charlie was outgoing and always had an answer on the tip of his tongue. Theo seemed far more restrained. Once again, Sarah turned the name over in her mind. If he wasn't Leo—which was too childishly rhyming to be a good choice—he must use another sign.

"How about Taurus?" she asked, thinking out loud. "Even if the names are chosen randomly, the Ts are not enough of a clue to discard the match. It might even be convenient..." She trailed off when she heard Theo drumming his fingers against the wooden surface of the desk.

"Miss Brecknell, I'm going to have to ask you to stop that."

"Stop what?"

"Guessing."

Something in his eyes gave it away. "I'm right, aren't I!" Sarah laughed in delight. "On the second try! That's not too bad."

He didn't look amused. "It's not a game, Miss Brecknell."

The laughter died in her throat. "I'm sorry. I won't tell anyone."

"Tell anyone what? I confirmed nothing."

Sarah leaned toward him. "So it's not Taurus? The assignment of names really is just random? An agent retires and the next one gets the code name?"

"Most don't retire," he said.

"But you can't have more than twel..." Sarah stopped, realizing his meaning. "Oh. They die."

Theo shook his head. "Can we discuss something else? Anything else?"

"Tell me about your family, then. That's safe enough, isn't it?" Sarah wasn't sure why she was so curious about Theo, but as long as she couldn't get him to answer the vital questions, she could learn something about him.

"I have four sisters and a brother. And my parents. It can get crowded when we're all together."

"You get to see them all? That's wonderful."

"Well, two of my sisters, the older ones, are married. My younger ones are still stringing a few suitors along, and my brother has no interest in society. He lives at our house in the country as much as he can. He wishes to learn how to run an estate."

Theo didn't need to add the reason why. While Theo, as the future Baron, would inherit the title and all the wealth of the family's lands, his brother was likely to need other skills to survive. Younger sons did not have an easy path.

"I wish I had siblings," Sarah said. "Mama always hoped for more, but she is stuck with me."

"She has nothing to complain about in you."

"You have not heard her! When I talk at parties, I tend to talk about Roman history, which does not go well among the *ton*. I am not a sparkling wit at the best of times. Mama despaired of my making a good match, until Charlie started courting me. Of course, he chose me because of my habits, not in spite of them."

"Speaking of courting, have you seen Lord Carlin since the dinner?" he asked.

"No," Sarah said, putting her head down. "Why?"

"He seemed taken with you."

"I'm sure he was merely being polite."

"He asked to call on you. That is not required by politeness. He wants to court you."

"Well, that is his choice."

"And yours," he pointed out.

"I…suppose." Sarah said. "In truth, I don't expect to marry."

"Why not? You were engaged once. And gentlemen are obviously still interested in you."

"It wouldn't be right."

"Are you so in love with Charlie's memory you'd remain a spinster for him?" Theo asked with a frown. "You don't owe Wolverton your life. You can start over."

"Oh, why should it matter to you what I do with my life?" Sarah retorted with heat in her voice.

Theo looked taken aback.

Sarah was equally shocked at her outburst. "Forgive me. I shouldn't have snapped at you."

"I shouldn't have raised the subject," he said. "I forgot my place. We're not as familiar with each other as it feels."

"Is that a common trap for spies?" she asked.

He paused. "Maybe. Relationships tend to be kindled quickly and one never knows how long they'll last. Friendships, romances, alliances. Doesn't matter. The rules just aren't the same as they are in polite society."

"Which do you prefer, polite society or your other world?" she asked, curious.

"Society is slightly less dangerous," Theo said with a wry smile. "But also less interesting."

"The trade off."

"I live in both worlds. So I don't have to compromise."

"But your family does. They only get half of you, and

they don't even know, do they?"

"No. They don't. Why do you ask?"

"I don't know," Sarah said. "I think about it all the time now. The Zodiac, I mean. I try not to, but I'm surrounded by it. These notebooks, Charlie's death, you, all the things happening in the world. How do you stand it?"

"You get used to it," he said. "I don't have a better answer."

Chapter 15

☿

THE SAME DAY, BEFORE ANYONE could call on her or divert her from her goal, Alyse went round to the Hotel Foster, where Elena was staying. She sent her card up and hardly waited a moment before she was shown to the suite of rooms Elena held.

Elena was waiting for her, standing by the fireplace. In the daylight, her hair was even redder, and she looked a little younger, perhaps because she was not dressed so formally. She smiled when Alyse entered. "Ah, the late night has done nothing to diminish you! You look like Sleeping Beauty just awoken."

Alyse blushed a little at the compliment. It was silly, and flattering, and strangely intimate. "I see that you have been awake for hours, too." She glanced at the desk by the window, which was covered in papers.

Elena followed her glance and rolled her eyes. "Oh, just the endless nonsense that accompanies any request for funds. I must write letters, and flatter my patrons, and beg them to pay promptly enough so the next dig can actually occur." She gestured to the long chaise in front of the fire. "But that is dull talk. Please sit, my lady. Shall I ring for tea?"

"That would be lovely. It's colder than it looks outside." Alyse sank down on the chaise.

Elena rang and gave the order to a maid, then moved to the chair next to where Alyse sat. "This cold is my nemesis. When I'm in the desert, I curse the sun, but I would take the Egyptian heat over this climate any time."

"Won't you tell me a little more of what you're planning next?" Alyse asked. "It would warm me to hear it."

Elena laughed and then talked about her upcoming journey back to Egypt. Alyse listened raptly, imagining the places Elena described, and feeling a strange ache in her chest. That was a world she might die to see.

"Alyse," Elena said after a while. "I have been talking about myself this whole time. How very rude of me."

"No! I like it. Your life is so fascinating. I could listen for hours."

"My stories are mostly sand, dear. It is your turn."

"But I have nothing to say," Alyse said, suddenly ashamed. "My life is so ordinary. I'm sure that's why you ran away—to escape the sort of life I lead right now."

"Ran away?" Elena raised an eyebrow. "Perhaps. But having an ordinary life is not the same thing as having an ordinary mind. Do tell me what you're thinking."

Alyse blinked. What she was thinking was that Elena looked beautiful…vital and happy. "I wish I could be like you," she said finally.

"That is halfway to telling me about yourself," Elena said, laughing. "But it is still too much about me. What do you do all day? What do you dream of doing?"

"They are not the same at all."

"Why not?"

"Because I suppose women do not often get to do what they want. Not that I dislike my life," she added hastily. "I am very lucky."

"How so?"

"Well, I live comfortably, and have a great measure of freedom. And I'll have a good marriage. Theo—Lord Markham—is really like marrying a friend."

Elena watched her with skeptical eyes. "And that's what you want? To marry a friend?"

"Better than being handed off to a stranger! A title is all well and good, unless it's used as a dowry. With Theo I know what I'm getting."

"You do not sound like a woman in love."

Alyse shrugged and looked away. "Perhaps I'm not very good at expressing it. It's personal, after all. I can't believe I'm telling you, actually. We just met!"

"Sometimes, a moment is sufficient to know you have found a kindred spirit," Elena said, a tiny smile playing around her lips.

"I do wish you intended to stay in London a little longer," Alyse confessed. "You are like a comet—here for a little while, and then gone again. And life will be duller after you go."

"I have never been called a comet before! How delightful."

Alyse warmed to hear it. Then she remembered something. "You know, I actually did go on one adventure. The objective was the North Pole, but we did not achieve it."

"That is a legitimate adventure, my dear. How old were you?"

"Seven."

"Seven!"

"Well, let me explain. When I was growing up near Cheltenham, one of my neighbors and good friends decided to go on an expedition to the North Pole, and he wanted me to come along. It was Theo, of course. Now I did nearly anything Theo suggested—he was a little older than me, and much cleverer, and has the nicest green eyes. He told me to pack a wool blanket and my warmest cloak, because although it was July, it would still get quite chilly at the Pole."

"You were walking to the Pole? From Cheltenham," Elena said in amusement.

"Yes. Theo estimated it couldn't take more than a week to be in Scotland, where we'd need to get passage on a ship, naturally."

"Naturally."

"He had Cook prepare my favorite sandwiches, so I thought we were adequately provisioned. Well, we started walking. I've always been good at hiking. But at around five in the afternoon, there was a thunderstorm. We were forced to make a hasty shelter. Wool blankets, you may not know, are horrible in a downpour. We were soaked to the skin, and it was several hours before anyone came across us."

"You must have felt frozen."

"Oh, Theo built a fire as soon as the rain stopped. He's very resourceful."

"But you did return home?"

"Yes. One of Papa's tenants drove by and smelled the smoke. We got a ride back in a haycart. Our fathers were furious. Our mothers too, naturally, but it was a father's wrath we feared most! After we were dried off and changed, they brought us—Theo and me—into my father's study, which was an intimidating room in the best situation. Both of them dressed him down in front of me. They told him he was a fool who should be whipped. I said I would run away if they did!"

"Your loyalty does you credit," Elena murmured, her lips quirking as she tried to keep a straight face.

"Finally, Lord Markham asked Theo if he understood what a terrible error he'd made. Theo said he'd reflected on his actions. He was very sorry for putting me in harm's way, and if he had it to do over again, he certainly would have brought both a tent and a dog along, which would have ensured the expedition's success." Alyse finished on that note, pleased at how vividly she remembered the whole afternoon.

Elena laughed in delight. "That is a marvelous failure! I wish half my digs ended so well. And you stayed friends all through the years?"

"Friends and allies. He *was* very sorry about the downpour, you know. After he got done with his punishment, he said, *Alyse, are we still allies?* I said, *always.* And so it has been ever since."

"And you are to marry him."

For a moment, Alyse was drawn back in time to the summer the betrothal had been decided on by their fathers. Alyse was still very young, but she was dimly aware of what the future would hold. Theo seemed the finest person in the whole world to her. She always liked him, and it didn't occur to her that she might someday differ in her desires or want to make the decision herself.

In fact, Alyse was never comfortable around the other girls who twittered and cooed over boys they admired. The art of flirting seemed byzantine and dangerous. Even more challenging was the notion of deciphering a young gentleman's intent. So to have it all handled for her was most reassuring.

That summer, Theo was only at home for a few weeks. He was grown up by then, while Alyse was still considered a child. He had begun working in government in some capacity. He seemed so distant and mature to her. She asked him about the nature of his work, and he only told her it was very dull, and she would not be at all interested. When she pressed him, asking why he should do it at all, if it was boring, he told her: "Because what I do will help others, Alyse. Most of them won't ever notice, or if they do they won't know who's done it. But I'll know. And that's what matters."

She half fell in love with him that summer. He certainly noticed that she had blossomed from a girl into a young woman. And when she confessed her curiosity about kissing, he obliged her. It had been eye-opening. She knew Theo was one day going to show her more of that, but he never pressed her or suggested anything indecent. Alyse soon realized how rare a situation she was in. She would marry a friend. What could be better?

"Alyse?"

She blinked, back in the wintry present. "Excuse me?"

Elena was watching her with interested eyes. "My goodness, he must have unusual qualities for a man. You were in a reverie."

"Was I rude?"

"If you were rude," Elena said, "I would not hope to see you again. Yet I find you intriguing, Lady Alyse, and I hope I learn more about you."

Alyse smiled, delighted. She wasn't used to being intriguing.

Chapter 16

♉

OVER THE NEXT FEW DAYS, Sarah and Theo worked in the little room for hours at a time. As it turned out, slipping away proved shockingly simple for Sarah. She evaded her absent-minded father with ease, and placated her mother by accepting invitations for events of the shortest possible duration and the smallest likely guest lists. She requested her friend Chloe go with her to the events, so she would have someone to lean on.

As a gentleman and an aristocrat, Theo didn't have to explain himself to anybody, so if he wanted to come to the Athenaeum every day for the rest of his life, no one would dream of telling him no. However, he told no one where he was going, other than his incurious driver.

Sarah didn't ask how he managed to get in and out with no one seeming to notice or care. She only hoped they would somehow find a clue to the cache of letters the man named Rossi wanted.

She was making some progress. She worked at one particular code for a full day and night, after convincing Theo she could be trusted with one notebook at a time to take back to her house. He conceded fairly quickly, all too aware they had little time. She broke it late that night, after realizing it was a two-step combination of a Caesar cipher and a substitution code. Once she understood what Charlie did, she was able to create a key. She stayed up all night to decode as many passages as possible.

She showed Theo her results the next day, and proved her method by showing him translated passages.

"Look. There's a whole section here on some items he bought and sold to a G. Villani. I'm not sure what. The cheapest item is ten pounds and the most expensive is one hundred."

Theo was delighted. His smile nearly took her breath away.

"Villani," Theo said. "That's an unusual name. Italian?"

"Like Matteo Rossi?" Sarah asked.

He nodded. "Exactly."

"You think there's a connection? It may be a coincidence."

"Or it may not. I'll check it out."

"How will you do that?" she asked.

"I may not be as intelligent as you," he said. "But I do have a few skills."

"Don't tease me."

"I'm not teasing. I'd cover a bet you could best nearly any of my old professors."

"They'd never let me speak," she said.

"Only because they know you'd show them up."

"Oh, let me work," she scolded him, though her heart warmed at the ridiculous praise.

They worked. Using her newly devised key, Sarah translated a notebook dating from the spring before Charlie's death. Most entries appeared to be personal notes. What he did, things he purchased, where he went. None of it seemed very important. Still, since any line might contain a hint, she worked out the passages word by word, and only read them through at the end. Then she found one that was not what she ever expected to read.

16 May — Spent night with G. She wanted me to stay longer, but had to leave to Fr. for assignment. Brought small oil by Ingres to sell there. Told G I'd buy her a present as well. She begged for emeralds — of course. She's becoming expensive to keep.

"Oh," Sarah couldn't stop herself from saying, as realization dawned on her.

"What is it?" Theo asked, his eyes alert.

"Nothing," Sarah said hastily. "That is, it's not related to what we're looking for."

"Sarah," he said, noticing her expression. "Tell me."

"It's just..." She closed her eyes briefly. "I think he had a mistress."

"Did he." He looked guilty, as if it were somehow his fault.

Sarah shrugged, trying to push the hurt away. "I'm not completely ignorant of the world." But Charlie said he *loved* her. He made love to her. Why would he have a mistress?

Theo took the notebook from her nerveless fingers and read the passage himself, using the key. "Hard to put a different interpretation on that," he concluded, with disappointment in his tone. "I'm not sure how to protect you from such revelations."

"It's not your duty to," she said. Her eyes were itchy, wet. She wiped her eyes surreptitiously. Not surreptitiously enough.

Theo said, too casually, "We should stop. We're losing all the light anyway."

"I'll...I'll go see if my father is still deep in his own work," Sarah said. She felt like running. Her body was completely tense. How could he have a *mistress*? she wondered again. What was wrong with Sarah that Charlie didn't want just her?

But she mastered her composure, and then crept down the back stairs. The whole building was nearly deserted. Her father was nowhere to be found. She returned to find Theo waiting patiently, his attention given to Cassius, who had arrived with the offering of a dead mouse, which now lay in front of the window.

"Oh, Cassius," Sarah said, happy at least something was working as expected. "Well done!"

Theo smiled. "That is not what any one of my sisters would have said on seeing a dead rodent."

Sarah laughed. "I'm used to it. Listen, Papa may have forgotten me. He's nowhere in the building, and I think he must have gone home alone."

"Does that happen often?"

"Occasionally. He's very devoted to his work, and it makes him forget little things like where he left his daughter. I can hire a ride home. I keep a purse in my office for such occasions."

"No, let me drive you. Since I learned who Rossi is, I don't like the idea of you being unattended, even for a short trip."

She agreed to that. Once they were in the carriage though, Theo had another suggestion. "Are you hungry?"

"I'm always hungry," she confessed.

"Then we should get something to eat." He stopped her objection before she could voice it. "And don't worry, no one will recognize either of us."

He drove her to a very respectable tavern offering several private dining rooms for guests. Theo requested one, and they were shown there immediately.

Sarah looked around the small room. A fire burned in the grate, making the small space quite warm. The table could have accommodated four, but only two places were set.

"You've been here before?" she asked.

Theo helped her out of her pelisse, and hung it up before he removed his own greatcoat.

"The food is good, and it's an excellent place to relax for a short while. You're working extremely hard on deciphering those notebooks. You need to take a rest."

"It would help to think of something else," she admitted. "I just know I'm missing an element somehow. Those passages I can't decode are maddening. No matter what method I try, I get only gibberish. There's a twist. He was so clever about that type of thing. I wish—"

"Sarah," Theo broke in.

"Yes?"

"Remember when I told you to think of something

else for a little while?"

"Oh, I see what you mean." She sat down at the table. "What should I think about?" she asked, feeling rather shy.

"How about dinner?" he suggested. "What do you like?"

"When it comes to food? Everything."

A server came in to tell them what was on offer. Theo asked Sarah what she favored and then ordered food, and brandy for himself.

"Something to drink?"

"Only tea," she said quickly.

The server brought the drinks. Sarah relished the heat of the tea, and Theo evidently enjoyed his brandy.

"You don't drink?" he asked.

"Not when I'm nervous."

"That's usually what starts most people off," he said. "Why are you nervous?"

Sarah looked up. "It's just that…you think you know someone so well, and then you find you didn't know them at all. As if you never even saw their true self."

"You mean Wolverton."

"And his mistress. I wonder what the *G* stands for." Sarah was still mortified at both the secret and her reaction to it. "Would he have kept her after we married?" she wondered aloud, before she thought better of it.

But Theo heard her. "He may very well have put her aside. In a happy marriage, he would have had no reason to look elsewhere. It's really not uncommon to have a mistress, though."

"You're speaking from experience because you have one?" she asked tartly, then put her hands to her face. "I can't believe I said that. Don't answer me."

He answered her anyway. "I don't. And if I did, I can't imagine keeping a mistress after marrying, unless something happened to make the marriage go very sour. But I expect to be very happy."

"Everyone *expects* to be happy," Sarah said, her voice sounding far more bitter than she intended. "Oh, Lord. Forgive me. I'm horrible today."

He reached over to take her hand away from her face. The feel of his hand around hers was absurdly comforting. "You haven't got much rest these past few nights, have you?"

She shook her head. "No. Not since I met Rossi, in fact. But what else can I do? I have to find some clue in those notebooks."

"You already have," he reminded her. "I'm going to search for this Villani person immediately. I already have someone investigating Rossi's whereabouts. You *will* find out where this cache exists. I believe it does... somewhere."

She smiled weakly at him. "Please don't be so kind to me. It's not good for you."

"What do you mean? Why shouldn't I be kind?"

"Because it makes me fond of you, and I shouldn't do that. Once this is over, I should forget I ever knew you. Isn't it safer that way?"

"Perhaps. But I don't abandon my friends."

"We're not friends," Sarah objected. "I'm just helping

you find these papers. I owe it to Charlie to help, since he can't defend himself anymore. If he was keeping something hidden, he must have had a good reason for it, don't you think?"

Theo sat back, those green eyes suddenly unreadable. "I'm sure he thought it was a good reason."

"So you don't have to humor me to ensure I'll help."

"Humor you?"

"Well…you never told me how silly it was to play with codes. Nearly everyone else has eventually told me women ought not muddle in such things."

"Sarah, I'm delighted you muddle in such things. If you had listened to any fool who counseled you to stop, where would we be today?"

The food was brought in then, and they stopped talking of spies and mistresses. Theo made every effort to distract Sarah from her concerns, telling her stories of him and Charlie at school, and all the old pranks they used to play. By the time he saw her home, Sarah was feeling infinitely better.

Theo made her promise to not think of codes until she returned to the Athenaeum the next day. "And by then, maybe I'll have some news about Villani."

"You're going to keep working all night? Right after you told me not to?"

"That's the difference between us. You need to rest because your work is all in your brain. I just need to slog through city streets and gather scraps of information. Any fool can do that."

"Be careful," she said, worried for him.

Theo took her hand and kissed it. "I will be. I promise. Now go inside. I trust you have an excuse ready if anyone was looking for you?"

"Of course. I was in the basement chasing after Cassius when whoever it was called for me. So I found my own way home." She was fairly certain she could make that lie believable.

"Excellent. I'll see you tomorrow evening." He released her hand, ready to let her go.

"At the Athenaeum? In the evening?" she asked confused. They always met in the afternoon.

"Have you forgotten tomorrow is Monday? Lady Alyse's party? You may need a day without the disruption of sneaking around. Tomorrow you should just behave normally, and I'll see you in the evening, at the party. You do remember being invited, don't you?"

"Yes of course. My friend Mrs Lamb is coming as well, so I'll have an ally. But I can't waste a whole day."

He opened the box of notebooks and handed over the few Sarah had been working on. "Here. Just keep them safe."

She was pleased he trusted her with them. "I will. Until tomorrow, then." Sarah climbed out of the coach and walked the short way to her home.

As it happened, her father only just remembered he'd left her behind, and was relieved when he didn't have to retrieve her. "Sorry, my girl, but I just got a new translation of Horodotus. Absolutely wonderful. You ate already? You always manage so well, dear. Your mother is out at some function, and I confess I forgot about dinner entirely."

"No need to worry about me, Papa," Sarah said soothingly. "I'll read for a while and then go to bed."

She went up to her room and rang for Naomi to help her get ready for bed. She was exhausted, and she knew she'd fall asleep as soon as her head touched the pillow.

Right before she closed her eyes, Sarah recalled what she said to her father. He had no need to worry about her. Which was true, because Theo was worrying about her. That was the most reassuring thought Sarah had in the past week. She wondered where he was just then, but sleep overtook her and she wondered nothing more.

Chapter 17

♉

JUST AS SARAH WAS FALLING into a dreamless sleep, Theo was staring at the window of a building in one of the neighborhoods of London known for its artists and galleries.

After seeing Sarah home, Theo decided to start pursuing the Villani lead straight away. There couldn't be that many people in London bearing the name. Charlie's entry also mentioned art, so Theo concluded Villani might well be either an artist or a dealer.

A few hours of diligent searching among the streets and the taverns of the most likely area—well east of the better galleries on Pall Mall—brought results. He ran into a group of artists drinking their way to oblivion in a smoky, overheated tavern in Suffolk Street. Theo bought one round and left a half hour later with extensive knowledge about several artists and their patrons, several terrible local brews, and several art dealers, including a Giselle Villani. He even got the street direction of the building where she conducted her business.

Normally, he would have waited until the next day to contact someone related to an assignment. It would give him time to develop a cover identity and a story. But learning Villani was a woman made Theo reconsider the situation. Especially because she was a woman with a first name beginning with G. Theo always trusted his gut on such matters, and his gut told him that there was no possible way Villani wasn't *also* Charlie's mistress, the mysterious, emerald-loving *G* who so upset Sarah.

He went to the building immediately. Since he planned to break in, he was a little disconcerted to see light coming through the windows. But perhaps the end result would be the same. After adjusting his jacket to ensure he looked presentable, he crossed the street and knocked on the door.

After a moment, the door opened, revealing a woman holding a pistol. "What do you want?" she asked, looking him over with no fear in her voice.

"I wanted to buy art," Theo said smoothly. "And if you feel the need to protect your stock with a gun, I'm suddenly much more interested."

She smirked as she lowered the weapon. "At this hour? The protection is for me." An accent was clear in her voice, as was a certain hint of sensuality that was likely cultivated. "Why don't you come back tomorrow."

"But I'm here now," he countered, deliberately putting more warmth in his own voice. "I promise I won't take up too much of your time."

She surveyed him, taking a while to do so. Then she stepped back and opened the door wider. "Come in. Welcome to my offices, sir."

Theo stepped in, noting that she made no move to put

the gun away. "You are Mrs Giselle Villani? Or would it be Miss?"

Her lip quirked. "In England I go by Miss Villani."

"Miss doesn't suit you," he commented.

He was simply telling the truth. Giselle Villani didn't look missish at all. She had a mass of thick hair the color of strong coffee, and large, languid eyes in a slightly lighter shade. Everything about her suggested the bedroom. That probably helped her in business dealings with men too distracted to pay attention to money when they had her to look at. He'd wager any amount she began as an artist's model and picked up a lot of information while men treated her like a doll.

Interestingly, she wore an emerald necklace at her throat.

"So," she said, noting his perusal and liking it. "You have my name, but I don't have yours."

"Lord Starling," he said, using one his aliases.

"A lord in my humble shop! How very impressive. Well, what brings you to me in the dead of night? Not the usual time to purchase art, is it?"

"I don't sleep," he said. "And I'm used to others doing what I ask. Since I'm a lord and all."

"That still does not explain why you came to *my* shop."

"You were recommended particularly."

"Recommended by whom?"

He smiled at her. "I'd rather not say."

"You keep everything secret as a matter of honor?"

"No. I just don't like giving information away for free.

Everything has a price."

Her eyes brightened. "I agree completely, my lord. Information is the most valuable commodity of all."

"Only if one knows where to sell or buy it," he said, turning away from her to look at the art in the room. Pieces were hung up, but many more leaned against the walls or were stacked carefully on tables. At the further end of the space, a large table was covered in wood slats and various tools for framing. Whatever else she was, Giselle appeared to truly be in business as a dealer of art.

"What information do you deal in?" she asked, shadowing him.

Theo debated how far to spin his lies. "Let us say, information of interest to speculators."

"Tell me more," she ordered, making her voice a purr.

"Tell me about the art first. I'm interested in diversifying my income. What artists would be good to invest in? Whose work might I sell for a profit in a few years' time?"

She pursed her lips, taking the question seriously. "I could recommend several. Calcott has been a popular name, and I expect more success for him in the future. Much depends on what you are willing to pay up front, and what you hope to recoup."

"Let's say I am willing to pay twenty pounds for a painting today, and I want sixty for it in three years. And I don't want to be hounded by other collectors while I hold the items."

"You have no preference for style or period?"

"Do you?"

"I am familiar with many Spanish and Italian artists, of course. But their work does not always sit well with an English audience."

"I'll sell to buyers on the Continent then. In France. Or Spain. Even Italy."

"Don't bother with Italy," she advised. "They're awash in Old Masters and great names from the Renaissance. They look to the past, and the market is fierce."

"You know your business, Miss Villani," he said, with complete honesty. "How much will that piece of intelligence cost me?"

She smiled saucily at him. "It will cost you nothing if you call me Giselle."

"Noted, Giselle." He looked at one painting on the wall, a lushly-colored portrait of a woman. The folds of her clothes were so vividly done that he could almost reach out and feel the fabric. "This one must be an artist worth considering."

"Indeed. Jean-Auguste Dominique Ingres. A young man, but connected to some of the greatest artists in France—though those names are also connected to the current government. So who knows how long such favor will last?"

"Ingres," he mused. "Have you sold other works by him?"

Her eyes narrowed. "Perhaps. Why do you ask?"

"Why should it matter?"

"Don't dismiss me. I am not just a pretty face, my lord."

He looked her over. "No, you're not." Theo wasn't

particularly moved by her silhouette, but he could see she relied on sensuality to dominate others. So he pretended to be impressed. "Pretty is not a word I'd use when describing you…though I could think of several others."

"Why not meet me for dinner tomorrow evening?" she asked. "We can talk more then. You seem intriguing, and I like to meet new people."

"Why not tonight?"

She glanced involuntarily at the door. "No. I cannot. In fact, you should go soon."

"Expecting someone else at this hour?"

"My business partner, coming with a shipment from the wharves," she said. "That is all. Come tomorrow night, say, ten o' clock? A late dinner, and then…"

Theo was already going to Alyse's party tomorrow night. But he didn't mind stringing the shrewd Giselle along, or keeping her waiting. "I look forward to it, Miss Villani."

"What have I told you?" she said with a manufactured pout. "I am Giselle to my friends."

"Who are you to your lovers?"

"Still Giselle. But said with more feeling." The smile she threw him that time *did* affect him, and he knew he shouldn't stay longer than necessary.

"Until tomorrow, Giselle." Theo left then, feeling the cold winter air like a tonic. Giselle would wear any man down after a little while. No wonder Charlie made her his mistress.

He barely crossed the street when he saw a cart pulling up to the larger set of doors at the side of Giselle's building. A huge man jumped out of the back of the cart and strode to the door. "Giselle!" he called, then added something in Italian. Theo watched from a sheltered spot as Giselle's figure appeared in the open doorway.

"Hey," another voice hissed in the darkness. "Over here!"

Theo looked to the side and saw Jem lurking in a shadowed corner a few doors down. As soon as both Giselle and the newcomer were inside, Theo walked over to Jem, grabbed him by the arm, and kept walking.

When they were out of sight of the building, Theo stopped. "What are you doing here?"

"Was going to ask the same thing, my lord. You told me to keep an eye on Matteo Rossi. That's just what I've been doing."

"That man is Rossi?"

"Missing fingers and all," Jem said confidently. "I just trailed him from the docks. He picked up all those crates from a ship just in, named the *Sirena*."

"Good name," Theo muttered.

"So you weren't expecting to see Rossi here?" Jem asked.

"No, but I should have. They're working together," he said. "Of course they are."

"Sir?"

Theo shook his head. "Never mind, Jem. Good work, by the way. You've done enough for tonight. Now that I know about this connection, I have some serious thinking to do."

Villani and Rossi, working together. Villani was Charlie's mistress as well as his connection to the art world, and Rossi was the man who ordered Sarah to find a cache Charlie left behind. Things were beginning to fit. Every time Sarah broke part of the code, another puzzle piece fell into place.

Theo only hoped she could break the rest in time.

Chapter 18

☉

SARAH WOKE UP REFRESHED, AND she surprised her mother by announcing she would spend the day at home with her. Sarah even promised to sit in the parlor during the hours Mrs Brecknell would be "at home" for callers. But every other moment she spent working on decoding the notebooks. And soon enough, it was time to go to the party.

Alyse's party would be the most well-attended event Sarah would appear at since the funeral. She was nervous, even though she was going with her old school friend Chloe and would know several guests there. She would feel out of place, lost amid the more confident, though younger, girls who now dominated the scene. She was not witty or beautiful enough to be of interest to anyone. And then, of course, there was her secret shame. If anyone knew how impure she was, Sarah wouldn't be allowed anywhere in society. At least her dress was pretty, she thought wryly.

The gown was made up last year but never actually worn. After Charlie's death, she ordered it put away, and then she'd nearly forgotten about it until Naomi unearthed it for that evening.

It was exquisite. The petticoat was a powdery, icy blue watered silk. Over it floated a cloud-like layer of white linen so fine it was nearly transparent. The blue underskirt looked like a shifting sky beneath the mesh of linen. And at intervals were stitched little clusters of seed pearls, so they caught the candlelight with a soft sheen. A few white peacock feathers comprised her headdress, simple enough that her blonde curls were what most people would notice. She wore gloves in an even lighter blue than the skirt.

Naomi was delighted with the results of her efforts. "Oh, you look divine, Miss Sarah. You shouldn't wear dark colors ever again. And you should stop by your mother's room before you leave."

Sarah did just that. Her mother had been napping, but she woke and smiled at Sarah when she saw her. "What a vision! You look like an angel. One would think it is your own coming out ball all over again!"

"No one will be confused on that point," Sarah said. "But I hope I will do."

"Any man would be dazzled," her mother countered.

"I'm sure I'll just sit with Chloe most of the night." Sarah plucked at her gloves. "In fact, she will be here any moment."

* * * *

As it happened, Theo was also speaking to his mother before he left for the party. He was dressed in evening clothes a shade fancier than his usual, though he adhered to his typical greens and browns.

"Oh, Teddy. Don't you look perfect," his mother said fondly.

"Please don't call me that," he begged her. "I'm not ten years old."

"No need to be short with your mother. What's the matter? You haven't quarreled with Alyse, have you?"

"Alyse and I never fight," Theo said. "Which might be a hint in itself that something is wrong," he added, before thinking better of it.

"I hope you don't expect me to understand that bit of nonsense. How can you object to *not* fighting with your future wife?"

He looked at his mother. "I fear I know Alyse too well. She is almost like a sister to me."

"But she is not," his mother said firmly. "Theo, darling, I do understand your point. But trust me, after your marriage, your relationship with Alyse will change…and grow. The birth of a child will alter your whole world, and I've no doubt that Alyse will be the wife you've always dreamed of."

Theo nodded, and said something suitable to put his mother off. Perhaps he once dreamed of Alyse, but certainly not for years. In fact, he'd caught himself thinking of Sarah more than once, a somewhat alarming fact he chalked up to spending so much time with her over the past week.

And when he saw Alyse that evening, looking regal in her deep red silk gown, he reminded himself he was lucky. Her dark hair was put up in curls, and the dress was cut perfectly to show off her slender form. She was a good-spirited person by nature, but tonight she sparkled. Theo watched as she greeted the far more understated Mrs Heath with a smile so bright it might melt the snow outside.

Alyse would always say the right thing, do the right thing. She was a perfect lady, and she was sweet and truly kind. Why was he having doubts? Stifling his darker thoughts, he walked over to her. "Good evening."

"Oh, Theo, you've shown up at last." She took his hand in hers and gave it an excited squeeze. "I was a little worried bad weather might prevent people from coming out."

"A groundless worry," he muttered. "Everyone is here."

"But I don't think your friend is yet," Alyse said.

"Who?"

"Miss Brecknell! I enquired about her to a few people. I heard the young lady was practically a hermit for months. Why didn't you say? I would have extended an invitation far earlier if I'd known. Can you imagine how she must have felt, sitting there all alone, with nothing but memories." Alyse shuddered.

"She has a family and friends of her own," Theo said. But he didn't know how true that was. The thought of Sarah mourning alone was far more troubling than he was prepared for. "I think she is retiring by nature, anyway."

"Perhaps. But I should have liked it if you told me about her. Sometimes I think you keep part of yourself very separate, Theo."

He shook his head, but Alyse was right. She rarely

came out and said things so bluntly, but of course she would notice. They *were* too close. One couldn't be near a person for years without seeing the truth. "I only keep the dull parts from you, Alyse. Besides, do you tell me everything in your life?"

Uncharacteristically, she blushed. "Perhaps not." Then she looked toward the entrance. "Oh, look. Miss Brecknell came after all."

Theo looked for Sarah, but didn't see her. "Where is she?"

"You're staring right at her," Alyse said with a giggle.

"There's no one who…" he trailed off.

At the entrance, a blonde woman in a blue dress stood watching the room. Her expression was aloof, the look a goddess gives mortals. The dress was molded to her upper body, then fell into a looser, concealing shape that only added to the allure. What could be under that fabric but even more perfect curves? He wished he knew who it was. Until he realized it was Sarah.

Theo stared at her, feeling like an idiot. In the light-colored gown, she looked like a different person altogether. When she saw him and smiled, she took his breath away.

"She's not wearing black," he said, stupidly.

"No, thank goodness!" Alyse agreed. "It didn't suit her coloring at all. The blue is just lovely, even if the cut is from last year. Oh, bother," Alyse said. "Mama is gesturing wildly. Will you go greet Miss Brecknell and tell her I will be over to chat as soon as I can extract myself?"

Theo was happy to oblige.

She wasn't alone, of course. Her companion was a lady who didn't appear much older than her, but who possessed the unmistakable air of a married woman, and thus a suitable guardian of morals.

Sarah smiled shyly at Theo. "Good evening, my lord. Are you acquainted with Mrs Lamb?"

Theo turned to the other lady. "Not yet, which seems an oversight on my part. Welcome to the Templetons's home, ma'am."

"Lord Markham is engaged to Lady Alyse," Sarah explained to her friend, "which must be why he's pressed into duties such as greeting guests."

"Not too onerous a duty," he said, "when the guests are so lovely."

"Miss Brecknell mentioned you are also something of a diplomat," Mrs Lamb noted, with a raised eyebrow.

"That doesn't mean everything I say is a lie," Theo protested. He looked at Sarah, "Do you intend to dance tonight?"

"If someone will partner me," she replied.

"I will, for one," he said. "And I'm sure you won't lack other offers." A tiny stab of envy needled him at the thought of other men courting Sarah.

The other lady offered him an approving smile, then turned to Sarah. "I will sit to the side, where it's a little cooler. Please join me when you tire of your partners."

Sarah nodded, and allowed Theo to lead her to where the dancing was to take place.

"I see you came out of your shell," he said, as they worked their way through the crowded room.

Sarah nodded. "It would have been rude not to come. I mean, I wanted to, of course…"

"Of course," he echoed, wryly.

"Excuse me. I'm nervous. I don't miss society at all. I couldn't bear to be seen at first. And then it was so easy to stay away…"

Theo stopped her. "If anything, all the gossips will be sympathetic. It's the sort of story society loves."

"Do you think so? I felt like I'd be betraying Charlie if I did anything."

"Betraying?"

"Well, showing a lack of respect."

Theo frowned. Charlie didn't deserve Sarah's respect, and certainly not at the expense of her avoiding the public sphere for months on end. "Never give those harpies a chance by showing a glum face. Hold your head high, and they'll never question a thing. You look beautiful."

Sarah smiled at him and gave a little toss of her head. He could actually see her straighten her spine. "You're right, of course. I won't let them get to me. I shall be like Caesar facing down the Gauls. One against an army."

"You'll have them eating out of your hand."

* * * *

Sarah did dance first with Theo, who was good, but not overly accomplished, a fact he freely admitted. "My talents lie elsewhere," he said, in apology.

"I knew that very well, my lord," Sarah said. "And I am grateful Lady Alyse spared you."

After the first set, Sarah was surprised to find other

gentlemen wanted to partner her. She almost asked Theo if he put some of them up to it, but in the whirl of the evening, she lost track of him for a while.

Her partner for one set was none other than Lord Carlin. He was a wonderful dancer, and so confident that Sarah was not in danger of once missing a step. Furthermore, he kept her laughing nearly the whole time. He had a gift for conversation.

"You must give me a breather," Sarah finally said, after he finished a story that actually had her breathless.

"Of course," he said. "Let me walk you through the glass gallery."

He led her to a room that functioned as a conservatory. It was filled with plants and trees too tender for the outdoors. He said, "I wish could take you outside in a moonlit garden, Miss Brecknell, to find a hidden place where I could steal a kiss from you."

Sarah stilled, unsure what to say.

"Ah, I have offended you," he said.

"Not at all," she said. "You merely surprised me."

"Have I?" He raised an eyebrow. "Surely I'm not the first man to tell you so."

Sarah blushed. "No."

"Nor can I be the first man to actually kiss you," he went on.

"I would prefer a different subject, my lord," she said hastily. "Please."

"Can it be possible?" he asked, teasing her. "Here we are in the middle of London, yet I have found a truly innocent woman."

Sarah looked away, her face flaming. Innocent was the one thing she wasn't.

"And the blush confirms it," he said. "You must first accept my sincere apology for upsetting you," he said. "Then I will regale you with a story that I've been saving for just such an occasion."

"An apology is not necessary, but I will accept it if you insist."

"Good. My heart is once again whole. Now, are you at all familiar with the creature known as a rhinoceros?" Within seconds, Carlin had Sarah giggling again with his account of a journey she suspected was wholly made up.

* * * *

Theo found Sarah with Lord Carlin. She was smiling at the man in a way that Theo had never seen before. Her whole face was open and joyous. He paused in his steps, arrested by a sudden and undeniable sense of jealousy. Why should Carlin get her to smile like that, when Theo could not? But then, the other man was paying her compliments, and taking her mind off the worry secretly plaguing her. Of course she would welcome such distraction.

Theo's interactions with Sarah were considerably more serious. He was trying to protect the empire. Carlin merely wanted to court the girl. As was obvious by the way he sat so close to her.

So Theo composed his face and continued on. "Miss Brecknell, I am sorry to interrupt your tête à tête here, but Lady Alyse wanted to have a word."

Sarah stood up immediately, but then turned back to Carlin. "Please excuse me, my lord. I am sorry not to hear the end of the story."

"Your hostess takes precedence, Miss Brecknell," he said graciously. "If you would like to hear the rest of the story, I should be delighted to tell you at the Wolvertons'. Miss Wolverton mentioned you would be riding with the group this Thursday."

"Oh, she mentioned that to you, did she?" Sarah asked, showing no surprise. "Well, I look forward to it."

Theo didn't clench his fists. He didn't frown. He didn't look upset at all.

"What's wrong?" asked Sarah, as they walked away. "You look rather put out," she said. "Did I do something I ought not? I suppose I should not have spoken with Lord Carlin so long. And Chloe, that is, Mrs Lamb, will wonder where I am."

"I have heard nothing untoward about Lord Carlin," Theo said, wishing it were otherwise.

"He is quite delightful to speak to. I wish..." she broke off.

"What?"

Sarah turned pink. "Nothing. He said he wanted to kiss me. I think I offended him when I refused."

"He had no right to even suggest it."

"It was nothing," she said. "Just a bit of flattery taken too far. I have been out of society too long. I forgot how people speak."

Theo wanted to punch Carlin.

"I wanted to ask..." Sarah began nervously.

"What?" Theo hoped she'd ask him to punch Carlin.

"Did you happen to discover anything during your reconnaissance last evening?"

Yes, I discovered who your dead fiancé's mistress was. But Theo shook his head. "A few things. Nothing I'd want to share yet. Did you have any more luck with the notebooks?"

"I got a bit further. Mostly more mentions of his art collection. Pieces he bought and sold. Some lists of his costs for framing and shipping. All so mundane!" Her tone was puzzled. "Why bother encoding such details?"

"You'll find what you need to know," he said in a low voice. "Now, you're riding with the Wolvertons?" he asked in a more conversational tone, getting back to a safer subject.

"Yes," said Sarah. "My mother has been at me to accept invitations, though I must have been addled when I accepted that one. I'm not a good rider at all." She looked over at him. "You are, I have no doubt."

"What makes you say that?" Theo asked.

"Something in the way you carry yourself. I remember thinking the night we met at the dinner, I was sure you were a rider."

"You happen to be right. And, just so you know, Lady Alyse and I are also going to be there."

Sarah brightened. "That's good to know."

Fortunately, they reached Alyse before Theo could do or say anything stupid regarding Carlin. Alyse greeted Sarah and began to chat. Theo mostly stood guard.

He mentally compared the two women as they spoke.

Alyse was animated and bright, where Sarah was polite and rather shy. Alyse looked vivid in her deep ruby gown. Theo remembered telling her how perfect she looked when he first saw it. Alyse had laughed and twirled around happily. Sarah's gown was less bold, but it was perfect for her, hinting at a subtle sensuality.

Theo stopped himself. Why the hell did he keep thinking of Sarah like that? He had long ago learned to rein in any passion around Alyse, even when they were alone. She was too well-bred, too aware of her role. And Theo, knowing his responsibility was to honor her, knew better than to press her.

Like most men of his class, Theo found ways to separate his love for his fiancée from his baser needs. He never had a mistress. He didn't want one…it seemed far too much work. But it was never difficult to find companionship for an evening. It was passion free of any entanglements, and he told himself that once he was married, it would be unnecessary.

But if just seeing Sarah in a gown was enough to lead him to more forbidden ideas, perhaps he wasn't nearly as enamored of Alyse as he assumed he was.

Then Sarah happened to catch his eye and smile, completely unaware of his thoughts, and Theo knew he had a problem.

* * * *

As the clock ticked toward the small hours, Sarah and Chloe decided it was past time to leave. Neither woman was particularly fond of crowds, and the party showed no signs of thinning out. The heat in the rooms was nearly unbearable.

Still, despite Sarah's heavy wool pelisse, it was a shock to step out into the freezing night. Chloe made a beeline for the carriage and laughed when they were safely inside. "My goodness, but it's chilly out! Still, if we stayed any longer, I might have withered away."

"It was warm," Sarah agreed. "And stuffed!"

"You made quite an impression," Chloe said. "Nearly all the ladies I chatted with wanted to know who made your gown, and how you managed to find so many partners for the dances."

"I suspect at least some of them were put up to it."

"Or they decided a lady noticed by a gentleman such as Lord Markham must be worth a dance."

"He was only being kind," Sarah explained. She hoped her expression wouldn't give her away. Her feelings about Theo were getting rather confusing, especially in light of the situation.

Sarah directed the cab to let her out at the corner of her street. "With the snow, the wheels may get stuck in our drive. Goodnight, Chloe!"

"Call on me this week, dear!" Chloe reminded her as the carriage drove off.

Sarah hurried through the icy muck to her house. She avoided the worst puddles on the drive and was just about to mount the steps under the awning of the front door when something swooped in behind her.

Before she could even scream, the huge form of Rossi clamped a hand over her mouth. "Been waiting for you," he grunted.

Sarah struggled against him. After only seconds, her lungs begged for air.

"What are you up to?" he said. "Dancing your way through the city? Don't you have more important things to consider?" He removed his hand long enough to let her breathe, but didn't let her go.

"Get away from me," Sarah gasped. "You have to be mad to accost me in my own drive!"

"Have you been looking for me?" he hissed.

She took another huge breath. "Looking *for* you? What do you mean?"

"A few too many strangers hanging about my place. Saw some last night. Asking about me, and my partners."

Sarah got angry. "Why do you look to me? Why should I care what other schemes you have going? The less I see of you, the happier I am."

He seemed a little cowed, but said, "Don't think I'll forget what I asked you to find. Where are my papers? Are you hard at work?"

"I've been looking!" She twisted as much as she could, but Rossi had his arm around her neck, and he was far stronger than she was.

"You don't appear to appreciate the gravity of the situation." He pulled her tighter against his body. "Do I have to explain?"

"I'll find them!" she said. "I promise! You told me I had until the 31st. Do they have to be found by then?"

"If you like walking on your own feet, they do," he growled. "Wait for my instructions. Don't try to find me before the meeting."

"I don't know what you're talking about! I didn't try to find you." Sarah inhaled to scream bloody murder, but he clapped a hand over her mouth again.

"Don't you dare. Anyone sees you, they'll see a little slut…not an innocent lady."

Sarah went still at the threat.

He released her. "Don't tell anyone about me. Just find Wolverton's stash. You don't want to attract more attention than you already have."

Sarah pushed him away, though mostly because he stepped away. She whirled and ran to the front steps.

"No one," he warned, from behind her. "Not a housemaid, not your mother. Not your father. No one."

Sarah watched him walk away.

She recovered her normal breathing before she lifted the knocker. She didn't want to alarm the house. Sarah remembered the key she always kept in her reticule and pulled it out. She couldn't risk anyone seeing her in her current state. Her parents were likely abed, but Naomi would be awake.

The key turned silently in the lock and she was able to slip inside. She locked the door behind her and stood for a full minute, her body shaking.

Rossi came to her home. He could come back. She had to let Theo know what had happened.

Chapter 19

♉

THE PARTY WAS STILL LOUD and chaotic, despite the hour. Since Sarah had left, Theo found himself feeling restless and annoyed by the remaining guests. Alyse was looking a little tired too. She was sitting to the side, surrounded by a few of her friends and the archeologist Mrs Heath. It was a delegation of women, and he wanted no part of it.

Instead, he drifted toward a side room where many of the gentlemen were gathered. Over the next hour, he managed to down more drinks than he had the whole first part of the evening. It didn't faze him in the slightest. It never did.

Sometimes, Theo wished he could get drunk. But something in his make-up appeared to negate all the effects of alcohol. At school, his friends professed the belief that the Scottish blood on his mother's side was to blame for the curse. Theo didn't agree that it was a curse, except when he saw how other men could drink and simply not care about anything for a while.

"Another?" one of his companions asked, seeing the empty glass in Theo's hand.

"Why not," Theo said dully.

Before the next drink could be found, a servant came up to Theo. "Lord Markham? This just came for you," the servant said, offering a note.

Curious, Theo unfolded the paper. It was not signed. But after a week of working by her, he knew Sarah's graceful and unadorned handwriting. The words, however, made no sense.

She wore a long ribbon last night.

He frowned. Sarah had told him what the phrase meant—*I need help*—but why send it to him in an actual letter?

Unless she actually needed help right then. And what could she put on paper other than the odd code? Officially, they were barely acquaintances. She didn't have the privilege to write to Theo openly.

The servant was still there, waiting to hear if a response was required.

"I have to go," he said. "Have someone find my coat." He should tell Alyse of his departure, but he had no time. He'd apologize after he discovered what happened.

He got to Sarah's home as quickly as the roads allowed. Not knowing what the precise situation was, he paused at the front door. How would it look to call on the house at such an hour?

Trusting his instinct, he walked around the side of the house, cursing the frozen ground as he went, and found one room with a lamp burning. He saw Sarah through the window, sitting in an armchair, staring into space. She was still wearing her ballgown. The pale blue silk and the white linen were mussed and crumpled. Theo didn't like it.

He tapped at the glass, and saw her start violently. But

she got up and hurried to the side door. After she recognized him, she let the door open a crack. "Theo?" she whispered.

"Can I come in?" he asked.

She opened the door wider and he slipped in. She bolted the door, pulled the curtain closed too, then turned to face him. "Thank you for coming. I had no idea what to do."

"What happened?" he asked, concerned.

"When I returned from the party, Rossi was here, right outside the house. He must have been waiting." Sarah repeated the conversation with her eyes distant, as if she were seeing it again in her mind. "He let me go after a minute, but..." She was shaking. "I'm just...I was so scared."

Before he even considered what to say, Theo pulled her against his body and folded her into an embrace. "You're safe, Sarah. You're just feeling the shock now, but it's over."

Theo lifted her chin up to see her face, looking into those wide grey eyes. He lowered his mouth to hers and kissed her.

Sarah made a tiny sound of shock and pleasure, but she didn't pull away. Her lips parted, and he took it as an invitation. Sarah's hands were on his chest, then her arms were around his shoulders, his neck. He held her closer. She tasted like lemon and sugar. She touched her tongue to his lips and tasted him, innocent but curious. And incredibly arousing.

He was drunk, he thought. It was the only thing that

made sense. He'd finally got just drunk enough to do something on pure impulse. Theo was ensnared by her mouth. He forgot why he'd kissed her in the first place. He only knew that he wanted to.

He took a breath, finding his blood up more than he could have imagined from a mere kiss. Sarah's eyes were half-closed. She looked both sweet and scandalous, her skin flushed and her lips reddened.

What the hell are you doing, Theo?

He let her go, and took half a step back. "I didn't intend to do that."

"No. I'm sure you didn't. Forgive me," she said, looking at the floor.

Her hair had come partly loose. He itched to undo the rest of it. "It's my fault," he said, trying to act normally. "You should be able to trust me."

Sarah was still looking down, but he saw an odd smile grow on her lips. "You're the only person I can trust. Isn't that funny?"

Considering he would bed her in a heartbeat? Yes, that was funny. And appalling. "I won't let it happen again."

"That would be for the best," she said, her voice tight. "Will you still help me find the papers?"

"Of course."

"I just don't want you to resent me."

"Resent you?" he asked.

"For behaving so shamelessly. I'm not myself tonight."

"Sarah, it was my fault," he repeated. "Not yours. I should be able to act like gentleman around you, not a pig."

She laughed, but still sounded sad. "Then we can begin again."

He tried to regain his equilibrium. "I'm glad you sent for me, but you must not do it again." Theo took the note from his pocket. "If this had fallen into the wrong hands, it could have been used against you."

"It wasn't signed."

"Your handwriting is distinctly yours. Even a hint of impropriety and your reputation could not recover."

Sarah paled.

He tossed the note into the fire. "I have another idea. Do you have any openings on your staff right now?"

"As a matter of fact, we're short a hostler. I should be attending to it, but with everything that's happened recently…"

Theo stopped her. He knew exactly who to use. "With your permission, I'm going to send someone over—trustworthy, and sharp enough to keep an eye on you and the rest of the house."

"When you say keep an eye…"

"I mean to protect you. Not spy on you. His name's Jem. You've seen him before."

"Your incurious driver?"

He nodded. "I guarantee he'll be a good servant. And if you should need anything, he'll be the one to contact me."

"Yes, that's much safer, isn't it?" Sarah said quickly.

Theo still needed some distance from Sarah, or he'd find a reason to touch her again. He deliberately walked to the side door. "Rossi was waiting for you, you said?"

"At the front door," she said. "It was dark, and I didn't see a thing until he grabbed me."

"Why push you for the papers? He's already given you a date to hand over what you find."

"He was certain I had hired people to follow him. He was crazy." She looked at him more sharply. "Unless…it was you, wasn't it? You have been tracking him down."

"Yes," he admitted. "I hired someone to follow him. Though there's no way he'd know who ordered it. He seems nervous."

"Oh, *he's* nervous? The poor dear."

"Sarah," he said. Without meaning to, he was standing right next to her again. "I won't let anyone hurt you."

She shook her head. "The only thing that will keep me safe is finding the papers in time."

"You will. You're getting closer. I know who Villani is."

"You do?"

"Charlie's art dealer…and Rossi's partner. There's obviously something more going on with both of them. We're going to see the end of this, Sarah. Just keep working with me, and trust me."

She took a breath. "I will. Less than a week, and you'll be free of me."

Theo nodded, not trusting himself to speak. Less than a week until Sarah vanished from his world as suddenly as she'd entered it. He had to keep his feelings to himself. He had to work, and he had to complete the assignment as soon as humanly possible. Before he did something he would definitely regret.

Chapter 20

☊

AFTER THEO LEFT, SARAH SNUCK upstairs to her bedroom, though she felt as if she'd never sleep again. First the stress of the party, then the shock of Rossi's appearance, and finally Theo's completely unexpected kiss.

She'd been so relieved to see him that she didn't think twice when he held her. It felt wonderful to be held, to be told she was safe. And then he kissed her. She tasted brandy on his lips, which accounted for the *why*. He never would have done such a thing if he was sober. But the *how* was another matter. When Theo kissed her, she nearly melted.

She remembered liking it when Charlie kissed her, though it had always seemed daring and exciting more than pleasurable for its own sake. With Theo, her whole body seemed to wake up. She ached with wanting more.

Which was impossible. Thank God Theo realized what happened and stopped it. Sarah wondered what she had done to make him forget himself like that. Perhaps holding her was enough. No real lady would let a man get so close to her.

Or perhaps it was the fact she sent for him at all. She

should have waited until the next day. It wasn't as if he had to be there. She just lost her head and did something foolish. Just as she had with Charlie when he took her virginity.

There was something fundamentally wrong with her, she decided. She lacked some moral backbone, and it would ruin her no matter what. The sooner she decoded those notebooks, the sooner she could end this. No one else would have to suffer from her disastrous decisions.

When Naomi woke Sarah up in the morning, her expression was disturbed. "There's a lad at the back door, miss. He says he's the new hostler. But who hired him?"

"What?" Sarah sat up, her head in a fog. "At the back door? You made a boy wait out in the cold?"

"Oh no, miss. He's in the kitchen now. But we're all rather confused."

"Get me dressed," Sarah said. "I'll go down and speak to him and straighten everything out."

In the kitchen, the stranger sat at the long table where all the servants took their meals. He'd been supplied with bread and strong tea by Bette, and looked perfectly at ease. He was lanky and rather tall. Brown hair and eyes were not particularly distinctive, but his glance was sharp.

He stood up immediately when she entered, then produced a sealed letter from his coat pocket. "Good morning, Miss Brecknell. I am ready to begin my duties just as soon as you approve my hire, ma'am."

He waited, quite sure of his welcome.

Sarah broke the seal and scanned the letter. "James Harper," she said, just learning his full name at the moment.

He nodded amicably. "Everyone calls me Jem, ma'am. As the letter should state, I've got my references there. I can act as hostler, footman, scullion,"—here he winked at Bette—"and all-purpose errand boy."

"So I see." Sarah looked him in the eye. "It will be reassuring to have a trustworthy lad at the house again. We've been too long without one."

Jem nodded with the right mix of eagerness and guile. "As you say, ma'am. Just give the order, and I'll see it done."

"Thank you, Jem." Sarah gave him a stern look. "I warn you that I tolerate no poor behavior in my house, no matter what recommendation you have. Further, any reference to the color of Naomi's skin or the quality of her heritage which may even be passingly considered cruel is grounds for dismissal."

"Understood." Jem's friendly nod to Naomi indicated he did indeed understand.

Sarah went on. "All servants have leave to attend church on Sundays, as well as a full day off once a month, as permitted by your duties. You will not consort with the other help, and you respect the privacy and honor of everyone under this roof."

"Certainly, ma'am."

"She means you'll be sacked if you even think about romancing anyone," Bette warned.

"As it happens, my heart is already taken," Jem said cheerfully. "Lucy is my love's name, and if you ask I'll tell you more about her than you'd ever want to know. It's my pining you'll have to endure, ladies, not my importuning." He gave a dramatic sigh.

Bette smiled despite herself. "We'll see. Meantime, I'll show you where everything is."

Sarah left the kitchen, confident Jem would fit in among the servants. Naomi followed her. Upstairs, Sarah endured her maid's gentle scolding for not waking her after returning home the previous night.

"I ought to have taken that gown to be checked for tears straight away, miss. And your hair! You didn't braid it last night, just slept with it loose again, didn't you?"

Sarah apologized. "I was tired."

"Was it a lovely night, miss? You haven't been to a real party in ages."

"The ball was very…interesting. I danced."

"Oh, with gentlemen?"

Sarah smiled into the mirror. "Several. Though not all at once."

"Oh, your mama will be so pleased." Naomi giggled as she finished pinning Sarah's hair back.

"Yes, I'm sure she will be," she said. "But I'll tell her about it myself."

Chapter 21

♉

OVER THE NEXT FEW DAYS, Theo tried to forget he ever kissed Sarah, meeting her as usual in the little room of the Athenaeum. She seemed content to work near him, saying she felt safer when he was around. So why push her away, he reasoned. He got carried away the other night, but it wasn't as if he needed to avoid her.

He watched her as she read through one of the notebook passages, her lips moving as she mouthed the words she was translating from the code to plain text in her head. Every once in a while, she would make a tiny *oh* of surprise, or an *aha* of triumph, or just a musing *mmmm*. It was fascinating, and more than a little intriguing. If he only had her voice to go by, he'd think she was doing something quite different. What sort of sounds would she make if he touched her?

That line of thinking was dangerous. If only he hadn't kissed her the other night. How many drinks did it take to lower his guard? He wished he remembered that fact as well as he remembered the feel of her mouth.

Sarah never mentioned it, and he knew the incident was an anomaly. *Just keep working, Theo.*

At the end of Tuesday afternoon, Sarah proudly handed him some papers. "Here you are. This should speed things along considerably."

"How?"

"It's a key. I replicated Charlie's original by working backwards. Match the format of the coded passages to the first example in each part of the key. Then just follow the steps and you can decode most passages on your own."

He took the pages, suitably impressed. "You're going to make me look like a genius."

"Well," she said, "Not all the codes are broken. I'm still working on this other one in particular. I feel it's important." She held up one small notebook.

But even so, they could now work twice as quickly. Once Theo left her for the day, he took the key and the remaining notebooks back home, where he worked late into the night, hoping to decipher important passages that would expose Charlie's methods.

Theo did uncover a secret, though it wasn't the one he was expecting.

29 Jun. Bought another Ingres piece today. Perfect. Cost to be recouped from G.

7 Jul. Bedded S today. Spontaneous, as she interrupted work and may have seen the letter. Pleasant duty. Should have done it a while ago. With luck, won't have to move date of wed up.

11 Jul. Arrange sale of new Ingres portrait to G. Profit less than anticipated. Need to sell next piece quickly.

15 Jul. S asked about latest coding exercise. Don't like it. Had to remind her of her sin.

19 Jul. S put me off today. Suspicious?

It took Theo several minutes to decipher the coded lines, and then several more to realize the implications. Did he really read that correctly? Yes. It appeared Charlie seduced Sarah. And not merely for pleasure, but with a very specific purpose of distraction, which she surely wasn't aware of.

Theo sat back in his chair, the revelation sinking in. Charlie *seduced* Sarah, only weeks before his sudden death. Suddenly her behavior at the funeral and afterwards made far more sense. She wasn't merely bereaved, she was likely terrified of the possibilities in her future. What if she had been pregnant? Charlie's death would have ruined her whole life, exposing her transgression with no hope of a hasty marriage to patch it over.

One thing was clear. Theo would have to make sure she didn't see the journal. Of course, he didn't anticipate Sarah's analytical mind.

The very next day, she noticed the gap in the timeline presented by the notebooks.

"Have you seen the notebook for June and July of last year?" she asked, in the middle of an otherwise companionable silence.

Theo froze, caught out by the question. "Um, no. Perhaps it was lost."

"All the other months are accounted for," she noted, with a little frown. "Are you sure you didn't put it somewhere?"

"It's possible," Theo hedged. "Perhaps I left it at my home. I'll look. Was there something in particular you think happened that month?"

"Oh, no. But you said yesterday that you were nearly done deciphering May's book. Did you discover anything interesting?" Her expression was hopeful, and entirely innocent.

"Nothing too unusual," he said. The fib nearly choked him. And he was normally so good at lying. "More discussion of his art hobby."

"Why did he insist on writing about that in code?" Sarah said. From her tone, it was clear the question needled her. "Dealing in art isn't a crime."

"I don't know," he said, wishing he had a better answer to what was a very good question.

"And one notebook missing. What if someone took it from him? He might have had it on him the night he died…"

"Don't think about that," Theo said hastily. "Just take the next available one and with luck we'll find the answer there."

"I do hope so."

She was diverted, but Theo didn't know for how long. And they still needed answers before the meeting with Rossi.

Chapter 22

♉

WHEN SARAH HAD BEEN ASKED to join the Wolvertons for a ride and luncheon, she accepted because she knew she'd never hear the end of it otherwise. Thursday dawned warmer than usual, and the clear sky promised good weather for a ride. And in truth, it might be good to get out of the stuffy rooms she'd been hiding in for so long, and to appear among others doing a perfectly ordinary activity like horseback riding. A bright winter day, a gentle horse…Sarah could manage that. She hoped.

Sarah arrived at the Wolvertons' feeling distinctly ill at ease. She had ridden in the past, since it was a common part of a young lady's education. But she never felt at home in the saddle, and she so rarely found a need to ride that she was quite out of practice.

She also lacked the correct outfit. Georgia was as kind as ever, naturally, and told Sarah to come a bit early so she could borrow one of Georgia's riding habits.

"Good morning!" Georgia called when Sarah arrived. "I had Annie put out two choices. Come upstairs with me and pick the one you like the best."

Upstairs in Georgia's room, Sarah saw the habits side

by side on the bed. One was a dull buff color. The other was ruby red, a velveteen that looked lavish and extremely bold.

Sarah immediately pointed to the buff. "That one will do. Thank you."

Georgia frowned. "Are you sure you won't at least try the red one? Just here in the room? I hoped to see it on you."

Sarah reached out to stroke the fabric. It was so lovely, and finer than anything she owned. The buff would be boring by comparison, but if it was just to try…. "If you insist, I can model it for you. Likely it won't fit me very well anyway, as it's been cut for you."

However, once Sarah was attired in the ruby-colored outfit, wearing her own black riding boots, it was evident the habit fit very well indeed. The tailored cut of the outfit emphasized curves Sarah normally hid beneath looser fabrics.

"Oh," she said faintly, looking in the mirror. "Thank goodness no one else will see this."

But the others didn't seem to think that way.

Georgia nearly shouted, "Annie, you're a *magician*! That cut. The color. Miss Brecknell looks absolutely perfect!"

"It is a good color, ma'am," the maid agreed smugly. "Quite fetching."

Georgia giggled. "And look at the time! We must hurry down to catch the rest of the riding party."

"But I can't wear this!" Sarah protested, her heart dropping to her stomach. "It's too bright. Too, um, trim.

And too fine. I'll ruin it."

"Oh, not to worry, ma'am," Annie said. "Never a spot I can't get out." A conspiratorial smile passed between Annie and Georgia. But Sarah could do nothing other than follow Georgia back down the stairs to the courtyard.

"Georgia," she hissed, just before they reached the door. "You planned this!"

"You look lovely. I'm sure Lord Carlin will think so, too!"

"Oh, but—"

And then Sarah was out in the courtyard. The cloudy sky did little to dim the light she felt was beaming down on her, making the red outfit appear like a beacon.

Lord Carlin stood there, speaking to Mr Wolverton. When he saw Sarah, a look close to shock crossed his face. "Miss Brecknell?"

"Who else could she be?" Georgia said impishly.

"Good morning, my lord," Sarah said nervously when she reached him. "Mr Wolverton, thank you so much for inviting me."

"Glad to see you out again, dear," he said, with a glance at the still mute Carlin. "Isn't that so, man?"

"Yes," Carlin said. Then he took Sarah's hand and kissed it. "Miss Brecknell, you leave me speechless."

"I hope not," she said, completely sincere. "I like all your stories so well!"

He laughed, finally recovering his usual attitude. Carlin asked her if she brought her own mount, and Sarah admitted she didn't own a riding horse. Carlin had already spoken about his interest in fine horseflesh, so she thought she disappointed him.

"I wish I had known," he said. "I just bought a new one you would fancy. I could have arranged for her to be brought here today."

Before she could respond, another voice called her name. "Miss Brecknell!"

She turned, and saw Theo standing by the stable door. "Miss Brecknell, you ought to come select a horse so the boys can saddle it."

"Excuse me," she said to the men, and then walked to Theo. "You needn't shout like a fishmonger," she reprimanded him when she came to the doorway.

He didn't apologize. Instead, he surveyed her. "I thought you said you didn't ride."

"I don't. This is Georgia's habit. She insisted I wear it."

"And for that, every gentleman here is grateful." He smiled at her in a way that made her knees wobbly.

Sarah raised an eyebrow, but didn't press him to continue. Instead, she looked over the horses still in the stalls. She was drawn to a white beauty, the prettiest horse in the stable.

Theo came up behind her. "Not that one," he said.

"Why not?"

"Lightning is a good field hunter, but has his own mind. You'll find Darling more to your taste." He pointed to a less impressive animal two stalls down.

"Are you sure?" Sarah asked, moving toward the dappled brown horse.

"Trust me," he said. "This one has a much better temperament. And she's smarter, too."

The horse he called Darling whinnied just then, as if in response.

Theo laughed. "See what I mean? She's listening."

He pulled a bit of apple from his pocket and handed it to Sarah. "Give her a bit and she'll love you forever."

"It's that simple?" she asked.

Darling smelled the apple and quickly accepted Sarah's offering. After a moment, Sarah stroked the horse's forehead, murmuring a greeting.

"Ah!" called Georgia, who just peeked in. "Darling will be perfect for you. Well chosen!" With a gesture of approval, Georgia ducked out again, calling to the rest of the party.

"*You* picked the horse," Sarah muttered under her breath.

"What does that matter?" Theo had stepped up closer to her again, and Sarah was terribly aware of him. The memory of his kiss the other night hadn't faded at all, and he looked as if he'd do it again, if given the slightest en-couragement from her. He'd already flirted with her when he told her how she looked in her borrowed outfit.

"We should rejoin the others," she said, her voice coming out breathier than usual.

"So we should." He escorted her out of the stable. Soon enough, all the horses were saddled and ready. Sarah was helped up by a groom, and hoped she did not look too ridiculous.

The beautiful white horse turned out to be Theo's. "I see why you were so proprietary over him," she said, laughing. Then she looked over the group. "Is everyone here?" she asked, hoping to delay the inevitable.

"Where is Lady Alyse?" Georgia asked suddenly, just realizing the other's absence.

"She sends her regrets," Theo said. "She was not feeling well."

"Oh, no. I do hope she recovers. She's never been ill a day in her life."

"No," Theo agreed with a frown.

So Theo had no fiancée to pay attention to, Sarah thought. Perhaps he simply had to waste idle flirtations on somebody, and she was available.

With Georgia in the lead, they began to ride, the group naturally spreading out as each horse and rider found their pace. Sarah dropped to the back, uncertain of her skills. She was also afraid to push Darling into anything rash.

After a moment, Theo glanced back and also slowed until he was next to her.

"I don't need to be shepherded," Sarah said.

"Who said anything about shepherding?" he retorted. "Perhaps I prefer to let the others go ahead."

"Then why did you have to slow down so much?"

He bit his lip not to laugh. "You are clever, Miss Brecknell."

"I'm sorry." Charlie once cautioned her against appearing too clever. Watch what you say, Sarah. Other men hate it when a woman trumps them. Sarah remembered his warning as if it had been branded into her.

"You often apologize for something that is not a fault. Who taught you that?"

"I…don't know." It was a good question. Sarah hadn't always done that. Or had she? Charlie often told her how adorable she was when she apologized, but he never told her not to do it. In fact, she seemed to remember feeling like she was always apologizing to Charlie for one thing or another. She apologized for worrying when he was late to call on her.

No, I said I would call on Thursday, not Tuesday. Don't you remember, Sarah?

I'm sorry, she would say, so afraid she had upset him.

Theo didn't say anything, but she could feel him watching her. They rode in silence for a few minutes. Sarah concentrated on handling Darling, and he seemed content to keep pace with her.

"You're doing very well," he said, after a while.

"Give me an assessment after I've faced a few challenges, my lord."

"Haven't you?"

Sarah looked over at him, well aware he wasn't talking about her riding skills. "I think the greater challenge lies ahead. The date I'm to present my mysterious friend with a document is in two nights. And I have nothing to give him."

"I've taken care of it," he said, offering her a smile.

"How?"

Theo negotiated a patch of mud, which brought him a little closer to Sarah. "Using my various resources, I've managed to procure a document that will work for our purposes. You'll meet Rossi, I'll learn what I need to know before detaining him, and you'll be free."

"You make it all sound simple."

"You don't believe me?"

"I want to believe you, but I reserve judgement until it's over and I'm still alive."

"Sarah, I'm not going to let you die."

"You shouldn't say my name," she warned him.

"I like your name," he objected. "But I'd never say it where—" He broke off, looking down the path. "Your suitor is coming," he noted, in a slightly annoyed tone.

Sarah turned to see Lord Carlin riding toward them.

"Miss Brecknell!" Carlin said, as he came up and circled around. "How are you getting on?"

"I am adjusting to it," she said. "Lord Markham has been kind enough to see that I have not fallen."

"Miss Brecknell exaggerates," Theo said. "She is doing very well."

"As much as the quality of the horse allows," Carlin said. "On a proper thoroughbred, you'll find the experience vastly better."

"Oh, I don't know," Theo disagreed. "I've found that the pedigree isn't the best indicator of quality. Lightning might not have a famous sire, but he's smarter than any overpriced warmblood, in my opinion."

"Perhaps your horse is suitable for a daily ride, but that's another thing next to showing or racing."

Sarah listened to the two men, wondering why the issue should matter so much.

Theo shrugged. "I don't care to show or race. Breeding means little if the match is poor. What do you say, Miss Brecknell?"

"I'm hardly an authority," she said. "I'm content with Darling here. She is quite calm."

"Excellent," Theo said. He turned to Carlin. "She's a natural, just as I guessed. Why not show her a faster pace, sir?"

"With pleasure," Carlin said, with a quick, suspicious look at Theo. "Miss Brecknell?"

"Lead the way, my lord," Sarah said. She glanced back at Theo. "Do you mind?"

He laughed. "Oh, I'll catch up."

* * * *

Theo watched as the red-clad woman rode away with Lord Carlin. He'd been astonished by the vision of Sarah in her pale ball gown the other night. But the riding habit revealed new facets of her. The vibrant red made the blond hair glow; her grey eyes were somehow deeper and more lovely too. The cold air made her cheeks and lips reflect the red of the habit, making her look more alive than ever. In fact, he contemplated how he might lose the rest of the riding party long enough to get Sarah alone for a moment. He wanted to kiss those lips again.

Which was a warning sign. Ever since Theo uncovered the secret in Charlie's notebook, he found himself reevaluating nearly every exchange he'd had with Sarah, searching for some hint that she was more worldly than she seemed. But whatever had actually happened between Sarah and Charlie—and Theo had a few bad dreams about the possibilities—Sarah was still essentially innocent. She trusted Theo to help her. And he had no intention of letting anyone else know the truth he inadvertently discovered. After this was over, he'd burn the notebook. Then Sarah would be safe.

He shouldn't even have flirted with her as much as he had, except that he couldn't seem to stop himself. Her reactions were so priceless. But Sarah was not a plaything. And he was not available. The thought angered him. Carlin taking Sarah away angered him. The idea of not seeing Sarah again angered him. And when he got angry, he needed to get it out.

Thankfully, he was already on horseback. There was no better way to turn his mind off than to concentrate on simply riding. Theo let his horse loose. The animal knew him well, and surged forward, overjoyed to be free on a crisp winter day. He rode at a pace which would be insane for a less skilled rider. But Theo knew the terrain and his mount. He took jumps and dodged obstacles without even pausing. After a while, he forgot there were others around, especially when he saw the large meadow open up though a gap in the trees.

There was a clear path to the fence cutting through the meadow. He urged Lightning to run flat-out, and jumped the high fence without slowing. Lightning landed perfectly and Theo grinned, finally feeling the last of his negativity dissipate.

A cheer sounded from somewhere across the meadow. Surprised, he glanced over and saw the main riding party at the edge of the trees. They had seen his final stunt.

Now calmer, he rode to meet them. When he slowed the horse to a walking pace, the beast's hide steamed in the chilly air.

He reached Sarah first. Her eyes were round. "You said you rode, but you didn't say you rode like *that.*"

"A gentleman must have a few talents. Riding is one of mine. Did Charlie ever tell you about his carriage-chasing?"

"Yes. He was wicked. That's so dangerous."

"I know. I was the other one who always rode with him."

"My lord! You shouldn't have done that."

Theo shrugged. "I know that now. When I was younger though, we thought it was fun."

"Fun." Sarah sniffed and looked away. "So you were a foolish boy after all."

Georgia rode up to them then. "If you were anyone else, my lord, I'd say you were showing off."

Theo smiled. "Just taking advantage of the day, Miss Wolverton. I was going stir-crazy with the cold. I needed to cut Lightning and me loose."

"Well, you certainly did that!" With a glance at Sarah, Georgia circled her mount around. "Now let's head back to the house. It's high time for something warm to drink! Ride with me, Sarah."

After a quick glance at Theo, Sarah nudged her horse forward to join Georgia and the others. Theo remained behind the group, not willing to strain his horse too much after the sprint. And it was clear Georgia wanted Sarah to have plenty of time with Lord Carlin.

* * * *

The relief Sarah felt at being outside, and momentarily free of everything pressing at her, evaporated on the return to the house. Georgia mentioned that Cook put together a "few bites" for after the ride. In fact, it was a feast on a level Sarah usually associated with holiday suppers. Virtually every kind of cold meat was available. Hothouse fruits lay on the sideboard, and an array of little pies—both savory and sweet—were there for the choosing.

Sarah permitted Lord Carlin to fill a plate for her. He brought her one nearly teetering over with food. "I fear I may have been excessive," he said in apology.

"Oh, no," she replied. "That looks just about right."

Bryony noticed the exchange. "I should have asked for more. But until my ball, I have to watch myself to fit in my gown."

"Bryony!" Georgia warned, upset at the subject matter.

But Carlin only laughed. "Your sister is perfectly correct, Miss Wolverton. She's young and needs sustenance. For myself, I have never seen the appeal of ladies looking half-starved. A bit of weight enhances feminine beauty." He looked at Sarah as he spoke, and she quickly dropped her eyes. Carlin wasn't being terribly subtle about his interest any longer. And shouldn't she be pleased by that? He was a very kind man, and she faced diminishing prospects.

"Tell me, my lord," she said, hoping to divert the subject to something slightly less personal. "How often do you ride?"

"Oh, frequently enough, though not so much in town. In Kent, I ride nearly everywhere."

That was enough to spark a more general conversation about where the best riding was, and Sarah could let the group talk without feeling she was at the center of it. The ride had brought out her appetite, and she ate nearly everything in front of her.

After a while, she excused herself, and went down a hallway without any particular aim in mind.

"Sarah!" a low voice called, from the opposite direction as the dining room.

She turned her head to see Theo standing in a doorway. "My lord?"

"Come here," he said. "You'll want to see this."

She walked to him, curious but a little nervous. "What have you been up to? You never came in to luncheon."

He took her hand and pulled her into a small room. It looked like it was intended to be a study, but it was filled with boxes covering nearly all the space. "What is all this?" she asked.

"Charlie's things, from his townhouse, mostly. I've been looking through it."

"And did you find anything?"

"Not yet. But with two of us, it should go faster."

"Theo, I can't be found in a room with you!" She hadn't forgotten how he looked during the ride, especially at the end, when he'd pulled such a daring stunt, and then looked so content about it. She finally realized that beneath Theo's often restrained demeanor was a daredevil, and she wasn't sure how she felt about being so close to him. "What if someone comes by?"

"They're all full on beef sandwiches," he said, dismissing the threat.

"I had the egg pie."

"Sounds delicious. I should have eaten something after all, but I didn't want to get snared in some dull conversation about this season's must-have hat."

After looking around, Sarah went to an unopened box and lifted the lid. "Do you have a particular item you're looking for?"

"No, unfortunately. I hope to find something new, that's all."

They fell silent, each searching on their own.

"This box has a lot of notes about art," Sarah commented. "Not in code, so it must be even less relevant."

They continued to search. Theo found a box of canvas and broken frames. "Why did they even bother packing this up?" he groused. "It's rubbish."

Before Sarah could respond, a shadow darkened the doorway. "I say, what is going on here?"

Sarah turned toward the door. The voice was Carlin's, and he sounded furious.

"Go away," Theo snapped back, in no mood to talk to the man.

"I will not. You've cornered Miss Brecknell alone in a room, and you expect me to look the other way?"

Sarah stood up, her cheeks already scarlet. "Please, my lord. He didn't corner me. He's not even near me."

"Miss Brecknell, do not think you have to defend this man. You are far too intelligent a girl to be in such a situation." He turned back to Theo. "I should call you out."

"Is that still the fashion?" Theo drawled, deliberately stoking Carlin's anger.

"Please!" Sarah said. "Both of you. There has been a misunderstanding. If either of you have any regard for me, you won't make an issue of this. I certainly don't want more attention."

She was speaking particularly to Theo, and she saw him relent, his expression softening.

"Very well," he said.

Carlin wasn't satisfied. "Miss Brecknell, please allow me to escort you back to the dining room."

"Of course, my lord," she murmured. She didn't even look at Theo as she took the other man's arm.

As they left the room, Carlin said quietly, "I did not expect to find you in a room with Lord Markham. What did he say to you?"

"He was not attempting to...harm me. We were having a private discussion, and I did not think my absence would be remarked on."

"What private discussion could you have with that gentleman?"

Sarah lowered her eyes, affecting more sorrow than she felt. "He had some news regarding my late fiancé," she said. "And I insisted on hearing it straight away. If there is blame to be laid, it must be with me."

Carlin shook his head. "It is always the gentleman's responsibility to consider the appearance of these things."

"As you have shown," Sarah said. "I thank you for your consideration."

Carlin pressed his free hand over her own. "You are worth every consideration, Miss Brecknell."

"I would appreciate it very much if you would not mention the incident again, my lord. Truly, it was of no consequence."

Carlin agreed easily, and seemed to go out of his way to turn the conversation to other subjects. Sarah noticed how he hovered near her, though, as if he were afraid Theo would return to sweep her away.

Chapter 23

♉

AFTER SHE PLEADED A HEADACHE so she would not have to join the group for riding at the Wolvertons, Alyse experienced a remarkable recovery. She felt guilty for deceiving her family and everyone else. But she didn't think she could take a day of pretending to be cheerful and carefree when she was anything but.

Instead, after spending far too long on deciding what outfit to wear, she visited the Hotel Foster yet again. She'd gone several times since meeting Elena.

She wasn't alone that day. There were a few other guests Elena entertained in her suite, two gentlemen associated with the British Museum and another lady who had expressed interest in funding Mrs Heath's next dig.

Elena's hair caught in the light, the red tones coming out. Alyse stared at her profile, particularly her mouth. Such a pretty, bow-shaped mouth. Her lips looked so smooth. What would it be like to be kissed by that mouth?

Alyse felt a sudden flush throughout her body and blinked in surprise. What was she thinking?

Despite the odd thought, she stayed until all the other guests left. She used her talents of keeping a conversation going to ensure that everyone was happy and satisfied when leaving. In fact, the guests were pleased enough by the visit that Elena was promised more funding by the end of the afternoon.

"That went well," Elena murmured once the last gentleman left. "And I have you to thank for it, Alyse."

"All I did was chatter," she protested.

"Don't be modest. There's an art to social chatter, and it's one I never mastered. I'm far too blunt."

"Well, I'm glad I could help, but I'm sure you would have persuaded them all on your own." Alyse paused. "You've never asked me to support your work."

"Haven't you done just that?" Elena asked, with a knowing smile.

Her hand rested lightly on Alyse's arm, and the touch warmed her flesh. *Stay there*, she willed silently. But Elena took her hand back, after a lingering moment of delicious panic.

"Will you stay to dinner, dear?" Elena asked.

Alyse shook her head, remembering she should return home before she was missed. "I am engaged tonight. But I wish I was not." Oh, how she wished she was not engaged at all.

Elena tipped her head, as if studying Alyse. "That is too bad. But you will come see me again, won't you?"

"Of course!" It came out in a rush.

Elena smiled at her vehemence. "Excellent. The days I see you are so much brighter than the rest."

Alyse glowed at her words. When she returned home, she put aside questions about her day, giving vague responses so boring that no one asked further. She abruptly decided to stay in that night, too distracted and moody to want to go out and be the butterfly everyone expected her to be.

After dinner, a maid found her and said Theo was at the front door to inquire if she was well.

"Tell him that I am now, but I just wish to rest," she said, remembering how she had played sick in the morning. Naturally, Theo would stop by to check on her. It was just the sort of thing he would do.

She felt a dark wash of guilt when she thought of her growing aversion to the wedding. It wasn't Theo's fault. He was the same man he'd always been. It was Alyse who was changing.

The truth was that Alyse was terrified of what the wedding night would bring. She was a well-bred lady, and as such, she knew what her own mother had told her, which was brief and highlighted Alyse's moral duty more than any actual description of the act. "Stay calm and unemotional throughout the process," her mother had warned. "It's distasteful and will hurt. There's no way around it. It is the price all women pay for Eve's sin, and you must accept it. But of course it is the only way to bear a child."

Alyse had always wanted children, so she said she would be brave and endure it. Her mother was obviously grateful that Alyse wasn't going to ask awkward questions. "Your husband will know much more than you. And I'm sure he will be as gentle as possible. But remember the act is for the purpose of creating a child. Do not look for any other purpose, and never, ever succumb to lust. It does not become a lady."

And Alyse was a lady. It had been emphasized at every stage of her education. Her duty was to bear children and pass on the blood of her line and her husband's.

Of course, Alyse was not totally ignorant. She had friends who gossiped horribly and told what Alyse was sure were lies about what happened in a marriage bed. It sounded horrific. Yet those same girls sighed over certain young gentlemen they knew and seemed to look forward to their own weddings.

Alyse didn't understand it at all. Thank goodness, she thought for the dozenth time, that she had known Theo for so long. He would never hurt her and surely he'd make sure not to embarrass her with any...passion. She liked Theo, but Alyse couldn't stop a little shudder when she thought of actually being bedded by him. How awkward. How humiliating. What women endured just to have a child!

Whether it was the underlying worry of the upcoming marriage, or the novelty of spending time with Elena, Alyse fell into a strange dream unlike anything she'd imagined before.

She relived all the horror stories her school friends told of the details of sex, but she relived them as if they were actually happening to her in bed. And it wasn't a man with her—it was a woman. No, it was a woman with reddish blonde hair and impish blue eyes and no trace of shame. Elena.

Alyse woke up with a gasp. The dream had felt so

shockingly real, she almost didn't believe she was alone in the bed.

And how could she have dreamed such sinful things? Except it didn't feel sinful when she dreamed it. It felt maddening and beautiful. To be touched like that, and kissed like that. Alyse quickly sat up. Her body was hot, and ached between her legs. A lady didn't have such feelings. She was ill after all. That had to be the explanation.

She looked at the clock on the mantel. It was the dead of night. She closed her eyes again, feeling weak. What had she dreamed? Elena's mouth on her skin, her hands on Alyse's body, touching her in ways Alyse had never even dreamed of being touched. It was so shameful to think that could be pleasurable. It was utterly wrong, to dream of laying with a woman in such a sensual way.

Alyse wondered if she had a fever. She was too warm, too restless. She was not thinking normally. She had not really been thinking normally since the moment she saw Elena, so bold and strong and alone up on that stage. Ever since then, Alyse saw the world differently.

Oh no, she thought. Is this what falling in love is like?

And if it was, how could she cure herself of it?

Chapter 24

♉

SARAH BRECKNELL HAD PROBLEMS OF her own that had nothing to do with love. The evening had arrived when Sarah had to meet a strange man at night, in order to hand over important documents she was supposed to have magically found. The previous day, a note arrived at her home with terse instructions on where to go. Sarah entrusted Jem to pass the note immediately to Theo.

For the meeting, she dressed just as Theo suggested, in a heavy, dark cloak. The dress beneath was dark blue taffeta in an empire cut. She wore black gloves and slippers, and a black ribbon in her hair. She had even thought to avoid wearing any jewelry that might shine in the light.

How odd she was not more nervous. Granted, she had Theo with her. The spy was familiar with situations like these, and he knew how to press what little advantage they had. They were presently hiding not far from the address where Rossi told her he'd be waiting, and Theo was going over some last minute instructions.

"Now, remember, you need to draw as much information as possible out of him, without making him suspicious."

"I know," she said. "But what makes you think he'll want to talk at all? Won't he simply take the letter and go?"

"No," he said. "This is one letter, and not the one he's really after. This letter will only prove you're a valuable resource. If he believes you can get the rest of the documents, he won't dare hurt you."

"But I can't get the rest of the documents," she protested. "We've had no luck."

"*He* doesn't know that. You must believe you will find the documents. Be confident. Smug, even. You, my dear, would be terrible at cards—you can't lie to save your life."

She paled at his statement. "Indeed?"

"Poor choice of words," he conceded. "But my point stands. You have to know you'll find the cache. And you will. I believe it. You deciphered those codes. You can do the rest. We just need a little more time, and whatever hints he might drop in this conversation."

"Very well," she said. "I'll try to get him to talk about his plans. What else?"

"No matter what he tells you, press for a later date for the rest of the hand off, if you can. Tell him the process is slow, or that you need to travel, anything. Tell him the moon has to be full. I don't care. But the more time you have to search the better."

"Yes." She took a deep breath, trying to calm her nerves. "I will get the rest of the documents, I just need time. And I will get him to talk."

"Perfect. And remember, I'll be right there. You won't

see me, but I'll be close."

Sarah felt a little better about that.

"I wish you didn't have to be the one," he said, frowning.

"But I do," she countered. "He accosted me. He thinks I'm doing this alone. If he sees you at all, we're in trouble. Isn't that correct?"

"Sadly, yes." Suddenly, his lip twitched. "But I do look forward to the moment when he finds out you're not entirely on your own."

"I don't think I want to be there for that revelation."

"Trust me, Sarah, you certainly do not."

She picked up the letter Theo had given her. "Are you sure this document won't cause anyone to be hurt once he takes it?"

"I'm certain. It's of the right age so Charlie could have had possession of it, and it's on a subject that would have been of great interest to someone last August, but moot now. The political problem it addresses is all over."

"What should I do if he asks more about it?"

"He won't. He only wanted you to retrieve what Charlie left. He can't be surprised when the information from a dead man isn't very fresh."

Sarah nodded wordlessly.

"I shouldn't have said that. I forgot…"

Sarah shook her head. "Don't. You're right. He is dead, and it's quite foolish to evade that fact."

He put a hand over hers. "It was badly put."

They had gone to the rendezvous point early, partly so Theo could check out the surroundings, and partly so they would not be surprised if the other man brought company.

Theo selected a hiding place out of the worst cold. They waited there, and Sarah soon learned another truth about espionage—waiting was inevitable.

"I don't see anyone," she whispered.

"Be patient. He'll come," Theo assured her grimly.

Sarah nodded in the darkness and tried to calm the singing of her nerves. It wasn't easy, especially with Theo beside her, lying in wait like some great cat.

The night grew colder and the wind picked up. Sarah began to shiver, despite her coat; Theo simply stepped behind her and put his arms around her, giving her his warmth. He'd unbuttoned his greatcoat, so she felt every contour of his body as she leaned back into him. That also did nothing to relax her.

About ten minutes before the official time, they saw a couple walking down the street. Theo went very still, and Sarah was afraid to even breathe.

"That's him," she said in the lowest voice she could manage. The words barely reached his ears, but he squeezed her shoulder to tell he heard.

The couple stopped at the door. The man unlocked it and led his partner, a lady in a hooded cloak, in before him. Then he looked up and down the street before closing the door again.

Sarah was suddenly far more nervous. "I don't think I can do this," she said.

"Yes, you can," he said. "If you don't, we don't know where he'll show up next…maybe the Athenaeum, maybe your home." He turned her so she was facing him. "Remember what we talked about. I'll be right behind you. All you have to do is raise your voice, and I'll run."

"But then they'll know I got help."

"Your safety is more important."

"Is that what a spy should think? One person is more important than the safety of a whole country?"

"Sarah, if I can't keep one person safe, I have no business trying to protect a whole country."

She smiled. "I hope I'm worth it."

"Nothing will go wrong," he promised.

"It's ten o'clock," Sarah whispered. "I should go in."

She left Theo and walked slowly toward the building. She knocked on the same door Rossi just entered. No one came to open it, but the handle turned easily. She went in, her heart pounding.

The space she entered was rough and unfinished, as though someone had meant to add interior walls for a home, but never managed to do so. Thus, Sarah saw only bare brick walls through the gloom. It was nearly as cold inside as outside. A light came from further away, but she would have to walk all the way in and turn a corner to see it.

"Hello?" she called softly.

"Come in," someone said. From the tone, it was the woman.

Sarah hesitated, then followed the voice. What choice did she have?

Around the corner, she saw two figures in the light of a simple oil lamp. The hulking figure of Rossi she knew all too well. The other figure was a stranger.

"Who are you?" she asked.

The woman turned and gave her a cold smile. She was beautiful, with a face that looked prone to pouting, accentuating dark eyes and a full mouth. "Think of me as a chaperone of sorts. You see, Miss Brecknell, we're not so barbaric after all. We don't want you to lose *your* reputation."

Sarah heard the stress, and was puzzled. Who else's reputation had been lost?

"You work with him," she guessed. "You both work together, on this scheme to get the papers."

"That's of no concern to you," That voice was Rossi's, low and rumbling. "Now show us what you brought."

Sarah pulled the letter from under her pelisse. "This is the only one I found so far."

"One letter?" he said, his eyebrows drawing together. "One little letter!"

The woman was reading the letter over. "Worthless," she spat out. "All this information, these figures…old."

"What did you expect?" Sarah said, trying to match the other's cold tone. "It's been a while, has it not?"

The lady looked at her with a modicum of interest. "You certainly don't sound like a grieving lover."

"We should just kill her," the man said. "She knows too much and she's of no use."

"That's not true," Sarah said quickly. "I am breaking his codes."

"Sure you are, missy."

"I taught him how to create codes," Sarah insisted. "Why else did you ask for my help? You can doubt me if you like, but there's one letter you didn't get on your own. *I* brought it to you. And if you want any more, you best keep me alive to track them down. One dead woman will get you nothing. One live woman might."

"Stay," the woman said, putting a hand out to the man. She started talking to Rossi in another language, though she kept her voice low.

The man jerked a thumb in Sarah's direction. "Dead is safer," he returned. The words were Italian.

Sarah listened to the two talk. She knew Italian, so she followed along with their conversation as best she could, but she kept her face blank, even confused, so they wouldn't suspect she understood them.

"But not smarter," the lady said, still in Italian. "We are in business, Matteo, and Arceneau will be here in less than one week. You think he'll be pleased with one use-less letter and the news we killed Wolverton's whore? If she retrieved one of the papers he stole, she knows how to retrieve the others. She's smarter than I thought to bring only one item here. She may have the others already."

"She may be lying."

"I don't think the girl is good at lying," the woman responded. "And we've had little luck so far. If Arceneau decides to take his irritation out on us, you think I'll be so pretty at the end? Or that you'll be able to walk?"

The woman put a hand on Rossi's face, staring at him intently. The gesture was so intimate that Sarah had to look away. It was as if they forgot she was there. They obviously assumed she couldn't understand a word of what they said.

All of a sudden, Sarah had a revelation. She nearly had to stop from shouting it out loud. Italian! Of course! That was the key. Charlie's unbroken code was so maddening because he wasn't translating into English, he was coding for *Italian.* Armed with that knowledge, Sarah could go back and decipher the coded passages within an hour.

If she made it out alive.

"What if she's holding out for money?" Rossi asked, his eyes locked on the lady's.

"If she was, she would have opened with it. Look at her. She's a naïf. She didn't have a clue what was going on. No, all she wants is to get out."

Rossi looked at Sarah, who instinctively stepped back. She remembered what he threatened her with the first night.

"Very well, my little angel," Rossi said in English. "You have another week to retrieve the rest of the documents he stole. All of them by Saturday next."

"How will I get them to you? Meet here again?"

The woman smiled at Sarah. "I don't think so. We'll send you word of exactly when and where to deliver your message, angel. It will be like a surprise."

"I don't need any more surprises," Sarah said.

"Well, do exactly what we say, and you'll soon return to your dull little life."

"And if I don't?"

"Then you can be buried next to your lover. Assuming the church will recognize your remains as human."

The woman bestowed a kiss on both of Sarah's

cheeks, and then swept out, laughing. Rossi followed her.

Sarah stood there, the conversation between Rossi and the lady repeating in her mind. They had said something important. Something *wrong*. What?

Then it fell into place.

Before she could even take a breath, Theo was there. Warm hands reached out to her shoulder. He spun her around slowly, his expression tight with worry.

"Are you all right?" he asked in a low voice. "You didn't come out after they did."

"No." The word came out in a whisper. Sarah was still dazed by her revelation.

"Why not? What did he do to you?"

"He did nothing. You did."

"What?"

She looked at him, blinking until she could focus on the face she'd grown to trust. "I have another week to find the rest of the papers he stole."

"That's good. We'll find them, Sarah. I promise."

"The papers he *stole*," she repeated.

Theo tried to hide his expression, but wasn't quick enough. "Whatever they told you, remember they aren't your allies."

"It was the truth," she said. "I know it was. And I overheard what they said to each other in Italian. I was a fool for not seeing it before."

"It doesn't matter why he had them. We just need to find them."

"You deliberately didn't tell me," she said. "You didn't lie, but you knew the truth and you said nothing, which is more or less the same thing."

He swallowed, looking away from her. "I didn't want to complicate things."

"Complicate things?" She glared at him, her fury building like a fire given too much fuel. "My life was threatened! My reputation *is* threatened! I have to choose between trusting you who lied to me, and trusting a man who laughed when he described how Charlie died."

"I never lied to you. And you can trust me."

She felt so angry she barely heard him. "I won't trust you again until you tell me the truth about Charlie. The whole truth. Now."

Chapter 25

♉

THEO HATED THE LOOK ON her face. Confused, frightened, and angry all at once. All feelings he wished she didn't have to experience.

"Sarah," he began. "It's complicated. And dangerous. It would only hurt you."

"Shouldn't I be the judge of that?"

He shook his head, and then took her hands in his. "Can't you just forget about it?"

"No, I can't," she said, snatching her hands away. "And at this point, I deserve to hear it."

He sighed. She was right. "I'll tell you," he said, making the decision. "But not here. We need to go somewhere warm."

He led her to the street and found a carriage to hire. A cold winter wind chose that moment to rush around them, and Sarah shivered. Theo cursed the weather. It made everything worse. He bundled Sarah into the dubious warmth of the closed coach, and then called a name out to the driver.

The carriage was off. Sarah looked at him, still angry. "Where are we going?"

"It doesn't matter. Somewhere safe, warm, and anonymous. That's all."

After that, she didn't utter another word. From the set of her jawline, she had plenty to say, and he was lucky she wasn't unleashing it all on him at that moment. But Sarah was too much of a lady to ever raise her voice in public. Thus, the silent condemnation. She wouldn't even look him in the eye, instead pretending he wasn't there.

There were very few places where a gentleman could conceivably take a single woman without causing comment. One of those places was a theater. Granted, a lady like Sarah ought to have a chaperone with her. But Theo knew there was a large gap between the ideal and reality. If he took her to a private box in his favorite theater, no one would raise a fuss. And if Sarah kept her face concealed until they actually got to the box, no one would be able to identify her. A paper-thin rationalization, considering all that happened so far. But it was the only thing he could think of.

It didn't take long to reach their destination. Through the coach's window, he glimpsed a poster on the brick wall. It advertised an old show, and the paper was now ripped and faded.

See the Remarkable Miss Finn!

Comic Actress Extraordinaire!

Now playing the role of Simple Simon in the rollicking romance The Three Magicians!!

The exclamatory text floated over the image of a

woman dressed as a boy, with cropped hair and colorful but ragged men's clothing. The actress was holding a bright red handkerchief in one hand and had just revealed a dove in the other.

Theo wished his life could be as simple as producing the evidence like a magic trick. He glanced again at the image and thought a woman dressed as a boy could be a nearly perfect spy. *I should mention the idea to Julian*, he thought, *though he'll probably call me mad.*

"Put your hood up," he said to Sarah, as the carriage rolled to a stop. "You don't want to be seen."

"Astute as ever, my lord," Sarah said sarcastically. But she obeyed him, drawing the hood up so her face was well hidden. "Where are we?"

"The Pavilion Theatre. It's not private, but it's close enough."

* * * *

"A *theater*," she said.

A theater was one step up from a brothel, as far as Sarah knew. It was one thing to attend the Theatre Royal, where strict standards were in place and even the King himself might conceivably attend a play. But most theaters were little more than indoor circuses, showing not serious drama—for which they had no license—but bawdy comedies and music and dancing and weird acts.

And that's what Theo called *safe*.

Sarah wasn't sure she dared take down her hood the whole time she was there.

"No one will see you," he said. "The lights are all directed at the stage, and it's difficult to see much of anything in the boxes. Believe me, I know from experience."

They entered the building, Sarah relying on Theo's escort, since she could only see what lay directly in front of her.

He guided her through a door to a private box. The little room was much fancier than she expected. The furniture was gilded, the chairs facing the stage were upholstered, and a lush oriental carpet was underfoot. There were unlit candleholders on the walls. It was empty save for them.

"You're familiar with this place," she guessed.

"Yes. I rent this box because it can be a useful place to meet people...or to hide from them."

She looked around, and slid against the back wall, as far as she could get from the rail, where patrons could look down onto the stage. From the laughter of the audience, some comedy was in progress.

"Sit down, Sarah. You look like a ghost."

"I will not sit down!" she said. "This isn't an evening out. I'm not staying long enough to sit down. I'm only here because you lied to me."

Theo stepped so he could look directly at her. "No. I didn't *lie*. I just didn't tell you the whole truth." His body eclipsed the light from the stage, so his face was shadowed. Still, she could tell he was angry.

Well, so was she. "Hiding the truth instead of outright lies? How is that different? Why didn't you tell me? Why?"

She was so furious with him she wanted to hit him.

But Sarah had never hit anyone, and Theo was so close to her that she'd never be able to raise a fist between them. She tried, but instead her hands only rose to his chest, her fingers balled up tightly. "Why didn't you say anything?"

He leaned even closer. "Because I didn't want to hurt you." His hands curled around her upper arms, still concealed by her cloak.

"Don't mock me," she warned.

"Watch your voice."

Only the proximity of other people kept her voice from getting louder. She wanted to scream, but hissed out, "You didn't answer me. It's because you didn't trust me, isn't it?"

"No, I never thought that. Telling you would have meant revealing a side of Charlie you never wanted to see, and I didn't want to hurt you."

By the look in his eyes, he *was* telling the truth. But it wasn't enough.

"Why? With stakes like this, what does it matter if I'm hurt? Why should that matter to you?"

He kissed her. Sarah knew he would. She knew it and she did nothing to stop it. She tasted his lips and then she was bending toward him, as if she had no shame at all.

The kiss wasn't gentle as the first one had been, but it was just as entrancing. She should stop. She should remind him she hated him.

But she didn't hate him then, not when his hands moved to slip under her heavy outer cloak to slide around her waist. Not when he held her so close she could feel the heat off his skin. Not when he parted her lips with his tongue and ever so slowly deepened the kiss, until Sarah was burning with a desire she hadn't thought she was capable of.

"That's why," he said, when he pulled away long enough to take a breath. "Do you understand?"

Sarah inhaled, her breath as shaky as her body. "No."

"I don't want to hurt you because you make me feel like this," he said, his voice hot with either desire or anger, or both. "How do you manage that? To be so utterly innocent I get irrational at the thought of you being damaged, yet all I can think about is getting you alone?"

"I don't do anything." She flattened her hands against his chest, intending to push him away. "You're wrong. You don't think of me like that. You're engaged, or don't you remember?"

"Of course I remember," he said bitterly. "But I've never felt anything for my fiancée like I feel for you."

At that confession, she completely forgot to push him away. "We barely know each other," she protested.

"Is that true?"

"What does that mean?"

"Sarah," he said, his expression perfectly serious. "When you saw me, at the dinner at the Wolvertons, what did you think? When you first recognized me, what *exactly* did you think?"

"That I knew you," she said, feeling faint. "But only because I met you at the funeral…"

"No," he said. "You hardly saw me at the funeral. I could have been dressed like Queen Elizabeth and you wouldn't have noticed."

Something in the absurd statement pulled her out of her daze. "No. To catch my attention, you should be Queen Boudicca. I prefer older history."

Theo just stared at her for a moment, then leaned past her shoulder so his forehead touched the wall behind her. He dissolved into silent laughter. Then Sarah couldn't stop from laughing too, collapsing into him. The whole evening had just been too much for her nerves, and once she smiled at the nonsense she said, she had to laugh, and then she couldn't stop. He held her, tightening his embrace until both of them were tangled together, weak with slightly hysterical joy.

After a moment, he straightened up to look at her.

"That remark," he said, putting one hand on her cheek and tilting her face to meet his, "is an excellent example."

"Example of what?"

"Why we're matched."

She stiffened, recalling the situation they were in. "We're not matched."

"Yes, we are." he said, growing serious again. "You recognized me."

"I felt as if I knew you from a long time ago," Sarah admitted, her heart beating wildly. "How could you know that? I've never mentioned it. I've never even written it down for myself."

"I know it because I thought the same thing when I saw you. I recognized you. I thought, *that's her*."

"You can't be serious. That's…mystic."

"It's instinct. Are you denying it?"

"I find you attractive. But that doesn't mean I believe

in fate!"

"I do." The way he looked at her made Sarah wish she believed in it too.

"If that's true—you believe and I don't—then it's evidence we're *not* well-suited."

"No. It only means we're complementary." He reached to undo the buttons on her cloak. "Take this off. You're too warm."

"That's not a good idea."

"Why not?"

"It's improper," she said, though it wasn't.

"Your cloak? It's not as if I intend to take all your clothes off."

She went still as soon as he said that. If he knew Sarah was ruined, he wouldn't be half as restrained as he was right then. She closed her eyes, trying to stop the picture from her mind. He called her innocent a moment ago. His attitude would change sharply if he ever learned the truth about her.

Even as he pulled the cloak away, she said, "I have to leave. I'm sorry."

"Quit apologizing," he growled. "We've already talked about how you shouldn't take the blame for things that aren't your fault."

"It must be partly my fault. I encouraged you."

"You did no such thing." He laughed softly, sadly. "All I know is that I can't think clearly when you're near me." He leaned toward her again, and kissed her neck.

Sarah sighed. Why did that feel so impossibly good? With one hand, he took hold of her neck and kept her skin under his mouth, not allowing her to pull away, to recover her better sense.

After a moment, she couldn't remember why she should not let him be so close. She felt drugged, a sweet haze enveloping her as she allowed Theo to devour her, his mouth working its way down her neck to her chest. She couldn't explain why it felt so wonderful, but she wanted to surrender to it, she wanted to kiss him back.

A voice inside her warned her she was being foolish. "Theo," she whispered. "Why are you doing this?"

"I've been dreaming of touching you."

"That is not true," she said. Sarah wanted to laugh, except that his expression didn't suggest a man who was joking.

"You know you make sounds when you're concentrating on something? Little *mmms*, and the occasional *oh*."

"I don't."

"I keep wondering what other sounds you'd make if I knew what to do."

Sarah wished that didn't sound so interesting. "I'm not a code to be deciphered," she said, uncertainly.

"Yes, you are."

She would have thought up an excellent retort if he hadn't bent his head and bit her neck then, making her gasp. Heat flushed through her. She'd done exactly what he wanted, reacting to his move with an instinctive little sound.

"Let me hear more," said Theo. Something in his tone made her aware of how *much* he meant it.

"I shouldn't," she said, even as she put her arms

around him, somehow afraid he'd move away. "Besides, I don't want to you to see my face." *What a terrible argument*, she thought. One would think she *wanted* to be convinced.

"That's all? Then take a step forward," he said, moving back from her.

Puzzled, Sarah did, and he shifted so he was standing against the wall instead of her, and he held Sarah with her back to his chest. "There. I can't see your face."

"What do you intend—"

He kissed her neck and slipped one arm around her waist, pulling her tight against him.

"Oh," she whispered, her head falling back onto his shoulder.

"I'm just going to listen to you, sweetheart."

Her legs went a little weak, and he felt her tremble.

Within moments, he'd slid down the wall so she sat between his legs and could lean her back against him and feel him breathe and know exactly how hard he was. The plush rug beneath them was as good as a bed, and the darkness of the theater box hid them from the world. Sarah felt scandalous like that, but didn't have the slightest inclination to move away.

He trailed a finger along the neckline of her gown, then edged the cap sleeves down her arms. He moved to cup one breast, earning an *oh* from Sarah, who didn't think it possible to blush more than she already was. He continued kissing her neck and shoulders, which he did with a very flattering dedication. Sarah moaned a little each time, knowing he liked to hear it.

With his other hand, he worked the skirt of her dress up until nearly all of her legs were exposed. He found the top of one stocking, and he ran his thumb along her inner thigh, pressing gently, until he reached the curls where her legs met. At her startled gasp, he reversed direction, stroking her leg down to the knee.

His hand slid to her stomach, gliding over the fabric of her gown. "Tell me to stop," he said in a low voice, his breath brushing by her ear. "You can."

"You really want to touch me like that?" she whispered. Yes, it turned out she *could* blush more.

"How else can I know what you'll sound like when I do, sweetheart? Tell me to stop or go on. Your choice."

She took a breath. "Go on."

Sarah heard his sigh of relief, and couldn't stop from smiling. So she wasn't the only one losing all sanity tonight. She put her hands back to rest on his hips. "Go on," she said again.

He stroked her legs with both hands, slow and sure. She shifted so her knees parted a little more. Sarah sank back when she felt his fingers on her thighs, caressing the skin so gently she almost couldn't feel it. Her hips moved in response, begging him to touch the center of her body, already growing warm. But still, he lingered, content to tease her with those feather-light strokes. She closed her eyes, breathing deeply, wondering how she had succumbed to him so quickly.

She knew he was smiling every time she made a sound, which she couldn't seem to stop doing. He used one hand to push her legs further apart, giving him freer access to her body.

She was utterly unprepared for the meltingly sweet feelings he created as he touched her. She began to murmur incoherent words as she felt herself reacting to him, spiraling into ever tighter circles with every flick and stroke.

He eased one finger into the heat of her body, drawing out the sudden flush of wetness there. "Theo," she gasped, her eyes flying open. She thought, *all this, and we're still fully dressed.*

"Yes, love," he said, his mild tone completely at odds with the bite he then gave her, his teeth raking the delicate skin of her throat, sending her temperature soaring.

"What are you doing?"

"Listening," he responded. "I like listening to you."

"What should I do?"

"You're doing quite enough right now, sweetheart. Just let me touch you."

There didn't seem to be any hurry, she noted in a daze. He lingered over her, building a slow fire inside her, touching her as if they had all the time in the world. When she tried to turn around, urged on by a wild instinct, he gently pulled her back against his body, murmuring soothing words she couldn't recall, promising her that she was deserving of this maddening, wonderful delay.

"Please, oh, please," she begged him relentlessly, hardly aware of what she was saying.

Theo felt the shift in her body, when she tipped over the edge to the inevitable conclusion. He then altered his touch, moving faster. Sarah was vaguely aware that his own breathing was coming quicker, and she knew she affected him too.

Sarah's breath grew ragged. She moaned softly when the subtle movement of the man surrounding her grew insistent, dominant. The wave threatening to overwhelm her broke then. He held her tightly as she came undone in his arms with a long sigh.

She turned her head to the side, and even though her eyes were closed, she tried to hide in the crook of his shoulder. She was so glad it was dark. She couldn't imagine feeling like this when anyone could see her.

Her body relaxed against Theo's, and he shifted so he could hold her more comfortably. All the tension between them was gone for the moment. Sarah would have been happy to stay like that forever, cradled in his arms.

She didn't recall how it happened, but Theo was sitting against one wall, and she lay curled up on him, her skirts now covering her body again. Her head lay on his shoulder, and she was grateful he couldn't quite see her face.

"Sarah?"

"Don't look at me," she whispered.

"Why not?"

"Because!" Sarah had no idea how she could ever have a normal conversation with him after that. She thought she had learned what men and women did together when Charlie seduced her. But this was completely different. It was far more decadent. And more intimate. "I don't know what to think..." she trailed off again, confused.

"You could think that you liked it, which you're fully entitled to do."

"I don't believe that's the usual argument."

He pulled away enough to expose her face. She kept her eyes closed, but he kissed her very carefully. Softly, placing no demand in the gesture.

Sarah responded after a moment, her body softening against him. She took a breath, then said, "It was quite shameless of me to let you do all that." She buried her head in his chest again, embarrassed. "Now you know how I sound."

He laughed softly. "I don't know half as much as I want to."

His words cut through the last of her daze. She sat up and looked at him, wishing she didn't have to say it. "Theo. Don't distract me any more. I need the truth."

Theo sighed, then nodded. He took her hand in his. "You won't like it," he warned her. "You must promise to tell no one. Ever."

"Of course."

"I'm serious as death, Sarah. Once I tell you, you'll know why. Do you give me your word?"

She took an unsteady breath. What could she say? "Yes. I won't ever speak of it."

"You must lean against me," he said. "Like you were."

"What?"

"Just do it, Sarah. I'll tell you what you've asked to hear."

She did. Her head rested on Theo's chest, and when he bent his head, his mouth was tantalizingly close to her ear.

"Now listen," he said quietly. "This is the truth. The night Charlie was killed, he was heading to Woodforde. But he wasn't attacked by highwaymen. You were right. It was a story made up on the spot—no one had time to do anything else. The truth is that he was killed by another agent of the Zodiac."

Sarah stiffened, but his arm tightened around her, anticipating her reaction. "*Not* me, Sarah. I swear it."

"Why was he killed?" she asked.

"He was a traitor."

The words seeped into her head, and settled there. Theo waited for a moment, letting the revelation sink in. She waited for outrage to rise up in her chest. Nothing. Perhaps she was still too shocked.

"Are you sure?" she asked.

"I wasn't there. But I'm told he admitted it before he died."

Again, Sarah waited for her righteous indignation to surface. It didn't. "Rossi said the papers he had were stolen. What did he do?" she whispered. "Exactly?"

On the unseen stage, a musical number began while the actors rushed back to change for the next scene. The dancing girls and cheery, bawdy music were so appallingly *wrong* in that moment Sarah couldn't even cry.

"He stole as many documents as he could, and then sold them to the highest bidder. He had been doing so for years—since before the time he proposed to you."

She wished it didn't sound like the truth. But it fit. All of Charlie's little mood swings, his secrets, his promises and threats.

"Sarah?" Theo asked, his voice tight with concern. "Are you all right?"

"Should I be?"

"I warned you," he said, but without censure. "I'm sorry I kept it from you, but I assumed you wouldn't help me if I told you the truth. And I truly didn't want to hurt you."

She was glad she wasn't watching Theo's face. She was afraid of what she would see. "You think because Charlie was a traitor I would have refused to help you? Do you think I condone that?"

"I think you loved him. I think you still do. And you wouldn't want to have damaged his memory, even if his outward reputation would not have been changed."

"I can't believe you'd think I would choose loyalty to him over loyalty to my country!"

"Love is a very powerful motivation, Sarah."

"Not if it asks you to betray your ideals," she hissed.

He said nothing to that, but held her until she relaxed again.

She still rested against him, but something else needled her brain. "The Italian," she said.

"What?"

"I forgot to tell you. I think I know why I can't make sense of the remaining code. I think he was using Italian instead of English. When I heard them talking, it made me think. If Charlie was connected to them, he might have been thinking like them...in Italian."

"You might be right."

Something in his voice made her look sharply at him.

"What are you really thinking?"

He shook his head. "I never should have let you walk in there. It was far too dangerous."

"It had to be me. Besides, it got me out of the house," she said, with a little shrug.

Theo shook his head, and laughed quietly. Without warning, he kissed her again, just below her ear. Sarah closed her eyes, wishing she had more strength, or less shame. She should either be outraged, or seduced completely. This in-between was torture.

Very pleasant torture.

Sarah realized with a painful start how infatuated she had become. She reluctantly moved away from him and stood up.

So did he. He found the cloak and put it around her, pulling up the hood himself, looking rather possessive.

Sarah watched his expression, and wished things were different. "We're not going to meet like this again," she told him.

"No." He didn't try to argue. "You don't have to see me again at all, if you don't want to. You can write, and Jem can be the courier."

"Don't be absurd. We can work together just as before." She held his gaze. "I want to find those papers. If I'd realized what Charlie was up to earlier, perhaps I could have helped then. Maybe stopped it before he… somehow. But at least let me help now."

"Keep going through those codes. Try the Italian. That's the best thing you can do."

He moved toward the doorway. "Come. I'll see you

home.”

“Is that wise?” she asked, remembering his comment of not being able to think straight when she was around.

“I’ll behave myself,” he promised. “And if I thought you were valuable before, I know you’re even more precious now.”

Chapter 26

♉

THEO GOT SARAH HOME WITHOUT incident. Leaving him behind as she went back into her home was both a relief and a disappointment. Sarah barely looked at him in the coach, too consumed with the onslaught of information in her head from that evening. Not to mention Theo's devastating seduction of her. He didn't even require her to remove a shoe before she came apart in his arms. How was she to live after *that* encounter?

Her parents had gone to sleep long before, so she had only Naomi to manage as she prepared for bed.

"And how was the performance?" Naomi asked, brushing Sarah's hair out.

Sarah stiffened, thinking immediately of the unsanctioned theater she'd been inside. But Naomi couldn't know about that! Then Sarah recalled she told everyone she was attending a musical performance at Chloe's home that night. "Oh, the performance. It was…well, it was pleasant enough. Nothing remarkable."

"And who was there? Any gentlemen? Lord Carlin, perhaps?"

"I didn't see Lord Carlin tonight," Sarah said. That

was true. She felt better when she didn't have to lie out-right.

"Well, I expect he'll call tomorrow. You get right into bed, miss, so you can be well rested."

Sarah didn't sleep. Why sleep? Nothing could be dis-covered in dreams. And she had a real puzzle to solve. After Naomi left her, she lit another lamp, till the room was artificially, painfully bright. Then she worked, using the clue of the Italian. She compared the scraps of lines, matching numbers to potential keys, noting which ones she tried, and then discarding the failures.

But she couldn't focus on the work for long. Why had Theo kissed her the way he had? What did he mean when he said he believed in fate? The embarrassment Sarah felt in the aftermath of sharing such an incredible, scandalous moment with him faded, leaving her with more difficult emotions. What did she think about Theo? Why did she feel so strongly that she had known him somehow?

And what would she do with the truth she gained? Charlie betrayed her. Sarah knew he'd done a far worse thing than simply seducing her, but the sting felt personal. She trusted him with her heart and her body. She had committed to spending her whole life with him…and she didn't even know who he was. It was appalling. How could she have ever had such powerful feelings for some-one so deceitful?

Was she just weak? Wasn't she doing the very same thing now? She could feel Theo when he entered a room. She knew he was going to speak before he said a word. She loved looking at him. She dreamed of being with him.

I am very shallow after all, she thought. Chance brought him into her life, and she was not content to let him go. She instead welcomed his interest and encouraged his attention. All the while knowing he was not available for any honorable conclusion. Marriage would be the only acceptable answer to Sarah's desires. And marriage was not something he could offer, even if he were interested in doing so.

And yet she dreamed. Sarah sighed. How had she ended up like this? At least tomorrow would be an ordinary day.

But as it turned out, it was not an ordinary day. When Naomi woke her the next morning, the maid's expression was worried. "Miss," she said. "You must get up and see your mother."

Mrs Brecknell had taken ill during the night, and a doctor had been called. Sarah hurried to her mother's bedside.

"Mama!" she said. "What has happened?"

"Oh, dear. You must not come closer." Her mother didn't look much different, though her skin and hair were dull, and she breathed with difficulty.

"Nonsense!" But Sarah backed up a few steps, at the urging of her father, who had just come in.

"She woke up in the night and couldn't catch her breath," he explained in a low voice. "She rang for help, and Naomi, who got here first, said she was nearly blue in the face by the time she entered."

"Oh, no," Sarah said.

"Like a weight, pressing onto my chest," her mother

said, her voice quiet. "I'd never felt that before. My heart seemed to slow down. I felt sure it was the end."

"What did Naomi do?"

Her father said, "She sat her up in bed and eased her breathing. The fit seemed to pass, but your mother is so weak. I'm not sure what can be done." His tone was fretful, uncertain.

Sarah put her hand on his arm. "It's just a brief illness. Nothing more. Mama will pull through. This was a fit brought on by a nightmare, or worry, perhaps. She needs more rest, and warmer air. It's too cold in here by half."

Her parents didn't seem to hear her. When the doctor arrived, he confirmed it was too cold in the room. "Add fuel to the fire," he said. "All night long if need be. Too cold air will weaken you further, madam."

Sarah was startled when Naomi carried in a tray bearing Lord Carlin's card later that day. She'd been absorbed with her mother's health, and she had forgotten all about the outside world.

"I'm not quite prepared for callers," she said. Indeed, she was still wearing her morning dress, and her hair was bound up in the simplest manner. She certainly did not look like a hostess ought to.

"He said he only wished to convey a short message."

"Send him to the parlor. I will be there as soon as I can be." Sarah hurriedly tried to make herself look a little more polished. She fixed her hair, and put on the jewelry she forgot to wear in the morning.

Still, she felt woefully unprepared when she saw the distinguished and very proper form of Lord Carlin in the parlor. "My lord," she said. "Forgive me for making you wait."

"Miss Brecknell," he said, turning to look her over. "I just heard your mother is doing poorly. Allow me to offer my best wishes for her."

"Thank you, I'll tell her," Sarah said. "But that cannot be what brought you here today."

"No, I actually wanted to ensure you were well, since I did not see you at the Lamb's home last evening as I expected to."

Sarah glanced behind her to see if Naomi was close enough to overhear. It would not do for her to realize Sarah lied about where she'd gone.

"Well, in fact," she hedged, "I did not feel so well either. I chose to stay away from the event. Though I think it was just something I ate. I am quite recovered."

"That is a relief. I confess I had hoped to entice you out this evening as well, but you may feel it necessary to tend to your mother."

"Entice me?"

"To the theater."

"The theater?" Sarah echoed. In a rush, the scandalous memory of last night returned.

"Yes. The Theatre Royal. There is a performance of *Henry IV* which is supposedly quite well done. As you enjoy history, I thought of you."

"Oh! The Theatre Royal. It sounds wonderful," Sarah said, with genuine regret, "but as you guessed, I would not feel it right to leave my mother until I have better news…or at least some news."

He nodded. "I expect so. Your devotion to your family does you much credit."

She looked down nervously. She was hardly a model daughter, and it felt wrong to hear praise for her meager efforts. "It is kind of you to say, my lord. I do wish I could have accepted your offer."

"Another time," he said, not quite hiding his disappointment.

"I am sure this illness will pass," Sarah said. "It must. I cannot dream of Mama..." she trailed off. "She must recover."

"Miss Brecknell," Lord Carlin said, looking closer at her. "You are distraught. Is there anything I can do to ease your worry?"

"Not unless you can heal the sick," she said. "I only wish it were spring already. Then Mama would recover much faster." Sarah sat down abruptly, thinking not just of her mother, but everything that happened over the past few weeks. "It seems no matter what I think of, the time is never quite right, and there's never enough of it."

Carlin sat across from her, his gaze on her face. "Are you speaking of your mother's illness? Or something else?"

Sarah focused on him, aware she had revealed too much. "I was just thinking aloud, my lord. I fear you overheard a thought too many women have all too often. I feel as if I have no option other than to wait, and it is maddening."

"But it is not unique to women," he said. "Things like illness—or news—we can't control what happens or when. We all must wait. Providence doesn't seem to care for clocks."

She smiled at him. "That is very wise, my lord. I shall try to remember it."

"Ah, my dear Miss Brecknell, it is just me rambling. Speaking of clocks, I will not take up more of your precious time." He stood up. "If you like," he said hesitantly, "you might send a note to let me know when your mother improves. I should like to pay my respects to her in person."

"Of course, my lord. I should be happy to." She knew full well Carlin also wanted to know when Sarah would be available socially.

After he left, she fell to brooding again. Carlin represented the world she ought to be trying to enter. He was stable, and safe, and unfailingly courteous.

Yet she kept turning to the darker world of the Zodiac, drawn into the secrets kept by the men she knew. She should be terrified of what it symbolized, but instead, she was fascinated by it. And by Theo, who to her represented what the Zodiac truly was. She knew he was unattainable. She had no cause to think otherwise. He never promised her anything, and indeed warned her to be wary of him. But the truth remained: if Sarah had a choice, she would turn to Theo before Carlin every time.

But choice was the one thing she didn't have.

Chapter 27

♉

THEO SPENT A RESTLESS NIGHT, occupied with thoughts of the search for the papers and of Sarah, and how he could rid himself of the infatuation he'd wandered into. Nearly seducing her and coming dangerously close to completely destroying her reputation was *not* the best method of doing so.

He'd been so absorbed in his task he hadn't been thinking or acting like himself. So Theo went around to see Alyse, assuming that spending time with his actual intended bride would remind him of everything he truly wanted.

The footmen and maids all knew Theo well, so he was shown in immediately, without the usual pretension of finding out if she was receiving callers. "Lady Alyse is in the side parlor, my lord," the maid at the door said. "Shall I take your coat?"

When he walked into the room a few moments later, he found Alyse alone, staring out the window, even though she had a book in her lap. "Morning, Ally."

"Oh! You came to call." Alyse looked surprised that he was there.

Theo was a little affronted. "You say it as though it's not a regular occurrence."

"I just wasn't thinking about guests."

"I didn't know," he said in apology. "The maid never bothers to announce me, but of course I should not assume anything. Do you want me to leave?"

Alyse put a hand up. "Of course not, Theo. Please stay. I've been out of sorts lately, and my temper is up since I got into a tussle with Mama this morning."

"Over what?" Now that he looked closer, Alyse did seem perturbed.

"She wants me to choose between the pink paper and the pink paper for the wedding invitations."

Theo shook his head. He must be missing some nuance. "They're both pink?"

"One is pinker."

"Then pick the less pink one and be done with it."

"That's precisely what I did! Mama accused me of being flippant and not caring about the wedding planning."

"And?" Theo asked.

Alyse gave a helpless little shrug. "She's right. I don't care at all. I've never been less excited about the trappings of an event."

"Should we postpone..." he began to say, then stopped, realizing his entirely selfish reasons for suggesting it.

"The date is out of our hands now," she said, her expression miserable. "I'm so sorry, Theo. I hoped to placate my mother by setting the date, but she's worse than ever. You'd think it was her wedding all over again!"

"Shall I speak to her?"

"I wouldn't wish that on you!" Alyse shuddered theatrically. "But she's maddening. No wonder some people elope." She shot him a look. "I'm *not* suggesting that, by the way."

He laughed at the idea of rushing Alyse off to the Scottish border, the usual destination for desperate couples. "The gossips would have a field day with that," he noted.

A disgusted look flashed across Alyse's pretty features. She hated gossips. The Templetons as a clan loathed anything that hinted of impropriety. "Mama would be even worse than she already is."

"If you want to avoid a repeat discussion, you should escape the house. Why not visit your friend Mrs Heath?"

Alyse looked sharply at him. "Why do you say she's my friend?"

He blinked in surprise at the sudden change in her tone. It was almost accusing. "Well, isn't she?" he asked. "I thought you got on so well after that lecture, and you have seen her since then. What's the matter? She hasn't asked you to fund her expedition, has she?" He frowned at the idea of anyone taking advantage of Alyse's kindness.

"Of course not! I mean, I would be happy to fund her work—it's fascinating—but that's not the point. She's certainly never suggested it. I shouldn't like money to intrude on our…friendship."

"Then what's the issue? She seems like an intriguing

person. She must have a pile of stories to tell. I could drive you around to her place myself. I don't like the idea of you moping around the house."

She offered him a grateful smile. "You're always swooping in to save the day, aren't you?"

He shrugged. "What are allies for?"

Within a few minutes, Theo ushered Alyse out of the house and helped her into his carriage. "Where is Mrs Heath staying while she's in London?"

"The Hotel Foster," Alyse said.

Theo nodded, called the name out to the driver, and climbed into the carriage. On a whim, he sat next to Alyse, rather than opposite her.

She looked over at him. "Is the other seat damaged?"

"No," he said. "But why shouldn't I sit by you?"

She smiled. "Whatever you like." She leaned toward the window, apparently interested in the passing scene.

Theo watched Alyse sidelong. She *was* beautiful. There was no question about that. He always loved her profile, and thought her deep chestnut hair was gorgeous. But she'd become like a picture to him lately, not a flesh and blood woman at all.

Sarah was flesh and blood. She was beautiful too, though not in Alyse's refined way. Sarah's charm was in her spirit, the way she lost herself in studying something or smiled suddenly at a joke. Theo could barely look at Sarah without wanting to touch her. Alyse, however, hadn't inspired that for a while.

Was he just distracted? Perhaps he'd forgotten how alluring she could be. He slipped one arm around her waist, and drew her a little closer to him.

Alyse turned to face him, surprise on her features. "Theo, what are you…"

He bent his face toward her. "When was the last time I kissed you?" he asked.

"I don't know," she said. Her eyes widened and her breath sped up. "Last week."

"That was a peck on the cheek." He continued to hold her, even though her whole body was tensing up. "Why not let me give you a proper kiss now?"

"In a carriage? With everyone to see? That's hardly proper."

He reached over her with his free hand and drew the shade on her side, then did the same for his. "How about now?"

"What's come over you?" she asked. "You never act like this."

"We're going to be married. Shouldn't I want to kiss you?"

"Well, yes. But that sort of thing is for after the marriage," she said, though her voice had dropped.

"We've been practically married our whole lives. And anyway, I've kissed you before."

"So why do it again?"

"I remember liking it."

Alyse took a deeper breath. "If you insist."

"I do," he said. He tipped Alyse's head up a bit, and kissed her lightly on the mouth. She didn't pull back, didn't resist. But she also did nothing to encourage him.

And he felt nothing. No heat, no sense of need. With

Sarah, he'd been ready to sell most of his worldly possessions just for the chance to feel her skin. Her lips had burned him.

Alyse's lips were soft and warm, but she plainly felt nothing. Or she was such a proper young lady that she'd forgotten how to feel a thing.

He ended the kiss, and saw her hand tense and her arm held too stiffly. He knew she wanted to wipe her mouth.

Well. He had insisted.

"Here." He offered Alyse a handkerchief.

"Why?" She took it as if it were some exotic specimen.

"You obviously don't care for the taste of me."

"It's not that," she said quickly, too quickly. "Theo. Please understand, it's not you. I love you so dearly."

She looked about to cry. Theo felt like a heel, as if he'd pressed her to do something terrible. He moved his arm to her shoulders, and drew her close to him again, though in a completely different way than before.

Alyse sensed the change in mood and relaxed against him. "I'm sorry," she said. "I just wasn't expecting you to kiss me."

He shook his head, and then bent to kiss the top of her head, the glossy sweep of her hair. It was how he kissed his sisters.

"I don't know why I did," he said, though he knew all too well.

"Please don't do it again." Alyse held the handkerchief tightly in one hand. It was now wet with her tears.

"I hurt you," he said.

"You can't hurt me, Theo," Alyse said, some of her usual composure returning. "Besides, it was just a kiss."

The carriage came to a halt. Theo snapped open one shade, illuminating Alyse's tear-streaked face. He reached out to wipe the evidence away.

She let him, then sighed. "Do I look frightful?"

"No, you look lovely, just like always."

Theo stepped out and then held out a hand to help Alyse. "Will you have any trouble getting home?"

Alyse shook her head, stepping onto the pavement. "No. The hotel's footmen will call a carriage for me."

Theo kept hold of her hand for a moment. "Alyse? Are we still allies?"

She smiled, looking somehow sadder than before. "Always."

Theo watched her until she entered the hotel, then he turned back to the carriage. The kiss revealed far too much to him. He didn't love Alyse the way he ought to. He loved Alyse in almost precisely the same way he loved his sisters, or Georgia and Bryony. The way he felt about Sarah was completely different, and he had nothing to compare it to. True, he'd defend any of those women to the death. But Sarah, he'd probably kill someone on her behalf. The thought of any other man getting her alone in a room, tasting her…Theo grew irrational at the thought.

Perhaps his feelings for Sarah would fade with time. Perhaps he wasn't in love with her at all. It was just a very odd infatuation.

Except he didn't think it was. Something about Sarah felt right. Even the first time he saw her—when she looked so distant and separate—he knew she was special. She was meant for him.

In which case, Theo told himself, why the hell hadn't *she* grown up near him? Why hadn't she been introduced to *him* instead of Charlie? Why had he not even met her until he was completely and utterly bound to marry someone else? If their love was destined, destiny had poor timing.

Worse, Theo couldn't shake a growing feeling that he would be poisonous for Sarah. And not just because his work was making her take risks. Theo felt like he knew Sarah, as if he'd known her in a previous life and just now recognized her again. But that brought with it a terrible feeling that he'd ruin her if he pursued her. He might even cause her death.

So where did that leave him? He still had to find out what Charlie had hidden. That hadn't changed. And he needed Sarah's help to do it. That hadn't changed. If he were smart, he'd keep Sarah at arm's length and then never see her again. Theo doubted he was that smart. Theo knew very little about romantic love. But he knew he loved her. And to lose her would kill him.

Chapter 28

ど

AFTER THEO LET HER OUT of the carriage, Alyse deliberately slowed her pace as she walked into the lobby of the Hotel Foster. She wanted to run. Whether away from Theo or toward Elena, she wasn't sure. Why had he kissed her? Was it a test? Did he suspect? Theo hadn't shown the slightest bit of interest in her for a long while. She'd discouraged it from a sense of ladylike propriety. At least, that's what she always told herself.

She was greeted courteously, and didn't even have to announce which guest she was visiting. They knew her there by then, and told her that Elena was receiving. It was good for business for the Lady Alyse Templeton to be seen in the Hotel Foster. Alyse went up the stairs, her heart pounding.

Elena opened the door herself. "Come in! It's Marianne's day off, so I must do all the serving myself." She laughed though. The effort of hosting a single guest was nothing compared to the sort of responsibilities she took on in her working life.

Alyse stepped in, and Elena shut the door after her.

"Have a seat wherever you like. I'm glad you could

come, dear."

"It was easy," Alyse said. "I have a chaperone for all the parties. I can't do more than take a turn around the gardens with a gentleman. But no one cares if I spend hours with you. Because you're a woman, and what could possibly happen?"

Elena's eyebrows drew together. "What indeed?" she asked speculatively.

Alyse sat down on the long chaise. She was still flustered over Theo's actions. "He kissed me," she blurted out.

"Who did?"

"Theo. He drove me here as a favor, and he was behaving so strangely. He kissed me as if he wanted to ravish me. He's normally so chivalrous."

"You say ravish. Did he hurt you?"

"Oh, no!" Alyse lifted her eyes and saw Elena's stormy expression. "I exaggerated. Theo would never, ever hurt me. It was just so surprising."

"So it wasn't cruel."

"No. It wasn't…anything." Alyse stared at her hands in her lap. "I felt nothing."

Elena sat down on the chaise as well, and she leaned over to take Alyse's hand in hers. "Are you upset because he took the liberty?"

"It was less about the liberty—we're about to be married, after all—but more that he did it and it was so meaningless."

"A kiss should never be meaningless." With those words, Elena raised Alyse's hand to her lips. She kissed the back of her hand, just where her first two fingers joined.

Alyse's heart raced. Such a simple gesture, yet she felt as if she were about to burst. "Elena."

Elena watched Alyse carefully. "How did that feel, by comparison?"

By comparison? There was no comparison. This kiss left Alyse weak. Elena's perfume enveloped her, and Alyse breathed in shakily when she smelled it, and the more subtle scent of Elena's skin lying beneath it.

"I…can't say." Alyse whispered. "I can't say."

"Ah." Elena loosened her grip, as if to release her hand. "Should I let go?"

"No!" It came out fast and breathless. "Don't let go."

"I will tell you a secret," Elena said, her voice warm. "I don't want to let go."

"That's the secret?"

"In light of what it reveals, my dear, it is quite a potent secret. Wouldn't you say?"

Such a revelation deserved an equal revelation. But Alyse was overwhelmed, and could barely say anything. "Please, I've never been so scared."

"Why? Tell me."

Alyse closed her eyes and fumbled for the words. *Love* was too dangerous, and too bold right now. "Because I crave you," she whispered.

Elena's eyes widened. "Crave? Are you hungry, then?"

"I've been hungry my whole life," Alyse said fiercely. "But I didn't know it until now. Always feeling what I was offered wasn't what I wanted, without having any words to say why. Always afraid, underneath it all, afraid that someone might know what I was dreaming."

Elena moved closer to her on the chaise. Moving delicately, almost like a dance, her arms circled Alyse. "Don't be afraid with me."

Alyse's body sang when she felt Elena touch her. Her skin tingled and she couldn't breathe properly. Her heart pattered with fear and only dimly understood desire. "I don't know what to do," she gasped out. She reached out and put her arms very hesitantly around Elena's neck. "Please tell me."

"Would you like a kiss?" Elena asked softly, her eyes intent.

"Yes," Alyse said. "Kiss me."

Elena leaned forward. Alyse closed her eyes. She felt breath against her cheek, and then a mouth over her own.

Alyse instinctually tightened her arms around Elena, drawing her closer, breast to breast. Delighting in the entirely new sensation of Elena's soft lips on hers, Alyse let out a sigh.

Elena drew away and smiled. "You taste like a dream."

"Can I kiss you?" Alyse asked.

"I'm dying for it," Elena confessed.

Alyse moved to kiss Elena on the mouth, and lost herself in the feeling. Her lips parted when Elena's did, and she gasped when Elena ran her tongue along her lower lip, tantalizing her. "Is this the right way?" she asked.

Elena held her and laughed. "There is no right way, darling. There's only whatever way makes you happy.

And I want to make you happy. I'd keep you here forever if I could." Another kiss, more questing, left Alyse flushed and trembling.

"Lord, I feel I'm being seduced," Alyse breathed.

"Well, I could say the same thing, beauty," Elena responded with a smile.

Alyse once drank a sweet wine until her head swam and she was amused by everything. Alyse found Elena's touch to be as powerful as that, with none of the sickening aftereffects. Instead, she felt like she was more awake than she had ever been. The minutes she spent with Elena seemed as precious and as rare as gold. Alyse wished she knew how to prolong them. Especially because she knew that all too soon, it would be over.

"I was afraid to tell you..." Alyse said, dizzy from Elena's kiss. "I didn't know if you would understand."

"I understand that, and more. The only thing worse than keeping a secret is telling it to the wrong person." There was pain in her voice.

"That happened to you?" Alyse wrapped her arms around the other woman, as if she could keep the pain away.

"Once. I told a woman who was my friend—oh, not that I loved her—just that I felt differently than most people do about these things." She paused. "I wish that day had never happened."

"She rejected you?"

"She looked at me as if I were a monster."

"I hope you left her."

"I quit the field," Elena said. "And not as victor, I assure you. The things she called me…. I even thought she must be right about some of them."

"No," Alyse kissed her again, trying to erase the past. "She was wrong."

"Depending on who you ask," Elena said. "Now you know why I always want to return to Egypt, to the desert. The rules are different there. No one expects me to act like a perfect lady. To a point, I can be myself."

"But aren't you lonely?" Alyse asked.

"Sometimes." Elena made an effort to smile. "But now I'm here. And I have you. Did you ever think such a thing, on the night we met?"

"I thought you were intimidating, and very splendid. I'm glad I know you better now." Alyse glanced at the time and grimaced. How had an hour passed? "Though I must go home soon. I have to be a perfect lady."

She got ready to leave, wishing she didn't have to. "I'll come back as soon as I can. Tomorrow."

"I'll be waiting," Elena said, smiling.

Chapter 29

♉

S ARAH KNEW I TALIAN AS AN offshoot from knowing Latin, so she stumbled a bit as she worked to decode the last few maddening passages. But Italian was the missing element, and later that day, she had produced three lists of words and phrases. She didn't know exactly what they referred to—but she knew they had to be correct.

The first list was mostly names: Ingres, Caldcott, Gainsborough, Sawyer, Rillings, and several others. She guessed they were artists, because the second list consisted of phrases such as "portrait of a young man in blue," "head of a saint," and "view from Bruges." They must be specific pieces Charlie either bought or was trying to buy. The third list made little sense, even decoded. It was just words and broken phrases: Charlotte, 10,000 north, personal from M. Causer. Perhaps they would make sense to Theo.

On Monday, when she presented the newly decoded parts to Theo at the Athenaeum, he nearly laughed out loud. "This is perfect. You did it. You broke the codes."

"But what does it mean?" she asked, hoping for a revelation. "Does it make sense to you?"

"Not yet," he said. But he smiled at her. "Don't worry, though. I can work with this."

"You're sure?" Sarah felt a thread of anxiety. "What if you can't?"

"I will," he promised. "And in plenty of time. Trust me?"

She nodded. She did trust him. "You'll let me know, won't you?"

"As soon as I can." Theo paused, and she knew beyond a doubt he was thinking of kissing her. But he didn't, and she wasn't sure if she was relieved or not.

* * * *

Armed with the list of artists and paintings, Theo did a bit of research on his own, and then arranged to meet Giselle Villani again. She reprimanded him for standing her up the other night, but he persuaded her that he was serious about purchasing art, so she relented. In a calculated decision, Theo also dropped the information that he knew Charlie, a fact that made Giselle's eyes gleam warily.

But even so, she was intrigued by what she thought Theo was, so he was able to get more information out of her over dinner.

Many of the pieces Charlie put into his coded list were works of art Giselle sold to him initially, though she didn't know their whereabouts any longer. Theo could tell she definitely wanted to know—the pieces represented a fair amount of Charlie's money.

"How did you meet?" Theo asked casually.

"He wanted to buy art. I'm a dealer in art. Is that so difficult to understand?"

"Did he say why he wanted to buy art in particular?"

"Why does anyone buy art? People like beautiful things."

"I've seen some of the pieces he bought. They weren't that beautiful."

"Ah, well. Any collector is liable to make mistakes in the beginning."

"Even with your expert guidance?"

"I told him what artists to watch for," she said with a sniff. "Can I help it that he did not buy their best work?"

"A matter of money, perhaps? He didn't have enough for the best?"

"I don't know," Giselle said, visibly irritated. "Why should you care?"

"Just curious. I've been impressed with Wolverton's taste in other matters. I expected to like his choices in art too, but I suppose we differ on that."

"In what matters did you admire his choices?"

"Women, for one." He was telling the truth about that, at least with regard to Sarah.

But Giselle naturally thought he was referring to her. Her pout vanished. "Yes, well. He was an intriguing companion, I must say."

"One might say the same about you."

"I would let you say such a thing, my lord," she purred. "But sadly, I am expected elsewhere this evening. If you go, my lord, do I have any hope that you'll return? Or will you vanish again?"

"Giselle," Theo said flatly, not pretending to be smooth or charming. "How many men walk away from you?"

"Very few," she responded, just as candidly.

"Then you'll see me again."

She accepted that, and Theo was able to escape. He would see her again, but not for the reasons she expected. Giselle was neck-deep in the situation surrounding Sarah, and Theo had long ago decided which woman deserved his protection.

Chapter 30

♉

THE NIGHT OF BRYONY WOLVERTON'S coming out ball finally arrived. Bryony had requested that everyone wear light colors—an implicit plea to help her forget her bereavement. Sarah didn't think she ought to wear the blue dress again, so Naomi aired out another gown, this one an ivory muslin with wide lilac stripes. Sarah willingly submitted to her maid's efforts to make her ready for the evening.

As usual, Naomi worked magic. Sarah's hair was curled and put up with an ivory pin. Naomi found a few dried lavender buds to tuck in as well. The overall effect was less elaborate than for Lady Alyse's party, but still made Sarah look more vivacious than any of her dark frocks could.

"Excellent, miss," Naomi declared. "These are the dresses you ought to be wearing."

"We'll see," Sarah said. She did enjoy the lighter feeling. Perhaps it was time to put off the mourning wear. Especially since she no longer saw Charlie when she closed her eyes.

She saw Theo.

Sarah put the thought away. "Hand me the ivory fan, Naomi. Mrs Lamb will be here to collect me soon."

Sarah stopped by her mother's room to show off the dress. Her mother was still in bed, but her color had returned. She smiled to see Sarah in a light color. "Just beautiful, darling. Your eyes are shining."

Sarah promised she would tell her mother every bit of gossip she heard. Though Sarah was feeling much braver about social engagements than even a week previously, Chloe once again joined her that night. She clucked with worry over the news of Mrs Brecknell's still delicate—though recovering—health, but she announced Sarah's outfit gave her hope. "You look lovely tonight. Like your old self."

At the Wolvertons' home, many of the guests had already arrived. Sarah looked around for Theo, but didn't see him before Chloe swept her over to introduce Sarah to a circle of her friends and acquaintances.

"So you are Miss Brecknell," an older lady said upon being introduced.

"Ah, the Miss Brecknell that Lord Carlin is so taken with?" another woman named Madame Osgood asked, peering at Sarah over a quickly moving fan—it was already warm.

"It is true that Lord Carlin has called on me more than once," Sarah said. "Beyond that, I could not say."

"So he has not proposed to you yet?"

"No, ma'am."

"Well, I shouldn't think it will be long before he does. Carlin has taken considerable time in remarrying. But of course, that is his privilege."

"His Christian name is Marmaduke," Chloe noted, with a wink at Sarah.

"Oh, I don't know if I could marry a man named Marmaduke," another guest said, laughing.

"Given name aside, it would be a fine match," the older lady said. "He has an estate in Kent that is said to be quite extensive, and though he has only eight thousand or so, that would be sufficient. And I'm certain he wants heirs to his name," she added.

Eight thousand sounded like a fortune to Sarah. "We have not spoken of such matters," she said. "Nor do I think it will surface as a topic soon."

Was that all these ladies chattered about: incomes and issue? She excused herself as soon as possible, pleading that she had to find something cool to drink. But on her way to the refreshments, she was hailed by Lady Alyse, who beckoned her over. She had come as Theo's partner, naturally, though she was standing by Mrs Heath at the moment.

"How lovely to see you again!" Alyse said. She looked especially flushed and happy. "But of course, you would be here, considering how close you are to the Wolverton family."

Sarah nodded. "Yes, though I have not yet been able to speak to Miss Bryony. She is without doubt the center of attention."

Mrs Heath said "Well, let her enjoy it. A young lady's coming out ball may well be her last night to be the center of her own life."

The tone of the comment struck Sarah as odd, but she brushed it off. She said, "I am glad you were able to come tonight, Mrs Heath. My father organized your talk at the Athenaeum, and I was there. I know little of archaeology as such, but it sounded quite fascinating. Will you return to Egypt to do more work?"

"I have booked passage already," she replied, with a sidelong glance at Alyse. "As soon as my business in London is concluded, I'll be off for warmer climes. I came here to seek out more sponsors, you see."

"I hope you have been successful. How do sponsors take to the notion of a lady archeologist? Does it frighten them?"

"Oh, it depends on the donor! The shrewd ones know it's good publicity. And the shrewder ones know I'm the best."

Alyse giggled at that. "Such confidence, Mrs Heath."

The other woman shrugged. "If I do not believe in my own abilities, who will? I have never found it advisable to wait for others to approve my own dreams."

Something passed between Mrs Heath and Alyse that Sarah couldn't quite understand—a look, or a hidden message. But the lady's comment resonated with her on a more basic level. How could Sarah be happy if she only waited for others to give her what she hoped for?

* * * *

Theo spotted Sarah speaking with Alyse, but before he could join them, a lady stepped into his path. By her determined expression, she intended to flag him down.

"Lord Markham," she said. "Do you remember me? I am Mrs Lamb."

He nodded. "At the party last week. Are you acquainted with the Wolvertons?" he asked.

"Not closely. I am here because Miss Brecknell wanted a friend she could rely on, though she is doing quite well on her own. Not that she needs to be watched. She always behaves like a lady."

Theo remembered the night at the theater when Sarah had behaved far more like a woman than a lady, and was glad he was skilled at controlling his expression. He smiled. "Then it's once again you I'll have to ask permission from if I hope to partner Miss Brecknell for a dance."

Mrs Lamb laughed. "As I recall, you were able to persuade her to dance at the Templetons' ball last week with no help from me. For which I wanted to thank you."

"Thank me?"

"Sarah—Miss Brecknell—has been shut in too long. I was gratified to know she could still enjoy a night of dancing. She has been more like herself these past weeks than for months before. Years, in fact."

"Years? So you knew Miss Brecknell growing up. Was she always so, ah...scholarly?"

"A bluestocking, you mean." She paused, reflecting. "I don't know if it was so all-consuming. We were girls, after all, and growing up was our main occupation. But she was always bright, always interested in everything, and her father encouraged it. She never mastered the social talent of aloofness, that is certain."

"No, she is not like most ladies."

"Not in the least. I am glad to see her recovered from her grief though. I was worried about her, when I heard of Wolverton's untimely death. I feared she might do something..." She broke off, aware she was speaking to a near stranger. "Something rash."

Theo didn't need her to say what she was thinking. Remembering Sarah at the funeral was bad enough. "From what little I know, she loved him in a way most men could never hope for." Without warning, jealousy uncurled in him.

"That's true," she agreed. "Though I wonder if he appreciated the fact."

"What do you mean?" he asked.

"Oh, I don't know. He had a certain air..." The lady paused to give Theo a sharp, considering look. "I didn't care for him."

"You didn't?" *Everyone* liked Charlie. That was his talent.

"Oh, I know it puts me in the minority. He was a charming man, make no mistake. But I knew Sarah before and after he met her, and I didn't like what happened to her in the least."

"How so?"

"She changed after meeting Wolverton. I knew she was in love with him, but she nearly severed all her other friendships once he proposed. I wouldn't be surprised if he suggested it."

"Would she have obeyed such an order?"

"She would have jumped into the sea if he asked her to," Mrs Lamb said flatly. "Sarah thought she was the luckiest young woman in the world when he started court- ing her. But I always thought him overbearing. He told her how to dress, how to behave. She once mentioned to me that he said she wasn't very smart."

Theo nearly laughed. "That's insane."

"I know! Sarah's one of the most intelligent people I've ever known, man or woman. Yet she was in awe of him and took his slightest whims as gospel. To be truthful, I was quite relieved when I didn't see her so much. It was like talking to a different person."

Theo felt a cold anger building up inside. Mrs Lamb's comments, along with the notebooks and Sarah's own innocent revelations all added up to create an unflattering picture. Charlie had been a manipulator, coolly using Sarah as both a resource and a decoy. He didn't care what happened to her. His actions didn't stem from desperation, or even a desire to better himself. Instead, it appeared Charlie acted as he did simply because it amused him. The money from his work as a double agent was merely a bonus. The real reward was the idea that he was better than everyone else.

Theo couldn't think about that at the moment, though. Instead, he ought to do exactly what Mrs Lamb suggested. "If you'll excuse me," he said. "I'll find Miss Brecknell and tell her you've all but ordered me to dance with her."

"Please do that, my lord," she said. "Don't let her slip back into melancholy."

* * * *

Sarah wasn't in danger of melancholy, but she was in

danger of a parched throat. She managed to get some punch, and then wandered into a less crowded room, though there were still plenty of people around.

She drifted closer to an opened window, where the air was slightly cooler. Without meaning to, she began eavesdropping on the conversation of two gentlemen nearby, as soon as she heard the word *art*.

"I'm put out about it, of course," said one man. He was about sixty, with a definite paunch. "I paid a pretty penny for that piece, and the emperor's lackey decides he wants it, so *poof!* The agent confiscates it, and I've just made a gift to the French Empire. I hope the whole bloody country gets trampled."

His companion chuckled. "You should have known better than to tempt the agents with a piece of artwork like that."

"Well, what else should I have done?" the fat one asked. "Bought a lesser piece by a lesser artist? What's the point of that? Fine art is *meant* to be impressive."

At his words, Sarah nearly dropped her punch glass. *A lesser piece by a lesser artist.* All along, the answer was staring her in the face. Charlie's taste in art was inscrutable, until she realized why he wanted it. He wasn't interested in the art itself. The pieces were all decoys. They existed for only one reason.

Charlie purchased art good enough to not be questioned as pieces worthy of collecting, but never so good that they might be noticed or confiscated by anyone before they reached their intended recipient. It was very, very clever. Only someone like Charlie could have thought of it.

She started to walk toward the main room, sliding her glass onto an empty surface without even looking. That was when Theo found her.

"Miss Brecknell, I was hoping…" His smile faded as soon as he noticed her abstraction. "What's happened?"

"Theo," she said in a whisper. "I know where the papers are."

* * * *

Theo froze for a second, and he gripped her arm with one hand. "What?"

"It's the art!" she said. "The actual artwork, I mean. It has to be. There's no other reason why he bought and sold the type of pieces he did." Realizing he had no idea what she was talking about, Sarah quickly explained the conversation she overheard, and her theory of the modest fame.

He nodded at the end. "So you think he hid the documents he was selling with the art as he shipped it around? Everyone looked at the art, instead of the papers with it?"

"Perhaps. We'll need to see how he packed the art. Or some of the pieces he still owned. The notebook listed several titles. They have to be somewhere."

"The hunting lodge," he declared. "That was Charlie's domain. Where else would he have worked on such a thing? Sarah, you're brilliant."

"It's just a guess."

He released her arm, aware he shouldn't have touched her at all. "You don't guess. Let me think about this."

"What's to think about? You just go there and look," she said. *You're a sign of the Zodiac*, she wanted to add. Locked doors didn't mean much to them.

"Come dance," he said. "Your friend practically insisted I ask you."

"I'd prefer not to. I can't possibly concentrate on the steps now."

"It's Miss Bryony's coming out, and we need to appear as carefree as everyone else. Just one set."

He led her to the floor and they lined up with the others. The dancing wasn't actually that onerous, though Sarah missed several cues. Fortunately, the crowd was such that no one noticed her lapse.

Except the lady with the fan who was so interested in her earlier. What was her name again? Oh, yes, Madame Osgood. Sarah saw her watching and felt cornered.

After the set ended, Theo excused himself, saying he had to attend to Alyse. Sarah intended to meet Chloe where she was sitting, but the lady with the fan fell into step with her.

"Miss Brecknell," Madame Osgood said. "What a pretty gown. Lord Carlin would approve."

"Is that so?" Sarah asked. "I'm afraid I have never gleaned his preferences on the matter."

"Oh, I have. We're *very* close, you see."

The implication in her words made Sarah look over at her. "If there is something you wish to say, madame, you ought to say it plainly. I am fond of mysteries, but not in conversation."

The lady only laughed. "What an original creature you

are, Miss Brecknell. I can see why he finds you refreshing."

"Lord Carlin, you mean?"

"Naturally. I was pleased to hear you don't have stars in your eyes about a marriage proposal. Of course, he may propose…he's been talking about it long enough. But he'll not give me up, you understand."

"Give you up," Sarah repeated.

"Must I spell it out for you?" the other lady asked, her eyes sparkling with mischief.

"That's not necessary," she said stiffly. "I'm not a child."

"Of course not. Ah!" Madam Osgood said, as they approached Chloe's chair. "And here is Mrs Lamb again! Well, I'll leave you two to chat." She gave a superior smile and then turned away.

"How are you enjoying the evening?" Chloe asked.

"It's been enlightening," Sarah muttered. "I may never leave the house again."

"Oh, dear. What happened? Something that Madame Osgood said to you? Don't put too much stock into her statements. You know, rumor is she was once an actress who bought her way into society."

"I would prefer not to speak of actresses." Sarah sat down beside her friend. "I'm still readjusting to society, that's all."

At Chloe's urging, they rested for a while, then walked slowly around the rooms. They were able to congratulate Bryony and chat with the family for a bit. But Sarah had lost her enthusiasm for the party long before.

It was just before they were about to leave when Theo found Sarah again. He pulled her aside on some pretext. "Listen," he said. "I'm going to Woodforde, and you have to come with me."

"What? I can't do that."

"What if there's another code to be broken? You're the one with the best chance to do it."

"I can't. It's impossible."

"If I find a way to make it possible, will you come?"

She closed her eyes briefly. "Yes," she said, knowing all the reasons she should have said no.

"Good. Leave the details to me. I'll plan a way to get us both to the lodge without being seen. And I'll do it so neither your safety nor your reputation will suffer."

"We need to act quickly," she said. "Rossi will contact me soon with the date of the final meeting."

"We may only need a few hours at Woodforde. Now that you know the secret, we'll find the answer there."

"I only think I know," she warned him. "We don't have proof of the theory yet. I could be wrong."

"No," he said. "I know you're right. I can sense it." He looked around. "You have to go before someone sees us together. Why do we have to creep around like criminals when we're the ones trying to do good?"

"None of these people know you're trying to save the country and the crown," Sarah said. "They'll only care that you were with a woman who isn't your fiancée."

"Then go. I'll get word to you via Jem."

Sarah left him. The situation was getting dangerous. She was with Theo too much, and the excuses were wearing thin. They had to finish this treasure hunt soon, or she would be ruined no matter what the outcome.

But when it was over, she would never see Theo again. Sarah would return to her dull life, only now she would be aware there was so much more out there, hidden currents beneath the surface of society. How could she be content with her life, knowing that?

Chapter 31

♉

SARAH ASSUMED IT WOULD BE impossible for her to be alone with Theo long enough to drive to Woodforde and back before someone missed her. But he was both a lord and a secret agent, and he exploited resources she didn't imagine.

Only a day after the party, Jem found an excuse to speak privately with his temporary employer. He explained that Sarah should rise very early on Thursday and wait by the mews behind her home, keeping in mind to dress for the cold and have everything she might need in her reticule for the whole day.

"A carriage will come for you then, ma'am."

"You're not driving?" she asked, puzzled.

"No. I've another task. Lord Markham has arranged it so that you'll seem to be at the Wolvertons in the morning, at the behest of Miss Bryony. Anyone inquiring about you there will be told you'll return as soon as Miss Bryony can let you go. In the afternoon, someone will cover for you at the Athenaeum—don't ask who. Either way, we've got a plan to make it seem that any caller insisting on seeing you will have just missed you. With luck, no one will notice, but your whereabouts shouldn't be questioned until well after dinner, by which time you'll be back at home with no one the wiser."

"How can anyone manage that?"

"It does become easier when one has money and a number of morally questionable folks to press into service." The way Jem grinned made it clear he was looking forward to whatever part he was to play.

Sarah promised to follow instructions, and the next morning, she was waiting exactly as she'd been told. Theo pulled up in a two seater he drove himself. "Get in," he said. He was dressed in a nondescript, dark greatcoat. A hat concealed most of his face. He could have been anybody.

They drove to Woodforde. Theo made sure Sarah was well tucked in against the cold, and kept as fast a pace as he dared, considering the frozen roads and tracks.

Sarah watched the trees go by, feeling the winter landscape was a dream. With Theo beside her, she felt perfectly safe…and also dangerously out of her depth. She had agreed to come because she *knew* the information had to be there. Charlie always had to be smarter than everyone else. His hiding place would be devious. How could it be anything else?

Woodforde was called a hunting lodge, but it had been part of the Wolverton family's property for so many generations that it was relatively close to the outward-creeping suburbs of London. No longer used for its original purpose, it had been converted into a retreat. Charlie claimed it shortly after he joined the Zodiac, and since then, the place had effectively been his own.

"You never saw the place?" Theo asked, as they drove through the frosted morning.

"No. Charlie spoke of it often. I knew he spent time there. He said he wanted to show me the place, but that until we were married, it would not be…ah, proper." She checked her words. Theo was doing precisely the thing even Charlie would not.

Theo heard her, and gave her a look. "Are you worried?"

"I trust you," Sarah said.

He laughed, a short, rather dark sound. "How reassuring. I hope I'm worth your trust."

When they reached Woodforde, Theo secured the horses and headed directly to the front door. "Come on," he said. "You should get inside where it's warmer."

"What if there are people here?" she asked, suddenly worried about being seen.

He shook his head. "Nothing to worry about. I grilled Georgia—subtly, of course. Woodforde never had a live-in servant. Charlie was too secretive for that, not to mention it's quite small. There's a caretaker who keeps an eye on the property, but he lives in the village, and makes his rounds here only after he attends church on Sundays. We're quite safe."

He opened the door with an ill-gotten key, and motioned Sarah in. "Can you get a fire going? I have to see to the horses."

She nodded. A fire was quick enough to start. The whole place felt as if it was just waiting for the owner to return. Even after nearly half a year, it didn't feel abandoned at all. If Sarah were superstitious, she might have expected Charlie's ghost to appear.

"Not that you've ever stopped haunting me," she whispered to the air.

She briefly explored the place, which was small by aristocratic standards, even for a retreat. The ground floor consisted of a main room dominated by a fireplace on the far wall, with a small kitchen and what looked to be a storage room or servants' quarters off to the side. A staircase above the main entrance led up to a floor containing a few smaller rooms, two of which were bedrooms. Though it was sunny outside, the curtains of these rooms were drawn tightly, making the spaces dark as night. Sarah hurried back downstairs, glad that they would not be there long enough to see how the place looked when night truly fell.

Once the fire started to warm the main room, Sarah was able to look around. Art surrounded her. Dozens on dozens of pieces were hung up on the two long walls of the great room, covering nearly all the surfaces that weren't windows. There was no order, no style, no sense of purpose. Medieval saints, renaissance princesses, and modern day landscapes competed for attention. She walked slowly around the main room, trying to match the names she'd uncovered to the images she saw. Some were labeled on the frame. Others were not.

Theo came in from the cold then, stamping his feet. He saw the walls and peered around in awed horror. "It's hideous."

"I have to agree," she said. "What was he thinking? If someone saw this place, they'd know he didn't care about the art."

"You truly think it's the key."

"How can you doubt it?" Sarah said. "Charlie wasn't collecting art because he liked it, or even as an investment. He used it to hide his real investment—the stolen documents." It was a clever plan. Who looks at a portrait on the wall and thinks there's anything behind the painting?

Theo nodded. "Then let's get a closer look, shall we?"

He stood on a chair to pull down a lower hanging piece Sarah pointed out, then laid it face-down on a table he had covered with a cloth. "I don't want to harm the art," he explained. "Or let anyone else guess what we've done."

He looked at the back of the piece, and made a disappointed sound. "There's nothing behind it."

Sarah stepped closer. "There must be. The notebook mentions this piece specifically." She leaned over the painting, looking carefully at the back of the canvas, which was utterly blank. Nothing had been fastened to it. She ran her fingers over the canvas, hoping to sense something her eyes missed. Then she propped up the piece to peer at the art, the back of the canvas, the frame itself. Was there a hidden compartment? Some message hidden in the paint?

"Even if it's not here now, it must have been here once. But no pins, no pocket, no cuts…just nothing," she said in frustration.

Theo frowned. "It doesn't make sense, does it? Why bother to mention the painting in code if there's nothing there to find?"

"I don't know," Sarah responded, her irritation rising. She had been so certain.

Theo noticed her reaction. "It's only one painting. I'll take another down. Maybe he meant to put something here but didn't have time."

She looked over the relevant pages, then pointed up higher on the wall. "Take down that one, with the lady in the silver dress. It's listed too."

Theo scrambled up to loosen the picture from the wall, and soon the empty hook swung from the wire.

He laid it down carefully, the painting side face-down on the table. But there was nothing on the back there, either. Only the same clean, blank canvas.

"Oh, no," Sarah said, feeling a lurch in the pit of her stomach. "I misinterpreted the code!"

"Don't panic, sweetheart." Theo bent to examine the piece. "There must be something here."

Anticipating work ahead, he shrugged out of his jacket and laid it across a chair. He turned his attention back to the painting, and so he didn't notice when the jacket slid to the floor.

Sarah stooped to pick it up. As she did, one of Charlie's notebooks fell from an inner pocket. She laid the coat aside, and flipped through the notebook, wondering which one Theo felt the need to bring along.

After only the first page, she knew it wasn't a book she'd seen before. A quick glance at the date showed it was the one Theo once said was missing. Clearly, it wasn't. So why hide it from her?

By that point, she had mastered Charlie's various codes so well that she could translate the words in her head. Sarah read silently as Theo continued to examine the painting, not noticing her distraction.

Bedded S today…

The words took a moment to filter into her brain. So Charlie did write about her. He wrote about *seducing* her. Humiliation washed over Sarah, followed quickly by anger. Anger at Charlie, for writing it. Anger at Theo, for knowing about it. And most of all, anger at herself, for being so foolish as to trust anyone.

"Sarah?"

She didn't even hear what Theo was saying. She couldn't rip her eyes off the page, reading the other damning phrases, the coded language not hiding anything after all.

Chapter 32

"SARAH?"

Turning from the painting in frustration, Theo found her standing very still, something held open in front of her like a prayer book. The notebook he had hidden from her.

Oh, hell. "Sarah. Put it down."

Instead she raised her eyes to watch him. "This is the journal you said was missing." Her voice was low, calm for the moment, but unlikely to remain that way.

"It's not important."

"When did you read this?"

He moved, ready to take it from her, as if that could do anything.

She gripped the notebook so tightly, the pages would rip if he tried. "When did you read this?" she repeated, her voice even lower.

"Sarah. It's not import…"

"When?"

He relented. "Last week or so."

"And you didn't tell me."

"What should I have told you?"

"It was about me! You let me go on, thinking…"

"Thinking what?"

"Thinking no one knew!" she burst out. Embarrassment warred with anger, and anger won.

"No one does. I didn't share the information."

"But *you* know."

"So?" Theo tried to appear calm, hoping she would match his tone. He should have burned the notebook immediately.

She glared down at the pages. "I can't believe he wrote that about me. On paper."

"Well, he did." Theo said shortly. "Whatever you think you knew about him, you can put it aside. He wasn't a hero. He was a liar, and a thief, and he betrayed you as much as anyone else."

She closed the book and handed it to Theo without looking at him. "I'm going upstairs. I have to lie down."

"Sarah…"

"Please leave me alone." Not looking at him, she fled up the steps.

He did leave her alone, for at least an hour. He pulled more paintings down, and tried to find some clue of what they came to the lodge to get. But she didn't come down, and he couldn't think about anything other than her. He kept looking up the stairs when he should have been looking at the art.

Giving up on the idea of solving the problem on his own, Theo went upstairs and knocked on the one closed door. "Sarah?"

After a moment, her voice came back, muffled and dull. "Go away."

"Come down where it's warm." The upper floor was distinctly chilly, and Sarah certainly hadn't lit a fire in her room.

"Sarah," he said again. He tried the handle and found the door opened easily. Feeling like he was intruding—mostly because he was—Theo stepped into the room, which was pitch dark despite the day outside. The open door illuminated a narrow sliver of the room, including the bed.

She lay on her side in the middle of the bed. She was on top of the bedcovers, though she had pulled another blanket over her against the cold.

"Can I get you anything?" he asked.

"No."

Theo turned to the fireplace. He'd light that, and at least she wouldn't freeze.

Within a moment or two, the flames gave the illusion of warmth, though it would take a while to dispel the chill. Theo saw Sarah's face now, staring at the flames… or at him.

"I'm sorry," she said.

"For what?" Of all the things she might have said, he hadn't been expecting an apology.

"Being so childish when you're doing important work."

"It can wait," he said, moving closer to her. He sat on the edge of the bed, but he was afraid to reach out and touch her at all. "And I should be the one to apologize. It was thoughtless of me to keep the book around you. Of course you'd be able to read the code."

"But you did know what was in it."

"I read the entries with the key, yes," Theo admitted. "I had to. He mixed everything up…the personal with the professional, that is."

"That's true," she said, with a laugh he didn't like at all. She shifted onto her back so she could look at him. "I was such a little fool. You knew the night I had to meet Rossi, didn't you? In the theater box. You already knew about me. But you didn't make me…"

"Sarah, for Christ's sake. What do you think I am?"

"What did you think *I* was? He wrote that down as if it were no more or less important than ordering a new suit. *Bedded Sarah, took her virginity, just to keep her in line.*"

"Don't think about it."

She only shook her head. "I thought he loved me. But he was just distracting me. Making me think of other things when I should have been thinking about what he was up to."

"He was good at persuading people to think what he wanted them to. That's why he was such an excellent agent. It wasn't your fault. He tricked you. He used you."

"I let him."

"You didn't know."

"How do you know what I knew? Or wanted? Maybe I begged him for it."

"Did you?"

She looked away. "No."

"Did he force you?" he asked quietly. Was it possible to kill someone twice? he wondered. If Charlie hurt Sarah like that, he deserved to die twice.

But Sarah was shaking her head. "No," she said quickly. "Nothing like that. He...persuaded me. Everything I knew came from books no one knew I was reading, and they didn't reveal much either. And he said I should know, and I was so pretty, and he loved me."

"You aren't pretty at all. You're beautiful."

"Is that meant to console me? I can't marry any man now. I should have known something was wrong. I'm not an alluring woman. I know it. Yes, I have nice features. Mama always thanked Heaven for that. But I don't know how to flirt, or..." She sighed. "Wouldn't it make sense that he only saw me as a tool? A thing to use for his design, and then...done. I'm unnecessary, and can be tucked safely away to be the invisible wife. Meanwhile he goes off onto other, more interesting conquests."

"Even if he was an ass—which he was—it doesn't mean there's a thing wrong with you."

"I'm *all* wrong. I'm compromised, ruined, and completely at odds with society."

"Ruined how? No one knows. You're safe."

"But I'm not..."

"That's your fear? That you're no longer a virgin? If you fell in love and lost yourself with the one you expected to marry, that's understandable. And not unheard of, by the way. You know how many brides are already carrying their first child when they speak their vows?"

"But I'm *not* a bride, am I? I never will be. And anyway, I knew it was wrong. Ladies don't behave that way. But he said he couldn't resist..." She closed her eyes. "Forgive me. Of course you don't want to hear this."

He didn't. Except that part of him *did* want to know exactly what Charlie had done to her, so Theo could do it better and destroy her previous memories.

Sarah opened her eyes again, and there was a different light in them. Something more determined. "Are you jealous?" she asked, with uncanny insight.

"Yes." Yes, he was, and he always would be. He did not want to be in competition with a dead man.

But he wanted Sarah. Leaning down, he kissed her. Sarah sighed just a little—and it worked better than any flirtation. He *wanted* her. Some dark part of him wanted to have her and keep her so only he'd ever get to see her. That was what obsession was, wasn't it?

Sarah melted under his mouth. He loved how sweetly responsive she was, how curious she was. Because she wanted him too.

That latent realization burst on him all at once. "Sarah, this isn't why I asked you to come with me."

"I know that," she whispered back. "But since we are here, I have a request." Her tone betrayed how shy she was feeling.

"What?"

"Could you make me forget him?"

She had a gift for telling him what he wanted to hear. "I will try, sweetheart."

Chapter 33

♉

SARAH NEARLY FAINTED AS HE kissed her again, opening her mouth to let him in. Then he gently pushed her back against the pillows. "One thing, sweetheart. This time I get to see your face."

Sarah nodded. Then she kissed him, and she reveled in that. *She* kissed *him*. She wasn't sure she was doing it correctly, but the way he held her suggested he wanted to keep her close. Sarah tried to cover every inch of his skin, moving from his mouth to his jaw to his neck. Her lips got scratched by stubble she couldn't see, but the sensation was exciting rather than irritating. By the time she reached the spot behind his ear, Theo's breathing was strained. He kissed her back until she felt far too warm in her clothing.

When her curiosity had both of them deeply entranced, she pulled back for a moment. "Theo, when we… I'd like to be naked."

"Of course," he said, laughing a little. "That's a given, sweetheart."

"Is it?"

His eyes narrowed. "Are you telling me that…and I'm

not going to say his name…when he seduced you, he didn't appreciate you enough to take your clothing off?"

"Ah…no," Sarah said, blushing furiously.

"A traitor *and* an idiot." Theo closed his eyes for a second. "Did…never mind."

"What?"

"Did he take your hair down?"

"No. Do you want to take my hair down?" she asked.

"God, yes. But I want you naked first."

"Oh."

Theo shifted, helping her to stand up at the side of the bed. He rose too, and Sarah let her hands fall on his chest. "What should I do?" she asked. "Please tell me what you'd like."

He bit his lip. "Where to start," he said, musingly.

"It's hard to get out of my gown until the buttons at the back are undone," she said helpfully.

He reached around to attend to the buttons at the gown's back, all the while watching her face. A little smile hovered at his lips.

"You're enjoying this," Sarah said, almost accusingly.

"You have no idea," he said. The gown suddenly felt loose around her bust, and Sarah instinctively caught at the fabric to keep it up.

"Don't do that," he said, pulling her hands away. He then tugged at the sleeves and the whole thing fell in a pool at her feet. She still wore her stays and the chemise underneath, but the fabric concealed very little. She hoped her figure would please him. She knew ideal women were praised for a sylph-like shape, but she was heavier and curvier than that.

Theo untied the ribbons of the stays, and soon there was only the cotton of the chemise, and her stockings. He looked her over consideringly, then knelt down to deal with the stockings first. He took his time, sliding his hand up each leg to roll the thin fabric down. He teased her skin along the way, until Sarah wasn't sure she could stand up without help.

"I can do the last part myself," she said. Then she paused. "It's not fair that you're still dressed. So won't you do that? For me?"

"It's not," he agreed with a sly look. He reached for his shirt.

She watched as he took off his own clothes. Despite her history, it was the first time she had ever seen a man's naked body. Theo was beautiful, she thought. His skin was a few shades deeper than hers, with hair on his legs and chest. He was sleekly muscled from riding. And he was completely aroused, she noted with shy glance. Somehow, she had done that.

She smiled, unable to stop a delighted laugh. "I'm glad I asked," she said.

"So am I," he said. "Now finish, sweetheart."

She gathered the fabric of the chemise and pulled it over her head, feeling Theo's hands on her waist as soon as her skin was exposed.

"You're beautiful," he said, surveying her, appreciation clear in his eyes. "Can I take your hair down?"

"Please."

First, he pushed the bedding aside, and sat back, leaning against the headboard, bringing her with him. With his hands still on her waist, he encouraged her to straddle his legs, kneeling so she faced him. Sarah thought the position completely scandalous, and also incredibly interesting.

He found each pin holding her braids in place and pulled them out one by one. He took his time, plainly enjoying the ritual. Sarah felt shy at first, but as he handed her each pin, she found she enjoyed it too.

On one level, it was always a relief to lose the pins. But now the relief combined with arousal, so that she could hardly wait for him to finish. When the pins were out, she pulled the braids over her shoulders to cover her chest.

Theo sat back again. "Loosen the braids," he said.

"You don't want to do it?"

"I want to watch you."

She threaded her fingers through one braid, loosening the three parts up from the bottom, until half her hair lay in waves over her body. "I should continue?"

"Yes."

She smiled. She could somehow make him so aroused he could barely speak. She didn't understand it, but she liked it. Sarah unthreaded the second braid, the gold hair coming loose in a growing wave until it concealed her torso.

Theo leaned forward. He swept her hair back over her shoulders, revealing her breasts. When he was done, Sarah's hair fell down her back and the fine strands floated over her skin.

"What…what do you think?" she asked.

His expression was enough to make her weak. "No man's ever seen your hair like this?" he asked.

She shook her head, causing the stands to glint in the dim light. "You're the first. And likely the only."

"Good," he said, his voice raw. "You're beautiful. All of you."

He ran his hands over her skin, already damp with heat. Sarah sighed when he grazed her breasts, cupping each one and teasing her nipples to hardness. He then stroked his hands down her stomach, sending shivers through her. But she gasped in surprise when he pulled her hips toward him, drawing her close to his erection.

"Shouldn't I be on my back?" she asked, suddenly anxious.

"Later, perhaps. I'm enjoying this far too much to rush."

She laughed, a trace of nerves showing through. "I'm afraid I don't know anything. It's funny. I did this once, which was enough to ruin me and forever make me impure…but I didn't learn a thing. I'm just as ignorant as before."

"You're not ignorant. You're innocent."

She laughed. "According to who?"

"According to me." His eyes were serious. "And I'm going to teach you a few things that have nothing to do with putting you on your back." He moved one hand to the curls between her legs, touching her until he found the most sensitive part.

Sarah sighed with pleasure. "Please keep doing that."

"That's *exactly* what I want to hear, sweetheart."

He continued to watch her reactions as he explored her. When he slipped a finger inside her, Sarah's legs went weak. She was shockingly wet. She could feel it.

"Theo…" she whispered. "Please."

She wasn't sure what she was asking him to do, but he kept touching her, asking her to tell him if she liked what he did. She answered in little gasps and moans, giving herself up to him until she rocked her hips against his body and came undone in a slow wave of pure bliss.

As the sensation subsided, Sarah bent over him, feeling his arms around her. "I liked that," she said. "I'm just a little light-headed. Can I lie down?"

"Whatever you say, sweetheart." He shifted to lay her on her back, and settled himself above her. He was still hard. She could sense the tension in him. And she knew she wanted more.

Yet Theo just kissed her, capturing her mouth with his. His tongue licked her lower lip until she sighed, squirming with pleasure. "Why are you waiting?" she asked.

"First," he said. "I'm not waiting. I'm enjoying you. I want to hear you, and watch you, and smell you and touch you, and I'm never going to get enough of you." He pulled back enough to smile at her. "Second, anticipation is a pleasure all its own."

She looked at him, knowing what really was in store for her. "It's all right. I know it will hurt."

He shook his head. "It won't hurt at all."

He positioned himself above her, pushing her legs apart with his body. He bent to kiss her again, his mouth hot against her throat. He told her she was perfect, and she wanted to believe him.

Then she felt his hard length just touching the center of her body. Sarah was so certain there would be pain, just like the first time, that she tensed up instantly.

"Take a deep breath, sweetheart," he said quietly. "Trust me. This time will be better."

She did, and her body relaxed. He went slowly, gauging her response. She felt everything: Theo filling her, the pressure of his body on hers, the heat they both generated under the blanket. But there was no pain.

"You're right," she whispered. "This is better."

He smiled a little. "You're just telling me what I want to hear."

"No! I can't lie to you, Theo. Not now. How did you know you wouldn't hurt me?"

"One, you were meant for me, and two, you're so deliciously, marvelously wet that I know you're ready."

She swallowed, going hot at the passion in his voice. "Is that a good thing?"

He shifted inside her, and his moan was answer enough. Sarah felt a thrill down to her toes that she could please him like this. "What should I do?"

"Come undone," he ordered. "Again. I want you to need me."

He moved within her, and Sarah forgot her shyness. The sensations were overwhelming, though, and before she even got used to the rhythm, she found her body aching for release. Her breath betrayed her, quickening until she once again tried to hide her face from him.

"No," he said firmly, tilting her head back to him. "You promised. And I love seeing you."

So she let him see her as her whole body shuddered with pleasure. His eyes went dark as he watched her, and listened to her gasp in relief. Her breathing slowed after a moment, though she still felt like a touch of his finger could destroy her.

After a moment, he moved again, reveling in her body. Sarah felt his own breathing speed up, but then he withdrew from her and abruptly gave one gasp of release as he came. She sensed both desire and disappointment in his voice.

"Did I do something wrong?" she asked, concerned.

"No, but I nearly did." Theo sighed. He turned onto his back so he could wrap her in his arms.

Then she understood. "Ah. That was for my benefit?"

"To protect you, at least to try. When we're married, I won't do that."

"Theo," she said gently. "I'm not the one you're going to marry."

He looked at her, but said nothing.

Then she said, "But we could pretend for a little while."

"That's a fine idea, love."

Sarah lay half over him, a pose that felt surprisingly natural, considering she'd never done it before. She wished it would be the first of many times. She supposed she should feel ashamed of her behavior. Perhaps she would be later. But it seemed foolish to do so right then, when she could simply enjoy having Theo next to her. She traced lazy circles on his chest with her finger, hoping to memorize him.

Perhaps Theo was right about his belief that they somehow knew each other long before they met. It couldn't be coincidence that her head could nestle so comfortably in the spot between his shoulder and neck. And it couldn't be coincidence that their bodies joined so perfectly. She tried to remember what it had been like the first time, but then realized it didn't matter to her any longer. What mattered was the moment she had now.

Smiling to herself, Sarah wriggled into an even more comfortable position on Theo, hooking one foot around his leg. He responded by bestowing a kiss on her forehead and tightening his hold around her waist.

"Imagine if we could stay like this," she murmured, not expecting an answer.

"I already am," he said quietly.

Chapter 34

♉

AFTER A WHILE, THEO FELL into a doze. Sarah didn't. She watched the flames in the fireplace, her mind awake and burning with questions. Unfortunately, too many of them had nothing to do with the man next to her. Had this whole excursion been for nothing, other than her complete ruin, of course? How could she have been so wrong about the role of the art? There were too many hints, too many connections. It must have some significance.

She eased out from under Theo's arm. He made a discontented sound in his sleep, which made her smile. She leaned over and kissed his cheek, as she imagined a wife would. Why not? She wouldn't have to face reality until they left.

She dressed hurriedly and then slipped out of the room. She went downstairs to where the paintings still lay face down on the table and the floor. The sunlight coming in the uncurtained windows blinded her for a moment. Was it possible so little time had passed?

She looked over the room. Where had she gone wrong? What had she misunderstood? And why did she think the answer would reveal itself now? What had changed?

She had changed. Though not a virgin before, she knew she wasn't quite the same woman she was when she'd run up the stairs a few hours ago. Theo said he believed in fate. Perhaps she had to believe in something too. Logic hadn't got her anywhere.

"What are you hiding?" she asked the painting lying in the center of the table. Once again, she ran her hands around the frame, feeling for some catch, something not right. She found nothing. Little flecks of oil paint stuck to the back of the frame, but there were no words, no clues, nothing to indicate the stains weren't perfectly normal.

Stains.

Sarah looked at the canvas back again. The frame was stained with numerous drips and a smudged fingerprint. She was not an artist, but she knew oil paints were by nature messy. How could the frame be so marked up while the back of the painting itself escaped? No paint had soaked through? No smudges touched it? Impossible.

Excitement shot through her. There *was* something wrong about the painting after all. She plucked at the tacks holding the painting in the frame, ripping her fingernail in the process. After a moment she managed to free the stretched canvas, and the back suddenly bubbled out a bit.

"That's it," she breathed. There was an extra layer. With trembling hands, she separated it from the original painting. A single sheet of paper was tucked between the layers, undetectable under the heavier weight of the canvas.

Sarah pulled the sheet free, and saw it was a letter written in French. Too elated to read it, she actually jumped up and down a little bit. Theo had to see it.

Sarah took the stairs almost at a run. Theo must have heard her, because he was already sitting up when she flung the door open.

"What's wrong?" he asked.

"Theo! Nothing's wrong! Look!"

She hurtled toward the bed and pushed the letter into his hands.

He caught her as she overbalanced and nearly crashed into him. "Calm down, sweetheart. What is it?"

"Calm? A letter! Between the canvas! From France!" Sarah knew she was babbling but she was too excited to stay calm. "Please look at it. Is it important? He must have reframed all the art to make the second layer…"

"Darling," Theo said, pulling her next to him. "Take a breath."

Sarah did, and suddenly blushed, remembering he was still naked under the sheet, and that she'd all but thrown herself at him. Again.

Fortunately, Theo didn't see her reaction because he was staring at the letter, trying to read it in the dim light of the dying fire. "Can you open a curtain?" he asked. "I can barely see this."

Sarah rushed to the window and flung aside one drape. A bolt of sunlight illuminated the whole room. She turned. "Better?"

Theo nodded, still lost in the letter. Sarah used the

time to steal a hungry look at him. She should be mortified by her behavior, yet all she could think was that he was beautiful and she was lucky he was the one to cross her path.

He finished reading the letter, putting it down with a sigh.

"Well?" asked Sarah. "Was it worth hiding?"

"Definitely. One could ask a few hundred pounds for this."

"Is that the going rate for such things?"

"It all depends on what it contains." He sat up straighter, realizing the full implications. "My God, why did you let me sleep? You found out how he hid the papers!"

She laughed, giddy. "Yes. There's an extra layer of canvas across the back of each painting. I was looking at them all, and I thought oil paints are so messy. The canvases shouldn't be so clean. So I ripped apart the one and found the extra layer. The letter was laid absolutely flat. There was no way to detect a bump or a line under the thickness of the canvas."

"Sarah, you're brilliant."

"No, I'm not. I should have seen it immediately," she said, embarrassed at the praise.

He held up the letter. "Come here and look at this."

She walked over to the bed to look at the letter, but as soon as she got near, Theo reached out with his free arm and pulled her onto the bed, so she was laying over him.

"What are you doing?"

He didn't loosen his hold. "You're brilliant. Say it."

"I'm not."

"Say it."

"Or what?"

"Or I won't let you go."

She smiled. "Perhaps I'm not keen to be let go."

He moved to kiss her, but just as soon as she started to respond, he repeated, "You're brilliant. I want to hear you say it."

"You're brilliant," she parroted.

"Sarah," he warned. "I'm an agent of a secret organization, I'm trained to be ruthless, and I've just proven to have the morals of a feral cat. Don't push me."

Sarah laughed at his threat, but finally said, "Very well. I'm brilliant."

"That's my darling."

He kissed her again, and this time he didn't stop for a while. Sarah only recalled herself when the crackle of paper intruded on her consciousness.

"Theo," she murmured. "I think you're lying on an important government document."

"Bloody hell." He shifted and reluctantly let her go.

Sarah rescued the precious letter from the bedsheets. "Don't you want to see if there are more?"

He nodded, his expression growing more alert. "Yes, I do." He looked around the room. "I don't suppose you could help me find all my clothes, sweetheart? I was distracted when I took them off."

Sarah blushed again—she seemed to do that constantly around Theo—and moved off the bed to retrieve all the clothing he shed earlier.

"I'll wait for you downstairs," she said. The idea of staying and watching him dress was somehow more decadent than the reverse had been.

Theo must have known exactly what she was thinking, judging by his sly look. "You could stay."

"Theo!" she said. "You're an agent of a secret organization, and you have work to do."

"Taskmaster," he grumbled.

Sarah fled the room before he might convince her to linger.

Moments later he was dressed and downstairs, totally focused on the issue at hand. Following Sarah's lead, he dismantled painting after painting. Sometimes he destroyed the art itself, but neither of them cared.

As they worked through the list of paintings, they amassed a small pile of documents, all carefully hidden the same way. Theo scanned each one before putting it aside. Sarah didn't ask to see them, despite her natural curiosity. If they were important enough to steal, their contents were surely confidential for a reason.

She looked around the room, and at the devastation they'd wrought. "Someone will surely think a gang of culture-hating vandals broke in."

Theo glanced around too, then shrugged. "Better than someone guessing the truth."

"We should clean it up."

"We'll take care of it before we leave." He pulled another paper from the painting he'd just dismantled, and was skimming it already. "Sarah," he said. "This has to be it. What Rossi was hoping to find."

"What is it?"

He looked over at her. "It's from an emissary of Prussia. A letter responding to a suggested marriage alliance between Princess Charlotte and Prince Frederick."

"She's just a child! And anyway, I thought it was hoped she'd marry William of the House of Orange."

"It seems someone thinks the situation is still to be decided. If this became public, even to know that it was considered, it would look very bad. The King would be seen as unreliable. Other nations would point to this as evidence that other agreements couldn't be trusted."

"You think that's what Rossi is after?"

"It's the most valuable thing I can imagine." Theo held up a few other documents. "This one negotiates the purchase of land for government shipyards overseas, but it's dated six months ago. This other document is a secret recommendation to better fortify the Port of Rochefort. That would have been useful *before* the French attempted to intercept a shipment of supplies to the West Indies last September." He put them all down again. "If I could only buy one of these letters, I'd buy the one about the Princess. It's the most potentially valuable and the least likely to expire."

"But perhaps they don't even know. They wanted the whole cache—Rossi and Villani. They were never negotiating for one of these. They just knew Charlie possessed something valuable, and they're gambling that what I bring them will be profitable."

He frowned. "That's possible. Actually, it makes things a bit easier. You can bring them all of these—with the exception of the Princess letter—and they'll discover their gamble didn't pay off."

"What will they do to me then?" Sarah asked nervously.

Chapter 35

♉

THEO STOOD UP AND LEFT all the papers on the floor. He walked over to her and drew her close. "Sarah, you can't imagine I'd let you be in danger for this. I'll plan it out so you're covered the whole time."

"How can you do that when it's just you?"

"Who said it would just be me?" He smiled. "Now that I know what to expect, I have a few reliable people to lean on. I'm not letting anything happen to you."

He bent his head and kissed her. He only intended to reassure her, but one touch of her mouth was enough to remind him of all that just happened upstairs. He wanted her all over again. There wasn't enough time to do everything he dreamed about doing with her. Frustration gnawed at him.

"What is it?" Sarah asked. "You have that look on your face."

"What look?"

"The one you get when you're deciding whether to speak or not."

How the hell did she read him so well? "Sarah, are you a mind reader?"

"If I were, I'd know what you were thinking. But I just know that you are. Won't you tell me?"

He almost laughed. "If you knew what I was thinking, you'd faint."

"I didn't faint before," she protested. "I was quite scandalous. Admit it. You were a *little* shocked by my behavior."

"A little. But I like it." He ran his hand lightly over one breast, drawing a soft *oh* from her. "I'd keep you here for days if I could get away with it."

"That sounds like an invitation for debauchery."

"It would be. But all the same, I'd do it. Once just isn't fair."

"You said spies don't use the word fair."

"I'm not speaking as a spy. I'm speaking as a man."

Sarah stretched to kiss him, then wrapped her arms around his neck. "Make me faint," she whispered. "Tell me what you're thinking."

Theo would make her regret that bit of boldness. "All right. Just tell me when you want me to stop." He slid one hand down her back and cupped her bottom before bringing her against him. Sarah gave a little gasp of surprise but didn't pull away.

"I am thinking that you'd look beautiful lying on that table, right where the sun is hitting now. I'd take off your clothes and have you—me standing up, you on your back, sweetheart—and I'd bury my face in your hair while you beg me for more."

Sarah's eyes grew round, but she said, "I'm not fainting yet."

"I'm just getting started." He shifted so he could touch her between her legs. "You like it when I touch you there."

"Yes," she said in a shaking voice.

"You'd like my mouth there even more."

"That's not a real thing," she said, disbelievingly. "People don't *do* that." She paused, her expression speculative and not nearly faint enough. "Do they? I mean, you want to do that to me?"

"Find out," he said. "Come upstairs with me."

She let him take her to the bedroom again. She let him take her clothes off and lay her back on the bed. She let him kiss her whole body. She let him lick her in places, some innocent, some not, until she nearly *did* faint, even though she denied it. At the end she sighed, her expression both peaceful and astonished. And through it all, she never once told him to stop. She asked him for more.

They lay together on the bed, warm under the covers. Sarah propped herself up on one elbow and kissed him sweetly.

He loved to hear her reactions, raw and unaffected. He wanted to be inside her again, but he doubted whether he'd be able to withdraw in time. Sarah was too arousing, too tantalizing. And she trusted him.

But then she touched him, and he remembered he could also trust her.

"You don't mind?" she whispered.

He felt her running her fingers along his erection. He felt slightly faint himself. "Just the opposite."

"I thought…because I liked it when you touched me,

that…"

"Keep thinking, sweetheart."

She smiled at his tone, and continued to touch him. He lay back, extremely willing to see where Sarah's thinking took them. She went slowly, which delighted him. She was an amazingly attentive student, and he was soon ready to explode.

"If you let me keep doing this," she said shyly, "will it satisfy you? I mean, earlier when you made love to me, you didn't want to…for my benefit…" she trailed off, not sure how to explain herself.

"Keep your hand on me," he said. "And yes, it will be satisfying." He came when she leaned forward to kiss him and crushed their bodies together. The combination of her skin and her mouth on his was all he needed.

She curled up by him afterward, saying, "Well. I wonder what I could say to make *you* faint."

"Don't give me more ideas, sweetheart." Theo resented every minute that slipped by. He kept her in his arms as she dozed, selfishly wanting to hold her as long as possible, even with the threat that they'd delay too long and destroy Sarah's alibi. He didn't care. Sarah was his.

But his better sense fought back. Ruining Sarah's reputation when he had no way of correcting the issue was a terrible way to treat her. He slipped out of the bed and dressed. If he was dressed, he'd be less inclined to want to return to the bed.

"Sarah, sweetheart, you have to get up," Theo said, putting his hand on her shoulder. "We have to go back."

She blinked, trying to wake up. "Is it time?"

"Sadly, yes." He smiled, though, hoping to stave off the inevitable.

She dressed while Theo finished tidying up the lodge. He had already cleaned up most of the evidence of the art destruction, burning what couldn't be hung back up. It wasn't perfect, but it would have to do.

"All right," he said, giving the place a final look in the dying light. "We can leave as soon as you've put on your coat." He moved around in a circle, uncharacteristically nervous.

"What's wrong?" she asked.

"Nothing. That is, nothing I can put my finger on. I just don't want to leave a trail."

"A trail for who?" Sarah asked. "Do you think someone else knows about this place?"

"It's not a secret he owned it. But anyone interested in Charlie's past had ample opportunity to break in." He still worried. "I just have an odd feeling."

"Then let's get moving," she said. "What will you do once you return to London after dropping me off? With the letters, I mean?"

"Take them to my superior. We'll find out if any of them still have value—beyond the one. And if needed, we'll destroy them."

"Good," Sarah said. "Though I hate to travel all the way back carrying such things. It's worse than carrying gold and yelling the fact out loud."

"I'll feel better when they're in a safe place," he agreed.

Sarah put on her boots and her warm cloak. She had

only her reticule to carry. "I'm ready to go," she announced.

He surveyed her, not particularly ready himself. "Sarah, when we both return to London, I can't promise you anything."

"I didn't ask you to promise anything," she said, her face set. "I'm quite capable of making my own mistakes, and I'll decide which ones I choose to regret."

"So I am a mistake or a regret?"

"You're neither. You made me happy, at a time when no one else could." Then, she opened the door and walked outside.

Theo stared after her, moving through the snow to the stable. How could she do that? Say he made her happy, and then just walk away? Theo doubted he ever made a woman happy before. Satisfied, probably. But happy?

He closed the door behind him, and made sure the latch was caught. The air was clear and cold, but not bitter. In the early evening light, everything seemed pure and still. They were a bit behind schedule, but he rationalized that Sarah's perennially distracted parents were unlikely to remark on her absence, even for a full day.

He passed Sarah on the way to the small outbuilding that served as the stable. Then a faint jingling sound teased his ears. Horseshoes. Just within earshot. "Sarah," he hissed. "Get over here now."

She stiffened at his tone, but came without questioning. "What's wrong?"

"Someone is coming," he said.

"It doesn't mean they're coming here," she said.

"What else is around here?"

"You think it's them," she guessed. "Rossi and that woman. Giselle."

He nodded once. The feeling in his gut rarely betrayed him. "I asked her about the art Charlie bought. It must have made her think too. She must have learned the location of this place and come out to look, just as we did."

Theo glanced at the stables. "Listen to me very carefully, Sarah. The carriage won't work now. If someone unfriendly sees us, we need to be able to move fast."

"Then what do we do?"

"I'll take one horse and ride away in the opposite direction from town. You hide here until you can't hear anyone. Then saddle the other horse—you can do that?"

She nodded mutely.

"Saddle it and ride to London. Don't stop."

"But where will you go?"

"I'll distract them from you. You're the more important person."

"I am? Why?"

"Because you'll take the letters to the Zodiac."

Sarah blanched. "That's mad!"

"That's exactly what they'll think." He handed her the leather bag. "Take the papers. If they catch up to me— which they won't—I'll tell them I didn't find anything."

"They won't believe that if they catch you!"

"Let me worry about that." He kissed her. "Be careful, but go as fast as you dare."

"But where am I going?"

"There's a large red brick building at Powell and Gate

Street. You'll find the Zodiac inside."

"What?"

"*Hide*, Sarah." He pushed her toward the stable.

"Theo," she said, fear in her voice. "Why would they trust me? I have no proof I'm connected to you. I don't even know your sign, for God's sake."

"Yes, you do. You already guessed it."

"Taurus?"

He grinned and gave her a final swift kiss. "Remember, it's a secret." He pushed her back into the darkness of the stable. "Wish me luck, sweetheart."

Sarah looked like she wasn't going to let him go without a fight, but all she said was, "Good luck, and be careful!"

He saddled the horse within seconds. He was seen before he could mount and ride away, though that was a good thing. He *wanted* to be seen. It was Sarah who had to be invisible.

A shout came from the woods. Rossi emerged, riding a horse giant enough to accommodate his massive frame. Theo ignored the order to stop, of course. He swung up and nudged the horse. Sensing pursuit, it needed no urging.

He wheeled about and rode away. Away from Sarah. Away from the papers. Away from London. Rossi and the other rider—Giselle?—followed close behind. Theo laughed to himself. He'd bet any money neither of those two could ride half as well as he could.

The trick would be to keep them close enough that they wouldn't give up the pursuit. Excitement built up in his veins. He wasn't reckless by nature, but when his back was to the wall, he could always call on his inner daredevil.

The pursuers were so hot blooded that Theo had no trouble keeping their interest. The horse navigated the snowy woods with ease, and Theo made sure to keep visible, offering a clear trail for them to follow.

A shot rang out, and the snow exploded about twenty paces away. He glanced behind. The smaller rider, who had to be Giselle, was holding a pistol out. So they didn't care who he was, not even to keep him alive for questions. They just wanted the papers he might have. Nevertheless, Theo had no intention of getting killed. He urged his horse to a slightly faster pace and darted through the winter woods. The light was draining from the sky, and soon they'd be chasing a shadow.

Chapter 36

♉

AFTER THEO CHARGED OFF, LEADING the other riders away, Sarah waited until all sounds had faded. Her heart pattered. Theo was gone. He'd saved her from discovery, but at what cost?

The building at the corner of Powell and Gate, he said. That was where the Zodiac held court. She had to get help from them. But first she had to get to London.

Surprisingly, there was one lady's saddle there in the little stable. She knew how to saddle a horse, but she was clumsy, and the cold air made her hands more awkward, despite her gloves. She managed to get the saddle cinched, and mount the horse with the aid of the fence to climb on.

There was still no sound or sight of Theo or the pursuers. She glanced around once, then took a deep breath. She had the satchel with the papers, and London was less than two hours' ride.

Sarah had a good memory. She retraced the roads, and was soon on the main road to the city. She was wearing her heavy cloak, but she certainly hadn't intended to ride all the way, and was soon shivering. But Theo said not to stop. She had to get the letters to the Zodiac.

The ride was brutal, the road dark, and the air increasingly cold. Sarah's hands seemed frozen. Her body ached from the saddle. By complete happenstance, she managed to get the horse to a smoother canter, and that made part of the ride bearable.

Once in town, Sarah rushed to the address Theo gave her, not knowing what to expect. When she found the building, she left the horse with one of the boys who made a living watching over people's mounts for a few pennies. She entered the lobby, though at that hour, the space felt empty and cold. She halted, stymied by the choices offered to her. Over two dozen names were listed as being inside, and naturally none of them were the Zodiac.

How could she possibly guess which one was right? It wasn't as if she could wander into each office and ask 'Excuse me, are you secretly a group of spies working outside the official jurisdiction of His Majesty's government?'

Think, Sarah, she told herself. Theo trusted her to find the Zodiac. There had to be a hint somewhere in the names, or he would have told her more than the street direction. So she dutifully began to look at all the names listed.

Barclay and Joseph, Solicitors. No.

Gashson Livestock. No.

Mrs Minsleydale, Ladies' Employment Agency. Definitely not.

Circle Imports. Suppliers to the Crown.

Sarah smiled. Zodiac meant circle of animals. And

how better to describe espionage than the importing of information?

"Hiding in plain sight," she muttered. "Actually, hiding on the fifth floor."

It took her some time to navigate the various hallways and staircases. Though it looked like a classically symmetrical building from the outside, the interior seemed to have been designed by half a dozen architects who all loathed each other.

After a dozen twists and turns, Sarah reached the correct door. She tried the knob, only to find it locked.

What if she was wrong? What if this was just an ordinary company? They'd think her mad.

No. Theo gave her the address, and the name was too suggestive. She took a deep breath and knocked on the door. Nothing happened. She knocked again, more forcefully. She was sure someone moved on the other side.

"Hello?" she called. "Please, open up. It's very—"

The door opened and she was yanked inside by a strong arm.

"—important!" she finished with a gasp.

The door slammed shut.

Sarah was held fast by another woman, who had ash blonde hair and a furious expression. "How did you get here?" she hissed.

"Taurus sent me," Sarah said. "He's in trouble, and I need your help."

"And he just told you where to go?"

Sarah pressed back against the wall, surprised and frankly undone by the ferocity of the other woman. Who was she?

"Please, Miss Chattan," a new voice broke in. "That's no way to treat a guest."

"We don't have guests," the woman named Chattan said. But she released Sarah's arm.

"No, we certainly don't, as a rule." The man who had spoken walked forward and put a restraining hand on Chattan's shoulder. "So let's not frighten this one away."

Chattan pulled back, and Sarah took a deep breath, sagging against the wall.

"You're freezing," the man noted.

"I rode from Woodforde. It's a few hours' ride."

"You rode?" Chattan asked. "Alone?"

The man put one arm around her shoulders. "You need to sit down. Chattan, is there a spare rug around?"

"Of course, sir."

"Bring it to my office. This girl is practically iced over."

She focused on the man. He was a little shorter than she was, with calm eyes and sandy colored hair. She couldn't place his age at all.

She cleared her throat. "Please. My name is Sarah Brecknell. I knew Charlie—Pisces—and…"

"I know who you are, Miss Brecknell," he said. He guided her to the open door he'd emerged from. "You should have a seat in my office. You need to warm up first, and then we'll talk."

"But Theo needs help *now*." She was too distraught to notice she had used his first name.

"And he'll get it," the man promised. "But not until

you start breathing normally again and I get some answers. Do you want tea?"

Sarah wasn't sure she'd heard right. "Tea?"

"Yes. Miss Chattan is excellent at making tea, even more so than defending the Zodiac. Myself, I never put the correct amount of leaves in."

Sarah blinked. *This* was the spymaster protecting the whole nation? He seemed so…ordinary. "Will tea help?"

"It never hurts."

"Then yes. I mean, yes please."

"Do you take milk?" Chattan asked, appearing with a blanket and tucking it in around Sarah as if she hadn't just threatened her with bodily harm.

"Milk? No."

"Good. We don't have any." With those words Chattan moved off, apparently domesticated.

The man sat down opposite her. She looked around the large but rather cluttered office, which was lit by several lamps and a small fire that felt divine.

"So, welcome to the Zodiac, Miss Brecknell," he said. "Speaking of which, did Lord Markham happen to mention any other names to you? For instance, mine?"

"He said nothing," Sarah began, "until he absolutely had to. Then he only told me the location of this building, but he had no time for more details. I deduced it was Circle Imports from the name, but I don't know who you are." She took an unsteady breath, looking at the man. "Who *are* you?"

"Julian Neville, at your service. I'm also known as Aries, which I expect you'll never mention," he said easily. Sarah actually calmed down a little. Whoever he was, however odd the whole encounter was, he somehow did inspire confidence.

She asked, "How do you know who I am?"

"As you said, you knew Pisces, and we tend to look into people associated with our agents." His face darkened. "I assume you now know why we're still interested in his doings, even after his death."

"Unfortunately, I found out. Oh!" Sarah reached into the satchel. "I have the papers he stole."

"Indeed?" Julian looked very interested then.

Sarah handed over the Charlotte letter first. "Lord Markham said he was going to bring them all to you, before he rode off."

"Rode off," Julian murmured, though he was already perusing the letter. "Holy…" he started to say. "Wolverton would have been able to get thousands for this."

"That's what we thought, when we saw it."

"So how did Pisces hide these papers so well not even a trained agent could find them?"

"He made them look like something they weren't." Sarah hastily explained how they found the papers hidden among Charlie's ersatz art collection, and how Rossi followed them there and forced Theo to create a distraction by riding away.

Chattan came in with a cup of tea, placing it silently beside Sarah.

Julian handed the letter to his assistant, and then focused on Sarah again. "Tell me exactly what's been going on, please. Don't skip anything, and don't lie. I'll know."

Sarah took a sip of tea—Chattan *was* good at making it—and recounted events from the evening Rossi first appeared in her office at the Athenaeum. Julian listened to her whole account with hardly any interruptions. When she finished, he leaned back in his chair, regarding her with blue eyes that didn't miss a thing.

"So it actually was you who broke Charlie's codes," he said.

"Well, Markham was the one to find the notebooks. Once he learned about what I knew, he enlisted my assistance."

"And it was you who discovered how the papers were hidden."

"I was just lucky."

"I find your responses intriguing, Miss Brecknell."

"Why?"

"Because you're so certain your contributions are not worth very much."

Sarah opened her mouth, then closed it again, aware that she was about to confirm his statement.

He went on, "In fact, you know as much or more than my agent did."

"I couldn't have done anything if he hadn't been there."

Julian raised one eyebrow at her comment.

Sarah realized again what she'd done, but laughed a little. "I'm sorry. But you must believe me. I had no idea what Charlie was up to at the time. If I'd known what Charlie intended to do with the knowledge…"

Julian waved her concern away. "He fooled a lot of

people. Including me, I'm ashamed to say."

She took a sip of the tea, nodding. Then she said, "Markham sent me here, and he said he would come back to London if he could…but I'm not certain he can. Won't you help find him?"

"We'll help. But it will cost you."

"It's already cost me," Sarah said warily.

"I suppose it has," Neville said, perhaps thinking of Charlie's many sins. "But still, I'm not doing this out of altruism."

"What is the cost, exactly?"

"We'll talk about that later. I assume you'll be missed soon."

Sarah nodded. It was hours past the time she was to be back home. It felt like days had gone by.

"Then leave this to us," he said. "If you want to help, you can do so by returning to your normal life and pretending absolutely nothing has happened."

She was taken back outside and bundled into a carriage by Miss Chattan, who told her not to worry about the horse, and wished her good luck. Sarah certainly needed it.

Her stomach tied itself in knots the whole way home. She was exhausted, and different, and overwhelmed. When her familiar house came into view, Sarah blinked as if she'd never seen it before.

When she opened the door, she expected to see her parents standing there, fuming at her absence and ready to lock her away to preserve what little was left of the family name.

As it happened, she found her father in the small parlor, lost in a book.

"Papa?" she asked hesitantly.

He looked up and smiled at her, his grey eyes blinking above his spectacles. "Oh, there you are, dearest," he said. "Did you stay late at the Athenaeum again? I must say, your mother may be right. You're spending too much time alone, after all."

Sarah gaped. She had left the city with a man she wasn't supposed to be with, discovered priceless documents her fiancé had stolen, been completely ravished—*twice*, ridden home alone, then met Britain's spymaster, and no one even noticed her absence?

"Papa," she began, then stopped. It was too much to comprehend at the moment. "You're right. Perhaps I will stay home tomorrow."

"Wonderful, dear. You are always so accommodating." He held up the book. "You know, this version of Herodotus is quite something. You should read it if you're feeling a vicarious need for excitement."

"What a good idea, Papa." Sarah wanted to laugh hysterically. What she felt was a vicarious need for peace.

* * * *

In the empty winter woods, Theo maintained a steady lead over his pursuers, keeping them hot on his trail but unable to close a gap. Once he was sure Sarah had ample time to saddle her own horse and get well away from Woodforde on the road to London, he had to make a decision. He could speed up, lose them, and cut away onto a different road back to London. Or he could draw them further onward, hoping to isolate them and get some answers once no one was around to stop him from questioning Rossi and his devilish companion.

Though there was an appeal to leading them to an out-of-the-way spot where Theo could interrogate them, it was a high risk for little immediate reward. He already knew they would be in place when they arranged to get the papers from Sarah, and he knew Arceneau would likely be there as well. On a practical level, going alone against Rossi and Villani was not a good move.

With a certain regret, he decided retreat was the best option. He urged his mount to a pace most fresh horses wouldn't match, and soon lost any pursuit. Night had fallen completely by then, and he was confident no one could track him. After a sprint, he turned abruptly onto another track, then circled back to the road to London. He couldn't risk returning to the hunting lodge. The carriage was still there, which was unfortunate, since it was evidence of their intrusion. But it was the price to pay.

A few hours later, he was within the boundaries of London. The horse was spent, so he rode slowly toward the offices of the Zodiac. He ought to have gone straight home, but he had to know if Sarah was safe.

He knocked on the door, and waited an eternity for Chattan to open it.

She said, "We've been expecting you."

He stepped in and she closed the door after him. "Is she here?" he asked.

"Not any longer," Chattan said. "We sent her home a

few hours ago. With luck, her rather long absence will be explained, but the young lady is now very much back in her own life."

He nodded. That was where she was safest. Away from him. "She brought the papers, though?"

"Oh, yes. Aries would like to discuss the next steps with you, by the way. Go on in. He's there now."

Julian waved him to a chair as soon as he saw him. "Sit. Your companion was most interesting."

"I noticed that myself," Theo said, in a neutral tone.

At Julian's request, Theo told him everything he knew about Matteo Rossi, Giselle Villani, and Arceneau. He finished with the news of Arceneau himself coming to get the cache of letters Sarah found.

"Which makes it too dangerous for her to actually be involved in this final exchange," he finished. "Yet, I can't think of how to avoid it. Miss Brecknell has been seen by both Matteo and Giselle. They'll know if someone impersonates her."

Julian nodded. "All such details will be worked out when we meet."

"We?"

"Certain people have been at me to allow the signs to work together. I can't imagine a better opportunity than this handoff with Arceneau. Go home and get yourself in shape." He handed a piece of paper to Theo. "Tomorrow evening at ten, go to this house on Spruce Street. Young Jem could tell you all about it. He's worked in that house."

"And I'll meet another sign there?"

"Why stop at one?" Julian asked. "You'll meet a few."

Chapter 37

♉

UNAWARE OF THE MACHINATIONS OF spies all around the city, Alyse suffered through the smaller frustrations of London society. She went to teas. She visited. She left cards and she laughed at clever jokes.

All the while, she felt like she was going to burst out of her skin with the secret she hid from the world. She was astonished no one could see the change in her. How could everyone be so utterly blind?

But then, everyone had their own lives to live. No one cared much about what was going on inside Alyse's heart…other than Elena. Her mother was giddy with planning the wedding. Alyse could barely speak to her on any other subject. Her whole family seemed to take for granted that she was delighted with her planned future.

Well, a few weeks ago, she would have thought so, too.

Whenever she could, she rushed to see Elena, eager to reclaim the illicit, dizzying happiness she always experienced with the other woman. Alyse stayed as long as she dared. Elena told her more about Egypt, and Alyse knew she needed to see it.

Elena held her close, and stared dreamily at the painting over the mantel. "It will be magnificent," she was saying. "You'll fall in love with the landscape, darling. Nothing but sand and sky. It's another world. And we'll be together, and no one can reprimand us or tell us what to do."

"It sounds like a dream," Alyse whispered. "I wouldn't have dared to even dream that."

"Well, you don't have to dream," Elena said. "Join me. We can leave dreary England behind and sail into the future. Our future. Beautiful, yes?"

Elena bent her head and kissed Alyse softly. Alyse felt so beloved she almost wanted to cry.

"Elena, darling. I…I can't come with you."

The other woman went still. "Why not?"

"I'm not like you, Elena. I'm not bold." Alyse shifted, sitting up, and then looked away. "I don't live for adventure. I was bred to be a lady and to learn to keep a house. It's my role."

"Your role? What do you mean?"

Alyse stood up and paced agitatedly from one side of the room to the other. "My role as part of the family. My mother is already knee-deep in paper for wedding invitations. I don't know what to do."

"Well, marry him if you must. It won't change anything between us. A marriage is meaningless."

Alyse frowned at her. "Not to me! I have a duty, Elena. I will speak vows that day. Should I break them?"

"Why not?" Elena gave a short laugh. "He will."

"Does that mean I should do the same? It's not right to

go into a covenant like marriage in bad faith."

"What isn't right is that you should be sold like chattel for the sake of your family's position in society."

"Oh, you don't understand at all!"

"No, I don't. What nonsense…hiding behind outmoded expectations." Elena sat up too. Her expression grew set, the way it did when she was preparing to argue her position.

"Don't pretend this is easy," Alyse said. "Don't pretend that I have no other considerations."

"What considerations? Markham? You were promised to this man while you were still a child, Alyse. What hold does he have over you?"

"Friendship, if nothing else. You talk like our marriage was some form of trade agreement. It was nothing so callous. Our families have always been close. If I don't love Theo the way a normal woman loves a man, do not imply that I do not love him at all. There are many types of love, as you should know."

Elena pursed her lips. "So tell him that. If he *loves* you, then he'll understand."

Alyse quailed. The thought of telling Theo the truth… he was her friend. But it did not follow that he would understand, much less condone her secret. "That's not fair," she whispered.

"It's not fair that you would compromise where he does not!" Elena's cheeks flushed with anger.

"He compromises as much as I do!" Alyse argued. "He'll be marrying a woman who will never love him in the way he deserves."

"Then you ought to tell him, so he can find a woman he deserves!"

"But I…can't!" Alyse wailed.

Elena stood firm, uncompromising. "You can."

"It's all very easy for you to say. You never had to make that choice."

"But you do, my love." Elena's voice softened. "Please come with me. You don't have to confront any- one. Just write after the deed is done. After you're free. Come with me. I love you."

Alyse shook her head. She tried to speak, but couldn't.

Elena looked at her, and then sighed. "I can't force you. But the ship will sail on the appointed date. My work requires that I be on board. I leave the decision to you, my love."

Alyse still couldn't respond. She went over to where her pelisse and hat were stored.

Elena watched, her face clouding. "Alyse. I'm sorry. Come back."

"No. I need to go home soon anyway."

"Come back tomorrow then."

Alyse looked at her, and saw Elena's skin flushed with both anger and desire. "I don't know."

"Please."

"I have to think. Good night."

She left the suite and the hotel behind.

Alyse felt like a noose was slowly tightening around her. Slowly, and not painfully, but a noose all the same. And eventually it would kill her.

The worst part was she could tell no one what was in

her heart. Elena listened, but didn't understand. She had already thrown aside her own respect for the society she grew up in, and she had no patience for those who were not so bold.

Her family would never accept the truth. Alyse would be put away in a mad house, assuming she wasn't forced to marry first.

And Theo. She had the sense Theo might listen to her…if only the situation didn't involve him! How could he listen fairly if it meant his own pride would be wounded? No, she couldn't hurt him that way.

She had to find a way forward on her own.

Chapter 38

♉

AT HER HOME ON FRIDAY morning, Sarah felt ill at ease. She'd done nothing but hide at home or in the Athenaeum for months. But a fortnight of clandestine sneaking around—and a forbidden romance—had completely changed her. She could not imagine anything worse than simply waiting for life to happen.

But at the moment, she had no options other than to play the role of dutiful daughter. She sat in the bright parlor. Sarah had put aside her book already, and was repairing a few items of clothing. Her sewing skills were mediocre, but the task was simple enough—just reattaching a few buttons and mending a hem. Naomi did all the more delicate work, but Sarah knew that she also had a responsibility to see to the household tasks.

Her mother was in the room too. She had rallied from her illness—which was never satisfactorily identified—much to Sarah's relief. She had gotten up from bed, and sat in the parlor by the fire, just as she had before. She was reading letters, though she took frequent pauses, complaining of a headache.

"You've been quiet, Sarah dear," her mother said suddenly.

"Yes," she replied. "I've been thinking."

"You're always thinking. What occupies you now?"

Sarah put down the mending. "I was thinking I may wish to travel this summer. I feel cooped up here in town. And even Wheystoke may be too confining. What if I could go a bit farther away?"

"Where would you like to go? Bath?" Her mother shifted, growing interested in this new conversation. Sarah had never suggested traveling before.

Before Sarah could answer, Naomi entered. "Lord Carlin is here to see Miss Sarah. Shall I show him in?"

Her mother smiled in assent. "Oh, how lovely! This brightens the day considerably, does it not?"

Lord Carlin entered. He was dressed a shade more formally than usual, and he carried a small poesy of hothouse lilies in his hand.

Sarah rose to meet him. "How kind of you to call, my lord. I apologize. I was not expecting you. Are those for me?" she asked when he held the flowers out.

"Naturally. I thought a bit of summer in midwinter might please you, Miss Brecknell. And the gift may forgive my calling without notice."

"You need make no excuse, my lord," her mother said indulgently.

"Oh. They're beautiful. How thoughtful." She inhaled the scent, then passed them to her mother. "Do smell them."

"Mmm. Just like spring." Her mother took the bouquet and stood. "Why don't I have these put in water for you, dear? Perhaps Lord Carlin would like a few moments to speak with you."

Carlin bowed his head to her mother in gratitude as she left the room, a wide smile on her face. Sarah's heart suddenly lurched. Her mother, of course, saw the hint she was too dense to pick up on. The clothing, the flowers.

He was going to propose.

Sarah tried to breathe calmly. "I...I was not expecting you to call today, my lord."

"So you said." He stepped up to her, smiling at her nervousness. "But I was thinking of you, Miss Brecknell. Indeed, I have been thinking of you rather seriously lately."

"Is that so?"

Carlin took her hand. "It will not surprise you to hear I am quite taken with you, Miss Brecknell. Though we have not known each other very long, I am constantly impressed by your wit and learning. It is still in my heart to marry again and have a family, and an heir to pass my name onto. It would honor me greatly if you would be my wife."

"Oh," she said, though it was not unexpected. "You are most kind. I fear that I am not suitably elevated to serve the role, my lord. I have no title, and only a modest dowry..."

"My dear Miss Brecknell, do you think I have not considered those things? I am not a rash man—evidenced by several years of living alone. I ask you for this honor because I feel you would be perfect. I do not require a pedigree. I am not a social climber. I am happy where I am."

When Sarah did not speak, he hurried on. "Of course, I don't mean to imply that you are in search of a title. Of course you are not."

"I only fear that I could not make you happy," she said in a low voice. "I am far less perfect than you claim."

"Because you were in love with another before?" he asked, his voice gentle. "I was married for twelve years, my dear. I would never ask you to forget someone you cared for. Such love makes us who we are. But life goes on. Why not embrace it?"

Sarah looked him in the eyes, and tried to smile. "I do see your point."

"Then why do you still hesitate?" He squeezed her hand lightly. "Do you worry about whether I can provide diamonds for you?"

"Oh, my lord," Sarah said. "You know I do not care at all about such things."

He smiled. "Precisely. I know that you value learning. Companionship. Family. I promise you all those things and more."

Sarah paused, her mind swirling. The unwelcome image of Madame Osgood and her knowing comments surfaced. "I...I have to consider my answer most carefully, my lord."

"I expect nothing less from you, Miss Brecknell. Please take your time. I will wait with every *appearance* of patience."

"You are most kind," she whispered.

Carlin bent and kissed Sarah's hand. It was a proper

and restrained gesture, but still held a certain appeal. "I will leave you now, Miss Brecknell. But I leave with hope."

She watched him go before she moved an inch from the spot. She felt frozen.

Carlin was not a passionate man. He didn't say that he was madly in love with her, or that she should be with him. But he promised stability, and companionship. And —though not in words—respectability. She would be a fool not to consider his offer.

For really, what other choice did she have? Theo wasn't ever going to propose to her. He was betrothed to another woman. And even if he weren't, lower-born, eccentric Sarah would hardly be a wise choice as the next Lady Markham.

No, Lord Carlin was her best option. If Sarah had any sense she would have accepted immediately, before he might think better of his offer.

But she would wait. She would think, at least overnight. One more night of dreams that her life might have been very different. And then, tomorrow she would write to Lord Carlin, and accept him, and begin the life she could have.

Sara's first proposal—from Charlie—had filled her with giddy excitement. This second one filled her with dread. Yet Charlie ended up a traitor and rogue, and Lord Carlin appeared to be a true gentleman.

"So why am I acting like this?" she asked herself.

"Well?" Her mother peeped in the room, with Naomi just behind her. "What did he say?"

"He proposed."

Naomi gave one yelp of triumph and embraced Sarah's mother. "I knew it!"

"Oh, Sarah!" her mother said, in relief. "How wonderful! I knew you could not pine away forever. Such a fine man. An excellent name and land nearby ours in Kent. This is marvelous."

Sarah looked at both of them. "I did not say yes."

"You did not refuse him," Naomi gasped out.

"No. I told him I must consider."

"What is there to consider?" her mother cried. "You can't be expecting another proposal."

"Not at all. In fact, I wasn't expecting this one. I was somewhat caught out."

"But you did not tell him *no*," her mother confirmed. She exhaled noisily. "Well. Thank heaven. Of course you will accept. He will understand a short delay. Your father will wish to be informed, of course. Not that he would have a word to say against it. And then all the formalities will be observed. Naomi, can you bring some of that sage tisane. I am overwhelmed."

"Yes, ma'am." Naomi rushed out of the room.

"She'll be telling Bette as soon as she steps in the kitchen," her mother observed.

Sarah quailed. Telling Bette meant telling Jem. And telling Jem meant Theo would undoubtably hear of the proposal.

When the next post came that day, Sarah found a letter for her written in a strange hand, different from Rossi's earlier note. She went to her room to read it. She was right to be suspicious of it—the letter was just a blunt list of instructions, ordering her to take a hired carriage to a certain house well outside the city on the ninth of the month, three evenings away. There, she was to hand over all the papers Charlie possessed.

The letter writer did not sign the bottom. But from the pretty, flowing hand, Sarah suspected it was from Giselle Villani. There was no way to respond to the letter. She had to follow the instructions, or face the consequences.

Too scared to leave the letter unattended, she slipped it into her pocket. Later that day, just the sun was setting, Jem found her.

"Ma'am, could you come to the stable, please? There's something you need to see."

Curious, she followed the boy, expecting a household matter that required her judgement. But instead, Jem told her to go in alone, and she found Theo waiting for her.

"What are you doing here?" she asked.

"I had to see you," he said simply. "After all, I did literally ride off and leave you alone."

"But you must have heard I made it to the Zodiac's offices, and then back home." Her voice dropped, and she moved closer to him.

"Hearing it isn't the same as seeing it," he said, looking her over. "You're all right? No damage?"

"I'm in one piece. You shouldn't be here," Sarah warned him. She hadn't dressed for the cold, expecting to be back inside the house already.

Theo saw her shiver and pulled her into his arms, the gesture meant to be comforting rather than sensual. Sarah relaxed against him for a stolen moment. "I am glad to see you, though."

"That's good." He laughed quietly. "So I didn't scare you away."

"No." She remembered the letter then. "Theo! I know where to go. Giselle sent this." She pulled out the note and handed it to him. "Is this enough? I mean, do you think you can plan something to—"

"—keep you safe? Count on it, darling." Theo read the words quickly. "Just in time. I'm going to see my colleagues tonight. I'll get word to you about what to do on the day of the exchange." His arms went around her again. "You're getting cold."

"I need to go back inside," Sarah said. "And you need to vanish."

"I know." But he still moved to kiss her.

Sarah reveled in the warmth the kiss, but she couldn't get carried away. She put her hands on his chest. "Enough. You have to go."

He nodded, giving her another look as if he was memorizing her. "Let me know if *anything* happens."

"I promise. Now *go*."

He did. Sarah returned to the house. Just a few seconds with Theo was enough to make her wake up. She responded to him so much more strongly than she did to anyone else. How could she seriously consider a proposal from Carlin when she knew it meant never experiencing such a connection again?

Chapter 39

THEO FELT BETTER ONCE HE saw Sarah safe and whole again, but he wouldn't truly relax until the whole matter with Rossi and Villani was finished. Plotting the exchange with the other agents should help with that. Promptly at ten, Theo arrived at the address Julian had given him, a house discreetly located in a quiet neighborhood. He was shown into a large room by a stocky butler who didn't ask his name or attempt to announce him. Like Jem, the man must be in the Zodiac's school for servants.

In addition to Julian and Chattan, there was another couple. He was a tall man with black hair. The woman was slim and sharp-eyed, with close-cropped hair. She had a distinctly continental air about her.

Julian greeted him. "Good evening."

"Glad you could come," the tall man said, with an easy smile.

"Is this your home?" Theo asked.

"No, it belongs Lord and Lady Thorne, who are safe in Cheshire. But Lady Thorne's disreputable servants use this place the whole year, and it's a useful place for the Zodiac to meet for skullduggery."

"It's called planning," Julian corrected.

"But I like to say skullduggery," the man protested.

"Of course you would," the woman said. She turned to Theo. "It seems introductions are a thing of the past. You may call me Sophie, or Lady Forester." She indicated the tall black-haired man. "This is Bruce Allander, Lord Forester, also known as Scorpio. I'm Libra, by the way."

"You're both agents?" Theo asked.

"I was forced to marry her during an assignment," Bruce explained. "Somehow I never got around to correcting the mistake."

Sophie rolled her eyes. "Naturally, he thinks that was a terribly clever joke." Her voice held hints of a French accent. "English humor is nearly as bad as English food."

"And yet you stay," Bruce commented in a mild tone.

"They're still practically newlyweds," Julian said. "Forgive them."

Something clicked in Theo's head. "You're *Libra*. You killed Charlie."

Sophie looked back steadily, her whole body subtly shifting to a fighting stance. "I did. To be fair, he tried to kill me first."

He considered the woman in a new light. Julian said Libra suffered multiple knife wounds during the fight. Whatever else Sophie was, she must be a formidable agent.

"You knew Charlie," she said, perhaps regretting her previous tone.

"No," Theo corrected. "I only thought I knew him. Whatever happened, don't think I blame you for anything."

Sophie tilted her head up. "Good. We are all signs. We should not be enemies."

When she sat back down, her husband took her hand in his without even thinking about it. "Well said, dove."

Julian cleared his throat. "To business, if you please. We have one opportunity to catch Arceneau, on this coming Monday evening."

The signs all instinctively turned toward Julian, accepting his leadership without question. Chattan had a small notebook out.

"What do you think we ought to do?" Bruce asked.

"Miss Brecknell has been told to bring the letters she discovered to the location given by Rossi," Theo began.

"What is that location?" Sophie asked, her eyes narrow and completely serious.

"A house north of the city. It appears to be unlived in, and has been offered for rent as recently as last week."

"So they intend to use it for one night, and then be gone. No trail," Sophie said. "If we let Miss Brecknell go in, then get into position, she'll leave a little while later, and we'll have Arceneau, this Rossi, and the letters all in one place. Easy. We move in as soon as she's outside again."

"I see a problem," Bruce said. "Once she hands the cache over, what's protecting her? Arceneau will have no further use for her, and he'll have her killed. You know that."

Theo said, "There must be some way to avoid using Miss Brecknell as the carrier. It's far too dangerous."

"I can impersonate her," Sophie offered. "I would love the chance to get close to Arceneau."

"I expect you would," Julian drawled. "But Miss Brecknell is British and blonde."

"I've been a perfect English miss before," Sophie said, in an accent that became prim and proper. "And I have a blonde wig."

"Do you speak Italian?" Theo asked her.

Sophie looked over at him, interested at the question. "No, just English and French. And a little Yiddish, for reasons I'll not get into. Why?"

"Rossi and his partner Giselle Villani do. Miss Brecknell understands the language—she overheard them, which is how we know about Arceneau in the first place. It would be useful to know what they say when they talk to each other—which they will." Theo gave Sophie a careful look. "And I hesitate to say this, but I don't know if impersonation would really serve our purposes. They know exactly what Miss Brecknell looks like. They've trailed her, they've spoken to her. As soon as they realize you aren't her, all bets are off."

Sophie frowned. "But I so wanted to ki—that is, capture Arceneau."

Bruce snorted. "There's a long line for that."

"So we're agreed," Julian said. "Miss Brecknell must be the courier."

Theo didn't like the idea one bit, but it seemed Sarah's presence was necessary to snag Arceneau. He nodded unhappily. "Yes."

"Then our second step is to decide how best to protect

her."

"There are three active agents here," Bruce said, looking around. "Taurus, Scorpio, Libra. Two of us can arrive before the courier and get into position, as close to Arceneau as possible. Inside the house, if it can be managed. I can slip in during the day and wait."

"Can you?" Theo asked.

"He's very patient," Sophie said. "More than I am."

Chattan made more notes, saying, "That step can't be planned very well. It will depend on what happens inside."

"I will follow Miss Brecknell as she travels there, to be sure she really does go inside and they don't switch the meeting place," Theo said. "Libra can locate Arceneau, leaving Scorpio to manage Rossi and Villani."

"That may work. And once Arceneau is in sight..." Chattan went on.

"He'll be detained," Sophie said.

"*Alive*," Julian emphasized.

Theo was still looking at Sophie's face and short hair, and realized something else. "You look like the actress Sarah Finn," he said, remembering the poster outside the Pavilion Theatre. "It's uncanny."

"There is an excellent reason for that." She gave him a nod of approval. "I knew I should have the Pavilion take those old posters down, but I was a bit sentimental about them. I didn't think anyone would put those two names together."

"Well, it did take an agent of the Zodiac to do it," Bruce pointed out.

Chattan put another note into her little book. "Regardless, it is a risk."

"You're going to see that the posters vanish, aren't you?" Sophie asked her, a bit sadly.

"It is my responsibility," Chattan said. "Given the choice between an outdated poster and a live agent, I'll choose the latter every time."

Chapter 40

SARAH TOLD THEO SHE'D WAIT for his message about how to handle the exchange. In the end, it was Jem who served as the messenger once more. "Here's an invitation from Lord and Lady Thorne to attend a dinner at their home Monday," he said, handing her the paper.

"I can't go…that's the night I'm to meet Rossi."

"Precisely. This is a cover. Just accept the invitation and let the Zodiac handle the details."

The details were simple enough. Jem would drive her to the location, and Theo would hand her the papers just before she was to meet Rossi.

By the time Sarah stepped into the carriage on Monday evening, she had no nerves left. She was not expecting Theo to be sitting inside, but there he was.

"Good evening," he said. "Again."

Just what she said to him the first night when she hid in his carriage. He gave her a smile, though, that made her wish everything was different. Theo waited for a response, and when she had none, he asked, "Are you scared?"

"Yes."

He moved to sit beside her, then handed her a knife in a sheath.

"This is supposed to make me less scared?" she asked.

"Take it. You can hide it under your cloak. Or in your boot."

"I can't take that," she said.

"You can and you will. Just holding it may make someone think twice about doing something to you. Please, Sarah. You can't go in without some protection."

"I'll have spies at my back, won't I?"

"They're less concerned about keeping you alive than they are about catching Arceneau. You need to rely on yourself. And me, of course."

Sarah took the sheathed knife and slipped it into the top of her boot.

"It will be all right," he said. "There *are* three of us. You may meet the others afterward. And we do know what we're doing." He took her hand. "How are you?"

"Nervous."

"You're brave."

"You've said that before."

"It was true then and it's true now." Before she could say anything more, he pulled her close and kissed her. Sarah didn't resist, too happy to be near him again. The feel of his mouth on hers made her forget the danger ahead. She wondered if her sudden urge to do something very scandalous in the carriage would qualify as something to make him faint. If only that was her greatest concern. Sarah tried to get as close as possible to Theo, hoping his strength would transfer to her.

But all too soon, the carriage came to a halt. Theo sighed. "We're almost there."

Her fear spiked. She had to go inside without Theo. She wasn't sure she could.

He took Sarah's hand in his. "Listen. Whatever happens tonight, I'll be very close by. I won't let anyone hurt you."

"I trust you," she said. "I've always trusted you, Theo. Ever since I first hid in your carriage and begged your help."

Theo gave her a large leather envelope with the letters bound inside.

"I suppose I shouldn't lose this," she said.

"That would be bad," he agreed. "Just be yourself, and everything will sort itself out."

"You still don't know me very well, do you?" she asked.

Theo leaned in and gave her a last quick kiss. "Everything I do know makes me want to know more."

Before she could think of a reply, he opened the door. "Step out, darling. Jem has to drive on. The orders are clear, and the carriage can't linger. Walk slowly toward the house. They won't expect you to rush in any case. That will give me time to be ready to follow you."

She stepped out, and watched the carriage drive away, Theo still concealed inside. She felt very alone, despite the knowledge that the Zodiac was somewhere around in the dark.

The house was set well away from the road, far enough so no one would hear a thing if she screamed, or if someone shot a gun.

She walked up the path to the front door. Sarah held the papers tightly to her chest, as if they were armor. In a way, they were. She was unlikely to be killed if the papers could be lost too.

"No one wants to kill you, Sarah," she told herself. She was unimportant. Only her connection to Charlie was relevant. Once she handed over the papers, they'd let her go.

She was almost certain that was what would happen. However, the other possibility—she'd be killed instantly because she knew too much—was a little too plausible to ignore.

At the door, she knocked three times, as instructed.

Giselle opened the door. "So you came after all."

"Did I have a choice?" Sarah asked. In a daze, she noted Giselle wore a single pearl around her throat, just like one she'd been given as a gift from Charlie.

Giselle beckoned her inside with an impatient wave. Sarah took her time, which earned her a derisive snort. "Oh, come along. It's a bit late to worry about your reputation now, isn't it?"

Sarah was led down a hallway to an inner room. "Go in," Giselle said. "He wants to see you."

"Who does?"

"Just come along."

Sarah did, having no other choice. An unknown man stood up and bowed when she entered. He wasn't very old looking, but his hair was completely white. "Good evening," he said, in a perfectly polite tone. "You are

Miss Brecknell, I trust." He had a strong French accent. His clothes were expensive, and he had that undefinable air of money about him.

"Yes," she said. Her voice was almost nonexistent. "Yes, I am," she repeated louder. "I have the papers."

"How wonderful," he said. With a sweep of his arm, he indicated a chair. "Have a seat, please."

"Is that necessary?" she asked. Theo had instructed her to not rush, in order to get the agents in place. But Sarah didn't like this man at all.

"Ah, it is, Miss Brecknell. I must look through those papers before I send you on your way."

"I see." She lowered herself to a chair. So faking the documents would have revealed the trick immediately.

Giselle stepped through a side door. "I saw no one," she reported to the white haired man.

"That is reassuring," he replied. "This young lady here," he said, pointing to Sarah, "Is she the same one as before?"

Giselle looked at Sarah with a scornful smile. "Oh, yes. That's Charlie's little bluestocking."

Sarah dropped her eyes. So it would have been equally foolish for someone to impersonate her. Arceneau was aware of nearly every potential trick.

"Good." He nodded. "Go find your partner," he said to Giselle. "Be alert. I don't wish to be disturbed as I look through these."

Giselle's expression was one of irritation. It was clear that she had orchestrated the retrieval of the papers after Charlie's death, and now she wouldn't even get to see them. Sarah almost pitied her.

But the other woman didn't dare speak back to Arceneau. She turned and left in a huff.

He had already opened the case and was skimming the top document. "You did well to find these, Miss Brecknell. How did you manage it?"

"Charlie left notebooks behind. A sort of personal diary. I read them and found out he concealed the papers with the aid of fine art paintings."

"Cleverly done." He smiled at Sarah. "There are advantages to being an intellectual. A bluestocking, as Giselle calls you."

"I don't think she used the term as a compliment," Sarah said in a low voice.

"No, but I did. You are an admirably self-possessed woman."

"Thank you for saying so." Sarah watched him. She found it hard to believe this white haired man could be a criminal mastermind who played European royalty off each other. Yet Theo wouldn't lie about that. And he had to be powerful enough to make Rossi step carefully.

"Ah," he muttered. He was reading what Sarah thought of as the *Charlotte* letter. "The crown jewel of this collection." He looked sharply at Sarah. "You have read these."

She could never lie her way out of that. "Of course. I was curious."

He smiled. "Curiosity killed the cat."

"I am not a cat," she countered. She wondered where Theo was. Would he hear her if she screamed?

"No, you are not. You say you read the notebooks Wolverton left behind. How did you do that? Others have tried to find the cache and failed. Why did you succeed?"

I had help, she wanted to say. Instead, she said, "Because I could decipher the code he used."

"You are a codebreaker?"

"Yes." She briefly explained the mechanism of the code. Arceneau listened with every appearance that he understood fully.

"How interesting."

She could sense him reevaluating her worth. Sarah as a pet code maker and breaker? Perhaps that would be worth it to him, enough to keep her alive.

Chapter 41

♉

JUST AFTER SARAH STEPPED INSIDE the house, Theo followed her. He moved as silently as possible. Any hint he was around would jeopardize the whole situation.

He had to trust the other two signs were in position. The front door was locked, but Theo hadn't wasted his time when he'd been at school. He learned to pick every type of lock he encountered, mostly due to the many pranks he pulled with Charlie so long ago. This lock was simple, taking no more than a few seconds. Theo slipped past the door, the hinges squeaking just a bit as he went.

The place was rather like a mausoleum inside. Cold marble floors and lofty ceilings kept the house almost as chill as the outdoors. Somewhere a fire burned—he could smell it— but not here. He was glad for his greatcoat.

He heard something to his right. Footsteps. He moved toward the sound, hoping it would lead him to Sarah.

Theo followed the noises for a little while, never quite catching sight of whoever was making the sound. Unfortunately, he was too eager to be suspicious of that little fact. Thus, Theo walked directly into a trap.

As he passed through a doorway into a new room, he

felt a sudden rush of air—his one hint of danger. Ducking, he sensed something whip over his head.

A muttered curse in Italian revealed his attacker. Rossi. Theo turned to where the man must have been standing in the shadows. Rossi was bigger than him, but perhaps not as fast.

Or perhaps he was. Theo made a grab for the dark shape, and missed. Rossi stepped out of the way and then swung a fist at Theo.

"So much for big and clumsy," Theo muttered.

Rossi heard him and gave a grunting laugh. "Just like everyone. You see me and think *he's stupid and slow.* Can't be stupid and slow when you fight wild animals for a living."

"Noted," said Theo. He deflected the blow—barely—and dodged out of the way of the next hit.

Rossi grazed him when he struck again, and Theo wasn't sure how long he'd last against such a fighter. They tussled for a few moments, exchanging blows. But the fight was largely silent until Giselle appeared.

"Matteo!" she gasped. She added something in Italian that Theo didn't understand, but he caught the anger and urgency in her tone.

He felt the urgency himself. He didn't like not knowing where Sarah was. He had to finish this and get to her. Rossi wanted to end it too. He stepped up his attacks, keeping Theo dancing just to stay clear.

But Rossi made a mistake. He pressed Theo too far, too fast, and the scuffle moved closer to where Giselle was standing in the doorway.

Theo saw his opportunity. He tricked Rossi into following him and then slipped near enough to Giselle that the other man reined in his movement and had to retreat.

Theo took one more step. He could avoid Rossi.

What he did not avoid was the large vase on the stand behind him.

Before he could make a grab for it, the whole thing teetered, hanging in space. Then it fell to the floor, where it met the hard marble with a resounding crash. Ceramic shattered and flew everywhere.

"Damn," Theo muttered.

Everyone was surprised by the noise. Theo recovered first, shoving Giselle back through the doorway she'd just used, then following her. She screamed as she stumbled back, but Theo had already turned the key in the lock and yanked it out.

"That should keep your friend for a few minutes," he said. "Now stand up."

* * * *

At a sudden crashing sound, Arceneau whipped his head away from the papers and toward the doorway, his eyes dark with fury. "You did not come alone, did you?"

"I don't know who it could be," Sarah said. She wasn't lying. She didn't know precisely which agent was there.

"Get up, Miss Brecknell. We're leaving this room." He gathered the papers up.

"Why? You don't need me now that you have the papers."

He drew a pistol. "I often take things I don't need, just because I like them. I said get up."

She rose shakily to her feet. "Please don't shoot me."

"Do as I say and I may not. Now walk toward that red door over there and open it."

He ordered her out of the room. Without a doubt, he was leading her away from Theo.

* * * *

Theo prayed the lock would hold for a little while. He faced Giselle, who was on the floor, scrambling for a weapon of some kind.

"Stop doing that and stand up," he ordered again.

Giselle saw his face, and followed his instructions. She rose to her feet and put her hands out, though her expression was hardly frightened.

"You should have killed me," she said. "But you didn't, because I'm a woman." She sneered.

"You wouldn't be the first woman I killed," he said. "But if you answer my questions, I'll let you leave here alive."

"I'm not interested in your questions."

"When did you meet Charlie?"

She glanced at him sulkily. "Why?"

"He kept you for over two years. What I want to know is whether you met him before or after you started working for Arceneau."

"Before." Giselle was watching him closely now. "Who do you work for?"

"I'm not interested in your questions," Theo echoed.

"When did Arceneau contact you about the cache?"

"Two months ago. Last year, one of his lieutenants was killed, and Arceneau spent a lot of time finding out exactly why. He discovered that the lieutenant's courier was Charlie. And that Charlie was selling more documents for money on the black market. Then he learned about me because Charlie and I were together. He found me, and offered me the chance to retrieve the cache. If I succeeded, I'd get paid."

"And if you didn't?"

She couldn't quite hide a shiver. "I'd be killed. Along with Matteo. Arceneau doesn't like loose ends. He gave me a deadline, and I knew I couldn't find it on my own in time."

A huge bang rattled the door. Rossi was trying to smash it open.

"So you had Rossi frighten Sarah into helping," Theo went on. "Why her?"

"Charlie told me all about her. How clever she was. He said she worried him sometimes. If anyone could uncover his clues, it would be her. She understood how he thought."

Theo shook his head. "Charlie kept his lives separate from one another. He'd never tell you what was happening in his other worlds. Not his work, not his espionage. Certainly not his social world."

Giselle tossed her head. "You don't understand, do you? He *loved* me. He talked to me about everything. He talked to me about that girl. He'd tell me how innocent she was, how naïve. He couldn't stand her. So he came to me, and I satisfied him. He planned to disappear with me after he sold enough of the documents."

"He would forego a respectable marriage to spend a life with his art model mistress?"

"Of course. He loved me. He would take me to Italy, if I wished. But we would also see India, China. Wherever we wanted to go!"

"India and China were also places he told Miss Brecknell they would go. Coincidence? Or was it just easier to talk about the same places when he lied to you?"

"How dare you. He wouldn't lie to me. He told me about the cache of papers, remember. He told me his plans for the future."

"But he *didn't* tell you where he hid the papers. And he never brought you to his hunting lodge. Face it, Giselle. He didn't trust you or like you any more than anyone else. You were useful to him, so he used you."

"He brought me gifts!"

"Let me guess. Your necklace was one of them. A single pearl—from Bahrain."

She looked uncertain for the first time. Her hand fluttered up to her throat. "How could you know that?"

"He gave a matching necklace to his fiancée."

"You lie."

"Why would I lie about that?"

"I don't know!" Giselle backed away, upset.

The door shook again, and splintered. Theo was prepared this time, and he stepped out of Rossi's path. The man barged into the room, holding a heavy pedestal, perhaps the same one that had been holding the vase.

"We're going to destroy this whole house," Theo muttered.

"Let her go!" Rossi yelled.

"I don't have her. She's right there," Theo said.

"Giselle!" Rossi saw her and ran to her, dropping his makeshift battering ram. "Are you all right?"

"I am," she reassured him. "This man and I were just having a little chat. You can kill him now."

Rossi turned to face Theo. "The lady suggests I kill you, and I think she's right."

Theo inhaled. Rossi looked furious, his blood already up from his assault on the door. Theo wouldn't stand a chance against Rossi in a fair fight.

Then again, he didn't see any reason to fight fair.

"She is undoubtably right," Theo said, keeping his tone agreeable. "She definitely wouldn't want you to know what our chat was about."

Rossi glanced at Giselle. "What's he mean?"

"Nothing," she said quickly. "He's just trying to stay alive."

"I don't mind telling you the topic of our conversation," Theo told the other man. "All you have to do is ask."

"Don't listen to him!" Giselle cried out.

"Tell me," Rossi growled.

"Gladly. I had a few questions about your lover's association with Charles Wolverton—the man whose cache you've been after."

"So?"

"Well, I just wanted to know what story he told

Giselle about taking her with him when he left the country. She believed he would—she was his mistress, after all…"

Rossi turned on her in sudden fury. "So it's true. You did cheat with him. You said you didn't, but you lied."

"No! I love only—" But her words were choked off as Rossi attacked her and put his hands around her throat.

Theo leapt forward to pull the man off, but Rossi was incredibly strong, and maddened by the revelation of his lover's trick. Giving up on the idea of being able to yank him away, Theo seized the knife he kept hidden, and stabbed the blade into the other man's side in a calculated move.

Rossi looked stunned for a moment, then howled in pain. He released his grip on Giselle, who choked in desperate breaths. She tried to speak, but no sound came out.

"Don't try to talk, Giselle," Theo advised. "You're lucky he didn't crush your throat. Just concentrate on breathing."

He turned his attention to Rossi, who was now awkwardly gripping his wound with one hand, and glaring at Theo. "You struck me while my *back* was turned."

"Yes, I did. Not very honorable, but I'm in a hurry. Don't take the knife out just yet. You might bleed to death if you do. You should thank me—I chose not to go for your throat."

"Why keep me alive? Why keep *her* alive?"

"You might be useful. Listen to me," Theo said. "If you know a single scrap of information about Arceneau, it may keep you from a quick death…or a slow torture.

Keep that in mind."

At that moment, Bruce appeared, pistol in hand. "I see you took care of these two already."

"Yes, but now I need to hand them over to you to watch. I have to find Arceneau before he leaves the house."

Giselle watched him with wide eyes. She lifted one hand from her throat to point to a door.

"What?" Theo asked.

She pointed again, more insistently.

"Arceneau is here now," Rossi whispered. "Right behind that door."

Bruce nodded. "Off you go. Don't worry about these two. I'll keep a close eye on them."

Theo needed no more encouragement. Within seconds, he was through the door.

Chapter 42

♉

Sarah walked as Arceneau directed, moving further away from the room he met her in, into a long hallway lit only by a few candles at the near end. The rest was in darkness.

She dearly wished she were an agent like Theo, who had skills and training. Sarah knew the knife was in her boot still, but she wasn't quick or skilled enough to be able to grab it before Arceneau would shoot her.

And even if she grabbed it, what then? She couldn't imagine hurting another person with a knife, not even someone who threatened her.

"Where are we going?" she asked, her nervousness making her voice high.

"Keep going down the hall. Open the last door on the right."

"What's there?" Sarah chanced a look behind her. In that moment, she caught her toes on some fold in the carpet and tripped forward, her hands coming out to break her fall. Pain ran up her arms as the impact brought her to the floor, her ankle twisted and she couldn't stop from crying out.

Arceneau muttered behind her, "Can't you walk,

child?"

"I'm sorry," Sarah whispered, real tears springing up in her eyes. "I can't think when I'm scared."

He held out a hand. "Come. Stand up. Now."

She had no choice but to obey him. She took his hand and let him help her up. She gasped in pain as she put weight on her ankle.

"Oh, Lord," he said. "You're crying. You are either a clumsy fool or the best actress I have ever met."

"The first," she said miserably.

"You can still walk," he said, using the gun to gesture. "Do it now. We have less time than before."

Sarah hobbled forward. Their progress was slower, but she knew that Arceneau would not tolerate another delay. As she reached the last door, she heard a sound.

"Sarah!"

Her head swiveled to the end of the hall. Theo had just broken through the door.

"Get in the room," Arceneau hissed.

Sarah saw him raise the gun to aim at Theo.

Just as Arceneau pulled the trigger, Sarah shoved into him with all her strength. Arceneau stumbled to the side, but didn't fall. His face went cold with fury. He moved fast, and kicked her injured ankle.

Sarah nearly passed out. Her legs seemed to turn to water and she sank to the ground.

"Stupid girl," he hissed.

Footsteps pounded toward them.

Arceneau grabbed Sarah and knelt behind her. He shoved the gun into her back.

"Stop where you are," he told Theo. "This gun holds two shots."

"That is unfortunate," Theo said, with a weak smile. He was empty-handed.

* * * *

Theo watched the white-haired man as he tightened his grip on Sarah, whose face was streaked with tears and pain. He didn't look her in the eye. He couldn't. If he saw her eyes, he'd go insane.

He focused on the man. "I'm assuming that you're Arceneau."

"He is," Sarah whispered.

"Shut up," Arceneau said.

Sarah made one soft sound of pain, and fell silent.

Arceneau looked at Theo. "You are an operative. Like Wolverton was."

"Yes," said Theo. "And I also want the cache. Hand it over, and I'll not pursue you."

Arceneau chuckled. "How typical. Brainless young men who think they're invincible. Bullets kill heroes too. Though you're more valuable alive. Tell me about your organization, and I'll not kill this girl."

Sarah shifted. "Don't."

"I said to be quiet, Miss Brecknell."

"No, you told me to shut up," she corrected. "A fine distinction, but still there."

Theo almost smiled. Sarah, precise to the end.

"So you have one shot left," he told Arceneau. "You already told me the gun only held two shots. Fire again—

at either of us—and your bargaining power drops considerably."

"I said it holds at least two shots."

"No, you didn't," Sarah corrected again.

Arceneau growled in annoyance. Sarah gave Theo a tiny smile, one Arceneau couldn't see.

She's distracting him, he thought. She's getting under his skin. Why?

"I'll ask the questions," Arceneau said. "What is the name of your group? Who runs it? What are your goals?"

"Goals?" he said. "That's easy. We're in it for the money."

"If that were true, Wolverton would not have sold the documents he presumably was hired to protect."

"Well, Charlie was always a bit of an odd duck."

"That's true," Sarah confirmed. She shifted again. "Can I sit down? I think you broke my ankle."

Irritated, Arceneau shoved her down.

She gasped in surprise, and slid one leg forward toward Theo, her booted foot peeking out from the skirt. The boot that held the knife he'd given her.

"How's the pain?" he asked casually.

"Stabbing," Sarah replied.

He nodded. "We'll have to do something about that."

"You know this woman?" Arceneau asked.

"Pandora deciphered Charlie's codes," Theo said. A little information would keep Arceneau from thinking too much about Sarah.

"Pandora. And Wolverton was Pisces. What's your handle?"

"Chiron," Theo lied easily. "The group is called Olympus, by the way. Because we watch from on high."

"How megalomaniacal."

"I thought that was your calling," Sarah whispered. "Running around the continent starting wars for profit." She put a hand toward her ankle, pulling up her skirt a bit, seemingly by accident.

Theo took half a step toward Arceneau, who was watching him with narrowed eyes. "Don't try—" Arceneau began to say.

From the end of the hall, there was a sudden shout. "Get down!" It was Sophie's voice.

Arceneau saw the threat and instinctively raised his gun to counter it. He should have kept it to his hostage's back, but by the time he realized what he'd done, it was too late. With no other choice, he shot into the darkness.

At the same time, Theo lunged forward and pulled the knife from Sarah's boot. He pushed her out of the way and leapt toward Arceneau, who was pulling the trigger again and again, as if the gun would somehow reload itself.

Theo didn't think. He acted. The knife went in easily. Arceneau looked surprised, staring down at his chest, where his white shirt grew red. He dropped the gun to the floor. Then he sagged backwards.

Chapter 43

♉

SARAH WATCHED IN HORROR AS the white-haired man fell to the floor. He murmured a few words in French—a prayer or a curse, Sarah thought. Then he slumped forward and collapsed.

Ignoring the body, Theo turned to her. "Sarah? Are you all right?"

"Is he dead?" Sarah asked.

"That's not my concern. Are you all right?"

"No." She winced. "I truly think my ankle is broken. Though that's better than being shot in the back."

"He shouldn't have threatened you," Theo said, helping her stand. He drew her closer to him.

"Is that why you killed him?" she whispered.

"No. I killed him because he was a target with sensitive information, who was better off dead."

"Is that what you'll tell Aries?" The other agent walked up, a woman, Sarah noted with interest.

"It's the truth," said Theo. "You're in one piece, so I assume he missed."

"Badly." She looked at Sarah. "You're alive? Good. I'm Sophie, by the way."

"Charmed," Sarah said. She took a tentative step and

immediately stopped. "I don't think I can walk on this foot."

"Then don't," Theo said. "I'll carry you out."

"I'm too heavy for that."

"I could find Bruce to help," Sophie said.

"Someone called?" The third agent appeared in the hallway. "I secured our Italian friends. Oh, look. Arceneau is dead."

"My fault," Theo said. "I should be the one to move him."

"Nonsense. You have to assist Miss Brecknell," Bruce said. He looked cheerful, considering the situation. Or he was trying to distract Sarah from the blood. He nudged Arceneau with a foot. "Deadweight *is* heavy. Just my luck. Taurus gets the pretty girl and I get the corpse."

"I didn't have a choice," Theo said. "Can I trust you both to clean up? Miss Brecknell should be attended to."

"Go. We'll handle this and then rendezvous with Aries." Sophie smiled at Sarah. "Welcome to the Zodiac."

Sarah was too overwhelmed to offer a response. Then Theo picked her up and walked her out of the house. A carriage waited outside, with Jem hovering nearby.

"Are you hurt?" he said, seeing Sarah in Theo's arms.

"Yes, but not mortally. I thought you couldn't stay here."

"I did move on, but only till I couldn't be seen. Then I heard a gunshot." Jem opened the door and Theo got Sarah inside, putting her down on one seat.

"Drive to her home," he ordered Jem, settling beside Sarah.

"Are you sure, sir?"

"Yes. She's not doing any more espionage work tonight."

Jem closed the door and jumped up to obey the orders.

Inside, Theo moved so Sarah could lay on the seat with her head and shoulders across his lap.

She looked up at him, finally feeling a bit calmer. "I don't think I'm cut out to be an agent."

"You did splendidly," he said, putting one hand on her hair. "But I'd prefer that you not do it again. The thought of you in danger makes me rather irrational."

"So I saw." She took a breath. "You got the cache though. And the enemy is dead or captured. It's over."

"Yes, it's over." He continued to play with her hair. His finger found the hairpins and loosened them. Her heart hadn't been beating normally since she went into the mansion, but now it was beating too fast again, for an entirely different reason.

"Your hair," he said, keeping it in his hands. "It's beautiful."

"Thank you."

"I hate the idea of anyone else seeing your hair loose like this," Theo said.

Sarah smiled at him. "I'll miss you." She couldn't think of anything else to say. There was no real way for them to be together. Not one that respected either of them.

"If you ever..." he began.

"...ever, ever need anything, I'm to come to you first. You're about to make me promise to do that."

"How do you know what I'm about to say?"

"Because," she said simply.

"So? *Do* you promise me that?"

"You already know, Theo." She pulled his hand down and held it in her own. "Of course I promise."

Chapter 44

ȣ

THEO HOPED THE CARRIAGE WOULD never reach Sarah's home, but of course it did. Just after Jem stopped the horses, he opened the door only to say he would go to the servants' entrance to find out how to get the lady back into her house without attracting attention.

That left Theo with a few more moments. Not enough time.

Sarah hadn't moved, but she was watching him with those alert, grey eyes. "I should thank you for everything you've done for me."

"Please don't," he said, thinking of the many things he'd done *to* her.

"I'm certain it would have gone badly for me if I hadn't been holding those papers earlier tonight. You were the reason we found them. At so many points, it would have gone badly if you hadn't been there."

He rested his hand on her shoulder, uncertain of what to say.

But Sarah didn't seem to expect anything. She gave him a smile and said, "I have a promise to ask you as well."

"What?"

"You must promise me that you'll work to be happy. In your life and your marriage and even in the Zodiac."

He shook his head. "No."

"Theo, please. I can't bear to think I'll ruin your life just because I asked for your help."

"No one can promise to be happy," he said. Especially because he knew that he wouldn't be seeing her again.

"One can promise to try."

He shook his head again, giving in. "I'll try."

"Thank you."

He wanted to tell her he'd discovered some way to dissolve his obligations so they could be together. But he hadn't. He bent and kissed her once, but dared not do more.

A moment later, Jem knocked once on the carriage door before he opened it. Theo saw the boy's face, and the face of a young woman behind him. She was dark-skinned and dressed as a lady's maid.

"Oh, no, miss!" the girl said. "You *are* hurt. I thought Jem was exaggerating."

"Sorry, not this time," Jem said.

Theo moved to help Sarah out of the vehicle. "Don't try to walk," he warned her.

Sarah nodded, leaning on her maid's body as soon as she stood on the ground. "Naomi will see me inside," she said, her eyes suddenly glassy with tears. "Thank you… for everything. You should go now. Jem will take you, yes?"

It was not the goodbye he wanted with Sarah. But he had to get used to not getting what he wanted. He gave her a nod. "Goodnight. And remember what I said earlier."

"I will, my lord." Sarah offered him a final smile, and let Naomi lead her back into the house via the servants' quarters.

"Don't worry," Jem said in a low voice to Theo. "Miss Naomi's been with the family for years and years. She won't let Miss Brecknell get hurt in any way if she can help it. She'll cover for her."

"She's lucky to have such loyalty."

"It's a good household. I'll miss them, but I imagine you'll be calling me back soon enough, now that this is done."

"Can they manage without you?"

"Oh, they'll hire a replacement. They did well enough before. Clever people," Jem said. "If a bit prone to gossip. Naomi cried the news of Carlin's proposal almost before the gentleman left the house."

"He proposed to Miss Brecknell?" Theo tried not to react to that. It wasn't unexpected, after all. But his expression was hard to control.

"That he did, sir." Jem paused. "She has not given him a reply yet."

"She'll accept." Theo hated to say it, but he knew it was the right thing for Sarah. Carlin would take care of her, even if he was too old.

"You think so, sir?" Jem asked.

"It is a reasonable and fair-minded match. Miss Brecknell is too intelligent to not see that."

"Ah," the boy said. "*Reasonable.*" He didn't bother to

hide his disdain. "Well, no sense standing around. Where to?"

"Spruce Street, where we began the evening. Miss Brecknell is out of the scene, but I am not."

Despite Jem's daredevil driving, Theo was the last agent to arrive back at the rendezvous. Bruce and Sophie were there first, along with Arceneau's body, now wrapped in a bedsheet. Theo handled the detention of Rossi and Villani with the assistance of Jem and a few more nameless servants. Like Jem, they all had pasts darker than the average maid or footman, and the holding of prisoners didn't faze them in the slightest.

"You got the easy job this time, lad," the butler told Jem.

"And I was due for it," Jem retorted. "Besides, the horses don't like you, Stiles. They say you stink too much!" Grinning, he evaded the butler's half-hearted swat. Then he left to return to his temporary duties at the Brecknell house.

Theo wished he could be as flippant. Julian was there, and he wasn't pleased that Arceneau arrived in a shroud.

"I had questions for him," he told Theo.

"I'm sure, sir," Theo said. "But I wasn't about to let anyone else get hurt on his account."

Julian closed his eyes. "An end is an end, anyway. We'll all get some rest now that he's dead. And Miss Brecknell is free of her final link to the traitor Wolverton."

"Another will take Arceneau's place," Chattan warned. "No one lets power like he had remain uncontrolled for long."

"It will take months to rebuild a network like Arceneau's," Sophie said. "Perhaps years. And we can keep an eye on the situation the whole time."

"Indeed," Bruce agreed, with a proud smile toward his wife.

"Not to mention," Chattan said, "We managed a short, joint assignment tonight where none of the agents tried to kill each other! I'd say it was a success."

It was all true, but Theo didn't feel like celebrating. As soon as he could, he left for home. His servants, of course, never questioned his comings and goings. That was Theo's great privilege at work. He said he needed nothing and headed to his bedroom, where he closed and locked the door to shut out the world for a few hours.

He fell asleep immediately, and slept until the sun was high in the sky the next morning. He didn't hear knocking at his door, or footsteps outside, or anything at all. He didn't remember dreaming, but when he finally woke up, he was certain Sarah should have been beside him. But she was not.

Chapter 45

♉

SARAH WOKE FAR EARLIER, BECAUSE Naomi roused her shortly after dawn. Sarah was in bed, examining her bound-up ankle. It still hurt, but Naomi had cleaned and wrapped it well.

When her maid saw her last night, Sarah was worried the girl might faint. But she bore up, and managed to get Sarah inside the house and up to her bedroom via the servants' stair.

"Your mama is asleep," Naomi had reassured her. "So you'll be safe until tomorrow morning. But miss, you can't be sneaking about any longer. Your parents have been noticing at last."

"Did they ask you about it?"

Naomi looked at the floor. "Not directly. But they will, miss, and I can't lie to them. You know that."

"I wouldn't ask you to. But will you do me a great service and talk with me in the morning? Before my mother is up, that is? I need to decide what to say to her."

"Of course, miss. I'll bring up your breakfast."

Then Naomi had left her to sleep. And Sarah did sleep. The events of the evening, and indeed the past few weeks, left her drained and somehow hollow inside. Was it possible it was truly over? Shouldn't she be relieved?

When Naomi brought a tray into her room, just as the morning light strengthened, Sarah felt no better. She confessed a few select facts to Naomi, mostly involving the truth of Charlie's personality and her need to clear up a few things with regard to her own involvement in Charlie's activities. She said nothing of the Zodiac, of course. She never would.

But Naomi was suitably horrified that Charlie was involved in some criminal scheme. "How wicked, miss. And he was always such a charming gentleman!"

"Too charming," Sarah said. "And even gentlemen need money. So he did something he shouldn't and people thought I was part of it."

"But they don't any longer?" the maid asked. "How did you do it?"

"I…I had help. The man you saw in the carriage last night. He helped me, and I'm grateful. But you see, I couldn't tell my parents what was happening. I couldn't let anyone know."

"This man you won't name," Naomi said carefully, "Was he…did he…oh, Lord, how do I ask this of a lady like you. Was he, um, a good man? In how he treated you?"

Sarah put her hand on Naomi's. "He is a very good man. I trusted him, and he did everything I asked, and I couldn't have wished for a better friend."

The other girl nodded. "Then that's all right. But you mustn't sneak about any longer, miss. He doesn't expect anything from you, does he?"

"Oh, no. We shall not see each other again."

"That makes you sad," Naomi said, looking at Sarah with keen eyes. "You're fond of him."

"It doesn't matter. What matters is how furious my mother is. What did she say?"

"Only that you can't be allowed to gallivant out on your own. She encountered Lord Carlin at a party last night, and she was aghast that you hadn't answered his proposal yet."

"And more aghast that I haven't accepted it with delight," Sarah said miserably.

"Is there a reason why you should not?" a new voice asked.

"Mama!" Sarah yelped.

Her mother stood at the foot of the bed, looking at them with a disapproving expression. "Do you not have duties in the morning, Naomi?"

"Yes, ma'am." With a guilty expression, the maid slid off the corner of the bed and hurried out of the room.

"You confide in the maid before me?"

"She's easier to talk to," Sarah confessed.

"Sarah! I'm your mother!"

"I'm aware of that."

"Don't be tart."

"I didn't mean to be. I'm not good at banter like you."

"No one has ever looked to you for banter, Sarah. A simple yes or no will do. Such as a yes or no to Carlin's proposal. You feel bold enough to entertain yourself with friends I have scarcely met—who is this Lady Thorne person? Never mind that now," she amended. "But you can't see fit to secure a husband?"

"Perhaps a husband isn't my goal."

"I don't understand you!" her mother said, exasperation in her tone. "What do you want, if not this?"

"I don't know!" Sarah burst out. "But I'm sure it's not what you've always wanted. It's easy for you. Everyone says you were always charming and witty. You always say the right thing. You're never at a loss in a conversation."

"Well, you will have your chance later this morning. When Lord Carlin mentioned your enduring silence, I told him to come around today to get an answer."

"Mama! You didn't!"

"It's poor form to keep a gentleman waiting for an answer, Sarah. Especially when you are not fielding other proposals as well."

"But I don't know what to say."

"Say yes."

"No!"

Sarah's vehemence finally broke through, and her mother blinked in surprise. "Truly?"

"He's too old."

"Then why didn't you refuse him immediately?" her mother asked, though with a new, thoughtful expression.

"Because I was surprised. And he's kind."

"He can support you."

"I have other reasons."

Her mother suddenly held out a hand. "Do you want me to be there?"

"Yes," Sarah said, taking it.

"Then I will be."

When the fateful hour came—eleven in the morning, to be precise—both Sarah and her mother were attired in pastel morning dresses, and Naomi had done their hair in true Naomi style: beautiful, glossy, and seemingly natural. The maid was so relieved mother and daughter were speaking to each other, and indeed *allied* with each other, that she would have done anything.

Carlin entered the room exactly on time. He exchanged a few pleasantries with Mrs Brecknell, but soon enough got to the matter he came for. "I asked you a question not too long ago, Miss Brecknell. I trust you have given it due consideration."

"I have, my lord. I do have one point, though, that I should like clarified."

He looked puzzled. "And what it that?"

She had rarely been so nervous. But she was quite sick of being told what she should be happy about. "If I marry you," she said, in a low voice, "what of your mistress?"

"Excuse me?" he said, eyes widening.

Sarah shocked herself by saying it out loud. Her mother raised an elegantly-shaped eyebrow, but said nothing yet.

"Would you keep her?" Sarah went on.

"That's hardly a wife's business."

"I think it is precisely a wife's business."

"Well," he blustered, with a disturbed look toward her mother. "That assumes I have a mistress. Who told you such a thing?"

"Madame Osgood. Your mistress."

Carlin closed his mouth.

"My lord," said Sarah. "You argued quite eloquently a few days ago in favor of the match. And I certainly enjoy your company and wit. I would be honored to call you a friend. But on a few points I confess we will never see eye to eye, and thus I must decline your proposal."

"I see," he said, looking half relieved, half offended. "You may wait a long time, Miss Brecknell, before finding a gentleman who will meet your demands."

"I dare say you're right, my lord." Sarah smiled at him, not bothering to hide her feelings. "But unreasonable as they may be, my demands are nonnegotiable. Such is my eccentricity."

"You approve of this decision, madam?"

"I trust my daughter to know her own heart," her mother responded, to Sarah's surprise.

"You have her future to think of," Carlin said.

"It is precisely her future that I am thinking of. Every day of it. I want her to be happy."

"Alone?"

"I am never alone," said Sarah. "I have books."

"You are unmoved, then," Carlin said. He bowed stiffly to her, then to her mother. "I will take up no more of your time."

"It is always a pleasure, my lord," Mrs Brecknell said, as if they hadn't just been discussing something terribly awkward. "I do hope we shall see you again around town or in Kent."

"Perhaps, Mrs Brecknell. Perhaps."

He left, and Sarah heaved a sigh of pure relief. "Oh, thank the Lord I said no," she whispered.

Her mother shook her head. "Well. Even I know not to argue with such confidence. Though I wish you'd hinted at your reason first. A mistress! What a thing to talk about over a proposal."

"I'm sorry, Mama, but I can never keep my mouth shut, even when I should."

"As you proved just now."

"Will he spread the story?" Sarah wondered.

"The story about how you refused him and openly discussed his private life in front of your own mother? My dear, the poor man will never breathe a word in public. This morning may as well have never happened."

"Oh, Mama. I'm never going to marry now. I'm so sorry. I know you wanted me to."

"Darling!" Her mother moved to hold Sarah in her arms. "Don't cry. I only want you to be happy and secure. Don't cry."

But Sarah cried anyway, in unpretty, unladylike sobs. Her mother held her the whole time.

* * * *

The next day, Sarah felt brave enough to return to the Athenaeum. She hoped the familiar surroundings would bring her back to her former peace of mind.

Of course, she also had plenty of memories of Theo there, but she resolved to ignore them when they came up. She did fairly well, until there was a knock at the door. Looking up, she saw Miss Chattan standing there.

"Good day," she said. "Would you mind following me upstairs? We have a matter to discuss with you."

"We, meaning…?" Sarah asked. If Theo was upstairs, she could not go.

"Just me…and Aries." Chattan opened the door wider. "Please come. Now."

Sarah was not surprised when Chattan led her to the same room where she and Theo had first started to break the coded notebooks. Now, however, it was Julian sitting at the table. Cassius was lounging on the table itself, his sleek black form taking up far more of the space than seemed possible.

"Thank you for joining us," said Julian.

"Well, you already went through the trouble of sneaking in and all the way upstairs. You both did sneak in, didn't you?"

"Of course. What's the point of having a clandestine organization if there's not going to be skulking about at every turn? Which brings me to the issue of the moment."

Sarah sat down across from him. "What issue?"

"Remember when I said that I was not an altruist, Miss Brecknell?"

"I do." She sat up straighter. "What is the price I'm to pay for the assistance of the Zodiac?"

"Your expertise. I'm going to hire you."

Sarah blinked in confusion. "What? You mean, doing what Charlie did? What Theo does?"

"No. You're intelligent, but a terrible liar. However, you know more about codes and hidden messages than most people could dream of. And you've been wise enough to keep your knowledge fairly quiet. So I'd like you to help me, and Chattan, to train our agents in those skills. Translate when necessary. Decode things we find. Teach us new ideas, things the enemy hasn't thought of. Help us be better. By doing so, you'll give every agent an advantage. And the country will owe you a debt of gratitude—not that you can ever tell anyone about it, of course."

"You're going to *hire* me? You're joking."

"Miss Brecknell, one thing I never joke about is making the Zodiac stronger."

"You would truly trust me to do that?"

"I wouldn't ask otherwise. And I should mention the position will come with a small stipend. Enough to live comfortably, though certainly not extravagantly."

The sum he mentioned then made Sarah faint with relief. It was just enough to live independently. Perhaps her refusal of Carlin was not the horrible mistake she had begun to fear it was.

"Very well. I can do that," Sarah said. "At least, I will try."

"Excellent. Taurus can be your contact."

"Can it not be Miss Chattan?" she asked quickly.

"I suppose it could be," Julian said. "Would that suit you better?"

"It would look less conspicuous," Sarah said hastily. "Once Lord Markham is married, he ought not be seen with other ladies, especially one like me."

"One like you?"

"I'm…rather eccentric."

"Indeed." Julian looked at her, and perhaps through her. "Eccentricity seems to be prized by the Zodiac's agents." He smiled. "Well, that's settled then. Miss Chattan will contact you in a few days with some more details, including a cover story should any more skulking around be required in the future. Do you foresee any issues with that, Miss Brecknell? An impending marriage to a certain Lord Carlin, for example?"

"How do you know he asked?"

"I'm a spymaster, Miss Brecknell. More prosaically, I'm also a member of one of his clubs. I hear things."

"Well, your information is out of date. I will not be marrying Lord Carlin. I refused him yesterday."

"How sad," Chattan remarked, not sounding sad in the least. "But it does make things simpler for me."

Julian stood. "I think that's all we need to know at the moment. Please excuse us, Miss Brecknell. Chattan and I have another appointment." At the door, he let Chattan through, and then turned. "I bid you a good afternoon."

"Good afternoon, sir. And thank you."

"Thank you, Miss Brecknell." He paused. "I suppose you need a code name."

"I can't be a sign."

"Nevertheless. I'll think of one. Goodbye, Miss Brecknell."

Julian left, and Sarah sat down again. A position. A stipend. She could support herself. She could do what she wanted. She could be close to the excitement of the Zodiac, without being in danger.

But how close could she be to Theo without endangering herself?

Chapter 46

♉

THEO HAD RECEIVED A SHORT note that morning from Julian, ordering him to appear in the Zodiac offices at noon. He dared not refuse it, even though the last thing he wanted to think about was another assignment.

In fact, Theo was thoroughly miserable. He hid it. But he dreaded his upcoming marriage to Alyse, and not just because he'd be closing the door to ever winning Sarah. How could he hurt Alyse like that? Yet, he couldn't tell her the truth. That would hurt her even more.

Marriage—and how to avoid it—was the only thing he could think about at the moment, so even when he arrived at the Zodiac's offices, he was distracted and short-tempered.

Julian asked him several questions about the previous assignment before casually mentioning that he actually hired Sarah to work with the Zodiac's agents.

"Is that wise?" Theo asked his superior.

"We'll find out. It's not as if she'll be in danger. She'll work primarily with Chattan."

He nodded. Of course Sarah wouldn't work with him. Was she avoiding him? Of course she was. Sarah knew how difficult it would be to pretend things between them were finished. Theo doubted he'd be able to pretend he didn't want Sarah if he got her alone again. She did the right thing. And he lost her. "And you're calling her what?"

"Consulting steganographer. Well, until I come up with a better term."

"I meant that she'll need a code name."

"Oh, that. Yes. Any ideas?" Julian asked. "You got to know her well. What would make sense?"

"Pandora." He said it without even thinking.

"Interesting. Why?"

"She was given something that shouldn't have been opened," Theo said slowly. "But at my request, she did open it, and nothing good came of it. Not for her, anyway."

Julian said, mildly, "If I remember, at the bottom of Pandora's box was hope."

"That was just a story."

"So you think that despite my offer of working with our august group, Miss Brecknell's future is hopeless?"

"Of course not. I'm sure she'll be an excellent consulting steganographer, so she'll enjoy that, and she's going to marry Lord Carlin, who's well off."

"No, she's not."

"She's not what?"

"Going to marry Carlin." Julian grinned. "Are you nursing some sort of malaise? You're usually quicker than this."

"How do you know she's not marrying him?"

"I'm a spymaster. Also, she told me."

"Oh."

"Oh? That's your response to hearing Miss Brecknell has turned down a proposal for no obvious reason?"

"He's too old for her," Theo said.

"You're not, though."

"I'm already engaged."

Julian shrugged. "Not like you to stop at such a meager obstacle."

"It's not meager," Theo objected. "There's nothing I can do."

"You're a sign of the Zodiac, and there's *nothing* you can do? What sort of agent are you? There's always something you can do," Julian said.

"My hands are tied."

"Then undo the knot. Cut it if you have to."

"Metaphorical knots are trickier."

"It's your life—and hers, of course. But how good of an agent will you be if you stand by and just watch as others make all your choices for you? If you don't like the situation, change it."

"How?"

"Well, it's a radical idea, but you might try the truth."

Theo looked up at him. "Let's say I do. What will you do when it fails miserably and I have to flee the country because all of society will vilify me?"

Julian held up a piece of paper that had been lying on his desk. "Overseas assignments are always available." He offered Theo a wry smile. "Good luck."

As soon as he left the Zodiac offices, Theo went directly to Alyse's home. He dreaded the conversation but he couldn't live as he was. Julian was right, as he usually was. For Theo to give up on what he truly wanted when he had any chance of attaining it was unworthy of an agent.

Of course, he didn't have any clue how to go about it, other than with the blunt instrument of honesty.

He walked slowly, but he arrived at the Templeton house with no clearer plan. It was just the end of the time in the afternoon for members of society to be at home to receive callers. Therefore, he was not the only person there when he arrived. However, social visits were usually quite short, so soon enough he and Alyse were essentially alone in the parlor.

She looked at him carefully. "I haven't seen you for a little while."

"I've been occupied," he said. "But I think we need to talk."

"Oh?" She stiffened. "About what?"

He took his time responding, hoping that something— anything—would allow him to bring up the topic of their marriage without seeming utterly contrived.

Alyse's expression was quizzical, then wary, then sympathetic. "Theo, would you like to walk me through the park?"

"That's a good idea," he said in a rush. Even alone in the room, it wasn't nearly private enough for what he wanted to say.

A few minutes later, they were outside, heading to- ward the park where he'd walked with Alyse so many times. The sky was already colored with twilight, and the clouds were turning pink and orange, a brief moment of beauty in the winter drear.

He was still not sure how to broach the subject of the marriage. "Alyse," he began to say. "You know I care about you."

Alyse stopped walking. "No. Don't say a word more."

She looked so upset he immediately looked around for a threat. "What? What's wrong?"

"I'm wrong," she said. "I can't do this, Theo. I can't go through with a marriage that is based on a complete lie."

He stood still. It *was* out then. Alyse had somehow learned about Sarah. And she was right. How could he marry her, forcing her to endure every day the knowledge that the marriage was nothing more than a contract.

"Alyse, I don't know what to say," he began.

"How could you know?" she asked. "It's not your fault."

"It's not?"

She frowned. "Certainly not. You're not responsible for..." She paused, searching his face. "Do you have something you want to tell me?"

Theo swallowed. "I never thought I'd have to, Alyse. But yes."

"Then say it," she insisted, her eyes suddenly wild. "For God's sake, be honest with me."

"I love someone else," he said quietly.

Alyse stood stock still for a moment, her eyes wide. Theo worried that he'd hurt her far more than anticipated. "I never intended to do it. Alyse, I swear I never meant to hurt you…"

Her words came out in a rush. "Oh, my Theo. You've just saved me."

"What?"

"Who? Who is she?"

"It's Sarah. Miss Brecknell."

Alyse's eyes widened further. "Do you love her truly? Even more, are you free to marry her…that is, if you were not engaged to me, would you marry her instead?"

"I would, yes."

Alyse beamed at him, tears in her eyes but a light in her face he had never seen before. "Then let me release you. Let me throw you off! Let me jilt you! Please, if you love me, throw our betrothal away."

"I don't understand." He frowned. Alyse had never seemed so fragile, or so determined. "I don't understand your part here. Have I treated you poorly?"

"Theo, it's nothing that you did. Don't you see? I don't want to marry *any* man."

"What's the other option?" he asked.

"To not marry at all. To suffer a life of spinsterhood." She glowed as she spoke. "I can do it after all. I shall go abroad. To wherever Elena's work takes her."

"Elena?" And then he understood. He understood everything.

"Poor darling, I'm shocking you dreadfully, aren't I?" Alyse laughed with her hands over her face, still giddy with her revelation. "Oh, my heavens! Of course I am. Theo, please forgive me…"

"I'm not a monk, Alyse. But this is unexpected. We're

engaged…you were going to marry me, despite having no interest in me at all?"

"How many marriages *do* have that?" Alyse asked. "Not many in society, you may be sure. For every couple like you and Sarah, there's twenty more who are only fulfilling a contract, or securing their title, or seeking an heir—like we would have been. How many times have you seen a debutante married off to an old man because the price was right?"

"Too many," he admitted.

"I love children, you know. If we had married and I could be a mother, I would have been content. But true love—no. That's something I could never offer you."

"Alyse…"

"Oh, I do love you, Theo. As my dear friend. But don't pretend you ever felt a great passion for me either. We would have gone our separate ways soon enough, once I got with child."

"You have a knack for puncturing myths."

"Perhaps. But it's also that I have no wish to deny you real happiness." Alyse took his hand in hers and squeezed it gently. "Sarah's your match. Of course she is! I did see the way you two look at each other. I was too distracted with my own thoughts, but I see."

"What will you say?" he asked. "I can't let you suffer for this."

"Who will care?"

"Alyse, everyone will care. On some level, we've been engaged for I don't even know how long. Years. To break this off will cause gossip."

"I won't be here to listen. I don't care!"

"I do. I won't let you get hurt over this. I owe you that."

Alyse sobered a little. "What can we say? How could I hurt you by accusing you of…well, running off with your Sarah? That's no way to start a marriage, I'm sure."

He said nothing for a moment, only holding Alyse's hand in his.

"I don't know," he finally admitted. "No matter what reason you give, there will be gossip, and…"

"Then I shall not give a reason," she declared. "Listen to me, Theo. I will cry off, and then leave the city. I'll tell Mama something, of course. Not the truth…she'd die of shame. But I won't blame you, and I'll be gone soon enough. She may be sore at you, but that's life. She'll come around eventually. Once Elena and I are together, we'll find the right words to tell the people who need to hear them."

"Are you sure?"

"I want you to be happy, Theo. Consider this my wedding present. But do me one favor. Say nothing to anyone, and do nothing, until after our ship sails on Friday. I want it to be *fait accompli*."

What could he say to that? "You're a treasure, Alyse."

"Yes, I am," she said. "And I'm your ally. Always."

Alyse spun around, her feet leaving a trail of prints in the snow. She hadn't looked so carefree in years. Theo watched her, his own heart growing lighter. Who would have thought that breaking a promise could give everyone involved so much joy? He couldn't wait till Friday. That was the day he'd see Sarah and ask her to marry him.

Chapter 47

ʘ

THE SAME DAY, SARAH LEFT the Athenaeum just before five o'clock, walking with her father to a waiting carriage.

"If I may say," he ventured, once they were settled in, "I noticed that you've seemed, well, a bit absent these past few weeks. Is anything the matter?"

Sarah had to bite her tongue to keep from laughing. "Oh, Papa."

"Then there is a difficulty? Is it that man?"

"What man?"

"That Carlin gentleman. Your mother said you turned him down."

"Well, I did, yes," she said.

"Any particular reason?"

She paused, then said, "His given name is Marmaduke."

Mr Brecknell shook his head solemnly. "My dear. You always did have such good sense."

"Thank you, Papa." Sarah tried desperately to keep a straight face, so she looked quickly out the window to avoid her father's expression.

They were just driving past a large park, the ground still mostly covered with snow, though patches of rough, muddy ground were beginning to show through. If Sarah had known what she would have seen while looking out the carriage windows, she would have drawn the shades, or possibly kept her eyes closed the entire journey home.

Instead, what she saw were the unmistakeable figures of Theo and Alyse, together in the wintry landscape. Lady Alyse was literally twirling around with joy. Theo stood with her, still but unquestionably *with* her. He must have managed to put Sarah out of his mind. She should learn to do the same.

All day long, she had been elated at the thought of working for the Zodiac, of using her odd skills to actually make a difference. But the sight of Theo being happy without her plunged Sarah back into the depths. How could she have been so foolish as to dream of some sort of happiness? She told Theo he had to try to be happy. She meant it, too. But why did he have to obey her wish so quickly?

Once she returned home, Sarah reverted to her reclusive self, though she had a new excuse. Her mother's cold had returned, and she was confined to her bed again, under strict orders from the doctor to rest.

Sarah tried to reassure her mother. "As soon as spring arrives, you'll feel better. A few weeks at most."

Her mother sighed. "Your cheeks are sallow. Tell me you are not succumbing to the same disease. Should I send you away?"

"Where would you send me, Mama? My duty is to be with you."

"Don't talk like a spinster! Perhaps I should have encouraged you to reconsider Lord Carlin's proposal. He obviously admired you."

"His is not the admiration I seek," Sarah said bluntly.

Her mother tipped her head. "What?"

Then, of course, Sarah had to tell her something of the past weeks. She explained how she met Theo—though she refused to share his name—and told how in attempting to solve a riddle of Charlie's past, she had become more and more enamored of Theo himself, until she knew she loved him.

"But it is pointless, Mama. He cannot reciprocate, even if he should want to. He is engaged. I was just careless with my heart."

"My dearest," her mother said. Sarah lay beside her on the bed, feeling her mother stroke her hair as she did when she was little. "I wish I had known."

"What could I say? 'I have stopped grieving for Charlie and now lost my heart to another inaccessible gentleman? I have turned down a proposal from a perfectly good man simply because I'm still hopeful that things might be different?' You can't reprimand me, Mama. I've already done that to myself."

"Dear, I would never. I forgot how really young you are yet."

Mother and daughter stayed that way for a while, and though Sarah wasn't sure what her future held, she was at least glad she had her family.

* * * *

The week moved slowly, day after day of sameness.

The weather improved—spring could not be delayed forever—but Sarah's mood was somber. She went to the Athenaeum most days, and she received one letter from Miss Chattan, explaining that there would be a short delay before her work could begin. Chattan hinted at some internal matter which required closure. Sarah merely continued her usual work, so that she might be ready to offer some useful knowledge of codes once she actually began her efforts for the Zodiac.

On Friday, Sarah got up earlier than usual. The sun was brighter that morning, and when she ventured to peek outside into the garden, the air was warmer.

Her mother was still recovering from her cold, so Sarah ordered Naomi to bring both ladies breakfast in her mother's bedroom. Though much of the past month had been nerve-wracking, one indisputably good outcome was that Sarah and her mother were closer. The petty squabbling over their different outlooks was largely buried. Sarah hoped the change would continue.

She sat on the edge of the bed, sipping tea while listening to her mother's gossip, derived from letters and visits from her friends. Even a cold couldn't keep her mother from a good story. Then, well before the time anyone would dream of making a social call, Naomi entered the room.

"Pardon me, but there's a gentleman to see you, miss."

"Lord Carlin?" Sarah asked in trepidation.

"No. It's a Lord Markham."

"Mama," Sarah breathed.

"That's him, isn't it?" her mother asked. "The one you

lost your heart to."

"Yes. But I don't know why he's *here*."

"Perhaps you should go and find out."

"But…I look ragged. And you're too ill to get out of bed, so you can't chaperone."

Her mother managed a delicate snort of disbelief. "Why do I get the impression that this would not be the first time you'd be unchaperoned with this gentleman? I order you to go down and receive him, Sarah. Hear what he has to say."

Sarah saw her reflection in the mirror as she reached the staircase. She was a fright. Her hair was only loosely bound in a ponytail falling to her waist, held back with a simple ribbon. The morning dress was not improper, except that it was horribly wrinkled after laying on her mother's bed.

But she couldn't make him wait.

Sarah dashed down the stairs. Naomi pointed to the drawing room door. "Shall I leave it open, miss?"

"Yes," Sarah said. "I'll ring if I need anything."

She opened the door and stepped through.

"Theo," Sarah breathed. "That is, Lord Markham."

"Theo," he insisted. He seemed to make the room shrink, just by standing there. He was as well turned out as Sarah was mussed, making her feel out of place in her own home.

"You look very well," she said inanely.

He looked her over from her feet to her head, clearly taking in her unkempt appearance. "How are you?"

"I'm perfectly well. Thank you. I haven't been receiving anyone. Forgive me. Mama is still very weak, and I've just come from sitting with her," Sarah was chattering, just as she always did when she got nervous. "Anyway, that's why I'm so…ah, messy."

Theo smiled, not at all put out by her stream of words. "You look beautiful."

"Oh. Thank you." Sarah wished he didn't affect her so much. "Why are you here?"

"That's a fair question. Can we sit?" He motioned to the two chairs facing each other by the fireplace. Sarah moved to one and sank down. Theo sat opposite her, leaning forward so he was as close as he could be without actually kneeling in front of her. It reminded her of the time in the theater box, when he told her all the things she shouldn't know.

Recalling that, Sarah inhaled and leaned back a little. "Has something happened?" she asked, suddenly worried.

"Yes," he said. But he didn't say anything else. Instead, he reached out and took her hand in his.

Sarah let him, cherishing even that touch. "Well? Can't you tell me? Why would you come to my house if you can't even say? Mama knows you're here. Naomi announced you. I don't know how I'll explain it. Any of it…"

"Sarah, will you be my wife?"

Sarah's jaw dropped. "What?"

"My wife. Would you marry me?" he asked, his voice low, almost pleading.

"But…I *can't*. You can't ask me that. What of Lady Alyse?"

"That's the thing that's happened," he said. "Alyse no longer wishes to marry me. It was her right to break off the engagement, and she has done so."

Sarah felt like the world was shifting away from her. Theo was free? "Is it…was it because of me?"

He shook his head. "Alyse had reasons of her own. Very sound reasons. I talked to her a few days ago, ready to beg her to break it off. But she already knew it wouldn't work out. We've been friends since childhood, and she knows me well. Better than a lot of other people. She pointed out that marrying her out of duty when my heart lay elsewhere would only invite disaster."

Sarah frowned. She could tell Theo wasn't offering a full story. But then she realized what he had said. "Your heart?"

"I love you, Sarah. And I don't want to lose you."

"Oh." She took a deeper breath, since her heart was beating faster than before. "I don't know what to say."

"*Yes* would work very well for me," he suggested. Then he frowned. "Tell me I'm not too late. You haven't accepted another proposal already."

"No," she said quickly. "No, I haven't. I could have, but he wasn't you."

His face cleared. "Then why do you hesitate?"

"I just can't quite believe we're having this conversation."

"We are. Trust me." He stood up, and pulled her up with him, so that she was standing toe to toe with him. His arms circled her waist, keeping her very close. "So what's stopping you?"

"Oh, Theo. This isn't simple. Would your parents approve of me? Would we marry under a cloud? What of your title? Would I make a proper baroness? Shouldn't you ask my father for permission? Will I still work for the Zo—"

Her last word was cut off by Theo's kiss.

Sarah's questions evaporated. Touching him, being close to him, was where she ought to be. She kissed him back, so delighted she could taste him. She lost all sense of propriety and wrapped her arms around him.

He held her next to his body, so tightly she could feel his heartbeat. Sarah sighed as he moved to kiss her cheek, her neck, her ear.

"We'll work all of that out," he said. "Everyone will love you. You'll do whatever work pleases you. And we'll be together. Do you have any other questions, sweetheart?" he asked in a low voice.

"No," she said.

He released her enough so he could pull back and watch her expression. "So you'll marry me?"

"Yes." She couldn't stop from grinning like a fool. "I love you. Yes, please."

"That's what I was hoping to hear," he said, with a pleased smile. "I promise you won't regret it, not for a minute."

"All I ask is that you love me, and that you hide nothing from me."

"I don't have anything left to hide, sweetheart."

She sighed, putting her head on his chest. "That's all I want."

"I say, what's happening here?"

At the sound of the new voice, Sarah raised her head to see her parents in the doorway, her father's arm around her mother to support her.

"Mama! You're up!"

"Curiosity is a great healer."

Sarah laughed. "Hello, Papa. Mama. Come in and meet my fiancé."

Her father stared at them, stunned into silence.

Her mother was only slightly less shocked. "Sarah, darling. Perhaps you can introduce your…friend?"

"Of course." Sarah made a half turn, but kept her hands locked with Theo's. "Mama, Papa. This is Theodore Drayton, Lord Markham. The next Baron Markham, actually. We're going to marry."

Her father put his spectacles up to his nose. "Markham? Have we even met?"

"Briefly," Theo said.

"Oh! Were you the gentleman at the Egypt lecture a few weeks ago?"

"Yes," he confirmed.

"Well," her father said. "That's all right." He turned to his wife. "Can't be a bad sort, can he? If he's part of the Athenaeum? If Sarah is content, then why should we object?"

"Whatever you think best, my love," her mother said, with a smile at Sarah. "Though I believe some details will have to be explained."

Epilogue

♉

THE WEDDING, SMALL AS IT was, was the talk of London, all the more so because no one quite knew the whole truth. Matrons spun out more fanciful versions every day. The only thing that was certain was the highly respectable Lady Alyse Templeton had thrown off the handsome and wealthy and slightly mysterious Lord Markham without so much as a by-your-leave, and had then vanished from the city for parts unknown. Rumor was that her tender heart was broken by some cruelty on his part.

This theory seemed to be borne out when Markham, far from showing the slightest contrition or shame, simply turned around and plucked another bride out of *nowhere,* as if that were acceptable. Mothers made ecstatic after hearing the first half of the story were plummeted to the depths when they heard the conclusion. How unfair of Markham to not allow the daughters of the *ton* even the slightest chance at catching him. How rude!

And who was this new bride, this bluestocking Sarah Brecknell? No one knew much about her. Granted, she was not a scandal herself. The most anyone could recall about her was she had been engaged previously but lost her own beloved shortly before her wedding. What her value to Markham could possibly be was a mystery. It certainly wasn't her modest dowry.

All these well-chosen rumors were spread by Zodiac agents and their associates. In particular, the efforts of one Sophia, Lady Forester, were key in establishing Markham as a cad and Sarah as a bewitched innocent. Sophie announced the girl was likely to regret marrying Markham, despite his wealth and status.

"I understand the heart," the Frenchwoman said haughtily. "Do not be surprised if the man wanders for weeks or months on end, leaving his virtuous wife alone. I will befriend the child," Sophie added. "It is the least I can do."

Sarah herself said little in response to the rumors. She was far too busy to bother about what the *ton* was saying. A new scandal would erupt in a week or so, leaving Sarah and Theo alone again.

And while she waited for the dust to settle, she had more important things to consider. Only a few weeks after the wedding, Theo had another assignment from the Zodiac.

"I don't fancy the idea of you carrying a secret treaty over to Vienna," she told Theo, once she learned of it. "Especially because you'll be alone."

"Then you'd better devise a good code to conceal the message, Pandora," he said, holding her close. "The sooner you do, the sooner I can complete my duties and return to you."

She smiled. "I should get to work."

"In a few minutes, sweetheart," he said, kissing her.

It was more than a few minutes, but Sarah didn't

mind.

ABOUT THE AUTHOR

Elizabeth Cole is a romance writer with a penchant for history. Her stories draw upon her deep affection for the British Isles, action movies, medieval fantasies, and even science fiction. She now lives in a small house in a big city with a cat, a snake, and a rather charming gentleman. When not writing, she is usually curled in a corner reading...or watching costume dramas or things that explode. And yes, she believes in love at first sight.